T0326753

The Salt Palace

Darren DeFrain

New Issues Poetry & Prose

Western Michigan University
Kalamazoo, Michigan 49008

An Inland Seas Fiction Book

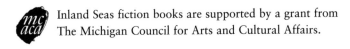 Inland Seas fiction books are supported by a grant from The Michigan Council for Arts and Cultural Affairs.

First American Paperbound Edition, 2005.

ISBN: 1-930974-31-0 (paperbound)

Library of Congress Cataloging-in-Publication Data:
DeFrain, Darren
The Salt Palace/Darren DeFrain
Library of Congress Control Number: 2003104650

Art Director:	Tricia Hennessy
Designer:	Matt Sia
Production Manager:	Paul Sizer
	The Design Center,
	School of Art
	College of Fine Arts
	Western Michigan University

The Salt Palace

Darren DeFrain

New Issues

 WESTERN MICHIGAN UNIVERSITY

For Melinda, Always.

The Salt Palace Roster

NAME	POS	SCHOOL
TEAM CAPTAINS		
Carol DeFrain**	PG	Hastings, NE '59
Dennis DeFrain **	SG	Nebraska '65
ROTATION PLAYERS		
Peter H. Walpole **	SG	Colorado College '93
Judy Fraser **	PG	Wichita State '80
Knute Fraser **	PF	Washburn '64
Dick Munzinger	SF	Colorado College '58
Myra Munzinger	PG	Ft. Hayes State '63
Kevin "Huck" Grauke & Catherine Collins	SGs	Texas '91
Chris "Beans" & Alecia Haven	SFs	Kansas '90
Jeff Greer & Kathy Poremski	Cs	Maryland '89
Pablo Peschiera & Andrea Martin	PGs	Hope '91
A.J. Rathbun	PF	Kansas State '92
Jonathan "Cha-Chi" & Jennifer "Monkey" Almy	Cs	Texas Christian '93
"Madrigal" Mark Munzinger & Carrie Lindsey	PFs	Wichita State '93
Ed Skoog #	C	Kansas State '93
John Lennon	PF	Penn '92
Jonathan Johnson & Amy Howko	SGs	Eastern Washington
Herbert Scott	C	Iowa

** denotes starter

# denotes rookie

2005–06 Coaching Staff

HEAD COACH
>Jaimy Gordon (Western Michigan)

ASSISTANT COACHES
>Stuart Dybek (Western Michigan)
>
>Debra Monroe (Texas State U)
>
>Tom Grimes (Texas State U)
>
>Steve Heller (Antioch)

STRENGTH-AND-CONDITIONING COACH
>David Dodd Lee (Western Michigan)

ATHLETIC TRAINERS
>Mike "Meek" Marchetti (Utah)
>
>Dan "Bluto" Nailen (Utah)
>
>Jeff Kissell (Utah)
>
>Carl Porter (Weber State)

SALT PALACE FAMILY DANCERS
>Under the Direction of Anna DeFrain & Lois Gunter:
>
>The Daughertys, DeFrains, Farrells, Jantzens,
>
>Johnsons, and Gunters

ASSISTANT TRAINERS
>Madchen & Ava DeFrain (College—TBA)

The Salt Palace G.M. would also like to recognize the generous support of The University of Wisconsin—Fox Valley for a grant to help finish this novel, and the additional help and support of Dean Jim Perry, Malcolm Allen, Scott Emmert, Judith Baker, Evelyn Li, Kathy Skubal, Becky Hoffman, and all the terrific folks at UW—Fox.

The author wishes it to be known that this is a work of fiction. Items presented within this fictional narrative as fact are always at the service of the story and should not be construed as definitive by any reader. Any numerical "data" was consistently averaged or approximated or guessed at when sources conflicted or were strictly anecdotal. Much of the information contained within was also frequently contradicted by the many good Mormon Elders who always seemed to happen by right when I needed more wisdom about some particular history or anecdote, further complicating matters. I would also like to thank the literally dozens of them who always took the time to try to answer my many questions. As for the larger questions they had of me, I'm still searching.

The author would further like to acknowledge that the details of Utah history were gleaned from many sources, but none more so than the very excellent *Mondo Utah* by Trent Harris, Dream Garden Press, 1996.

Contents

I. First of America

On days like this the sky stiffens, as if to say that summer will never come. Those sweet April showers, each one riding the tail of the one before, migrating through Kalamazoo without a warm week, chase the longest winter since I've been here. And now it rains, and rains, shining the cold, black tarmac where the cars have not yet come in. Just beyond the parking lot there is a delicate mist hanging on the grasses and between the pines, bending the sleepy Dutch tulips and daffodils who didn't know it wasn't time to wake up yet, and I wonder why I can no longer sleep.

And so, in the First of America[1] parking lot, the sun comes up and I sit in my old broken-down Bronco watching the short, short skies over the black glass and brown brick of Corporate Woods. All that raw land behind rolls in one believable bulge, twenty hours by car, back to the Wasatch Mountains. All that road, all those people still in their dreaming. The morning sun won't be out there yet. Only hours earlier, it tucked the shores of Great Salt Lake in, pulling the shadow-blanket across the valley as it hesitated before fading off behind the blue mountains of Nevada. I've watched that sun go down so many times that even in the gray mist of a sleepless Michigan morning it plays clear in

---

[1] First of America, one of the largest and newest banks in West Michigan. The building mentioned by Brian is the Corporate Woods Complex; the F.O.A. name is left off the complex so as to make the building less readily noticeable to unsolicited salespeople, infuriated customers and enraged former employees. F.O.A.'s other principal hubs include Indiana, Illinois and Florida.

my head. I think of Jaimy Sizemore; I even think of Joseph Smith[2] and what I never found there or here and why. I think of Jaimy Sizemore.

My father's words come to me now: "If you have faith," he always says, "your past will save you." Maybe it's his voice calling me back. Maybe it is His voice calling me for the first time in my life.

---

[2] The founder of the Mormon church. In 1829 Joseph Smith, along with ten other men, was visited by the angel Moroni carrying the golden tablets. These tablets, or plates, were about six inches wide, eight inches long, and about the thickness of common tin. Only Joseph Smith could look upon the tablets, using the breastplate with Urim and Thummim (a device similar to reading glasses), and translate these books. If he showed them to anyone else, he would be destroyed. He proceeded to translate the tablets, through a curtain, into *The Book of Mormon.* This "new" text extends the works of the Bible to the Americas in the period roughly from 2300 B.C. to A.D. 400. According to the book, the Lamanites, referring to Native Americans thought to be one of the Ten Lost Tribes of Israel, were preached to by Jesus Christ when he visited this new kingdom of the lost Israelites. This first church of the Americas flourished until it fell into apostasy. It remained that way until, as foretold in the golden tablets, the kingdom could be reclaimed by Joseph Smith.

Mark Twain, referring to the not-always-successful biblically-appropriated tone and language of *The Book of Mormon,* once described it as "chloroform in print." God also commanded Smith to revise parts of the Bible that had been, according to Smith, corrupted by Christians and Jews over the centuries. Many of these changes and additions were aimed at helping the two books justify and support each other.

I don't want to think it's the green numbers on the dash clock that pull me out of my nostalgia and into the rain, but the pit-a-pat song on the radio has ended. A song from ten years ago (ten years!) that stretches something inside me back to the dry mountains, fading away as I cross the parking lot, trying to outpace one of the Snack-Machines (Kitty's term of endearment, but like loads of everything else, something I've taken to using in spite of the fact it's not mine) to the revolving door, and I let her beat me to it. At times I think it's a meat grinder we all arrive at to meet the same fate: it chews our rolls and lumps and crushes our bones and joints into sausage, then stuffs that undigested flesh into plastic bank tubes. I've come to hate my life this much.

And this is the great mystery. The folding inward, the premature collapse. How have I come to empty myself of promise, of what little altruism I may have had once, a short time ago in Kaysville, two thousand green miles from the reflective black glass of a revolving door? "Lies and promises start off on the same road," my father always says.

I nod at the short, ruddy-faced and dandruffed guard who will spend most of the rest of the morning tending his prostate condition in the men's room, and I turn down a short hallway, on the ground floor, to the CONSUMER LOAN DIVISION. Most of the Snack-Machines are there, shaking down their coats or walking the aisles of carpeted cubicles prospecting for morsels of double-fudge brownies, peanut-butter pie, angel food. They are 'wonderful-nice,' the Snack-Machines, masterful calendars and caretakers of the office, spending their extra hours in their kitchens loading and unloading ovens of birthday squares, baby cakes, and retirement pies. I truthfully didn't have a drop of animosity toward this corpulent society until I found myself fat. A rubbery tube of flesh hangs over the lip of my belt-line and snaps inward like a minor under-tow when I bend down. At least I can still get to my shoes.

There's Dee Dee, who smells of lotion and whose thighs rub together so hard when she walks that she now wears spandex pants under her skirts to keep her skin from rawing over, and I hear her huffing up and down the aisles of computers and people dispensing reams of research and loan requests—schweep, schweep, schweep, schweep—"Good morning, gooooood morning"—until she stops at a desk near mine. It's Kitty's birthday today. I am to begin sneaking the card and I remove my coat, shake the small round drops stupid enough to cling to my hair, and flop down into my pigeon-hole to think up something cheering. I know that every last one of the Snack-Machines will have brought Kitty some food to share, and that Geoff, L.T. and I will be the only ones without an offering, and so it should be something sincere, something cheering. It reads: *Happy Birthday, Kitty! Everything was getting smaller and smaller until you came along. Here's hoping next year finds you in Arizona, away from this God-awful place.*

I leave off the last part and pass the card back to L.T. Since they've changed our desks, (again!) I'm so tucked away I can no longer see the clock, so I turn on my computer and type 'TIME' and my computer responds: "'TIME' IS NOT RECOGNIZED. 04/24/96 08:07.54." And I spend the next two minutes and six seconds tapping my RETURN key to watch the clock roll around to 8:10 A.M. From where I sit I can now see the tops of the black glass windows that look out onto the parking lot and I see they are spotted with rain.

Rhoda and I are living in separate apartments again, ever since I told her my roommate Phil was out of town. And he was, as far as I knew. So she gets out of bed after a session to go clean up in the bathroom and there's Phil coming out of his room, having mixed his nights and days again by driving down in a snowstorm from Traverse City the previous night, and he and

Rhoda come face to face, only she's nude and he's not and my seed's starting to drip out of her. It used to be that I was jealous of another guy seeing what Phil saw, as if one of my secrets had been given up, decoded. But I know Rhoda's been much more decoded than that by people I like a lot less than Phil.

I drove past her apartment this morning on the way to work, hoping there was something clairvoyant between us. I parked the Bronco in the morning drizzle and tried to think her out of bed. Tried to think whether or not she was alone or with Mr. Mysterious again—the man I know visits her nights her answering machine tells me she's not home, this Mr. Mysterious shedding his body hair in her sheets, whose very face I've had to create in my own mind. She's a student, Rhoda is, and when she *is* alone she doesn't rise until the sun hits her window, which, this time of year, in this part of the time zone, would be late enough anyway, but she's got these twin pines looming over her apartment. When nothing happens I whistle at her window, but it echoes across the street instead and I'm back in the Bronco on my way to work before my whistle fades from the dark, wet street. Rhoda's Catholic and I wonder if that's what makes me think of Jaimy again, if there is something unresolved I've squirrelled away which, like the ignorant tulips outside F.O.A., has come out of hibernation to bloom.

When I met Rhoda last year I told her I was a Mormon, though that's a lie as much as anything. It seems, outside of Utah, that being Mormon is something I'm compelled to announce as if I'm a lottery winner or suffering a contagious infection. And outside of Utah it's as much announcement as substance. There's a ward house near my apartment, but I can't bear to go any more. It's like going to a movie by myself. Church has always been, in large part, about the family dynamic, and by myself I no longer hear the call of the Angel Moroni's golden trumpet; the sound doesn't carry all the way from Salt Lake Temple[3] to my red ears in Kalamazoo. It's become enough for me, in the Midwest, to announce myself as Mormon and wonder what kind of chills or thrills that word brings to Gentile ears.

When I was home and the shoe was on the other foot, Jaimy and the few Gentiles I knew would announce their religious affiliations with a cross dangling around their necks. They weren't being antagonistic, most of them. There was a need for order you came to appreciate, something to help avoid embarrassing questions about what ward you belonged to and who your Bishop[4] was.

---

[3] The Temple in Salt Lake City, Utah has a solid gold statue of the Angel Moroni blowing his trumpet perched on its highest spire. Disturbingly, when the statue was last taken down to be cleaned it was discovered that it had been shot at several times. It is the ambition of all good Mormons to sanctify their marriage in the Temple, where, in a secret ceremony attended only by the Temple elders and the bride and groom, they are bound together for eternity.

[4] Unlike most Christian-based religions, the L.D.S. Church is a church without a professional clergy. Instead, they rely on a centralized, though incredibly organized, authority operating out of Salt Lake City. The Church is ruled by a hierarchy controlled by unanimous vote at church conferences. At the top of this hierarchy is the church president. Like the pope, the president serves until death. However, unlike Catholicism's College of Cardinals who lose their power to vote in a new leader, the same life-long tenure applies to the next tier in the Mormon hierarchy; the Quorum of the Twelve Apostles who generally "vote in" the longest-serving of their members. Gordon B. Hinckley was sworn in as church president a little time before the start of Brian's story. There was some

controversy that Hinckley had actually served longer when his predecessor, Spencer W. Kimball, became seriously disabled following a third brain operation from 1981 until he died in 1985. Kimball's successor, Ezra Taft Benson, who took office at the age of 86, was said, by his grandson, Steve Benson, the Pulitzer Prize-winning political cartoonist for the *Arizona Republic,* to be struggling with senility, and functioning only to "perpetuate the myth, the fable . . ." that he was capable of acting as the living prophet of the Mormon church.

The lower levels of power in the Mormon church fall entirely to appointed "volunteer" leaders, most of whom come from the business community and who have little to no formal theological training or education. The regional unit, called the stake after the poles used to hold up the sacred tabernacle where biblical Israel worshiped, is similar to a Catholic diocese. The smaller wards, the term used for subdivisions of municipalities in Joseph Smith's time, is similar to a parish.

Overseeing these wards are bishops, with the divisions being entirely geographic. A bishop's ordained power, however, should not be underestimated based on the privileging of his business acumen over his religious training. A bishop's discretionary powers include the granting or withholding of temple recommends that members need in order to, among other things: be admitted to a temple; allow a father to baptize his own son; have a marriage blessed in the temple; allow parents to give the traditional talk as their children depart for their missions; or be accepted for missions. Members must meet annually for an interview with their bishop to receive these important recommends.

The Mormon Church demands a heavy commitment from its members. To receive their recommend members must tithe ten percent of their income, abstain from smoking and drinking, give up two meals each month and donate the money saved to their highly effective internal welfare system, and young men must commit to a

Though I've always been put off by the wearing of the cross and by the crosses I see stuck onto the steeples of churches like the Dutch Reform Churches of western Michigan, I think it helps things along if everybody knows where everybody is coming from. But I also think that if a friend of mine were shot to death saving my life I wouldn't hold up the bullet as a sign of his suffering and sacrifice. It seems to me the bullet would be the last thing I'd hang onto. Rhoda tells me that's simplistic and that it overlooks our role in Christ's death. Catholic guilt, I say, though I don't doubt that I'm simplistic.

Dee Dee comes huffing back around with my print-offs and I start ordering my research, making sure the customers from my bank—having secured and paid off loans for cars, boats, jacuzzis and occasionally a vacation—aren't getting any money back they haven't already paid us. I used to let a claim slip every day—just one—some small amount, until I realized that the bank was willing to spend three bucks per customer to get their money back. $1.29. $3.42. $14.02. I calculated that in some obscene First of American way I was driving up the interest on their loans and I quit doing it.

The refunds are ridiculously low given what they pay me to track them down, justify them, and send them out to the people who sent them in. And the names spin by in the thousands. I remember them all, it seems, and some nights the people in my dreams assume their names, as their identities, and sometimes, as pathetic as it sounds, their loans. One of them is Mr. Mysterious,

---

two year mission that their families must pay for. Without a temple recommend, members are essentially second class citizens of the Mormon Church.

I tell myself. I once had Bobby Hansen's name come across my desk. Hansen was an NBA journeyman from the state of Utah who picked up a championship ring with the Bulls after escaping from the floundering Kings in the '91–'92 season.

"Brian," L.T. says right on cue from behind his carpeted wall, his voice cut by the oscillating fan at his desk, "you think your Jazz[5] gonna get outta the first round this year?" L.T., an avid basketball fan, comes down on me like a cold rain after a Jazz loss. He knows I'll bet Jazz no matter who's on deck and he cut me out of $100 last year when the Jazz faded at home to the Houston Rockets in the first round. It pissed me off, but at least he has

---

[5] The National Basketball Association team the Utah Jazz. The New Orleans Jazz entered the league on March 7, 1974, as the 18th member of the league for a $6.15 million expansion franchise fee. In a trade with the Atlanta Hawks the Jazz acquired future hall-of-famer 'Pistol' Pete Maravich as their first player. Maravich, along with being the Jazz' top scoring threat, was a showman. He wore a signature pair of floppy good-luck sweatsocks that always appeared to need washing. He shot the ball from everywhere and anywhere, and he never made a simple pass when he could make an entertaining one, so his assists regularly came from behind the back or through the legs.

After the 1978–79 season the struggling Jazz' ownership announced plans to move from New Orleans to Salt Lake City, Utah. Around the league the news was received with raised eyebrows and predictable jokes about taking a team named the Jazz into the staid atmosphere of Salt Lake City. The term 'jazz,' indisputably African American in origin, originally referred to sexual activity in addition to its obvious reference to the New Orleans based musical style. The

Geoff and me over to his house every other Sunday for a genuine Texan bar-b-que. L.T.'s displaced like me, and we watch a game and talk about anything but the bank. We call ourselves the Amigos after the movie *The Three Amigos* with Chevy Chase and Steve Martin.

So L.T. made me pay up, and after, as we were finishing another six pack, he was rambling and doing his shtick, that straight-in-the-eye don't-mess-with-the-black-man humor of his, about how his father cut out on him and how he can't settle down with just his one girlfriend, Jane, a beautiful woman with a ten year old boy who loves L.T. with a passion, who admires all L.T.'s stories and tall-tales about how he can dunk standing still, and suddenly I snapped: "You live your life out a window, L.T. And you're going to find yourself stuck at F.O.A. in twenty years, balancing loans."

---

term gradually came to refer to any vigorous or enthusiastic activity, and appeared in print for the first time in 1913 in a reference to a baseball team.

When the team made its move to Salt Lake it was so broke they didn't believe they could afford the cost of new uniforms and a name change. The name, however, was embraced by the community and stuck, becoming one in a long line of moves by the predominantly Mormon state to help redefine its reputation and character.

Maravich, who was eventually waived by the Jazz in 1980, missed seeing the Jazz's rise to respect. Eight years after being waived by the Jazz, the splashy, exciting Pistol Pete Maravich suffered a fatal heart attack during a pickup game of basketball in California. He was 40 years old.

Now L.T. chides me again. "They're gonna slide right into the fifth seed. They're tough at home, I'll grant you that, but fifth seed's gonna mean Karl's[6] hauling sheep all summer long."

"They'll suck it up. This is their year," I say. This is one thing I believe in. One place for faith in my life. "They're due." L.T. says nothing. The Amigos talk about three things at work: sports, movies, and music. Geoff talks about the car he's restoring, folding and unfolding a car-buff magazine he's had for more than two years loaded up on pictures of reconditioned cars and order forms for more parts, but the Amigos don't talk about Geoff's car. Geoff talks about Geoff's car.

"Did you guys hear that P.L. Travers died last week?" L.T. asks. He's playing a game the Amigos like to play. I hear the click-click-clack of the keyboards all around us. The carpeted cubicles can't drown out their ruckus.

"One hint, L.T." Geoff says.

---

[6] Karl Malone was drafted out of Louisiana Tech as the 13th pick in the 1985 NBA Draft. He's originally from Summerfield, LA., population 200. At 6'9", 256 lbs, he had the size and inside moves to attract a lot of attention, but had consistent trouble at the free-throw line in college. After several seasons with the Jazz, Malone purchased a black eighteen wheeler, complete with a mural depicting Malone on horseback herding cattle on a mountain range and an enlarged portrait of Malone in a cowboy hat on the side of his truck. In the off-season Malone likes to make runs in his truck, especially into Idaho where his wife is from. She and her twin sister are beauty queens, Karl's wife winning the Miss Idaho pageant a year before they married. Malone has since expanded his trucking company into a fleet of trucks, and has used the profits to help finance a hog farm his family operates in Arkansas.

"Think Disney. Think Australia. Think about a strange wind blowing . . ."

"Jesus," says Geoff. "Not the Mary Poppins lady!"

"Good call, Amigo. She died last week at age 96 in Queensland." Silence again. L.T. scours the entertainment pages in his off hours. *Entertainment Weekly, Movie Fan, Cinema.*

"That bothers me," I say. I look back at the top of the windows and we have our own strange winds to worry about. I can see the glass go concave—as if the building were aspirating—and then ease back flat. The wind has picked up so much the rain drops are moving along the tops of the windows leaving tracks like veins. It is like being at the end of a car wash.

While Kitty is off entertaining her nicotine addiction, Dee Dee and some of the other Snack-Machines decorate her desk with balloons, crepe paper streamers, and cakes, cupcakes, brownies, Rice Krispies treats, and two pies. "Oh, what the fuck?" Kitty says when she comes steadily back from her smoke.

"Happy Birthday, Kitty," Dee Dee says and begins a chorus of the birthday song. Other Snack-Machines begin singing and moving from their desks, converging on the sugary foods, like the chorus in a musical about chocolate.

Kitty is, as usual, put off. "Whose fucking idea was this? Dee Dee?"

"Yepper-Depper-Stepper-Doo," Dee Dee says and begins slicing smallish pieces of cake onto paper plates.

"You look more beautiful every year, Kitty," L.T. offers, then pinches her butt. L.T. can do this. More of a grab, really, given the enormity of L.T.'s mitt and the straight-legged smallness of Kitty's backside.

Kitty doesn't flinch, "You don't want to go there, L.T."

"You're old enough now. No more foolin' around. When we gonna go out, Kitty?" I could never figure out if L.T.'s flirting was rooted in actual desire. But then, Rhoda likes to tell me, I'm not all that perceptive about people and their moods; mostly I try not to care. When I first took this job—and L.T. and Kitty and Geoff were all new faces to me—I called my father and told him I didn't think I'd last out here, in the east. There was a conspicuous communication problem with everyone I met my first few weeks in Kalamazoo. They acted like they had to sound out everything I said in their heads, slowly, to understand me.

And there's a void where their dreams should be. This seemed so brutally obvious to me when I arrived for work my first day. I was fresh from college when my big brother Zach, who had done his mission[7] in Battle Creek and made a contact with F.O.A. and come aboard in '82, got me this job. I would ask what

---

[7] Young boys are encouraged to begin saving their money when they are in junior high so that they might get accepted to and finance a mission for the L.D.S. church. They're the kids you see riding around town on their bicycles in tandem in dark suits, wearing name tags that read 'Elder Peterson,' 'Elder Berry,' what not. They are sent to homes to home teach and to assist new converts. Largely because of this missionary system the Mormon church is one of the most aggressive and fastest growing churches in the world. While young girls are not directly discouraged by the church from going on missions, they are rather encouraged to obtain the illustrious promise ring (a ring essentially promising their engagement upon the missionary's return) from a departing missionary and work on filling their hope chest (not a literal chest, but a collection of necessities for married life—china, quilts, trivets). Once recommended by their bishop and accepted by the church for a mission the prospective missionaries are sent to M.T.C. (Missionary Training Camp) in Provo for a crash course in missionary work. If the prospective missionary

everyone did with their weekends, and Kitty, L.T., and Geoff, all several years older than me, said they liked to go to the bars sometimes, go to movies. I don't know exactly what I thought when I got out of college, but I knew there had to be more to life than going to work and going home at night, maybe a bar, maybe a movie. There had to be more important destinations ahead, plans to be hatched, things that needed doing that were yours to only do and that you could only do *now* that you had a real job and a real paycheck. But paychecks can't stretch *that* far. They can't turn into something they're not. At best, they pile up enough so you feel safe, and one week turns into one month. One month turns into one year. Two thousand miles, I think, must turn into two million.

So I made friends at work. But when I would try to broach the subject of my dissatisfaction with Geoff or L.T., I knew right away they wouldn't understand. L.T. wanted a job in one of the upstairs offices; Geoff wanted to fix his car and drive it. He wanted his softball team to win a trophy. These aren't dreams, though; these aren't things that anyone needed some singularity or deeply held belief to accomplish. They're goals, hopeful ambitions, at best! Like thinking the Jazz can win the title. It might happen, but it never really happens. And when I told my dad about how depressing it was to live so much of my life this way, he told me I was about to learn a hard lesson. We didn't speak to one another for more than a year except through my mother. It was the same way before I went to college, having blown my mission calling. We hit a dry spell then, and didn't talk to each other for two years.

---

shows an affinity for foreign languages, he is quickly and effectively taught a foreign language, complete with local colloquialisms and idioms, and sent to a foreign country. The swift and effectual teaching of languages by the M.T.C. is admired the world over.

I learned, as time went on in Kalamazoo and at F.O.A., that Kitty dreamed of owning a trailer home in Arizona where her brother lives, and that Geoff wanted his little girl to go to college. Everyone is like an onion, my father would probably tell me, and I've got to peel it all back before I go deciding there's nothing in the middle. Maybe it's the act of knowing, no matter the process, no matter the outcome, that I resent. Knowledge is limitation, belief is possibility, and faith and hope, somewhere between the two, is what I'm after.

"You *do know* what L.T. stands for, don't you."

"Loose Testicles?" Kitty says and begins to laugh, hard.

"Long Tongue," L.T. says. "Long Tongue."

"Save it for your lesbian friends, L.T." Kitty says.

"We'll get a room at a nice hotel, the Radisson . . ."

"Keep dreaming, L.T."

"You know what I hate about nice hotels?" L.T. says, leveling out.

"When," Kitty asks, "have you ever been in a nice hotel?"

"When they put those chocolates on your bed. When they put those chocolates on your bed and you come in late and you're drunk and you don't remember there might be chocolates on your bed, because, frankly, why the fuck would there be chocolates on your bed, and you wake up in the middle of the night and you reach down and you think 'Oh my God! I pooped the bed.'"

"You stole that," Kitty says, though she's laughing in spite of herself.

"Even if I stole it, that means it's still mine," L.T. says, and I pretend not to be listening.

The wind outside dies down. The window, still streaked with veins of raindrops, has stalled against the charcoal sky. I imagine the skyline below, the thick forest of evergreens and pines holding their colors against the looming gray, the web of birch branches crackling in the delicate rain. I envy the grounds crew, even in the chill rain, sucking at the moist air, hauling chipped pine and cedar and tending the bulbs that woke up too early this year and, in spite of several slow freezes, had been blinking their cat-eye yellows, fleshy peaches and blues, the past two weeks.

I often joked with the Amigos that the grounds crew sprays for birds. The Corporate Woods are surrounded on three sides by an occlusion of trees and yet, on the lunch patio, on warmer days, you can not hear the song of a single bird. L.T.'s theory is that Upjohn-Pharmacia dumps its chemicals just behind the trees, and he has imagined, in some detail, featherless and overgrown birds, so mucousy from sores that discarded pine needles adhere to their oozing, lopsided bodies, perfect for camouflage, their beaks cracked and jagged as teeth, stalking the woods like wolverines, feeding on equally scant squirrels and mice. It's only because of their uncanny ability to be absolutely silent that they are able to survive.

Despite the lack of sun I know Rhoda is probably awake, and while everyone is huddled around Kitty's desk picking apart and devouring Dee Dee's spread, I turn my back and call her. Rhoda answers after two rings, gravel-voiced, and obviously not yet awake. "Hello?" I am quiet for a moment, projecting myself through the phone and picturing myself curled up behind Rhoda under her warm cotton comforter. Then I picture her alone.

Rhoda is large, but not round like Dee Dee. Rhoda is angular, olive-skinned, imposing, with wide hip bones that jut out like the ivory handles on my grandmother's bureau. I often tease Rhoda that her strawberry blond hair is as coarse and wild as a tumbleweed, something she has never seen except on the television. Her face sometimes looks as if it is literally swimming through that hair, which smells sharp and tart like her kelp shampoo. Her soft lips are as pink as the inside of a conch shell.

"Brian?"

Her voice, scratchy, tentative, chills me and I hang up. It sounded like Jaimy's voice, and suddenly I am haunted by an image of Jaimy—spectral and rising, lone and pale.

Jaimy, like Rhoda, was angular, but more fragile, and taller—almost six feet of ghostly limbs and translucent flesh waiting to spin or break apart. Sometimes it seemed she was standing over me, floating away, or hovering. But that sense that she was breakable made her seem smaller somehow than she was at the same time. I remember the blue veins in her breasts and how I would trace them toward the skin covering her breastbone, beneath which her heart beat (I'd place my ear to her there and listen).

The last time I heard her voice was a call at three o'clock in the morning the year I moved to Kalamazoo. "Hi Brian, it's Jaimy," the voice had said. A long pause—"My mother has died." I was drunk.

Kitty reached over me and deposited a plate saturated with the sugary bric-a-brac. "Here, Momo, I'm not going to eat all this shit." She calls me Momo or worse. The grease seeps from the desserts into the paper of the plate like a halo or an aura.

"Thanks, Kitty," I say. She knows I've sworn off the stuff. She picks at a piece of cake and smiles over at Dee Dee, who is grabbing at another brownie. Dee Dee reminds me of my aunt Katrina, on my mother's side; warm and positive in an earthy, maternal way—a Venus-of-Willendorf way. Dee Dee was the first person who seemed genuinely interested in anything I might say when I moved to Kalamazoo, and I always have felt kindly toward her for that, for simply seeming to care. Her onion has a center, I think, and I don't need to peel it back any farther.

Carly, the supervisor, walks down our aisle. She wears red, F.O.A.'s official color, every day. She's just returned from having her hysterectomy, and I wonder if there's an appropriate sentiment for such a procedure. What does it mean to have your reproductive organs removed when you're still young, like Carly? "Happy Birthday, Kitty." It's insincere. She would fire Kitty if she could. She is like a hyena arriving amongst a group of vultures, and the Snack-Machines fill their plates again and fly away, one by one, back to their desks. Caw. Hiss. "How old are you today?"

"A day older than yesterday and still younger than you." Kitty offers Carly a plate and then clears a place to resume her research. "What did you get me, Carly?"

"Another smoke break."

Kitty looks at her watch and then at Geoff and L.T. and me, bouncing her eyebrows, grabs her jacket and says, "Well around here sugar melts, but shit floats." She sails out to the loading dock where she'll light her cigarette and suck it ashless in under five minutes. She does most everything like she's killing snakes.

That was one of the first things that struck me when I came to Kalamazoo. People smoke here. They sell cigarettes in Utah, certainly, and you occasionally see people light up—at concerts, at ski lodges, at places where a lot of people gather and where it's assumed people might smoke. But in Kalamazoo nearly half the people I've met smoke, they drink hard for nights on end, and fly in the face of most of the Words of Wisdom[8]. There are nearly as many smoky cafes as there are bars.

---

[8] The Words of Wisdom, often mistakenly seen as simply a kind of tea totalling mentality, advise Mormons not to drink hot beverages, not to drink alcoholic or caffeinated beverages, to refrain from smoking and premarital relations. While disregarding these Words is not 'sin' in the eyes of the L.D.S. Church, they are so strongly discouraged that in certain circles and locales (Brigham Young

My dad never minded having the occasional drink, though, and in fact his favorite Mormon joke went like this: Q: 'Why do you take two Mormons fishing?' A: 'Because if you just take one, he'll drink all your beer.' Ha ha. I learned to drink from my father and improvised the rest.

When Carly leaves with her haul, I redial Rhoda. "That was me earlier," I confess. "I could hear you, but I guess you couldn't hear me, so I hung up. It was a bad connection."

"I needed to get out of bed," Rhoda says, her voice smoothed over by now. I know Mr. Mysterious isn't there because there is no pretend in her voice. I imagine she has risen and turned on her hot water. I have convinced her to wean herself off coffee and she has agreed to cut back to morning tea, though I feel it is only better for her because it's more transparent. I told her, after we visited a cafe for one of our first dates (a date spent criticizing the way patrons slumped over their mocha-lattes trying to look très-chic) that I liked these people better when they were all drinking alcohol. (There are bars in Salt Lake City and I know most of them.)

Rhoda will have brushed her rawboned, frosty teeth; they are attractive, and she tends them like prize roses. I imagine her flipping her hair, can hear it brush against the receiver, and I want, more than anything, to be crawling from her bed myself. I tell her

---

University, for example) they are strictly enforced by the Powers that Be. When Jim McMahon (the quarterback of the Superbowl Champion Chicago Bears the year Brian graduated from Davis High School), a non-Mormon from nearby Roy, Utah, was attending B.Y.U. he was often, much to the embarrassment of the school and church, very vocal about the Words of Wisdom and did his best to break every one of them while he was breaking NCAA passing records. He was generally perceived as a 'charming Gentile.'

I will call her again soon, when I'm not flooded with work. "It's good to hear your voice first thing in the morning," she says, and hangs up.

Kitty slings back into her seat like a gunfighter's piece into its holster and talks to me while she orders her research. "Hey Momo, did you hear about Carly's hysterectomy?"

"No," I say. "I don't think it's something I need to know about."

"Her husband sent her flowers and a card that said, 'CONGRATS! IT'S A BOY!' Isn't that a hoot?" Kitty tries to push my buttons, and I let her. It's her birthday. "We went out with my sister and her kid last night. He's a little doll. A fucking doll! He's only two and she's got him standing on the table at Chianti's telling the waitress 'Well bite my teeny weenie!'" Kitty begins to laugh. "Bite my teeny weenie! Ha! Ha ha!"

"That's hysterical," I say.

"Say it for the woman," L.T. cuts in, his voice chopped by the fan. He has been trying to get me to say "Don't love me like you do, ladies" for months now. He saw this in a movie and thinks it would be funny to hear it come from my mouth. Kitty and Geoff think it would be funny. I don't.

I fade out, hearing only pieces of Kitty's story. I hear "Hey Mabel—get off the table! The dollar's for the beer!" several times. I hear L.T. say "Ice Princess," the fan cutting his voice.

I can feel myself taking shape in Rhoda's empty bed, my body assembling under her comforter. I can feel the nylon stitching on my naked shoulders and the clean sheets ripple under my heels. When I call Rhoda I will tell her to remind me to call my father when I get home tonight. I imagine my way through the rest of the day and in the late afternoon I make my way through the exiting Snack-Machines to my Bronco. The sun is breaking the clouds apart like a rescue team breaks the ice, pulling victims from an avalanche. But there is still so much rain and snow.

II. Gentile Women

My parents don't know about Rhoda, though by their comments I know they suspect I have returned to dating Gentile women. I could tell them that I have been to the Stake Center stomps[9], and I have been to church, and I have met some nice women. Like Liz, whose father is a bishop in nearby Paw Paw, and who is very attractive; terrific figure, eyes big and brown like a bird's. Liz is so unbelievably attractive, in fact, I wondered what she was doing still living at home, unmarried at her age, until she showed me a photo of her son Jacob.

Liz, like some L.D.S. girls I knew in Kaysville, had her son before she graduated high school. Jacob's father, who I know nothing about, excepting the obvious influence of his genes, is black. There aren't a lot of blacks in Utah[10], especially in

---

[9] A Stake Center is a larger meeting house for several wards. They often have mixers for single Mormons and 'stomps' or dances. These 'stomps' are designed for the younger crowd as a way to get young people together, before and after they have gone on their missions, under the aegis of the church elders, and to help build a sense of community among church members.

[10] When Karl Malone first came to Utah in 1985 he says he drove around for hours 'without seeing another brother.' When he finally did see another black man, it was down by the train yards in Salt Lake. He asked the man, a vagrant, if he wouldn't mind going out to get something to eat, as the story goes, so Karl would have someone to talk to. In fact, Malone's thick Louisiana accent was so bad when he arrived that the usual endorsement prospects for a first round draft pick were slow in coming.

Kaysville. I'd only ever seen a few of them down by the interstate pumping gas into their cars with out-of-state plates. As far as I know, there still aren't many blacks in Utah, owing probably to the fact that the Church didn't have their revelation allowing blacks to hold the priesthood[11] until the late 1970s.

Before that revelation we were told all blacks directly descend from Cain, and though it's no longer taught, the belief lingers. I feel it's something that shadows me; even here in Kalamazoo. When I am introduced to a black person as 'Brian the Mormon,' a ridiculously complicated tension springs out of my assumptions about what that person might assume I'm assuming and hangs there, preceding any conservation or first impression. It's a part of my burden, my dad would say, and that I must accept it all.

There was a general anxiety that swept through my high school, when several of the girls mysteriously started having

---

[11] The 'revelation' Brian is referring to occurred when the U.S. government threatened the L.D.S. Church with losing their tax exemption status if they did not allow blacks to hold the priesthood. In 1978, soon after the threat of taxation, Spencer Kimball, then president of the Mormon church, had a revelation from God allowing blacks to hold the priesthood. Even many Mormons had mixed feelings about the convenience of this 'revelation,' and the questions surrounding its impact on a decidedly Anglo-American religion. While blacks can now hold the priesthood, an absolute necessity to receive temple endowments, matrimonial sealings, and the ability to ascend to the highest tiers of the Celestial Kingdom, the descriptions of the Lord's curse against those of "black" skin still remain in *The Book of Mormon*.

mixed-race babies, and it wasn't until I was at the university that I had any first-hand experience with blacks. All the blacks I knew there were on the football and basketball teams and they all dated the white girls; but then, there weren't any black girls for them to date. Even Karl Malone used to come to my dorm to pick up this pretty girl with glasses from California who I never saw after my freshman year. A couple of times I thought about asking for an autograph while he was waiting in the lobby, but I remember how intimidating Malone is up close. He's like a Frankenstein's monster, each limb so massive you'd think he'd need a block and tackle to swing it along. He's a good head taller than I am but tremendously wide bodied and muscular like a bodybuilder[12]. And yet he still walks around like a normal person; light on his feet and unfettered. A body like that makes you believe in all kinds of things.

Karl stopped getting out of his truck, a jacked-up black pickup truck with tinted windows all around, and would just sit out front, his black truck shining under the white glare of the parking lot lights, and wait. I could look down from my window and watch her cross the lobby from the girl's dorm, pretending to ignore the stares as she climbed into the cab of the Mailman's[13]

---

12 Malone was recently voted, by the strength and conditioning coaches of the National Basketball League, the strongest player in the NBA The coaches noted that while there may be bigger, even more muscular players than Malone, no one of his size and muscularity can run the floor as well and play with as much finesse as Malone.

13 Karl 'The Mailman' Malone. So named because he always delivers. In early January 1984 a couple of grad assistants in the Louisiana Tech sports-info office were brainstorming marketing ideas for one of the most accomplished basketball players ever to emerge

truck. She was one of those campus goddesses, more than six feet tall and blonde, and like most guys in the dorm I always had a thing for her, but she wouldn't give me the time of day. Her name was Christine.

After she started dating Karl she wouldn't give anyone the time of day. Why would she? My roommate (Shellac-head, I called him, why should he have a real name?), would watch her with binoculars from our third floor dorm window as she undressed in the mornings and at night. He was a strange, zitty kid who would put so much Vitalis on his head at night that he didn't need to tend to it in the morning; it would shellac his hair to his head like a helmet. Like G.I. Joe hair.

One night I was telling some friends of mine what Shellac-head did at night and they suggested I get even, so I tracked down my friend Cliff from the football team. He was a tight-end and big, like Malone. But Cliff was really dark-skinned. The other football players would chide him and call him things like the Grinch that Stole Blackness and Saudi Soda and pretend they couldn't see him when it was dark outside. I knew that wouldn't matter, though, since Shellac-head didn't care one bit about Utah sports.

I told Cliff what was going on and one evening, when I

---

from the Pelican State. Malone, who happened to be in the hallway during this marketing session, had been referring to himself as the "Rim Wrecker" because of the number of backboards he had been shattering in recent weeks. Tech basketball coach Andy Russo had swept up the fiberglass shards and thrown them in a box. The grad students glued fragments onto index cards outlining Malone's achievements and mailed them to 1,000 members of the news media nationwide. The cards were stamped "Special Delivery from the Mailman."

knew Shellac-head was at work with the binoculars, Cliff dressed in Utah Jazz sweats and walked down into the parking lot and yelled up at Shellac-head. He called his name several times until Shellac-head stuck his head out the window. Cliff called him out: "I hear you been peepin' my girl! I'm gonna come up there and rip your fucking arms off, pervy-boy!" Shellac-head hid under the bed and didn't go to class for three days, convinced that Karl was waiting for him in the parking lot. Whenever that shiny black truck would pull into the lot, Shellac-head would high-tail it up to our room and lock himself in.

The little time I'd spent with Cliff made up most of my experience with black people before I moved to Michigan; the most memorable of which was just a laugh over a beer with Cliff after terrorizing my voyeur room mate. Now that I think about it, there were the Wilkersons, back in Kaysville, who lived four houses down from my parents when I was in elementary school and who had two children my age. When the Wilkerson's children would be let out to play it was always time to come inside, and I never got to even talk to them because they moved out after three months. I don't believe anyone really talked to them.

There were, however, a lot of blacks at nearby Hill,[14] and

---

[14] Hill Air Force Base, located just North of Kaysville in Clearfield, Utah. One of the largest Air Force Bases in North America. In the late seventies the so-called Hi-Fi killers were stationed there. They were two black men who, under the influence of drugs and alcohol, broke into the Hi-Fi stereo store holding several employees hostage while they conducted their robbery. One of the men then decided to rape, torture, and kill the victims, forcing them, among other things, to drink Draino, and stomped a stereo jack into the ear of one victim. His accomplice did not assist in these crimes, but was sentenced to death, and died by lethal injection at the Foot-of-the-Mountain (the

we had seven girls at Davis[15] end up with black babies—'mulatto babies,' the bishop called them. These GI's were really less scandalous than they were mysterious; like the Wilkersons, we never saw them come into or leave Kaysville, never saw them with the girls from our high school. There were rumors that they floated in like ghosts to exact revenge against Mormons in one of the most Mormon of communities. One GI supposedly fathered three children before he was transferred. We called him the Father of our Country.

Unlike the women back in Kaysville, Liz kept Jacob and is raising him in the Mormon tradition. Those Kaysville babies just disappeared like their ghostly fathers and I don't think it ever occurred to me to ask where they all shipped off to. It was assumed that's what happened to black babies in Kaysville back then. Like they were all little soldiers themselves and their transfer papers

---

same prison where Gary Gilmore demanded to be executed in the seventies) in the late eighties. His lawyers claimed the State of Utah had a racist agenda when it came to the death penalty. The Hi-Fi killers' horrific crimes had a lasting affect on Utah's relationship with Hill. Brigham Young taught and firmly believed in blood atonement. This is a belief that some sins, such as murder, are so serious that the atonement of Christ can not provide adequate grace for forgiveness for the sinner. Only the spilling of the blood of the offender can offer redemption. This practice is not Church doctrine, nor has the Church ever practiced this doctrine, but Young's ideas have long colored the beliefs of the faithful.

[15] Davis High is so-named because it serves Davis county, the fastest growing county in Utah. Their mascot is the Davis Dart, a scowling cartoon dart with heavily muscled arms and legs.

came through not long after they met their mothers. Liz mentioned the importance of a good father figure for Jacob one too many times and I backed right off. Nobody's that beautiful.

I met Rhoda not long after I met Liz, and our path seemed to be smoother, less complicated. There wasn't marriage and fatherhood waiting up ahead like a destination we were aiming for, we just kind of rambled along. And in that rambling I've stumbled into moments when she's absorbed in her physics or astronomy homework, when I've seen her lay her finger down on a single page and pull a pencil from her tumbleweed hair and caress it with her teeth before bringing it down to the page, when I feel most in awe of her because I know that she's absolutely engaged in things that are universal. That even if I try to project myself into the center of her thoughts, the universe always wins. She will look up at me, in my interruptions, as if I were some memory, some ghostly love that deserves a smile. And then I'm gone from her. But with every moment like that where her life eclipses my own, with every spectral, dismissive smile, she brings more heat to my want.

I was reluctant to go all the way with Rhoda, but she was insistent, and things I promise myself when I'm alone with my thoughts can melt furiously with the stroke of one hand, the caress of the backs of Rhoda's nails along the ridges of my body. When the deed has been done, I feel fresh, too, not at all guilty, like I've done something for myself that's between me and God and Rhoda and no one else. My parents, my bishop, my brothers and sisters suspect, certainly.

I imagine my brother Zach and his wife Michelle pulling and tugging at his fettering garments[16] and I'm glad that's not me.

---

16 Garments are similar to a Union-suit, worn under the clothing by missionaries and return missionaries (hereafter referred to as R.M.'s) acting as a blessed shield against the failings of the world. And,

If I'd done my mission, I think, I'd have folded my garments away like a soldier puts away his uniform.

Zach first donned his garments when I was in high school. Our bishop gave me the calendar[17] and I remember Zach telling me, when he saw how many black crosses I'd filled my calendar with, that it'd be easier for me not to fall to temptation once I got my mission call. But what Zach doesn't know, will probably never know, is that it gets easier all the time.

After work, when Rhoda stops by my apartment, I meet her at the door and soul kiss her and pull her toward my bedroom, undressing her in the living room, the hallway. When she resists I convince her I've checked, we are alone, but she still tries to drag her clothes along with her foot as we finally move into the bedroom.

After, while she sleeps, I notice the rain has stopped outside, and the lilac evening comes strong through my window. I rise and open the blinds. There are two women down in the parking lot looking into the sky I am surveying, not looking up.

---

should missionary or R.M. momentarily forget himself in the heat of passion, the cumbersome design of the garments serves as both reminder and deterrent against proceeding uninhibited. Brian, of course, having never served a mission, would be without garments.

[17] Bishops often give teenage boys calendars when they suspect they have been masturbating. When the boy feels the urge to tug his member he is asked to take out the calendar and look at it. If the desire become too strong and he jerks off he is supposed to mark that day with a large black 'X' or cross. At the end of the month the bishop will call several boys in to the church and they will share their calendars with each other and discuss methods of control.

They do not see me, even with the blinds open, standing nude near the window. I try to direct their stares to my window with my mind, but they exchange words and one gets into a white car and drives away. The other, a muscular girl in sweats and spandex, cocks her head, trying to pop her neck, and walks into my very building. She looks up, briefly, but I'm unsatisfied that she has seen me and I think it is just as well.

The violet light makes Rhoda's hair auburn, the roots and shadows blue. She turns slowly in the bed, exposing the snaky curve of her back and the soft, round backside. Rhoda's skin is so smooth and dark it looks like the slickrock of southern Utah, and I think about making myself small and climbing her body like canyon walls, sheltering in a cave. There is nothing ungodly about Rhoda's body, but I know I cannot attest to her mind or soul. She, I know, feels these things about me.

It is late when we wake again, the parking lot light shining hard through my window. I hear my roommate is home again, and he heads straight to his room and is silent. His life has become a mystery to me. I feel as though I have slept, but I think I have just stared at the ceiling so long my sense of time has come up useless. Rhoda dresses and I have to check the hallway before she will try to recover one of her socks. Somehow she managed to drag all of her clothes, except the stray sock, into my room.

We eat dinner at a restaurant near the university and Rhoda sees so many people she knows while we eat that I feel suddenly distanced from her, from even the act of knowing people. This is not the universe I want her to know. But what is? Utah? F.O.A.? We never see people from work when we go out.

Rhoda asks me what's wrong, as she drops me at my apartment, and I tell her I am merely tired.

"Are you still not sleeping?" she asks.

"No. Not yet."

"You should try some of that melatonin. My mother passes out from it."

"No," I say. I am strongly against taking anything to *make* me sleep.

"Prozac, maybe then," she says flatly. "Call your father." She kisses me goodbye.

When I am alone and the apartment is so quiet I can hear the tit-tit-tit of the lightest rain flickering against my window, I call my parents. My mother answers the phone and I think of Jaimy and wonder how it must be for her to call home. Empty. There is something grim and heavy about how Catholics handle death. It hadn't occurred to me that my parents could actually die. "Mom," I say. She knows it is late for me, near midnight, so she tells me to go to bed.

At night I am certain I do not sleep. I hear every click of my clock, every drop of rain and every peep outside my window long before the sun comes up. I drive by Rhoda's apartment again on the way to work and nothing happens, there is no mysterious car parked in front of her apartment and there is nothing out of the ordinary, like the nothing the day before and the nothings all the way back. Some days the sky just gets lighter and lighter, hot pinks all morning, soft flesh, a little rain, nothing, or nothing else. It doesn't make me love Rhoda any less that she cannot sense my presence, but it doesn't make me love her any more, either.

The morning moves at mid-week's pace and I drive to finish my first batch of research so I can call Rhoda before my break. But I find my mind returning to Jaimy more and more often. It feels wrong, as if I am cheating Rhoda somehow, ignoring her. And yet there is a fundamental rightness to this return, like my innards are a rubber band anchored in Kaysville and I have been stretched out here with the physical knowledge that I will soon snap back. Each time I return to these memories, these ghosts, I bring something more into the light, some forgotten feature, some habit or movement, like the restrained, lightning-quick way she tucked her hair behind her ear.

A scream cuts through the office like an indoor thunder clap, stopping everything from functioning in its normal mode. There is never a reason for loud, piercing noise at F.O.A., or any noise at all, really. Everyone on my row is standing beside their desks, trying to look over to the next row and the rows behind that. I feel a tightening in my gut—has someone come in with a gun? It is something I always fear, and I look out toward the window and try to look into the sky in case it might be my last chance. I do not want to die in Kalamazoo, Michigan.

"Somebody get a doctor! Please, somebody get a doctor!" That sends everyone running toward the sound, only Kitty has stopped and returned to the phone.

It is Dee Dee. I can see her white tennis shoe and her leg, wrapped in black spandex, twitching on the ground. The entire office is huddled around her, looking down at her and whispering among themselves. I can only see one of her legs, but she is face down and when that leg begins to move back and forth, it appears as though the crowd is picking at her, pulling her apart. "Okay, let's roll her over onto her back," a voice near the center says.

I can hear their efforts, and someone asks Dee Dee if she can hear, and then tempers begin to give way. "Will everybody get back so we can roll her over!"

"Get out of the fucking way!"

And "God damn it! Has anyone called the paramedics?"

I can see Dee Dee better, as I inch my way forward. Her legs bouncing off the ground as if she were kicking off an invisible blanket on a hot, uncomfortable night. Or she's having a nightmare. Her eyes want to escape from under their lids. They rage against the thin, bluish skin. Her arms, though, do not move except in tandem with her torso, which seems to pool outward; she is melting. Her face is as white as copier paper, water coming out of her eyes like her head is an overfilled water balloon someone stuck with a pin—it's no mere crying. She begins to vomit, and as she sucks for air, I can hear the vomit being sucked back in.

I feel myself grow weak at the knees, but I think, as I watch her die, about her soul entering the tertiary heaven[18], and I tell myself *don't worry for her,* because I know, given the right circumstances, finding our common link, I could eventually baptize her. For the first time I appreciate the importance of baptizing the dead[19]; it's all I can do. Watching and waiting.

When she stops vomiting I see a man I barely know reluctantly begin fishing things out of her mouth. I decide I might be most useful directing the paramedics through the maze of cubicles in our office and I go out to the front, where the guard is supposed to be. No one is there and I don't know how to buzz the door open, though I can see through the rain streaked windows into the still sea of cars that no ambulance has arrived.

I go into the men's room and call out to the guard, whose small feet I can see under the end stall reserved for the

---

[18] The Mormons believe in three physical heavens. The tertiary, or lowest, heaven is assigned to the unbaptized.

[19] The Mormons have one of the most extensive collection of genealogical records in the world. They believe that the souls of the unbaptized can be saved by being baptized. If a person were to convert to Mormonism and was concerned about the souls of their ancestors not realizing the highest heavenly plane, they could find their blood link and baptize the spirit of the dead relative in the name of Jesus Christ.

handicapped. "Dee Dee's dying. We need to buzz in the paramedics."

I can hear him panicking in the stall, "Oh Jesus. Jesus, Jesus, Jesus . . ." I hear him furiously tearing at the toilet tissue. When he emerges he has a magazine folded under an arm and is walking quickly past me, as though I were an impediment to his job. He smells coppery, like blood.

The paramedics are pulling up just as we come back into the lobby. He buzzes them through and I tell them to follow me. They are carrying only a tool box of medicines and implements and I know it will not be enough. When we turn the final corner of the maze I see dozens of women are crying. But Carly looks like she is restraining an urge to create order.

The word comes down and we are allowed to go home, if we want, after the paramedics haul Dee Dee outside. Geoff and L.T. help them maneuver her body through the maze of cubicles. She is strapped onto a gurney and they are respirating her, but everyone knows she is dead.

As I walk back to my desk I hear a man I barely know say, quietly, "I guess no one gets out of here alive." I stop, the impulse to attack him comes raging up through my body, and I turn to face him. His smirk seems to melt from his face and a woman near him whispers, "You're awful. Just plain awful."

My first thought is to let him have it, but then I think that for the most mediocre mind there is sometimes epiphany in cynicism and I let it all be.

III. The Family Home

For a long while I sit in the parking lot watching my officemates pull themselves out of the building. I sit until I feel the unnecessarily complicated extraction has come to some conclusion. It seems even the confused souls from the other offices have gotten wind of what's happened and begin making up their minds to stop standing around uselessly with their hands floating around their chins and get back to work. Every one of us looks so overwhelmed by emotion, and even the simplest maneuver looks awkward from where I sit. In the parking lot a light drizzle like glitter-dust covers their heads and drooping coats. They stand around until the dust sinks into their hair, and they become wet.

A person has disappeared from my life and the finality of that thought makes me shudder. Dee Dee wasn't the kind of person I always thought I'd hang onto, like I thought Jaimy might be, or like I sometimes now think Rhoda might be. But Dee Dee was always kind to me and had more good will bottled up inside of her than all my friends put together. Dee Dee was like a child that way, like a big smiling baby. I can't help but take it farther back now, and think of Dee Dee still curled up in the womb of her cubicle, all that doomed hope trying to make its way into the world.

The Western Michigan University campus is alien to me, like a new city, a new port-of-call. The students mill about, even in the cold drizzle, like the people from my office, and ignore my presence, my ratty old Bronco a passport to this place. I drive past the athletic building, a sprawling yellow 'W' painted onto the roof, like the stone and concrete letters on the mountains around Salt Lake—the monolithic 'U' at Utah, the divining 'Y' in Provo, a hundred smaller letters in the foothills announcing 'V'iewmont, 'B'ountiful,

'P'leasantville. One letter occupying so much mountain space it can be seen from the air.

I strain to find Rhoda's mass of hair bouncing through the drizzle, knowing, should I find her, my presence will be shocking— embarrassing, maybe. I think I might find her arm-in-arm with Mr. Mysterious and I imagine pulling the Bronco onto the curb, whapping the door shut as I jump out, brushing past Mr. Mysterious as if I could ignore him into oblivion. Or better still, I follow them until the very moment he leaves Rhoda alone and, when she fumbles for something to say to cover the awkwardness of the moment, I will say to Rhoda, before she recovers, "Dee Dee died today," or, more matter-of-factly: "Something terrible has happened,"or, frightfully: "I needed to tell you something disturbing," or, ominously: "I needed to talk to you, Rhoda." I imagine I tell Rhoda we need to drive out to Utah together, and she gets in the Bronco and we drive all night and all day.

There is a brunette with a bob, and then another, and a blonde with hair down her back, a hippie girl with wild strawberry blonde hair like Rhoda's and then I am to the Bronco Mall where I find a metered stall and let my clattery engine wind down. The college students look so young to me, like children standing in the rain, too cold and wet to play, too spirited to go back inside.

I disembark and head into the Union. It smells of rain and cologne and dust, and still no one notices me. I have never been in the Student Union before, but it is the same as the Union at Utah, at Utah State, at BYU. Bookstore, bowling alley, video games, billiards, kids. There is a cafe downstairs and a lot of open seating, and I remember that I am looking for Rhoda. I don't know where the physics building might be, where her classes are, and I don't have the energy for that kind of search. In fact, I think, I might need that kind of desperation if she's with Mr. Mysterious.

I realize I don't have any money and I see they have a F.O.A. branch built right into the Union. The people there don't recognize me either, and I focus in on the teller with the lupine face—the yellowy eyes and pointed nose—trying to impart to her what has happened to one of ours, the way I've heard wolves know instinctively when one of their own dies. I suppose I thought the howl from Corporate Woods would've echoed to this tiny branch by now and I'm worried that maybe it already has.

The girl over at the cafe counter is sweet, full-faced and smiling, as if she likes her job and I think I'll do something I've never ever done before—order a coffee. But then I realize I have no idea what to order and there are people standing behind me who don't know me and seem to *need* their coffees as soon as possible to get to class or to get back to work and a strange feeling creeps into me that I am doing something terribly wrong. That I will be caught. "What's good?" I say.

"The cafe mocha latte is good on a day like this, if you like chocolate."

"I'll have one of those, please," I say, snapping the crisp bill in my hands like a New Year's popper. I smile back at her and I can feel my own smile wilting on my face.

"Regular or Double?" she asks.

"Double," I say, feeling braver, feeling like I should do it right.

"Decaf or Regular?"

"Oh. I'll have a regular," I say. Her questions reinforce my feeling that I'm doing something wrong, but I'm on auto, answering things I don't think about.

"Two percent or skim?"

"Skim?"

"Here or to go?"

"Go?"

Her process is complicated but sophisticated. She turns handles, pulls knobs, smacks and flips metal containers, swirls a carafe into a hissing, steaming machine, and I think how unnatural the whole coffee thing really is. Who invented this process? How could someone possibly see all of this in a coffee bean? If you make the body impure, the Words of Wisdom say, you are that much farther from God.

The styrofoam cup feels warm against my hands, hot even, and I shift it backwards and forwards as I walk back into the vomitorium. There are plenty of chairs but they seem to be taken by drifting singles, slumped over books and magazines. I walk past a wooden map of the United States and see there is a hook on Utah with a handwritten tag: *Seeking ride to Ogden, Moab, or anywhere in between. Will pay 1/2 gas. Randy Hansen.* On the back of the tag is his phone number.

Hansen[20] is a common name in Utah. Like Peterson it doesn't carry the weight of Young or Smith, but is a good Mormon name none-the-less. The coffee begins to burn my hands and I feel a frantic need to sit down. I find a table near the cafe where I can survey the room and the doors. If Rhoda comes into the Union, I will see her.

I pop the lid off my double-mocha-latte-with-skim-milk-to-go, and the steam escapes like it does on television and in movies. Suddenly I am not so sure why I have ordered a coffee and I stare into the steaming, black concoction. I can see my eyes floating in the black and when I blink, the eyes blink back at me, dark and sharp. The girl at the nearest table stares at me, looking down into her magazine when I look at her. Just past her, two boys

---

[20] When the Mormon church was in its infancy, around 1870, some 38,000 English citizens and 13,000 other Europeans, mostly of Swedish extraction, had joined the church and come to the United States.

in baseball caps and thick woolen sweaters stare at me and when I look at them they resume their conversation as if they have not noticed me at all. I take a quick, scalding sip of the coffee.

It is not at all what I expect; it is smooth, sugary and, aside from burning the roof of my mouth, does me little harm. I sip again, peering over the lip of the cup with all four eyes. The girl is turning pages and the boys are leaving. I sip again, and I feel warm, better, centered. New boys move into the recently departed table and I stare at them.

The farther I move into the cup, the cooler it becomes, and when I arrive at the syrupy bottom I am ready for another. It is an expensive habit, more costly than beer, and my ten has nearly dissolved after my second. I feel good. I mourn for Dee Dee, but I feel alive, away from work and into life. When I order my third, my ten reduced to a sprinkling of change, the full-faced girl asks, "Are you sure?"

This caffeine is powerful juju and I can feel it taking over my blood, my thoughts. I remember when Jaimy had her wisdom teeth out, the day I took her to my parents' house the first time, or rather, the first time my parents were there. We were in college and I had taken her to get her wisdom teeth extracted and they doped her up and told her to avoid alcohol but they didn't say anything about caffeine, which Jaimy drank by the gallon back then, putting off studies and staying out late with me most nights, but still getting up at the lilac crack of Utah's dawn to go to work and school six days a week. And so Jaimy slugged down a half pot of coffee because, she said, she was *out of it* and didn't want to meet my parents while she was *really out there*. But I insisted, because this was a window of opportunity for us since it would be one of the few times my parents would both at home without any of my siblings around.

Jaimy was jumpy and talked a lot, but I thought that might just be nerves at first and things were going all right, given my mother's comments about Gentiles and my father's inquisition about her family history in Utah: *What were they doing in Kaysville?* And Jaimy asked me, quietly, whispering intimately into my ear on the couch in front of my parents, if she could go put some water on her face, she was feeling flushed, and I said sure and announced her intentions to my parents and pointed Jaimy to the *ante-room,* we called it, just under the stairs in the front of the house. It was for freshening up, and had a sink and a medicine cabinet and no toilet and I was proud of her when I watched her walk down the hallway in brisk, confident long-legged strides and turn and smile at me before she opened the door as if to say "Everything's going to be all right," before I had to go back to the icy stares of my parents who I knew would sit there silently until Jaimy returned.

Jaimy was gone several minutes and I was worrying that she was getting sick from the medicine like they said she might and then a loud, slow crash came from the bathroom followed by another, then a tremendous thud, and my parents and I were up in a flash, tearing toward the hallway. I knocked on the ante-room door and there was no answer. "Jaimy?"

My mother piped in, "Jaimy, dear? Is everything all right?"

I peeled open the door and Jaimy's head rolled out, beautiful, pale, and unconscious, and I remember thinking how much she looked like Sleeping Beauty from the Disney cartoon. She was unconscious, and unconscious of the fact that her pants were pulled down around her ankles and so were her panties and she was lying on top of the ante-room sink, next to the medicine cabinet, the towel rack ripped from the wall and clutched in her white hand, and there were small pieces of plaster stuck in her pubic hair and my impulse was to brush them away before my mother let out a gasp and my father chided, "Cover that girl with something! Oh for Pete's sake, please cover that girl with something!" She woke soon after, before I could cover her from my father's probing and disapproving eyes, which to this day, I believe, soured me on our potential, Jaimy and mine, to be together.

It seems that Jaimy had gone to put water on her face and had a nearly uncontrollable need to urinate and there being no toilet and things going, she said, terribly in the other room, she decided to try for the sink, which then gave way, and she grabbed at the only things she could to keep from falling, the towel rack and the medicine cabinet, and the next thing she knew she was with me in the emergency room (at mother's insistence), and she said she had to go again, it must have been all the coffee. Jaimy and my parents never recovered. And now I have to piss. . . .

I'm in and out and I still don't see Rhoda come in or go out with the tides of students. I feel better walking around. 'Large and in charge,' as they say. My half-finished third hits the trash can when I begin to feel an acidy sag in my stomach. My vision collapses, my periphery fuzzing over and fading out but my focus, my aim, becomes unbelievably sharp. I feel I can burn through the things I look at; table, linoleum floor, map of the United States, the unhowling girl. I pick up a copy of *USA Today* with some of the remnants of my mocha change and peel through the red sports section. The regular season ended and the playoff brackets have been set and, just as I thought, Utah is home against Portland and Portland's ancient rookie[21] phenom for the first five. *USA Today*

---

21 Portland's rookie center Arvydas Sabonis, sometimes affectionately called 'Arthritis' by his team-mates, came over from the European leagues as a thirty year old rookie. Arthritis can shoot from

gives Utah an out-in-four against Portland[22], citing Malone and Stockton's[23] age[24], in spite of the fact that this is an even year for the Jazz[25]. But then again this is the same rag that just two weeks

---

the outside, pass extremely well for a big man, and is a wide body in the lane. He presents some real match-up problems for the Jazz who have a soft-spot at center with the inconsistent rookie Greg Ostertag, Felton Spencer (who had been playing the best ball of his career before tearing his achilles the previous season) and the seldom-used Greg Foster. Brian, because of KU's recent success against his alma-mater in all sports, is a died-in-the-wool Jayhawk-stompin' University of Kansas-hater. During the off-season last year L.T. bet him that the Jazz would draft Ostertag, the all-time shot blocker at University of Kansas, given Utah's low draft pick, need for a shot-blocker, and proclivity for white, country-boy types. Ostertag showed up at training camp at nearly 300 lbs and complaining of asthma during coach Jerry Sloan's rigorous drills. Sloan said of Ostertag, "I've never seen someone so fat and out of shape in my life." And benched Ostertag for most of the early season. But Malone and Stockton and some other players took Ostertag under their wings and encouraged him to make the most of it. Ostertag slimmed down and by mid-season started playing more of the solid defense Sloan demanded. After their first play-off series Ostertag said, "I know when I came in here I had a lot of guys mad at me, but I'm trying hard now and things are coming together for me."

[22] The first round of the NBA playoffs is a best of five. The team with the better season record gets the home court advantage with the first two games played in Utah, the second two (if necessary) played in Portland, and a fifth game to be played back in Utah. While Utah has had its share of trouble in the playoffs, including a first round loss to Houston the previous year, the fact that a national publication

like *USA Today* would pick Portland in four, a team playing mediocre ball near the end of the season, to win on the Jazz' home court is a terrific slap in the face.

23 John Stockton, the 16th overall pick in the 1984 draft, was a little known player taken out of little known Gonzaga University. At 6'1", Stockton was considered by many too small to make it in the NBA. But the year of Brian's story Stockton became the NBA's all-time leader in assists (a pass to a teammate who then scores a basket) and steals (just what the name implies). Though the tandem of Stockton and Malone is unequalled in NBA history their allegiance to the small-market of Utah has seriously hampered Malone's endorsement contracts in the age of Nike, Reebok, Wheaties, McDonalds, and Gatorade, while Stockton refuses to endorse anything. Subsequently the two are seldom given much national attention or respect in the NBA in spite of their success. When Brian first came to Michigan and played some pick up games down at the Y and on the playground near his house, the black kids would tease "Pass me the ball John Stockton! Pass the ball John Stockton!"

24 While they are two of the leagues' veterans, Malone and Stockton are also two of the leagues' most durable players. During their careers they have missed only eight games (four a piece) between them. Their patented play, the pick-and-roll, whereby Malone will set a pick and feed the ball to Stockton then roll around the player he just picked off to receive the ball near the basket, is still the most consistently effective play in the league. If the Trailblazers hope to have a chance against the Jazz they have to isolate the pick and roll and stop Stockton and Malone.

25 The Jazz have made the Western Finals in '92 and '94. They lost in '94 to the NBA champion Houston Rockets and in '92 to the Portland Trailblazers.

ago named Stockton and Malone as two of the dirtiest players in the league[26]. The words and numbers on the page begin to read like the microfiche at the office and I restack the paper and feel an overwhelming need to stand up, to get moving.

I withdraw some more money and play a video game. It's a hitting game, three dimensional, and though I have no idea what I'm doing it's a blast; pop, kick, punch, and then my spine is torn from my bloody stump. My eyes dry up and I have to feel happy I learned a secret move—left, left, down, left, and an optic blast incinerates my opponent, a busty Korean girl in a leotard. I move on to the bookstore and the slicks from the magazine rack draw me over like a moth to a porch light. *How to Teach Him to Satisfy Your Needs,* sings out to me. The blurbs on women's magazines call out to me like Sirens: *The Real Secret Behind Better Orgasms, Is He Sleeping Around?* Rhoda? But none of the women around me look anything like Rhoda, and I decide it's time for one more sweep through the Union and then I should go home, and wait for Rhoda to call me.

There's a slip of paper under my windshield wiper and for a moment I'm certain it's a note from Rhoda, but it's from the

---

[26] *USA Today* polled many of the NBA's players to find who was the dirtiest player, and though Dennis Rodman, the outlandish rebounding sensation for the Chicago Bulls, was the run-away favorite, Stockton and Malone were the next two most frequently cited dirty players. Other players claim Stockton's choir-boy looks and low-key demeanor allow him to have more calls go his way, while Malone's infamous slap, knocking the ball from an opponent's hands when they lower them, was cited as both painful and generally uncalled by the referees: An anonymous player was quoted as saying "Apparently the sound of Spalding leather and the flesh of a human arm sound remarkably similar when slapped."

parking services instead. As I let my Bronco warm up I look out over the campus through my shimmering, drizzled windshield at the campus, the golden bricks and green glass buildings, the college kids teasing each other, the daffodils leaning into each other in front of a pulsing fountain, and I wonder where Rhoda is, breathing amidst all this chaos.

When I get home Phil is asleep. His door is open and he is sprawled across his mattress, his arms thrown over his head with the pillow squashed under them. I shut his door, jealous and disgusted, and check the answering machine.

There is a hang-up and then a call from Zach. "Brian," Zach's tinny voice says, "I tried and tried to reach you at work but you never picked up. You've gotta remember to put your phone on voice mail or you're going to get in some serious trouble. Listen, I just got a call from Mom that they're selling the house . . . Did you know about this already? They're moving to Park City[27] to a condo to retire near the Olympics. What in the heck is this all about? Call me."

Then there is another message from Zach, less tinny. "I heard what happened at work. Call me when you get home."

---

[27] Park City Utah, home of the 2002 Winter Olympic games thanks to a huge lobbying effort from the Utah State government and several local celebrities; most notably Steve Young, quarterback of the San Francisco 49ers. There were more than a few concerns by the Olympic committee about Utah's stringent drinking laws, but those fears were apparently put aside in favor of 'The Greatest Snow on Earth.' Park City's a short drive up Big Cottonwood canyon from Salt Lake City and home to the U.S. Ski Team and several of the best ski resorts in the country. Brian and his family generally ski the Ogden resorts, however, because they're closer to Kaysville and much more affordable for a family of nine.

I call Rhoda and she's home. "Are you at work?" she asks. Somehow she knows I am not.

"Can you come over, Rhoda? I need to see you."

"Right now?"

"Right this minute," I say. "I've had some coffee today and I don't feel myself."

IV. A Distant Family

Rhoda looks older than she did the night before, like she too has been without sleep. I can feel my coffee wearing off in the worst way. I tell her about Dee Dee and I don't leave out anything. Rhoda turns pale, like she might be sick, and says, "How can you possibly go back?"

"I have to," I tell her. "It's my job." Rhoda leans into me, and though she doesn't look as good as I want her to right now, she smells terrific, like someplace warm, dry, and clean. I start to unbutton her blouse, but she takes my hand away and looks me in the eye like she can't believe what I want from her. "It might make things easier on me," I tell her, but she holds tight on my hand.

Then all at once she lets go and draws back nervously. "What about Phil?"

"Out like a light," I say. I know the direction has changed and where we're headed and it feels powerfully focused, like I can shake what's happened and though Dee Dee is there, tugging at something on the fringes, I can feel myself moving away, into everything Rhoda. I move slowly, like I'm being quiet, and pop her velvety buttons with my thumbnail and the pad of my finger—one, two, three. She wears these bras that undo in front, something I like, and I unlatch her, watch her breasts fall softly onto her ribs. I kiss down her stomach, tasting the soap on her skin, smelling the spice of her perfume. Her slacks are loose and I pull those apart and off and her satiny panties come away from a swatch of hair that is as wild and strawberry as the hair covering her face, wild over her lips and eyes. I kick off my shoes. Then the phone rings and she tenses, arching her back, pulling away as if to rise, but I grab her hips underneath and slide her onto me, willing her to relax, which I can do now—*she does relax*. She slips back onto the

51

pillow, unclenching her muscles, one, two, three, until they are as loose as warm water under her warm skin.

"Brian, your brother is on the phone." Phil's voice cuts through the room, and the bond I have with Rhoda breaks open like someone has let the water out of a bath; her muscles begin tensing as Phil's voice is followed by three loud knocks against my door. "You hear me? It's Zach. He says he's got to talk to you."

"All right, all right, all right," I say. Rhoda clumsily buttons her shirt, I look for something to cover myself with, a book, and slip out of my room to the phone in the living room, "Can I help you!"

"Where the heck were you? I've been trying to get you all day long," says Zach, always impatient.

"What?"

"Mom and Dad are selling the house."

"You said."

"Did you know about this? Did they tell you already?"

"Do you really think they'd tell me before they told you?"

"You're right. I'm just really shaken up about this whole thing." There is a dramatic pause in Zach's voice, a void he wants me to fill.

"Why are you so worried about this?"

Another pause. "It's the family house, Brian! What's the matter with you?"

"We don't live there anymore," I say. Though I understand what he means I'm not at all prepared to go there. "What do you really want, Zach?"

"I talked to Mom this afternoon and she told me that they're not taking much of their furniture to this new condo and they want me to have as much of it as I can take."

"Why do they want *you* to have the furniture, Zach?" The conversation suddenly becomes significant for me, though looking around my living room I know these feelings of jealousy are perfectly useless. What am I going to do with another couch? An armoire?

"Because I have a new house with several unfurnished rooms and besides . . . we're expecting."

"I don't have a big new house, Zach, but that doesn't mean . . ."

"You pinhead. We're expecting a child!" Zach says again, as if I hadn't understood him the first time.

They've got four kids already and they're not out of their thirties. I know the church says to have a lot of children[28], that it's God's will, but having grown up in a family of seven kids I know there are limits, and Zach is pushing those limits, especially outside Utah where two and three kids aren't unusual. And some perfectly healthy, happy couples only have *one* the entirety of their marriage! I, for instance, have always fantasized about being an only child. I say, "Congratulations." Then there is a long silence. I look back to the hallway and see that my door is still closed, the rustling sound has stopped, and I picture Rhoda sitting on the bed, cursing me for being on the phone.

"I talked to Mom and I named a bunch of furniture and stuff that she's going to set aside for me, but I need to get it from there to here. There's some of your old stuff out there, too."

---

[28] The church of Jesus Christ of Latter Day Saints believes very strongly in the power of the family and what better way to demonstrate your belief in this faith than to have a large family of your own. Various church presidents and leaders have advocated large families as recently as this decade, and have recommended that women stay home to tend to these children.

I don't like where this is going at all.

"I thought if you could drive out there with your truck, I could have a U-haul hitch waiting for you in Ogden and you could bring it back out." There is another pause and this one is all mine. "I'd pay you for gas and your time, and I talked to Carly over at Consumer Loans and given what happened today she didn't have any problem at all with giving you some time off. Sorry to hear about that, by the way."

"You talked to Carly? What are you doing, Zach?"

"I heard what happened. It was all over the email this afternoon, and I called over there. Don't get weird on me, Brian. Not now."

"You've got me leaving work and running errands and you're discussing this with my boss." I want to hang up. "This is my time-off we're talking about! I worked for it!"

"All right. You're upset. But I want you to think this through before you come to any decisions. This is our parents' house, Brian. The house we grew up in, for Pete's sake! And they've just up and put it on the market without asking any of us." Zach goes soft, suddenly, and I can't hang up on him, if only to get through the novelty of this dynamic—him needing me for something. But I can't say a word, either.

"You just think about it. It's a paid vacation for you. I can work something with Carly so it won't all count against your days earned. You can even bring a friend if you want. Mom and Dad say that's fine." He means Rhoda. They've been talking about Rhoda.

"How long have you been discussing this?"

"Don't get weird on me, Brian."

"Why don't you just go out and get the stuff yourself, if you're so hot to have it in your house?"

"Brian."

"Jesus Christ, brother of mine, a woman I work with just died, understand?" Sitting alone in my living room, coming down hard from the coffee, reminds me again of the last time I spoke with Jaimy, how the enormity of a person's death is so relative.

"You think about it and I'll call you back tomorrow when you've had a chance to get your head clear. Goodbye."

I hang up the phone and look down the hall, two closed doors and not a sound from either, not a clue.

"The family home," I say out loud. "The family friggin' home . . ."

V. Companion

When I get back into my room Rhoda has the covers pulled up to her chin. "You were gone a long time," she says.

"Get dressed," I say. "We've got to get out of here."

"What's the matter?" she asks, slowly moving from the bed, peeling the covers from her naked body like she's breaking from a cocoon. Rhoda looks out of place in my bedroom, I think, the dark wood of the floors, the shadows from the street light cutting in half the room and my crumpled forest green comforter, her pale skin and hair like white sand dunes and tumbleweed rolling across a movie screen. I know it's not fair, but her still being naked irritates me.

"I need to get a beer or something. I need some leveling off from that caffeine—what terrible stuff. I'm as jittery as . . ." I look at Rhoda; she's studying her panties in the weak light of the room. "Did we do it?" I ask.

"Not really," she says, turning the panties inside out and bending to step into them. "You're acting weird. Maybe I should just go home." I grab her from behind, my fingers finding her hip-bones as if I'm mountain climbing, hanging on, pulling, maneuvering. I steer her up against the window and she grips the sill hard, her long nails clicking across the painted wood, her hair falling down her back and bristling against the blinds. The muscular woman happens to be exiting her car in the parking lot, walking toward the apartment, and I concentrate. I concentrate. When she slows for a moment, I know I have her. I will her to look up at me, and then I release her, because I realize I don't know what to do with her now that I have her attention.

A cold shiver shakes me free and Rhoda collapses back onto the bed, her face hiding behind her hair. "Brian?" she says, tearfully.

"I need to shower," I say, and I leave her. I am across the hall and into the bathroom before I realize that I am still aroused. But Phil is closed up in his room and I am alone, safe.

Our apartment has a wealth of hot, cloudy water, and I let it pour over me, so hot I can feel it cleansing my skin without soap. So hot my skin turns red, like a sun burn, and I scald myself until I can't feel anything at all. When I am through it is so quiet I can hear the steam settling, and I think back to the shores of the Great Salt Lake and a morning I spent camped in the back of my Bronco along a crusty inlet.

Jaimy wanted to spend the night by the lake, though I told her the black flies and the mosquitoes and the smell of the dead brine[29] would make it a miserable experience, even drunk. I woke early that morning to relieve myself, before the black flies and the mosquitoes rose and found my naked body. Before Jaimy,

---

[29] The only creature that can survive in the waters of Great Salt Lake is the brine shrimp. While several species of marsh birds feed on the shrimp, their numbers are largely unregulated and they wash ashore in the millions, rotting in the desert sun, and drawing equal numbers of biting black flies and gnats. There are few mosquitoes in Utah, but the few there are likely to be near the Great Salt Lake marsh.

Utah folklorist Trent Harris reports that in 1862 Moroni Dawson was gunned down in the Streets of Salt Lake City for trying to escape after his arrest for a vicious attack on then governor John Dawson. Dawson had made advances on a widow, who had beaten him with a shovel. Dawson tried to keep the whole affair out of the press and quietly get out of town. But Moroni and some friends tracked the governor down near Mountain Dell and beat him and then, to add insult to injury, robbed his stage. When it came time to bury Moroni, Henry Heath, a policeman in Salt Lake, took pity on

sprawled across the back of my Bronco like fishing tackle, woke. I watched the purple shadows of the mountains recede across Great Salt Lake and the mist drop away, and the sound of absolute silence was the same as it is for me now. I don't know if I want to have Jaimy creeping back into my memories like she is, but until I know better what I should do with her, I let her; I give her the keys to the place.

In Michigan you hang your towel in the bathroom, I discovered, because a wet towel molds and mildews in less time than it would take to dry through and through in the dry Utah air, and the smell creeps in, so I peek out the door to make sure Phil's door is closed, and it is, and I start toward my room when I hear the phone ring again in the living room. I feel it is Zach and I think I won't bother, but then I think I will and decide to just tell him I'll

---

the recently departed and bought a new set of clothes for the poor man to be buried in. Moroni's family was absolutely incensed by the entire proceedings and decided that the least they could do was move Moroni's body closer to home. But when they dug him up they found Moroni lying naked in his coffin.

It turned out that Jean Baptiste, the local undertaker, had been hoarding boxes full of clothes, shoes, and other items taken from the bodies of the dead. The accused was sentenced "out of court," and, according to Harris, Baptiste had his ears cut off and the words 'GRAVE ROBBER' branded to his forehead. Then he was placed in a ball and chain and taken out to wild and uninhabited Freemont Island in the middle of Great Salt Lake. Near the turn of the century some duck hunters found a skeleton with a ball and chain locked around its leg. The ghost of Jean Baptiste is thought, by some, to haunt the shores of Freemont, dragging his ball and chain and moaning his worst Dickensian moan in the bright moonlight of Great Salt Lake.

call him back in a few minutes, but then Phil's door opens. He stares at me and then he stares down there. I'm still naked and my entire body is beet red. "Do you want me to get it?" he says.

"No," I say and he draws his attention back up to my face and the phone rings again.

"Are you going to get it?"

"No," I say and the phone rings once more.

Phil waits for the fourth ring, which does not come, and then he looks me over once more. "All right, then." He goes back into his room and closes his door and I return to my room and close my door.

"I feel better," I announce.

Rhoda is dressed and lying on her stomach on top of the bed, her face obscured by her hair. "Good, because I think you're being a real asshole." she says. Then she repeats "a real asshole," only she says it so softly I can barely hear her.

"Do you want to get something to eat?" I say. I find some clean clothes in the closet and as I pull on my chinos I think I may have overdone the hot water.

So Rhoda comes with me to The Up and Under, a sports bar near the university, but is quiet most of the way there. The Up and Under is crowded, with university kids mostly, and I think how much I have begun to slip back into their culture today, how easy to be somebody else, somebody young. I feel as though I can walk over to any one of their tables and strike up a conversation, and then I look over to Rhoda who is sullen and tugging at her hair, unhappy with it, unhappy with me.

"What's wrong?" I ask.

"What's wrong with you? We just do it and you run off to take a shower and then out to a bar? Is that supposed to be cathartic? Romantic? What? I'm not your fucking absolution, you know."

"I was upset," I say; maybe she'd rather be with Mr. Mysterious and I wonder if maybe he's here, making her nervous. Or if it's just me. "I'm better now. In fact, I feel pretty terrific. And look . . . game one is going to be on here. That's some luck." I order some beer and the waitress comes back with our pitcher before Rhoda thinks to say something else negative to me. She has very small hands for someone her height, I think. Long, thin, beautiful fingers, but small hands.

"What did your brother say?"

"What do you mean?" I ask.

"You were on the phone a long time and when you came back you were acting kind of shaken from the phone call." She reaches across the table and takes my hands in her little hands. "Did he hear about Dee Dee?"

"My parents are selling the family home," I tell her. "They're moving to Park City."

"Does that upset you?" She's playing therapist and I cannot abide the condescension that goes with that role.

"No. But Zach wants me to drive all the frickin' way out to Utah to pick up some furniture they're going to give to him."

"And that bothers you?"

"No," I say. "Zach called *Carly* today and *made arrangements* for me to have some time off to run his errands claiming, I think, that I was upset about Dee Dee and needed some time away from the office."

"So, are you?" she asks, and then, "Do you?"

"No." I finish my beer and try to follow the game. The Jazz don't have the comfortable lead I'd like them to have. They're a third and fourth quarter team, and I know it's in the third quarter that they really give it the gas. But I also know they can't let Portland get out too far ahead, and then WHAM, Arvydas Sabonis nails a three pointer from way outside the arc—what the world's coming to when a big man can sink the three like that I don't know—and I can hear the announcer going bananas though I can't make out what he's saying over the jukebox and the noise from the bar. "Yes. Yes, I am upset. But you don't think the rest of the office is upset about Dee Dee? That's not something you get over, someone you know dying right in front of you, and right at the bank for Pete's sake! And I'm going to get special treatment because Zach wants the armoire and some china? It's dishonest."

"Nonetheless, maybe it would do you good to get away for a few days." Rhoda takes a dramatic pause. "How long does it take to get there?" And this time Rhoda drinks her beer and she drinks it fast. She drinks like a man, I think, and I'm pretty sure that's something I don't like about her.

"They said I could bring you along." Rhoda looks surprised and I know it's not so much what I said, but that I looked so surprised saying it. And now I know I'm into something and there's no nice way of getting out of it.

"To meet your parents, then?" she says, sipping her beer this time as if she's already practicing. "Jeez, Brian."

Hornacek[30] rims one out and I get edgy, thinking of *USA*

---

[30] Jeff Hornacek, Utah's shooting guard, whom they acquired in 1994 from the Philadelphia 76ers, sending their other Malone, Jeff Malone, in hopes of finding a guard with better passing skills and a greater range to his jumper. Hornacek played a good deal of his career with the Phoenix Suns, but was reluctantly traded by that club to the struggling 76ers for Sir Charles Barkley, the Round-Mound-of Rebound. Hornacek is a quiet, unassuming role player with a deadly three point shot and a great fit for a Jerry Sloan team. Hornacek, however, has been known to go into a funk occasionally, and the Jazz can ill afford to have their three point threat eliminated heading into the playoffs. Hornacek, when he's hitting from the outside, frees up the Mailman in the paint where he does most of his damage.

Today, of L.T., of Dee Dee, of Zach, of my parents, of Rhoda. I try to think of something that will put this off until I can get my head together but the more frantically I tear up my mind the more I come back to the idea that a little time off *would* be nice. Would get me out of my funk at work. But it's still not enough.

"I don't know if I can get away from school right now, Brian. Do you need to go out right away, or is this something that can wait until after finals?"

"There's no putting it off, I'm sure." Pushing. "It's coming now." The Mailman plows through Sabonis, the shot goes and he steps up to the line; they close in on his face and I can see him muttering his mantra[31] before sinking the free throw.

We drink our beers and I come down harder and faster than I want to. Rhoda doesn't say much and I don't say much. We just drink and sit in the bar and I can tell I'm getting drunk and want something to happen.

"You don't want me to go. Do you?" Rhoda says, firmly.

"Don't be ridiculous," I reply, and I can tell neither of us wants to play this out.

"Okay. Why don't you just say so? Don't be such a pussy about this!"

"The mouth on you sometimes."

"And quit muttering, it makes me nervous . . ."

---

[31] While no one but Karl knows what his mantra consists of he repeats it every time he steps to the line, before he takes his shot. When he came out of college his free throw percentage was a joke, but with practice and the advent of his free throw religion, which he has shared with no one, he is now one of the most consistent players at the line, getting nearly one third of his points there every game.

"Look. I don't even know if I'm going yet. This probably isn't the best time for me to be leaving the office, and I'm not exactly excited about the prospect of running errands for Zach."

"What could you possibly do at the office? The woman died, Brian. Don't let Zach make the decision for you. But if picking up some furniture for him buys you some time to get over Dee Dee, I think you should do it."

"What's that supposed to mean?" The waitress stops by and picks up our empty pitcher and asks if we want another. Rhoda says, "No thank you," but I want another.

"Why don't you just order a beer instead of a whole other pitcher?"

"Why don't you let me make up my own mind?" I say, and Rhoda takes her hands from mine, slaps them flat on the table, and goes to the bathroom. The waitress just stands there as if nothing has transpired and I finally have to say, "Another pitcher," and then rescind, "No. One more Bell's Amber is enough."

Rhoda comes back out of the bathroom. Her eyes and nose are as red as tomatoes and I get a little angry and embarrassed watching her cross the bar back to our table with her red face, making a production out of everything. I'm thinking if Mr. Mysterious is not watching all of this unfold she'll probably tell him about it later. "You're upset," she says before her butt hits the booth. "I can appreciate that. But you're acting like a garden variety asshole right now, Brian. Don't you see how you're treating me?" She knows I don't abide the "a"-word, and that's twice already this evening.

"I just ordered the one beer."

"Do you want to talk about Dee Dee?"

"No." I look up and Rhoda is wiping at her eyes with the backs of her hands, getting mascara all over. Then she just stares at me, really stares at me.

"Do you want to talk about Dee Dee? Are you sure?"

"Look," I say. "I said no. And I mean no."

"Why don't you want to talk about Dee Dee?"

This is Rhoda's trick to get me to talk about things I don't want to talk about. I can feel the cynicism building up inside of me, something fetid and seething that's been polluting my gut for months now and I want to stifle it before I say something I'll really regret. I know Dee Dee's death is making it resonate through me as if I were just a body of water and I picture myself floating on Great Salt Lake, naked, like that morning I camped out with Jaimy and a jet from Hill came booming across on a training run and I could feel the sound coming through the water, the water so saline that I floated almost on top like on a waterbed, the sound of the jet coming through me, waking Jaimy in the Bronco and splitting the sky, opening God's big eye and reminding me that I was floating naked on a lake on public grounds and I was ashamed, then and now[32]. "I don't want to end up like that."

"Like Dee Dee?"

"I can feel what I'm becoming and as much as I want to say it's my job or this place I know it's something else. Something that's been put in motion a long, long time ago inside of me."

"What . . ."

---

[32] When Jaimy called to Brian, and he knew he had to come back to the shore, he realized his nakedness for the first time, and realized that while he and Jaimy had had relations for several months, she had never seen him in his nakedness. He tried covering himself with his hands as he returned to shore, his back and legs covered in the itchy muck from Great Salt Lake, pulling at his every step, and when he was close enough and it was obvious that Jaimy would not avert her eyes he yelled out at her: "Don't look at me!"

"That could have been me lying face down on the carpet at the bank, all the life spilling out of me, and for a minute I felt as far from God as I've ever felt and I hated Dee Dee. I *wanted* her to die. I *willed* her to die . . ." Dee Dee's ghost is like a screaming baby. I can't, don't want to pick her up, and I can't walk away from her.

"You did not. That's ridiculous! You had no control over her death. You're just upset."

"Of course I'm upset. Of course I am." I can tell Rhoda is trying to think of something to tell me.

"You didn't even know her very well, did you?"

"Sure. I saw her every day. She was nice. She made me a cake for my birthday every year. She was nice. And that's just the size of it. She was nice and now she's dead. There are so many other people I would rather see dead at work."

"You don't mean that."

"Of course I mean that. Why couldn't it have been Carly? Why couldn't it have been any of those jerks over in documenting?" Why couldn't it have been Mr. Mysterious? And I think about what I've just said and feel the finger of God hovering like a baseball bat over my head.

Rhoda looks at me and I can feel what she's thinking and there's no way I can change anything, even if I wanted to, because she's drunk and I'm drunk and I think again about how alcohol takes you farther away from the purity of God and I wonder if it also protects you from God that way too. Takes you far enough out of His realm that you're on even footing, you and Him across the chasm.[33] I picture myself going toe-to-toe with an old bearded man in white robes and know this is the worst thing I have thought in years, but nothing happens. There's not even any lightning.

---

[33] Mormons believe that God is a physical, though perfect, presence.

I feel my feet are getting smaller when Rhoda says she thinks I've been through too much today and maybe I need to go home and get some sleep, though we both know that's still impossible, and also to clear my head, she adds, so I agree. She says we'll talk about going out to Utah tomorrow, but not to put too much faith in it, and then she asks the most amazing question: "But let's just say for a moment that it just won't work out and I can't come with you. Do you know anybody else who would be interested in going?"

"Randy Hansen," I say, as if I've been prepared to say it all night. "There was a name on the tote board at the WMU Union asking for a ride out to Utah. I could give him a call, I suppose." I'm not much for clichés but what descends on us is stunned silence. And the more I let the idea of Randy Hansen float around the room, the more it seems like the right thing, and I know that Randy Hansen will materialize from a scrawled name on a tote board at a school I don't belong to into a traveling companion and into a friend. It sounds like the best idea I've ever had, divinely inspired perhaps, and I can feel it making me burn, like red Roman candles exploding, spiders across my insides.

It's a pretty great sensation and suddenly I find that dwindling feeling that I'd been shambling after for the past several years, that somewhere along the line the pearl will be handed to me, flare up again in the pop of the blue centerlight and right on cue the television screen behind Rhoda's head goes all white. Leave Rhoda to Mr. Mysterious for a while; if she's there when you get back it's the real deal, the centerlight says. Go West, it says. Go West and come back to find your life again, it says. Find some faith.

When I step out of the car at my apartment I take in the wet spring air and walk out toward the field at the edge of my apartment complex and stare into the dark, sinewy patches of trees beyond, and I wonder what the spirit of the woods is doing. A big, ugly thing like L.T.'s pine needle birds. Rhoda comes up quietly behind me, leaning her face into my shoulders, and puts her arms around me as if she could open my chest like a closet door and let everything bundled up behind out into the pitch. Fuck you, spirit of the woods, I think, I'm going back to God's country.

I know Rhoda's hurt by my quick change of heart, so I close the doors of my heart and turn around and put my arms around her. Her big, white teeth are beautiful in the dark, wet night air and I kiss her on the mouth. When I look up from where we're standing in the parking lot I can see the room to my window, the white glare of the parking lot lamp shielding my room from view. Protecting it. No one sees me up there.

I want to sleep so that I can get up to campus and secure Randy Hansen's phone number before he finds another ride. Rhoda asks, "Will you be leaving soon, then?"

"No," I tell her. "Don't worry." As she drives slowly out of the parking lot I find myself worrying about Mr. Mysterious again. I worry about what it would be like to lose Rhoda. Who would I talk to? What would I do? She's the only one here who lets me into myself, lets me into the world, I think. But I think I must have thought something like this when Jaimy and I were falling out of love for the last time.

VI. The Calling

The caffeine has given me a hangover. And it feels strange not to be going to work in the morning. A picture of Dee Dee's empty desk flashes in my head. And I feel strange about not driving by Rhoda's house in the morning. Like I'm abandoning my rituals, cheating on work and relinquishing Rhoda to Mr. Mysterious. Dee Dee seems more real to me right now than Rhoda and I try to think my way into Rhoda's bed. Try to imagine her lying there next to me, and try to imagine her lying there alone. But then I'm at the Western Michigan campus again, the golden W hovering above me in the foggy morning like a great, golden bird, or an angel.

A blonde girl with legs too tan for this time of year locks her car door, tugs at the handle to make sure, and then jogs across the pedestrian walk in front of me. She smiles and I can see the flesh on her legs alive with goose bumps. They look bird-like. I smile back at her and we exchange looks, one or two beats longer than a glance, and it feels like we connect before she disappears behind the sheen of a half-dozen glass doors. Just that small, shared connection gives me hope.

I remember "Hopelessness." It's one of my father's favorite poems. "Whatever hope is yours / Was my life also; I went hunting wild / After the wildest beauty in the world."[34] Dad would quote poetry to us, and the scripture: "For I, the Lord God," Dad loved to assume His voice, "delight in the chastity of women." How these things come rushing back to me! But like the girl with the tan legs, it's all water over the dam.

---

[34] Wilfred Owen's "Strange Meeting."

When I'm back in front of the tote board I trace the distance from Michigan to Utah. I go straight across with my finger at first, dodging the hanging tags and hopes in between: Indiana, Illinois, Iowa, Nebraska, Wyoming, Home. Then I trace the line where I know the roads should be with my eye, until I end at Randy Hansen's tag. Half gas.

I imagine Randy will look like one of the kids slouching through the union in the morning. An R.M. maybe. More like me, if I'm lucky. It's a long, long drive to Utah. Three, maybe four days. Longer coming back through the mountains with a trailer full of Zach's new furniture. And I'll be alone again then.

There's a pay phone behind me next to a couple of newspaper vendors carrying *USA Today* and yesterday's *Gazette*. In the upper left hand corner of the *USA Today* there's a teaser for the NBA playoffs with a picture of Arthritis Sabonis, but I drop a couple of quarters in and take a copy anyway. *The Gazette* won't have coverage for another day, and even that will probably just be the box score: Portland 102, Utah 110.

I think it's a good idea to call Randy from the campus, like somehow that's going to facilitate our connection. It's still early, maybe nine o'clock, but not too early. If he's not in class, he should be home. While I wait for the line to connect I've got to fight off this silly feeling in my stomach.

His voice is deeper than I thought it might be, and scratchy, like he just woke up. And he's gruff. "What do you want?" I can hear a train passing in the background, somewhere outside of Randy's house, and I wait for it to clear the air before I try to speak.

"I," I say. "I'm calling for Randy Hansen."

"And this is . . . who? Who are you?" He's not really straining to be polite.

"My name is Brian Peterson," I say. "I got your number from the tote board on campus. I was wondering if you still need a ride to Utah?"

"Utah?" he says, like maybe he hasn't heard me right.

"Utah," I say.

"Are you from Utah?" he says.

"Originally, yes," I say and there's quiet on the other end of the phone. "Kaysville." Two kids in WMU sweatshirts, wearing their baseball caps backwards on their heads, a style that was on its way out when I was an undergraduate, stand behind me with their hands in their pockets. One of them exhales loudly and I try to hunker down into the phone.

"Yeah. I been there," Randy says, then there's a long pause again, as if he's remembering Kaysville, evaluating it. "Fruit-pickers, huh[35]? That's where you'll be going, then?"

"Yes," I say. "Park City, maybe."

"When are you leaving?"

"Well," I say. "Should we meet first or something?" This isn't unfolding at all like I expected. One of the kids says to the other, "C'mon man," and, thankfully, they leave.

"Are you L.D.S.?" Randy says.

"Yes," I say. "Are you?"

"You sound all right to me," he says. "I can go whenever you want." He says this like the decision is entirely his. Like I'm the one being interviewed. "You a dorm rat, then? Caller ID says you're a WMU number."

"No," I say. "I'm calling from the union. My girlfriend goes to school here and I just saw the tag."

"Give me your number then," he says. Before I can think I spill out the seven digits to him, not once but twice. "Maybe we

[35] Kaysville and nearby Fruit Heights are known for their cherry orchards.

should meet. I'll call you back later, I've got some things to take care of before we can go. And you've got my number, I guess." And he hangs up the phone without even a goodbye.

VII. The Introductions

"And then he said, I'll call you back later, and he hung up the phone," I tell Rhoda. She's dressed and her wet hair is pulled back in a ponytail. It makes her look younger. She looks like someone else's girlfriend without her halo of hair.

"Not even a goodbye?" she asks.

"Nope."

"I don't know, Brian. You don't know anything about this guy. He sounds kind of weird. Is he a student at Western?"

"I just thought he must be," I say. I don't tell her that I've been picturing him in my head, filling in the background of his life. First he was an R.M., then he wasn't. Then he was a jock at WMU, there on scholarship. Then he wasn't. And I realize that Randy's becoming more like me, the more I make him over. It's a dangerous game to play.

"Listen," she says. "Are you sure you even want to do this? Maybe someone else can go with you. Maybe Zach could go. Someone you *know*."

"What are you saying, Rhoda?" I say. "Because if you want to go, you should just tell me. I never said you couldn't go."

"I'm just worried about you driving all that way in that car of yours with some guy you don't even know. He could be some kind of mass murderer."

"So you don't want to go then?" I say. I feel as though I'm baiting her into going, and I can't help myself.

"It's not that I don't want to go, Brian. You know that. But I can't just drop classes and go to Utah." She says Utah like it's Mars, and for the first time I consider just how like Mars it must be for Rhoda. Or how like a Martian she might be to my family. What was I thinking?

"So don't go then," I say. "I'll take this guy with me or I won't." There is a new packet of pictures lying on the top of her television. I wonder why she hasn't shown them to me.

Rhoda is a picture fanatic. She has more photo albums than most people have books. Is Mr. Mysterious in the photos? There are photo albums Rhoda has full of old boyfriends that she pulls out now and again to help illustrate her stories. Like the time she went on the swimming trip out to Gull Lake[36] and Tom, her old boyfriend, and a couple of other guys skinny-dipped. She has pictures of these naked men in her photo album. They all stare out of the photos as if they know that their naked flesh will haunt the imaginations of men they'll never meet.

"Oh, Brian," she says, and hugs me. My head lies against her breasts and I can smell her skin, but the familiar scent of her hair is gone, tied behind her.

Rhoda's right, I understand, that I don't know a thing about Randy Hansen. It's only a feeling, a little jingle in my insides, but I know he's not dangerous in the way she thinks he might be dangerous. But there are a lot of other problems I haven't really considered in taking a stranger more than halfway across the country.

I call Randy again when I get back to my apartment. Our conversation is short, but he seems to be in better spirits. The train comes by again in the background. We wait, listen to it pass. It's a long, long train, and I can hear it shaking things where he lives. Plates maybe. Pictures on the wall? He tells me he has some

---

[36] A small lake north east of Kalamazoo. The Kellogg family maintains a house there, as do many other of the area's wealthiest residents.

questions, and we agree to meet at the Corner Bar. It's a bar down near the industrial parks in town, but it's a good place to meet. Families go there. It serves fried food, and the beer is cheap. There's no game on tonight.

So that settles it, then. I am going to Utah. I want to call some of my old college friends, but as I go through the pages of my address book I decide it might be more fun to just drop in and surprise them. Make it an adventure.

The phone rings just then. It's L.T. He hasn't gone in to work today, either. "You doing all right, Amigo?" he asks.

"Yeah. I'm good," I say. "I really am."

"I'm okay too," he says. "It's just . . ."

"I know," I say.

"Doesn't seem right. She was nice."

"When are you going back?"

"That's another reason I called," he says. "When I called in this morning Carly told me the promotion went through."

"The directorship?"

"No, the other one."

"In Consumer Relations?"

"No. No. In Development. I'm moving upstairs."

"Wow," I say. "That's something, isn't it?" The Amigos are finished, I think.

"It's strange, though. Coming when it did. I can't help thinking Dee Dee . . ."

"Oh c'mon, man. They wouldn't have bumped you up just because of that," I say. L.T.'s applied for every single job that has been posted in the past nine months.

"No. I mean, I can't help feeling that maybe Dee Dee had something to do with it all. Like helping out . . ."

"Like supernatural stuff?"

"Like an angel."

"Could be," I say. We talk some more about what he's going to do when he gets his bigger paycheck. He says he's going to take his girlfriend and her son to Detroit for a hockey game.

"I fucking hate hockey. Cracker sport," L.T. says. "But they dig it."

When I get off the phone I call Geoff, but his wife tells me he went to work. "You're kidding," I say.

"No," she says, like it's strange that I would think any other way. I never did like her much, I think. I think about calling him at F.O.A., but I can't imagine what we'd talk about. So instead I clean the apartment. Wash the dishes Phil has left in the sink, wipe up the dust on and around the television set, soak whatever's splattered behind the trash can with some 409, sort my laundry and run it down to the basement, and pull out my luggage (a hand-me-down tweed carry-all and a brown vinyl garment bag with the hook torn out of the top).

It's a warm day outside for this time of year, though the fog is still visible at the edge of the woods. It's like the breath of the woods, held inside the trees today, and tonight it will slowly exhale over the cars in the parking lot, my apartment complex, Rhoda and Mr. Mysterious and L.T. and Geoff and Kitty and every one of us left. For now I open the windows in the living room and let whatever's left of the big inhale into our apartment.

Zach calls while I'm changing the laundry in the basement and asks me why I didn't call in to work this morning. He says he cleared it for me, but that I've got to call them and tell them what my plans are. "Carly's understanding," he says, "but I don't want you to lose your job."

I fold my clothes and put them away. They're mostly button-down shirts and slacks. Not the kind of stuff I'll need to wear for the next week or so. The trip seems to be the best thing that's happened to me in a long time. And now there's just Randy to think about.

I leave early for the Corner Bar. I've got nothing else to do and the waiting is bothering me. I figure if I can get there early enough I can have a beer and relax. The sun still sets early in Kalamazoo, but I can feel the difference from the week before. By the time I get to the Corner Bar the sun is gone, though it's still light out, and the fog is spilling back out of the woods. I can almost hear the sigh that's sure to follow.

I sit at a table near the back. Behind me the owner, who wears suspenders and shorts year round, is ushering a motley crew through a sliding accordion door into a larger back room. It's the cigar club night and I can hear the patrons as they come in and out of the walk-in humidor in the back of the room exchanging information like they're still at work. I'm on my second beer when my table is shaken by the crack of a metal hook right on the edge nearest the back room.

"Brian?"

"Yeah?" I say. The hook is actually two flat hooks connected to each other by a spring. The two hooks are connected to a flesh-colored arm, flesh the color of GI Joe plastic flesh, and the arm is connected to an unshaven man with what looks to be a handlebar moustache and a red baseball cap with the word CO-OP sewn on the front.

"Geez. You about jumped out of your skin," he said. "You ain't that jumpy behind the wheel, are you?"

VIII. The Renunciation

Randy's face is pockmarked beneath his whiskers and I would think they were the result of some bad teenage acne. Zach has some, these acne scars, but Randy's pock marks spray up his neck and onto his face on the same side as the metal hook. His real arm and hand are covered with tattoos. The tattoos are hard to make out and mostly done in thickish blue outline. They look as though they have been deliberately muddled.

His teeth are white and perfectly straight and he has light, almost gray, blue eyes that are startling. He stares straight at me and smiles.

"I figured it was you," he says. "Most of these other cocksuckers are here to chew their tobacco dildos. Damn, I hope you're not a cigar smoker." He waves his good hand at the waitress and holds up two fingers that he then motions between the two of us. He does this like he's done it a million times before, and the beers appear before us remarkably fast.

"You're from Utah?" I say, because it is the only thing I can think to say.

"I grew up in Moab[37]," he says with some satisfaction. "But I've been a lot of other places since then."

"Oh," I say.

---

[37] A town in the southeastern corner of Utah. Named after the place in the Bible where Moses goes to die, which in turn is named after the unnatural son of Lot and his daughter. Moab is known now chiefly for its slickrock. It is close to several national parks and hosts an annual Jeep rally and several mountain bike races.

"Did you get a mission call?" he says.

"No," I say. It's a lie, but I don't think I want to get into all of that with this guy.

"I was in Palermo for most of mine. F.I.G.M.O.[38], you know? A real bear-fuck start-to-end, if you know what I mean."

I shake my head slowly, though I have no idea what he is talking about.

"Look, nothing personal, but I've just got a couple of questions for you." He pats his pants pockets with his good hand and then fishes inside for a small, wrinkled piece of yellow paper. "Got a bad case of C.R.A.F.T.[39]" he says. "Until they come out with memory drugs, these little Post-it thingys'll have to do. Now, you said you weren't a college student?" This is clearly a place for me to answer something more than no.

"No, I graduated from the U," I say. "I'm working at a bank now."

"Which bank?" he asks, but something in his tone tells me he doesn't really care, partly because he won't let me answer. "Why're you hauling your ass out west then?"

"Something like that. I've got to get some furniture for my brother."

"You've got to go to Utah to get some furniture for your brother?" He lays his list on the table and picks up his beer and drinks half of it at once.

"Doesn't it sound stupid?" I say. There is, I'll grant him, something as conspiratorial as it is easy in talking with him.

---

[38] Primarily used as a military interjective. Literally: "Fuck it, got my orders."

[39] Can't remember a fucking thing.

"Monkey fucking a football, I'd say. But it's your wheels, your life. Or is this your brother's car we're going in, too?"

"No. It's my Bronco. See, my parents are moving out of our family home and they're getting rid of a lot of their furniture."

"They're not heading to one of those raisin ranches, are they?"

"Raisin ranch?"

"You know, where they sit around until somebody comes to slog the shit out of their diapers."

"No," I say. "They're retiring. They've got a condo in Park City . . ."

"Oh," he interrupts. Like I've said something wrong.

"What?"

"Nothing. Just sounds like you come from money." This time he sips at his beer.

"Not really," I say. "My dad worked for the city and my mom was a teacher."

"Cop?"

"No. He worked in the treasurer's office."

"All right then," he says. "All right."

"So you did a mission?" I say, though I regret opening this door immediately. It's just that he's like no other R.M. I've ever seen. I've met a few wild ones, but none so down-and-out looking as Randy Hansen.

"Yeah, my garments are at the cleaners right now. Listen," he says, "speaking of all that jazz, you mind if we dip down to Nauvoo[40] just a bit? It's off the beaten track, but I've got someone I've got to see down there before I head back to Moab."

---

[40] Nauvoo, Illinois. The birthplace of both the Latter Day Saints and the Reformed Latter Day Saints.

"Yeah," I say. "I guess so. But I'm not going all the way to Moab, you know."

"That's fine, that's fine," he says, motioning to the waitress for another beer. "Is Ogden okay? Can you take me there? I can get somebody to come pick me up there."

"Yeah, I suppose so," I say. I don't know any nice way to say that I need to think about spending any more time with this guy. "When did you do your mission?" I figure I'm buying time until I can say what needs to be said.

"Years ago, and several me's ago. You know?"

"No," I say.

"I've been, well, finding some different paths than the one I started out on back then. Jesus, that must've been close to fifteen years now . . ."

So he's only a few years older than I am at most. He seems much older.

"I guess I've come back too close to where I started in a lot of ways and in a lot of things, but I don't see myself going all the way back to where I started out. Was a bit of a dry fuck really, all that."

"What? The Church?" I say. I feel indignant in a way that isn't really me.

"Yeah, but no more so than a lot of things. A lot better than most things out there, I guess. There was some . . . ah . . . competition for my attention a while back that took me somewhere else, and now I'm just done with the whole lot of it. Renounced my membership in the human race so long as there is a system and a leader. You know?"

"I think so," I say. But I only know about thinking about renouncing things.

IX. The Commitment

I can't stop staring at Randy's metal hooks. They are two spring-loaded hooks, laid side-by-side, that look like they can grab or pinch or scratch or stab in any number of ways, and he deliberately leaves them flopped out there on the table for me to study. "I've got one that looks like a human arm," he says. "But it's fuck-all worthless, and I don't think it's fooling anybody. No hairs, no shape, and it looks like a dead man's arm."

Randy shuffles his empty glass around the wet table like a hockey puck. "I don't believe in maxims," he says. "But I believe the only evil in the world is the incomplete." He insists on picking up the ticket, even though I had a couple of beers before he arrived. He pulls an enormous roll of tightly wound bills out of his pocket. The bar is smoky now, not just from the cigar club in the back, happily munching on their finds, but every table seems to have an ashtray going, like little soldiers huddling around their dying fires during a military campaign. Two men near the door shamelessly trade in Cubans brought across the border in Detroit.

Randy walks out with me and follows me to my truck. "This is what's getting us out there?" he says.

"What's wrong with it?" I say.

"Looks like you drove it through the fucking front lines." He leans down and pries a piece of rust loose with his hook.

"It didn't start doing this until I moved out here."

"So you think it likes the mountains good enough to get us there?"

"Engine's good. Tranny's good. No air, though," I say. I feel as though I've given up putting some distance between us for the time being. I do a quick mental inventory of the information I've given out this evening, though, trying to make sure I haven't disclosed where I live.

"Shouldn't be too hot," Randy says. "Well . . ." I feel as though I'm on a first date with him, and we're at that awkward final moment when we either kiss or try to part quickly and painlessly. Randy kicks at the back tire and then extends his hook to me to shake. I stare at it momentarily and then he laughs, "Amputee humor." He pats me on the shoulder and walks out past my rusting Bronco and onto the sidewalk. There are insects out this night, and a few smaller, transparent-seeming bugs clink against the parking lot light.

The fog has come back in while we were in the bar. I feel as though I've had a good time. Randy is rough around the edges, but he's friendly and he doesn't hold back. I could tell him most things and feel like it wouldn't be strange. Maybe because we both come from Utah. "You need a lift home?" I call after him, but he's already across the railroad track down the street. The red lights of guard rails begin to flash and lower, making Randy and his metal hand appear to pulsate in the night glow. I can feel the train through my feet, and then it is there, wonking its horn and blowing the fog from the street. Randy is on the other side.

I get into the Bronco and drive back to my apartment. I see my car in a different light, after Randy peeled a piece of the body away with his hook like a dentist might scrape a stubborn piece of tartar from my tooth. When I was with Jaimy it was in good shape. The body was solid, the seats didn't show their wear like they do now. The dash wasn't cracked and dusty.

After Jaimy and I turned serious with each other, she would let me drive her up to the Layton castle's[41] parking lot. We

---

[41] In the nearby city of Layton a real estate developer built a castle high up on the mountain, during the Reagan years. He built the castle directly above his ex-wife's home. It is clearly visible from anywhere in the Kaysville-Layton area and the grounds—including a riding

would kiss and sometimes she would let me take her panties off—
her long, white spidery legs rising up off the seat, her knees
invariably clunking against the dash as I groped around and tried
to convince her. But we never did it up there, though I wanted to
so badly I had to fight myself off. I think she thought she was
helping me, letting me do *some* things, letting me *almost* get there.
Mostly we just talked and watched the sun come down, the sky
stoking up like a furnace and giving us all its reds and oranges
before cooling to a slow purple.

I remember Jaimy's pale face soaking up the color like a
bare canvas. Her mouth would move with such care when she
spoke. She was uncertain about what she thought, and uncertain
about what I would think about what she thought, but mostly she
was just a careful person. She would ask me careful questions
about where I could see us in the future. And then, like now, I
imagined her, instead of us, really. I would try to picture her getting
older, more frail. And like now, I could only see her at that age, her
smooth legs, her long feet perched on the dash of my car.

And then she would surprise me with something like, "I
can see us being really kinky in our old age."

I thought she meant that we would move slowly toward
more and more adventurous sex together, but maybe she meant

---

stable, small, private zoo, and dramatic floral arrangements and
landscaping—draw hundreds of visitors each year. There is a state run
parking lot leading to several mountain trails in front of the castle
where teenagers sometimes come to "park." The view from the
castle's parking lot, beyond the former owner's ex-wife's house, is of
Antelope Island and Great Salt Lake. The sun sets in that direction,
making the spot all the more desirable. As with much of the country,
the owner's investments collapsed in the later Reagan years and the
castle has remained the property of a real estate company.

that we would slowly grow more and more desperate for pleasure. There was a lot about her I couldn't have known, and I wonder if this has something to do with her haunting me now. I think about what L.T. said about Dee Dee's ghost helping him out, and it seems weird that Jaimy would visit my thoughts so intensely just before I'm to return to Utah. But then, maybe, it's just that I'm going to Utah because she's been so much on my mind lately.

When I get home I climb out of the Bronco and look down at the spot where Randy picked away a piece with his silver hook. It didn't seem so important at the time, but when I stand in the light of my own parking lot it seems like an awful invasion. The rust is much worse than I thought it was, speckling the underside of the car like Appaloosa spots. Most of the spots have eaten through in the centers, and near the back panel it is more air than car.

When I get inside I know I have to call Rhoda. There are four beeps on my machine. Three are from Zach, one is Phil's mother. I've got to feel brave to do this, I think. There's something down inside of me that feels like a lie. Something that's telling me I might not be coming back and that I should pretend that this is the remotest possibility to me. "A snake hatched in a clutch of chicks will eventually eat its way to the mother," my father would say. But then he'd have a lot more to say if I came strolling into our old house with my Gentile girlfriend.

"Well, when are you going," Rhoda says. She wants to gain some control over this by having all the details.

"In a couple of days, probably," I say. It seems sudden to me when I say that. "I'll be back quicker that way, you know."

"You're coming back then?" Rhoda says. She doesn't say this like it's a concern, more like she's just checking facts. The conversation is driving her to this general journalistic tone, it seems.

"Why wouldn't I come back?"

"And this Randy guy? You think this guy isn't some kind of wacko?" I don't tell her about his silver hook, and I hope that I can swing it so that we don't cross paths on my way out of town.

"He's fine. He's an R.M. He's safer than me," I say before realizing that if something does happen they're probably not going to go searching for the right guy. But I know that I feel good about Randy. I feel better and better about the trip, about how it will cleanse me, clear the fog.

"If he's not a student, and he has the money to pay half your gas in that piece of junk car of yours, why doesn't he just take a bus or something?"

I don't know why, and it bothers me that she seems to know the right questions to ask about this kind of undertaking and I don't. "It's not such a piece of junk," I say.

"So okay, then," she says.

"So okay."

"Do you want me to come over tonight?"

"I've got to get some packing and stuff done tonight," I say. "Look. Tomorrow's Saturday, why don't we go out tomorrow night and we'll have a little party and celebrate this thing. Send me off right . . ."

"I thought you were doing this because of Dee Dee," she says.

X. The Light

At night I lie in my bed and watch the shadows on the ceiling. The moon is rising or falling outside and its fullness cuts through the shades of my window. The light from the moon, I notice, after hours of noticing these things, is quite different from the parking lot lights, more blue, more a part of the ceiling, than the parking lot lights, which are different, like the paint itself is different from what's underneath. This light is not so different from the car lights.

When I see a car's lights on my ceiling I get up from my bed and go to my window and stare through the slats of the shades. The fog has made itself comfortable, by this hour, and is leaving its snail's trail on all the cool cars of the parking lot. A young woman steps from her car, a small German car, and she falls back against the door when she is free from it. Her coat slips from her shoulder and she studies the keys in her hands for a moment. Her hair is dark, and from this distance I can see it is disheveled—it falls onto her face and she deliberately pulls it behind her ear.

She looks up into the sky, which is as thick and dark as if she were looking into a basement without any lights. The stars, she believes, are there, behind the gray clouds, and the moon is there too. I try to imagine the sky opening for her, ripping itself apart, finding a middle and spreading it open like steak being cut to the plate and pushed aside with a fork and knife, until she can see the pattern on the plate. But she grows tired of waiting for me to perform these rites and she looks back at the keys in her hand, tosses them a few inches into the air and snatches them back, and walks to the door of her apartment. She is drunk, and she walks as if against a sideways wind.

A new kind of light comes into my room, and I'm sure I have not slept at all. What I can't understand about this sleeplessness is that I'm never sure I didn't sleep. I worry that I've dreamt of the ceiling all night long, the waxing and waning light from outside my window, the drunk woman walking like a crab back to her warm apartment in the cold, damp morning.

The phones rings and it's Zach. "So you're going, then?"

"Yeah, I'm going," I say. I feel pushed into this again, suddenly. I think Zach is getting to me with his persistence. "And I've got somebody riding along on the way out."

"Is it that girl," Zach says, accusing.

"No. His name is Randy. He's an R.M."

"Where'd he serve?" Zach asks, suspiciously, as if Randy already has something to prove to Zach.

"What do you care?"

"Brian, Brian, Brian . . ."

"I'm going on Monday or Tuesday. Oh, and we've got to stop in Nauvoo for something," I say, remembering Randy's request.

Zach sits on the other end of the line, breathing out of his nose. "I don't know, Brian. Maybe this isn't such a good idea . . ."

"Darn it, Zach, you can't be like this now. I've decided I'm going and I'm taking Randy along with me. If you're so keen on being part of this why get that trailer set up? Or at least clear things up for me with Carly?"

"Clear things up with Carly? What things do you need to clear up with Carly? Did you call in yesterday?"

"No, Zach," I say. "I didn't, and I don't want any grief from you about it. You said you'd set it up so I wouldn't lose vacation time for this, so just do it. All right?"

"For Pete's sake, Brian," Zach says.

"That's right, Zach. For Pete's sake."

"How long will it take you to get there, then?"

"About three days."

"You're not going to drive at night, are you?"

"Of course I am," I say.

"Where will you sleep?"

"In a motel, you dink! What's this all about? You act like I'm six years old."

"Well, where is this Randy supposed to stay?"

I'm itching to tell Zach about Randy's arm because I know how much it will bother him. "Where ever he wants. He's a grownup, Zach, like you might be one day."

"He's not coming back with the furniture, is he?"

After a few more minutes I get off the phone and stand in the shower. Even this increases my growing sense that I might not be coming back to Michigan. The shower feels different to me because it's one of the last times I'll be in here, touching this hot water, which has a certain oily texture to it compared to Utah water, and smelling the smells of this bathroom: Phil's vanilla cologne, the bitter scent of rot beneath the sink, the sharp, burnt odor of the ceiling fan.

I dress carefully, again happy that I won't be wearing a tie or a button-down for some time to come. I wear clothes that Rhoda has bought for me. A black shirt she bought me for my birthday, and a loose fitting pair of jeans she picked up at Mr. B's Wearhouse sidewalk sale at the beginning of the year.

It's still early, so I drive down to Portage[42] to get some maps for the trip. Portage reminds me a little of Salt Lake, up near

---

[42] Portage, Michigan. Originally a satellite town of Kalamazoo that has boomed since the 1970s. Its main street, Westnedge, lined with miles of strip malls, is the second busiest street in the state of Michigan.

Trolley Square and 4th South where I worked at the Chuck-A-Rama[43] for a while when I was a freshman. Nauvoo, I think, is somewhere I'd like to see.

---

[43] Directly behind the Chuck-A-Rama buffet-style restaurant in Salt Lake City is Gilgal. Stone mason Thomas B. Child's Gilgal is named after the point in the river where Joshua led the Israelites into Canaan. When priests, carrying the Ark of the Covenant, touched the water of the river Jordan, the waters stood completely still and they remained that way while the forty-thousand armed Israelites marched into Canaan. To mark this crossing, twelve stones were piled at Gilgal. The first Passover in the promised land was celebrated at Gilgal and a mass circumcision was performed for all of the men born in the wilderness. Gilgal means, literally, "Hill of Foreskins." Child's Gilgal is guarded by a twenty-foot-tall statue holding a sword and nicknamed Boulder-head by locals. He is a granite representative of the giant in King Nebuchadnezar's dream. Child's collection, however, contains foremost among its many stone carvings a Joseph Smith Sphinx (an Egyptian Sphinx about the size of a small automobile with Joseph Smith's face). It is perhaps inspired by Brigham Young's claim that before Joseph Smith the priests of the world were as "blind as Egyptian darkness."

More likely, however, it was inspired by Smith's claims that he could translate what he called "reformed Egyptian." In 1835, a traveling salesman, having heard of Smith's claims, was selling his wares in Kirtland, Ohio. His wares at that time included several authentic Egyptian mummies and some papyri, and had drawn quite a large and enthusiastic crowd at every stop on his journey. Perhaps recognizing the power of tourist dollars at the time, Joseph Smith and the Kirtland church put together the substantial asking price of nearly $2,500 dollars and purchased the mummies and papyri.

Like now, ancient Egyptian antiquities captured the American imagination, and were certainly quite a draw. But Smith had more than a pedestrian cultural curiosity about these artifacts. What excited him most were the Egyptian scrolls that he believed contained the writings of Abraham and Joseph of Egypt. Smith and his company of scribes went to work on the papyri. They came up with a work titled: Egyptian Alphabet and Grammar. Smith claimed the papyri were another lost book of the Bible written in Abraham's own hand (speaking to polygamy, plurality of gods and other explicitly Mormon ideas). These works were eventually published as part of the Pearl of Great Price in 1851.

The Rosetta stone had been discovered in 1799 and translated in 1822, but the key to the hieroglyphics would not be published in Europe until 1841, making it nearly impossible for Smith to have been familiar with their conversions. Smith's translations have long proved problematic for the church. Many prominent Egyptologists have attempted to show that the papyri were merely common funerary works, and have pointed to the many anachronistic errors in Smith's translations (the use of the term Pharaoh, for example, was not in use until hundreds of years *after* the time of Abraham). Most troubling, no doubt, is the long-standing, collective doubt that something written by Abraham, a figure vital to the rise of Judaism, Christianity, and Islam, would be entirely lost by the Israelites, preserved by the pagan Egyptians, and then embalmed with an Egyptian priest.

The church's stand on many of the elements from these papyri (discretely placed in the church's holdings) is that they are a work of literary merit and that they act more as catalyst for inspiration rather than as historic documents.

When I came out to Kalamazoo I had a map Zach sent to me. One side was a mosaic of little diagrams of the interstates I needed to take to get to Kalamazoo, each one highlighted in yellow. There were recommendations for motels along the way, mileage estimates, and places I should probably eat. Zach's map took me right to the steps of my apartment building, and I hadn't needed a map since. The few times I went home for Christmas I rode with Zach and Michelle and their kids. First there were two kids, then three, finally there were four of them and there just wasn't room for Uncle Brian in their Chevy Suburban anymore. Now they've got another one on the way and there won't be room for it either.

John Rollins Books has maps and I go in there. I love the smell of book stores, especially when they don't have cats. I half expect to see my path highlighted for me as I pick up the maps and unfold them. I turn them this way in the light, and then the other way, feeling like I'm measuring out the world by the length of my arms, when I feel a tap on shoulder.

"Hello, Brian," she says.

"Liz!" I say. I'm not sure what to say after the obvious. I haven't spoken to her in a long time.

"How have you been?" she asks.

"I've been okay," I say. She really is so beautiful. I find it difficult to talk to her. My father would call her a Calendar Girl[44].

---

[44] Aside from the obvious reference to calendar girls, Brian's father would also be referring to one of the aforementioned steps to overcoming masturbation printed in a pamphlet written by Mark E. Peterson, Council of the 12 Apostles, Church of Latter Day Saints. Sometimes jokingly referred to as Peterson's Field Guide, the pamphlet claims that by following its nine guidelines and 21 suggestions anyone can be cured of masturbation. Aside from

"No," I say. "I guess that's not all true. A friend of mine died at work a couple of days ago. She was fine one minute, and the next," I clap my hands together, "she's down on the floor."

"Oh, Brian," she says. "That's awful." She reaches out and touches my hand. Her skin is soft and she smells like patchouli. I think, that can't be right, but the smell of patchouli is definitely coming from her. She stares at me for an uncomfortable moment.

"Yeah, it was really terrible."

"I'm sorry, Brian. I've got to get back to the cash register, but I want to talk to you about this. Really." She squeezes my hands and starts toward the register where several customers and a fortyish year old man with a salt and pepper ponytail behind the register, are giving her the eye.

"You work here?" I say.

"Yes. Just . . ." she keeps walking and I follow her, but Liz clearly is not one of those people who does two things at once. I can tell she wants to chat, but the customers and the guy with the ponytail are making her nervous. She smiles to each one of the customers and gives them a bookmark and says something comforting about their purchase, and I can tell I'm not the only one smitten with her charm.

I've got a map in my hand and so I get in line, hoping to get a few seconds of Liz's time to tell her I'm heading back to Utah.

---

keeping a calendar and marking each episode with a black star, the pamphlet gives such advice as tying one hand to the bed frame or yelling "STOP!" when one feels overcome with the lonely passion. Bishops (like Liz's father, for example), however, chiefly encourage the young men of their ward to keep calendars. There is no real accounting for the success of these suggestions, except that it is still in use.

I know she'll be envious, because she's never been there and the few dates we did have were mostly spent dealing with her questions about the mountains and the temple. Was it really as beautiful as she imagined it? Having no idea how potent Liz's imagination could be, I always said it was. Did I feel closer to God and the Son and Joseph Smith when I walked the temple grounds? I think she had it in her mind that most people spent every waking second either trying to get into the temple or thinking about being there, but I couldn't play along with that one, and her disappointment always showed. I could never tell if I had offended her ideas about me, or if she thought enough of me that I might have actually offended her belief. She made me tell her about the Christmas lights[45] so many times I began to feel blind reimagining all those little bulbs.

---

[45] The Salt Lake Temple puts on a spectacular light show every Christmas season, encouraging Gentiles and the faithful alike to stroll through the Temple grounds meticulously decorated with scenes from *The New Testament* and *The Book of Mormon*. The church also strings hundreds of thousands of Christmas lights every year to augment these displays, and the glow from the Temple can easily be seen from several miles away.

But clearly the most anticipated presentation is the annual caroling by the Mormon Tabernacle Choir. The Choir began touring in 1893, starting with an extremely successful performance at the Chicago World's Fair. The touring became such a successful public relations coup that it forced the development of a tourist kiosk and full time tourism staff back in the Salt Lake Temple. The first year tours were given of the Temple and the Tabernacle over 100,000 came to hear the free recitals. Now more than 1,000,000 visitors come to the Temple every year, most hoping to hear those same free recitals.

When I get to the front of the line Liz's friend tries to ring me up. "I'm waiting for Liz," I say.

"She's not on commission," he says and takes my map from my hand and scans it. "$5.95."

I pay him and when he's done giving me my change he grabs a bookmark from one of the piles near the registers and tucks one inside my map. "In case you get lost," he says. And then he turns to Liz, who is helping her last customer, "We need to straighten in fiction when you're done here." He disappears into the yawning shelves of the store.

Liz gives her comely goodbye and then extends her left hand toward my face. "I'm getting married," she says. She says it flirty, almost as a taunt or a challenge, though I know, with Liz, that's not the case—it's just me. "Shane just moved to our ward from Layton," she says. "Isn't that where you're from?"

"Right next door," I say. She keeps her hand floating in front of my face like it's tied to a string in the ceiling. "That was quick," I say. "How's Jacob taking all this?"

"Oh my goodness," she says. "He absolutely loves Shane! And Shane is so good with him." She pauses for a moment and looks down at the ring on her finger. It isn't so big, but the fluorescent light must be right above her because it shines an incredibly white light. I can see a small rainbow of azure and gold that I swear shoots from Liz's hand down onto the red Formica of the counter. "What about you?" she says before holstering her ring.

"I'm all right. I'm seeing someone. She's nice. You'd like her." I hear the name SHANE called out in my head just like at the end of the movie, SHHAAAAAAAAAAAAAAAAAAAANE!

XI. The Dark

Rhoda's apartment is at the front of a beautiful child's-wagon-red Victorian with white trim and angel cornices in the Stuart Street neighborhood. The houses there are part of a tussle; some undergo reclamation by historical societies or people with enough backing to run something big through my office, while others get slum-lorded into seven or eight apartments for students. One burns to the ground almost every year, it seems. The images from the local news—cub reporter Kelsey Carlson leaning forward into the camera and clutching a microphone in one hand, the other brushing her hair out of her eyes and waving a quick acknowledgement back to Jamie and Judy at Studio Three—of one of these houses turned into charcoal stumps, smoldering under a white spray from a fireman's hose, stay with me like definitions of fire loss, like what crosses my mind when someone says the word 'light' or 'dark.'

The rooms in Rhoda's apartment are so small, and the ceiling so tall, it seems as if the place has been turned on its side. Inside it smells nice and it's always the right temperature. She has flowers in a vase on the table and I poke around in them, looking for a stray tag from Mr. Mysterious. There are tiger lilies popping out all over town now, though they won't bloom until the warm surety of May. I like tiger lilies, even from Mr. Mysterious, the dark stripes teasing the eye down into the heart of the flower.

"I picked those up at Meijer's," she says quickly.

"Really," I say. "They're nice."

"Carnations mostly, but only three dollars," she says. "Did you want to watch that Jazz game tonight?"

I'm surprised at this. "Do you?"

"I don't mind," she says. "This is the playoffs, right?"

"Yeah, it's the playoffs." Rhoda never suggests watching games, but she's always tolerated them. "I just thought you'd want to do something else. Since I'm leaving."

"You're coming back," she says.

"It's just a week is a long time."

"Not really," she says.

"Maybe more than a week," I say.

"Well then, how long, exactly, Brian?" she says.

"Two weeks tops, I'd say. You know it's a week just to get out there and back, especially pulling that trailer full of Zach's junk. Probably a day or two to load it up, and I'm sure my folks'll want me to go through some of my old things before they toss them out for good. I want to visit them, you know?"

"I know," she says. But I wonder if she does. Her parents live in East Lansing.

"My brothers and sisters are mostly all there, and they'll be around too, I guess."

"I know," she says. "Maybe this will do us some good. To be apart a little bit. Figure out what we want."

I don't like how she's using the imperial 'we' at all here. "What are you saying?"

"You know perfectly well what I'm saying," she says. And I have to think this is the same kind of thing Jaimy and I went through. The same kinds of talks. Only Jaimy seemed more desperate for a definite result. Rhoda seems pretty sure she just wants the time. Time to spend with Mr. Mysterious to see if he's really any better to be around than I am? I'm worried he might be.

"You've never been like this before, Rhoda."

"Neither have you, Brian." She goes to the refrigerator and extracts a couple of cans of soda: a Pepsi for her and a Sprite for me. She places the Sprite in front of me on the table and says, "Or are you drinking Pepsi now?"

"No," I say. "Call that a failed experiment."

"That's what I mean," she says. "Plus, I'm getting ready to graduate at the end of this summer. I'm not saying I want any kind of long-standing agreement here, but I sure as hell don't want us to be some kind of failed experiment, either." She wipes a piece of hair from her mouth after a sip of her Pepsi. The sun has already moved west enough that the house next door throws a shadow over the window behind Rhoda's head, and her hair acts like some kind of late afternoon luminescence. It seizes the light of the room and holds it against the growing darkness outside. It's sexy.

"So you want to watch the game tonight, then?"

"I don't care." She seems exasperated with me.

We decide to go for a drive before the game and we take my car. I can tell Rhoda is being critical of my car as I drive. She cringes when the gear shift lurches us forward a little; she puts one hand to the cracked dash when brakes whine to a stop at the stoplight out past Meijer's. I have no lack of faith in my old car, though.

We drive down M-43, heading due west, past the orchards and blueberry farms, to South Haven and Lake Michigan. Rhoda says she just wants to watch the sun go down and sit and talk for a while, though she is silent for the most part on the drive out of town.

I'm not so sure we'll make it out there before the sun gets down. And as we drive into town, I can almost park my truck in the shadow of the car in front of me at the light. "It's going to be kind of chilly out," I say.

"We can stay in here," she says, and she takes my hand. Her hand is strong and a little moist. "Just pull in in front of the church down there." There is a road in South Haven that runs alongside a very steep cliff overlooking Lake Michigan, and on the other side of the road there is a Catholic church whose front doors open out to the lake. The lake is immense, like an ocean really. Even Great Salt Lake has beaches at the periphery, but if you stand

101

on the cliffs of South Haven, the wind coming up at your feet, you feel as if you are flying.

The sun is low in the sky and the sky is pale white; it comes through Rhoda's hair like a wind. As the sun drops, the sky darkens and takes on new colors, oranges and yellows stolen from Rhoda's hair, purples from the corners of night, and the water nearest the horizon lightens before it swallows the sun. Rhoda looks beautiful in all of this. She is not, I realize, a stunning beauty like Liz, but she is something else entirely: an enduring beauty, like Jaimy. Consistent as a setting sun, rather than insistent like that purple and red corner of the sky that I know I'll never see just the same again.

"It's a game two," I say. "So no hurry. We can stay as long as you want."

"Sun's gone," she says, finally. And there she is, in the lights of my dashboard, her white teeth and moist mouth glistening in the leftover light. I kiss her on the mouth and rub my hand up and down her back. "He's watching," she says, and pulls away from me.

I turn and see the silhouette of a priest standing in the open doors of the Catholic church across the street. He looks as if he has been expelled by the motor of some giant cuckoo clock, like he might give us the time, perhaps a warning, and be drawn back into the yellow glowing bowels of the church. "He's just watching the sun go down."

"That's all he's going to see go down," Rhoda says. I like it when she gets a little raunchy.

The drive back is full of stars, like you can only see in the country, and I wish my windshield was cleaner, or that I was the passenger. Rhoda told me once that the lights we see aren't even there anymore; they're so far away in the night sky that they'd have all burned out before the light we see will have reached earth. "The light of most things outlasts its origins," she says. "So when we see the light from the stars, we're taking some of that light away from what's left, absorbing the last glimmers of the starlight."

Rhoda leans her head against the glass and calls out the constellations to me: Cassiopeia, Orion, Pegasus, and then the harder ones: Chameleon, the Chameleon; Horologium, the Pendulum Clock; Coma Berenices, Berenice's Hair. She's pointing in all directions, and in spite of her best efforts I haven't learned to see any of them. They're like telling one wave from another in the lake.

Rhoda's knowledge of the universe is amazing, and she tells me a little something of each of these: "Berenice was an Egyptian queen who offered her locks to the gods for the return of her husband from battle. Her hair contains a multitude of galaxies. Nearly thirty stars . . ."

"Hang onto your hair," I say. "I'm only going to Utah."

"You'll come back," she says, and then she traces her long, hard fingernails up the denim thigh of my pants.

When we get to her apartment we go to her bedroom and Rhoda leaves the light turned off while she undresses. She is completely naked before I have my socks and pants off. She pulls my shirt to her and I find my way through the nebulous cloud of her hair to her waiting mouth. She is sweet and tart, like honey and salt, and I run my hands up and down her bare skin. She is cold and I can feel how tight her skin is, I can feel the goose bumps under the fine down on her lower back like Braille.

We fall into her single bed. I will miss this while I am gone. "I love you, Rhoda," I say when we are finished.

"I know," she says.

I don't say this to her very often, and she seldom says it to me. She doesn't say it tonight, apparently. The room is so dark. I can feel the tickle of her hair and I can hear cars passing in the street outside. Above us, in another apartment, a stereo turns on and I can hear the Replacements' album *Tim* coming through, falling down onto me.

I can't see the ceiling, or where it meets the walls, and for a while the only thing that lets me know the blue-black in front of me is not the clouds of my sleep is the chorus of "Here Comes a Regular" struggling through the floor. Then there is the sound of bed springs, clear and rhythmic and out of sync with the song. Building to a crescendo, and then the knocking of a head board or of a head against the wall that runs straight down to the wall I rest the top of my own head against. In the black dark, Rhoda breathes slowly beside me, and asleep or engrossed in the orchestrations above us, I feel I'm between two worlds: a world of the flesh, of Rhoda's flesh, of my flesh, and a world of some closeted memory, of a time with Jaimy, that hangs up above me. I know this album like I know my own thoughts turning in the dark. It came out when Jaimy and I were dating, and I remember playing it again and again, while we found each other in the ways they're finding each other up there. The way Rhoda and I almost found each other tonight.

"I think your game's on," she says. She climbs over me, finds her way across the room, and opens the door, casting her shadow across the room. She lets the door frame her nude body and the light comes through the hair between her legs. Each stray hair shines white against the black of her shadow; her body looks black in shadow. And then she turns and steps into the light and I can see her long, strong body in full as she walks away.

I hear the television come on. I hear the channels being changed. I hear "Malone for two! Thunderous, tomahawk dunk." I hear her move around some more and then the light turns off.

I pull on my boxer shorts and follow the glow of the television out to Rhoda, who is reclined on her couch, nude and sexy and putting off signals that we've not even begun for the night. The game is in the second quarter and the Jazz have a comfortable lead, and I feel like I'm in very familiar territory.

XII And on the Seventh Day . . .

When the morning comes I am alone in Rhoda's bed, clinging to the side of the mattress like I've just pulled myself out of the ocean and onto a small piece of wreckage. The morning light is still here, so I know I haven't lost the day yet, though that might not be such a bad thing. We opened some wine last night, I remember. And then I remember the beers and the last of a bottle of Jack Daniels Rhoda had tucked away in her cupboard. I remember the game, but not the result[46].

Rhoda's room is small, but very nice in a way only a woman can make something nice like this, I think. Things are orderly. The blues in the covers of her astronomy books seem to match the bedspread that complements the bright orange hues of the afghan her grandmother made, and that lies over the rocking chair her great grandfather constructed from the leftover oak tree they had to raze to make room for a house for him and his bride. I know Rhoda's history this well because I'm growing so weary of my own.

I'm alone in the room, and I don't remember Rhoda leaving. I've slept, though. Or maybe I've just passed out. Maybe, I tell myself, I just need out of my apartment to get some serious sleep. The smell of Rhoda's pillow is the smell of her hair. I look at it for signs of Mr. Mysterious—a stray hair, an unfamiliar scent. I inhale the pillow case like a dog, trying to find some bit of sweat or cologne. I can smell detergent, and I know that Mr. Mysterious can be washed away, just like I can be washed away.

---

[46] Utah wins this game 105 to 90 and takes a two-game lead in the best of five series.

Rhoda is in the kitchen sipping tea. She is wearing a silk robe I've never seen. It has a blue and silver floral pattern and looks luminous against her olive skin. I can barely see her downturned face, her hair tumbling down as she scans a book titled, plainly and threateningly, QUANTUM PHYSICS. "Good morning," I say.

She looks at the clock on her microwave before responding, "Good morning." She puts the book on the table next to her tea saucer and looks up at me. "You slept a long time."

"Yeah," I say. "A little bit of a headache, but I feel pretty good."

"You really hit that beer last night. I had a twelve-pack in the fridge before you came by and there's just one left."

"I'll get you some more before I leave," I say, and take a seat at the tiny kitchen table.

"No, no, that's okay. Do you want some tea?"

"Please," I say. "Why did we drink so much?"

"We?" she says, rinsing a cup out in the sink and then filling it with tap water.

"All right," I say. "I think I'd better get going. I need a shower and a change of clothes."

"Am I going to see you today?"

"Yeah," I say. "I need to pack, though. Can it be late?"

"It always is," she says.

Back at my apartment there is a message from Randy. I'd nearly forgotten about Randy. "I'm ready when you are, Bub. Give me a call and let's get going."

I realize that I'm in this thing with him now. I remember his silver hook of a hand. It's the kind of thing that I'd be freaked out by normally, but he swings it around with such grace, as if it's the most natural thing in the world to have a hook for a hand.

There's a message from Zach as well asking if he can pay me back for the gas for the trip. If I absolutely have to have it before I go, he says, then he can scrape it together.

It's always been this way with Zach. He puts me in the position of having to do him favors. Of all my brothers and sisters he's the worst. Little things, but even Dad always said that you should imagine every penny you borrow like it's in a bag and you have to carry it around with you wherever you go; imagine every little favor weighs one pound. Zach's creating a whole new gravity with the density of his gratitude, as far as I'm concerned. But Dad wouldn't see it that way. He'd say I've got a few tons worth of payback coming for my job.

I feel like I should leave Phil a note that I'll be away for a week or two. And then I think I should just see if he notices when his dishes pile up. But then I think that's unfair, even to him, and I jot a note on the refrigerator, "*Phil, I've got to go to Utah for a week or so. See you when I get back, B.*" and stick it behind the magnet holding the picture of Phil and his family.

Phil's family is small, by Utah standards; just Phil and his sister, Madison, and their parents, John and Dottie. The picture next to my note is of the four of them in Colorado, a green mountain in the background with the shadow of the photographer creeping toward them across the gray rock.

My family doesn't feel so large to me. It's what you're used to, I suppose. There's Zach, and Rachel and Luke, who are older. And Jessica who is a lot younger than I am. She's still in school. She was the only one of us to really leave the nest right out of high school and she's studying psychology at U.N.L.V. I haven't seen her for years.

I was eight when she was born, and my mom decided she was going to have Jessica at home since she was absolutely going to be the last one. Mom had joined a natural childbirth class with some of the other mothers from the church, "The Unshaven Hedge-Hugging Hippies of Upper Zion" Dad called them, but he tolerated Mom's newfound naturalism and so we tried to as well. For the entire pregnancy we'd been force-fed wheat germ and couscous and more vitamins than I could count. I remember the midwife was a large woman from our ward who wore white support hose and white nurse's shoes all the time. She wasn't married in spite of everyone's best efforts in the church.

Zach had deliberately told me that she was a wet nurse instead of a midwife and I carried that confusion with me to the birth, announcing to the house that "The wet nurse is here!" when she drove up into our driveway. My mother, who for some reason had climbed up onto the kitchen table to engage her labor, didn't pay me any attention, but my father pulled me sternly aside and said, "Look here you! If you're going to be a goof-off during this glorious moment you certainly have my permission to stay in your room!"

"He doesn't know any better," Zach said.

"Well he's going to learn in a hurry," my father said. I thought he meant that the coming birth was going to be the kind of life changing miracle that he'd been threatening us with.

I stayed back, not sure what I needed to be doing that wouldn't be some kind of screw-up. Rachel dabbed at my mother's forehead with a wet washcloth, Luke fed her ice chips, and Zach pounded the ice out on the porch with a hammer wrapped in a dish towel. I can still remember the insanely joyous look on Zach's face as he smacked the ice again and again with my father's favorite blue-handled hammer. The water from the ice sprayed up onto the base of the glass door leading out to the porch and Zach seemed almost to keep time with Mom's breathing. Smack, smack, whew. Smack, smack, whew. Dad held Mom's hand in his and recited verses from *The Book of Mormon* at first, then the Bible, then poems he remembered, then, when he seemed to run out of things to remember, song lyrics. I remember "Shadow dancing . . . Shadow dancing . . ." A song I couldn't believe my dad knew, but he had that kind of memory, even if he heard something just once, and there he was whispering the lyrics out to my mom as she pushed Jessica into the world.

My mother had gone through what my father said was her immodest phase. Seeing her naked wasn't so shocking, but the fact that she shed her clothes and paced the living room even though the curtains were wide open and the neighbors were all coming back from church was. Dad laid some old bed spreads on the kitchen table and ordered us all to fetch the pillows we'd practiced retrieving for the big moment. I carried my pillow like it was the baby because I wanted so badly to be an important part of the birth. To carry with me a little more knowledge and understanding.

When the midwife arrived it seemed to me like everyone knew exactly what they were supposed to be doing except me. My mother lay up on the table, a big elephant-legged table that has been in our family for generations, and that Zach has designs on, no doubt. Her legs were apart and she was naked except for the towels that kept falling down on her. My father, on one of his singing breaks, turned to Luke and Zach and me and arched his eyebrows as if to say: "This is where you all came from. It's where we all came from. Pay attention."

It seemed like it ought to be a source of some mystery, some deep, dark place with a light at the end of it showing me something I'd forgotten. I stared and I stared and I stared until Mom told Dad to get us out of there, she was going to have a b.m. and she didn't want us to see it. When we were allowed back into the room Jessica's head was pushing through like an egg from a magician's mouth.

After she was born the midwife began working feverishly down there and then covered Mom with some blankets. "Show's over," Zach said, out of earshot of my mother and father. We were supposed to leave my mom to rest and bond with the new baby, but I snuck back in to ask her if she was okay.

"Oh, sweetie," she said to me and reached out to touch me. She was still propped up on the kitchen table with every pillow and blanket we could find in the house. She looked like she was brimming over with cotton, spilling out from the table like a cornucopia, exhausted and pale and shaking. I had never seen her cry so much, never heard her scream out in pain. "This is the miracle, and miracles take some doing. It was like this with all of you, and you should know that no woman would or could go through with this without the joy in the heart that the Lord has given me. The joy the Lord has given you," she said, and she showed me Jessica's squirmy little spider body.

The phone rings, and it is Randy Hansen. "I am ready to get the fuck out of Dodge," he says.

"I think we can leave tomorrow," I say. "If that's not too soon."

"Where do you want to meet me?"

"What do you mean?"

"Where should I meet you?"

"I can just pick you up at your place, I guess."

"That won't work," he says.

"Why won't that work?"

"My landlord doesn't like people coming by," he says. It's a terrible attempt at a lie, but I can't really call him on anything. I'm thinking now that we should just get on the road and get this over with so I can get back to Rhoda.

I suggest we meet at the Corner Bar, and he agrees. It's a little late to get on the road, but I tell him we can't leave until

11:00 A.M. I want to see Rhoda once more before we go. And I need to run the car by Uncle Ed's for a lube and oil. Randy's not in any position to argue and tells me if he's not in the parking lot he's inside having one for the road. "Let's not fiddlefuck around too much though, unless you want to drive all night."

It takes me about thirty minutes to pack and about four hours to get rid of my headache from last night. I feel nauseous and hung over, but oddly rested. When I find myself compulsively looking around the room for that something I know I forgot, some essence of Dee Dee (who I now picture curled up in a baby's car seat that I'll need to remember to load in the morning), or just some piece of my life in Kalamazoo, I call Rhoda.

"Can I sleep over there tonight?"

"Sure," she says. "But no drinking tonight, okay?"

"No problem," I say. "I just need a good night's rest."

"That may not be part of the deal," she says.

XIII. A Peculiar People[47]

We're a peculiar pair, I think. Me, a tall, baby-faced, babe of the First of America. And Randy, not one mile outside of Kalamazoo, tow-headed hurly-burly silver-clawed man of the world. And still, nothing pleases me more. The road is open, the fog has lifted and retreated as we rumble past the walls of trees toward Indiana and then Illinois. I drive past Paw Paw and think, there is Liz's father and his ward, tucked in amongst the orchards and the vineyards, budding and unfurling in the mild spring air. There are wineries in this small town and they advertise all along Interstate 94, offering free samples of their vintage that come in small,plastic cups with cracker pieces to cleanse the palate. It reminds me of my time at Catholic mass with Jaimy, watching parishioner after parishioner step forward to be absolved and take Christ into their mouths and into their lives.

Driving past the vineyards struggling to open their leaves and unburdening themselves of the grapes that spring from the water of the air, the fog-berries, I, too, feel absolved of my life. It is as though I have given myself over to the highest power who will

---

[47] "But ye are a chosen generation, a royal priesthood, an holy nation, a peculiar people; that ye should shew forth the praises of him who hath called you out of darkness into his marvelous light"

—I Peter 2:9.

"For thou art an holy people unto the Lord thy God, and the Lord hath chosen thee to be a peculiar people unto himself"

—Deuteronomy 14:2.

have me, and I'm setting sail for the plains and the mountains beyond. You have to close a door to open it again, my dad would say.

"Can you swerve a little fucking more?" Randy asks without raising his head from where he has nodded off against the glass. He raises his silver hook and scratches at his moustache and then rubs his eye with the loop of the hook.

"Sorry," I say. I slept for almost ten hours last night, and when I woke Rhoda had made me a breakfast of eggs and bacon and pancakes. And then we did it once more before I got into the Bronco and drove to the Corner Bar where Randy was sitting on the curb with a large, olive-drab canvas bag with a shoulder strap.

"You're missing this incredible day, here."

"I'm missing my hand," he says, still stuck to the glass. "I'm avoiding the fucking day, Pollyanna."

"All that fog and those gray days," I say. "And now this, as we're leaving."

"The irony is killing me. Let me suffer in peace and die, will you?"

"Did you have a rough night?"

"Is there any other kind?" he asks. I notice the knuckles of his hand resting on his thigh are swollen, and beginning to bruise. Deep, greenish and black bruises. I look at his face for the first time since I picked him up and I see that his lower lip is a bit swollen and looks split in front of his canine. Could it have been like that before, I wonder?

"You want an aspirin, or anything?" I ask.

"I'll take something stronger if you've got it, but I've been chewing fucking aspirin since four fucking this morning."

"You have a little bit of trouble last night?"

"You could say that," he says.

"Want to tell me about it?"

"Girl scout kicked my fucking ass over some Trefoils and Thin Mints. Now let me saw some fucking logs before I put your ass on her mailing list, Oprah."

It makes me nervous, not knowing what kind of trouble Randy might be into, but then, I think, that's the great thing about leaving a place. You don't take your troubles with you.

"I've got to land a yam in the yam-yard when you get a chance," he says after some time.

"What?" I say.

"Drop the kids off at the pool, visit the Munger Potato Fest[48], put the Lincoln logs on spin cycle, squeeze cheese, you catching my drift?"

"Land a yam in the yam-yard," I say.

"Yeah, float a Baby Ruth, grand marshall the ass parade."

"Light the stinky cigar," my dad would say.

"When you get a chance, there. Chief."

We haven't gotten very far, but there's an Amoco shouting out its welcome to me not far past Paw Paw and I pull off. I figure if Randy's had a hard night it's probably coming back on him in lots of ways. As I slow the Bronco, Randy lifts his sticky face from the glass of the passenger window. That's one irritating habit already, I think. The window, I see in snatches, is occluded with his sheen. "Not here," he says, watching the Amoco intently.

"Why not?" I say. "Thought this was a pressing issue?"

"Not here," he says. "There's a rest stop up the road about forty miles. I need to stop there."

I can't believe the pomposity of this guy. As I pull back onto the interstate I see a black billboard with a simple message written in white letters: "I don't think you're not real," it reads,

---

[48] Quite a popular festival in the Upper Peninsula, actually.

117

and it is signed "God." The Baptists, I think, have been putting these up all over the interstate. L.T., I recall, used to be a Baptist. I look at the sign, looming over the highway in black and white, white and black, the graying sky moving behind it, us moving beneath it. Can this possibly chasten anyone into God's house? "And people think Mormons are weird," I say.

"We are weird," Randy says back from his slumber.

I turn on the radio for the last few stitches of WIDR F.M., the Western Michigan campus station. It's a good college station, I think, but there's nothing so good here I couldn't live without it. Almost nothing, anyway.

Jaimy and I used to go to all the college shows down at the Speedway Cafe in Salt Lake. It was a converted warehouse under I-15 and right next to the methadone clinic. There would always be some Indians lying around in the dirt, high on their methadone or waiting to come down from their smack before picking up their methadone tabs. One crawled out of the dust while Jaimy and I were waiting to get into the Fishbone show and told her she was a ghost walking. He didn't seem too panicked, but he was serious. "You look dead, girl!" he said. It really upset Jaimy, especially since there was the usual collection of Goths, punks, and ska-kids hanging around down there with their white make-up or their Sputnik hair or their black wrap-around glasses.

The punks and the Indians of Salt Lake City had some kind of connection back then. The Indian center would host a lot of the punk shows. They'd find the biggest Indians they could find and they'd wear black T-shirts and stand, arms folded across their chests, at the back of the hall, while the punks did their thing up near the stage; skanking, pogoing, slam-dancing. Nobody bumped the Indians. If anyone got out of hand, a couple of the big Indians would come and drag them outside. I never knew if they roughed them up or not. There would always be some Indian women sitting on folding chairs behind the big men, talking over the staccato rhythms of the music and swinging that one foot, slung over one of their chubby legs, gently in time to the music.

Jaimy and I would stand near the back at these shows, and sometimes I would dive into the fracas. There were some rules in the pits. You were not supposed to hurt one another. You just shoved each other around. No one threw an elbow or a fist. No one groped the girls who were brave enough to give it a try. And if someone fell down you helped them up. Sometimes a poseur would break a rule and the verdict from the punks was always swift, the justice merciless. The punks turned on the interloper like white blood cells attacking a virus. When they'd roughed them up enough they tossed them from the circle like garbage, face down onto the Indian center floor at the foot of one of the big Indians. They'd always say something like "tsk tsk tsk" and then drag them out the front door.

Jaimy was too frail to get into the pit, but she loved going to the shows. "This is the best thing I've ever seen," she said. And her look started to change as we went to more of the shows down at the Indian center. She never went punk, but she started wearing shorter skirts, tighter tops, more dark makeup around her eyes. And she'd always obsess about the eye makeup: "I don't look dead, do I Brian? It doesn't make me look dead?"

I remember coming out of the pit one night, covered in sweat, my T-shirt and pants clinging to me like I'd just come out of a hot lake, and I saw Jaimy standing at the back of the hall. The front door was open to let some air into the hall and to facilitate the rejection of the gropers and poseurs. It was a hot night and tempers were exploding every few minutes. Jaimy had worn a short, short black skirt and the light from the front door was coming straight through it. She looked like she'd just walked out of a movie. I never thought of her as sexy, but there she was.

As I was walking toward her, a punk with a pink mohawk came up behind her. "Hey, Spooky."

Jaimy said hello and I kept coming. "She's with me," I said.

The punk looked at me and looked at Jaimy, who just looked down at the ground. When the punk walked away, Jaimy asked me, "Why'd you do that?"

"Do what? That guy's a creep."

"That was rude," she said.

"I don't like you wearing all that black stuff," I said.

"You were rude. He wasn't doing anything."

"He was going to try to pick you up," I said. The hall was loud, the noise from the band was bouncing off of the walls, but it was small, and I felt the eyes of the hall upon us. The Indian at the door was staring at us.

"You should apologize," she said. I was sure she'd been too flattered by the punk's greeting. It was just a hello.

"You stupid Catholics and your apologies," I said. Jaimy was always making me apologize for things. She was always apologizing for things. "All right," I said. "Then can we get out of here?"

She looked really stunning, I thought. I could see why the punk might take a chance. "You're not having fun?"

"I'm soaked through to the bone with a bunch of other people's sweat, I'm sore, and I'm about to make a complete ass of myself. Isn't that enough for one night?" I walked over to the punk, who was standing in front of a small queue of other punks trying to make a pipe out of an empty can of Mountain Dew. "Hey," I said, tapping him on the shoulder.

As he turned around I felt a hand grip me by the shoulder and jerk me, with one swift yank, backward. The hand spun me around like I was small child. It was the Indian from the door. "You're out of here," he said.

"I was just going to apologize," I said. It sounded whiny.

"Out," he said, and he grabbed me around the elbow with his one big hand. His hand was calloused and large enough to swallow my entire elbow. I could hear the punk laughing at me behind my back as we walked out to the street. I could hear the click of Jaimy's heels as she navigated the slippery steps of the Indian center after us.

"Here's the one, Chief," Randy says. The travel center advertises free Michigan apples for each visitor.

"You sure this is the place?" I say. I feel I can give Randy a hard time, like I've known him for years.

"You got a pen in here?"

"A pen?" I say.

"You know, something to write with?"

"What do you need a pen for?" I ask.

"To dig the krungus out of my ass," he says. "What do you think I need a pen for?" I point to the glove box and Randy finds a ballpoint pen from Schaefer's flowers, where I ordered Rhoda a dozen roses for Valentine's Day.

"I'll be right back," Randy says, shifting the pen over to his hook so he can wrestle the door open. I cut the engine and watch him walk into the brown brick structure. It's the last stop in Michigan, and I can see the Indiana state line over my shoulder. I think I'd better go, too, my last chance to crap in Michigan. And I want my free apple.

The rest room is huge, but nearly empty when I get in there. I walk down the rows of stalls, and to my surprise I see Randy bent over the toilet in one of the stalls, staring intently at the wall and copying something down onto a piece of toilet paper laid across his plastic arm. I cautiously backtrack to the urinals and turn into one of them. Someone has written, in a sloppy hand: "Bucks with shorter horns stand closest to the trough."

"Hey Chief," Randy says from behind me. "I gotta make a quick call and tell someone I'm coming. I'll see you out in the truck."

"Get me one of those apples, will you?" I ask as he leaves.

I zip up and walk back to where Randy was studying the wall. There are pictures of penises, some erect and ejaculating, some big, some small. There are the standard rhymes about only being able to fart, and a few phone numbers offering blow jobs. There are a few city names and one, I notice, is Nauvoo with what looks like a circle with the letters Z.O.G. written inside of it in heavily stylized, almost gothic letters. It is written in the same thick, black ink as a nearby offer of someone named Cindy's sexual services and what is apparently her seven-digit phone number.

I stand and walk out of the stall and there is Randy, coming back into the rest room, with two shiny red apples pinned between his silver hook and his shirt. "What're you doing, Chief?"

"I had to get some paper to blow my nose," I say. "You make your phone call already?"

"Yeah, I'm good. Hope you're not coming down with something," he says, and he stands his ground until I walk past him and out of the building.

XIV. Randy's Mission

Randy's mood seems to have taken a dive, and he's gone into himself, sitting quietly, pulling on the corners of his moustache, until we get to the Chicago traffic. "If we'd left a little earlier we'd have missed this cluster fuck," he says.

"You never can tell," I say. "Pretty smooth sailing until we got here, though." The cars are funneled into two staggering lines of traffic, lurching and slumping their way a few at a time. They have set the cement median so close to the outside lane that I couldn't open my door if I had to get out.

"Monkeyfuckers," Randy says, to himself I think.

"Where'd you do your mission," I ask. Trying to pass the time, trying to draw Randy out of his anger. I know now that I am stuck with him at least until Nauvoo, and probably all the way across the plains into Ogden, so I don't want this mood of his to leave Chicago.

"The armpit of the world," he says.

"I thought you said you were somewhere in Italy?"

"Palermo," he says, spitting out the word like a wormy bite of apple.

"I've never been to Europe," I say. "You didn't like it, huh?"

"You like getting your ass beat day in and day out by the local Cosa Nostra's brats?"

"The mob?" I ask.

"That's no bullshit down there. And they all act like they've got a Papal seal granting them inquisitor's rights on missionaries. Shit, half the houses our bishop sent us out to, they'd be waiting for us when we came out. The other half they'd get us on the inside, their little, dried-up old grandmas cussing us out in

Italian while they played kick-the-elders'-berries. I fucking hated that shit, and I was paying my own money to get my ass kicked."

"It wasn't all like that, was it?"

"No. Sometimes we'd get some old fart who couldn't hear a car bomb in his living room, and he'd let us in to do our shtick. Those were the days you looked forward to, let me tell you something."

"Did you convert anybody?"

"Yeah, I got six while I was there, but five of them went back to Catholicism. They sent me letters, apologizing. Fuck 'em. I knew a kid in Rome who had them lining up for the baptism. It put me in a bad place when I came home."

"What do you mean," I ask. The fumes from the Bronco are leaking into the cab and I crack my window.

"You fart? Give warning, man. I don't want no Dutch oven action here. That's one thing I won't take on this trip."

"It's the traffic," I say. "Don't worry."

"What about you?" Randy asks. "Why didn't you go take God to the people?"

"I blew my mission calling," I say. "I don't really want to go into it."

"How the fuck do you blow a mission calling? I knew kids who'd fucked their bishop's daughter on the way to the airport—and they still went." Randy thinks this is really amusing.

"I just did," I say. "You know, you don't talk like an R.M."

"That's cause I'm about a million miles from all of that," he says, wistfully. "But you know what?" he says. "I'm coming back, I guess. I'm going back to Moab, and that's something. Who knows how this will all end up? Maybe it'll end in fire, maybe ice, you know?"

"Have you been in Michigan a long time, then?"

"Michigan? No. I've been in New York for the last four or five years. There and Toronto, back and forth a lot really."

"What were you doing in New York?" I ask.

"I knew some people there," he says. "You've got a lot of questions for a banker."

"I'm not a banker," I say. I resent the term like I resent the job, I suppose.

"You should open your mouth when you speak," he says, and pulls the front of his cap down over his eyes and slides down in the seat.

"What?" I say. I can't believe how this is turning out, and I know if I have to sit in the traffic with this guy for very much longer I'm going to start getting claustrophobic.

"A-NUN-CIATE," he says. "Don't mumble your fucking words all the damned time."

The radio's gone all staticky again, and I look out to see we're crossing over some sort of quarry, whole pieces of the world taken away, leaving white and lime-green rings descending farther than I can see from the road. I try to imagine this guy knocking on doors in a little Italian villa, on a warm spring day, the sky above the yellow stucco walls peppered with argent clouds. "Ciao, baby. How're you-all stupid dagos doing today?"

We're past the exit into Chicago now, and the traffic picks up some. Rhoda and I spent our first, expensive Valentine's Day in Chicago. I hadn't known her all that long yet, but it was easy enough to ask her to spend the weekend together. It's the kind of thing that would've seemed impossible at any such early stage back in Utah, but that's no doubt due more to the years and the relationships in between than to the modesty of the place. After traveling so many failed relationships, like Liz, like any number of other women I dated since Jaimy, there's a boldness that comes with knowing that failure doesn't come from boldness. It comes from everywhere else, but never from boldness.

I took Rhoda to the Science and Industry Museum[49]. Or rather, she took me. Rhoda listens to N.P.R., and she calls into the science show almost every Friday hoping to get her voice on the air. Her voice, she told me, has coursed over Utah and parts west more than my own. Travelled the universe and is still echoing and fading out past the heavens.

I held Rhoda's hand for the first time while we walked the museum. Her hand was soft, but like the rest of her, generous and muscular. She never clenched my hand, but I knew that her hands were strong hands.

Late in the day, the two-and-a-half-hour car trip weighing down on us a little, I think, we began to talk less and less and to hold onto each other's hands a little more. We would draw closer together in front of the exhibits of the locomotive engines, a working hatchery, a giant human heart we could walk through guided by the sound of the rushing blood. Rhoda's hair smelled so wonderful, and I remember the insane thrill bursting through my arm when I braved to touch it, to brush it past her shoulder.

In the Body Worlds room, we paused and leaned against each other until I could almost feel her heart beating beneath her thin sweater. I found the rhythm of her breathing and kept it with mine. The room contained more than two hundred authentic human specimins, whole, posed bodies and transparent cross-

---

[49] After the Chicago Bulls won their sixth championship, their second in a row at the expense of the Utah Jazz, the trophies were put on display in a number of Chicago locales, including the Science and Industry Museum. The trophies were placed behind glass, like all the other exhibits, and patrons could travel a length of red carpet and velvet ropes to gaze on the trophies as if they were any number of humanity's achievements, man's success against the universe.

sections preserved with special plastics. Among them were two displays of a real man and a real woman, each sliced razor-thin and pressed between sheets of glass and hung up, floating above the rest of us, the light shining through their organs and bones. We stood before these two for nearly an hour, like most of the museum patrons, I think, transfixed and enchanted. There were guides to what we were seeing; this is the liver, this the brain, the heart. But I wasn't at all interested in any of that. I held Rhoda's hand the entire time and stared into the cross sections of two people, each one so beautiful, like stained glass in a cathedral, like kaleidoscopes of the human soul casting their glow on the two of us.

"Do you have a girlfriend, Randy?" I ask.

"You could say that," he says. "Something like that," he says.

"What do you mean?"

"I got a wife out in Utah. But I haven't seen her in a few years. She doesn't even know about this," he says, holding the hook up and turning it, somehow (I can't figure out how he turns his hook, how he clenches and unclenches it).

Suddenly I've got two questions I want to ask at once, and I know he won't answer either of them. "Are you going to see her?" I ask instead.

"Now, that's not entirely up to me," he says. "And besides," he says, "there's a lot of road between now and then. What I tell you right now might not be the same thing I tell you then."

I nod. I'm getting smarter about Randy, I think. About how to question him, how to understand him. "You a Jazz fan?"

"Basketball?" he asks.

"Yeah," I say.

"You know, I been following those chumps for years now. Years. I used to go to the games when I lived in Salt Lake, back when tickets were only a couple of bucks for the nosebleed seats over at the Salt Palace[50]. Dr. Dunkenstein, Dantley[51], all those fools. Man, I used to really be into those guys. But you know what? Those fuckers just might have what it takes this year. If they can get Jaimie Watson[52] back and going, and that Baby Huey out of Kansas[53], they've got the best guard-power forward tandem in the game right now. I mean, fuck the Bulls. They could do it this year, you know?"

I'm dying to ask Randy when he lived in Salt Lake, but I like the vibe we're on and I just say, "We'll have to catch the next game when we stop over in Nauvoo."

"We might just make a man of you yet, chief," Randy says. "I got my eye on you, you know," and he returns to his window. We are past Chicago and I feel the pull of the plains, the tilt of the earth down into Missouri.

---

[50] The former home of the Utah Jazz, located in the heart of downtown Salt Lake City. Seating only about 12,000 it was the smallest venue for an NBA team before the Jazz brokered a deal for the Delta Center, located a bit west of downtown, but closer to I-15. It is located next to the Triad Center, a visionary multi-multi-million dollar mall thought to be the future of Salt Lake and built by Adnon Khashoggi, the richest man in the world at that time. During the Jazz's early, financially difficult years they even tried to broker a deal with Khashoggi offering limited stock options and even partnerships. Khashogghi refused to disclose his finances, however, and it turned out to be one of the best deals that never was for the struggling Jazz. Over-invested and overly involved in illegal arms sales, Khashoggi quickly plummeted from multi-billionaire to wanted man. By the late eighties, his reflective copper-

colored Triad center sat mostly empty, visible from nearly anywhere in Salt Lake City. The Salt Palace now serves as a convention center.

51 Darryl Griffith, aka Dr. Dunkenstein, one of the league's most exciting players in the early eighties. He led the league in three-point shooting the same year that Adrian Dantley won the second of his two scoring titles, averaging over 30.6 points per game and winning the Comeback Player of the Year award.

Griffith and Dantley were electrifying, explosive players who started to draw record numbers to see the Jazz play. But Dantley, arguably one of the best players in the history of the NBA, had a history of not getting along with coaches and staff and even other players. He was once fined, by coach Frank Layden, thirty pieces of silver for being a "Judas." And he once told a young Karl Malone to avoid diving for loose balls in practice because it might cut short his career. Malone, whose work ethic is legendary in and out of sports, was not amused. Dantley still has not had his number retired by the Jazz organization (standard fare for a sports franchise to acknowledge players of Dantley's abilities) because of lingering hard feelings. However, Dantley was recently inaugurated into the Utah Sports Hall of Fame.

52 Jaimie Watson, once thought to be the missing ingredient in the Jazz's formula for success, was a player with a flair for up-tempo, run-and-gun play, and tremendous leaping ability. But as the terms of his contract were drawing to an end, he suffered a knee injury that seemed to keep getting re-aggravated. Malone, speaking obviously of Watson's chronic injury, lashed out at his team during their lone losing streak of the season: "We got people of this team listening to their agents saying play or don't play instead of listening to the doctors. If you don't want to play, get the hell out."

[53] Greg Ostertag is often called Baby Huey. Because of his large frame and flattop, he does bear a resemblance to the cartoon lummox, but it is his inconsistent, sometimes lackadaisical play that often makes the name seem fitting.

XV. Like Masons

We're past the Chicago traffic, and it feels as if I'm really leaving now. "You know some people in Nauvoo?" I say. The road opens up outside of Joliet, and the distance between mileage markers is less and less occluded with exit ramps, gas stations, and signs.

"Some friends who owe me something," he says. "We used to be a little bit like . . . like some fucked up Masons[54], you could say. If you're a Mormon with a sense of humor, that is. And I need to make sure everything is all tidied up before I head back to Utah."

"How long is this going to take?" I say. It'd be a rude question with anyone else, but I think I'm starting to find an etiquette with Randy. Straight talk.

"Not long," he says. He fishes through his shirt sleeve and unhinges his arm and slides it off. There is more flesh and bone there than I would have imagined, but it is wrapped very neatly in white gauze. It is withered, not half the size of Randy's other arm, and the texture under the gauze is bumpy, irregular. "Awww . . . that's better, isn't it?" He flexes the arm and stretches it out like a

---

[54] Joseph Smith, himself a Mason, was fluent in the Masonic rituals, and they would have been fresh in his mind, his having recently been inducted, when in May of 1842 he performed the very first "endowment" in Nauvoo for a group of church leaders. His ceremony included all the usual Masonic trappings of secret handshakes, sacred names, washings, creation drama, cryptic symbols and, importantly, penalty oaths. Most of these Masonic-based rituals have found their way into contemporary Mormon ritual.

baby bird's wing. "You're going to want to take 55 South up here," he says, and he points out through the windshield at the grass-green sign with his bird wing. "I still see fingers at the end of my arm," he says. "Sometimes just the middle one, but you know, I can feel them there sometimes too."

"How'd you lose your arm?" I say.

Randy looks down at the plastic arm in his lap. The straps and padding look like a woman's undergarment, like something my mother might wear. "Let's just say when they tell you to keep your hands inside the ride at all times down at Lagoon[55] . . . you'd better do it."

The pock marks up the side of his bird wing and along his face and neck, submerged by his whiskers, tell me he's lying. "Really?" I say. "What happened?"

"Can you think of anything more personal than the loss of someone's hand?" he says. His tone is changed again, and I know

---

[55] Lagoon Amusement Park, located between Brian's hometown of Kaysville and Salt Lake City. Lagoon is modest by amusement park standards, but has been in existence for years. Every spring through fall it employs hundreds of area high school students to operate its rides and work as barkers at its many games-of-chance booths. It has, as Randy implies, seen its share of accidents on its roller coasters.

Historically, it was there that Louis Armstrong, scheduled to perform in the 1950s, threatened to leave if blacks weren't allowed to see his show. His demand was met.

Nefariously to some residents, the park is also known for its annual "Gay Day," where gays and lesbians are encouraged, either unofficially by the park or by the various gay and lesbian organizations in Utah, to attend. Salt Lake City was once said to have the highest gay-to-straight per capita ratio outside of San Francisco.

I've overstepped a boundary. "I know you're thinking, *Well if I lost my pecker, that'd be something.* . . . But let me tell you, try wiping your goddamned ass with a metal hook sometime. Try flogging the dolphin with a rubber hand and an arm that works like a block and tackle. Try getting through one fucking night without that phantom hand, those ghost fingers, creeping around in your sheets. That's a personal loss of the highest magnitude. Now what makes you think, all indebtedness for your bucket-of-bolts aside, that I'd let go that kind of pain in simple conversation?"

He means for me to answer, but there's nothing I can think to say. "Nothing."

"Open your mouth when you talk, will you? If there's one thing I can't abide it's a marble-mouthed mumbler. *Nuttin',*" he says, mocking me. "*Nuttin.*'"

I see a sign for Coal City, and one for Dwight. But nothing for Nauvoo. I realize I haven't any idea where Nauvoo is, other than it must be near the Missouri border and it must be small. "How far is Nauvoo?" I say, as clearly as I can.

"How're you doing on gas?"

"We need to stop up here somewhere," I say, again conscious that I bite at all my syllables.

"Take the Gardner exit. There's an Amoco there," he says.

"Does it have to be Gardner?" I say.

"It should be," he says, and we press on.

My father was like this on the few long road trips we took together: short with everyone, quick tempered, and absolute about where and when we would stop, regardless of how much gas was left in the tank, or how much urine was in anyone's bladder. He kept an empty coffee can he'd purloined from one of the Gentiles at work, and if you were unlucky enough to have to urinate before one of his random-seeming stops, you had to crawl into the trunk space of the hurtling green station-wagon, straddling the luggage and spare tire, and try to bring it out and empty your bladder before the next carload of teenage kids came careening by, honking and jeering. It was the worst for Rachel, who was in her puberty and who always looked as if she were mooning the passing traffic. Compounding all the embarrassment and the quiet ridicule of my siblings was my father's stern warnings and stares in the rearview not to spill a drop in the car. Finally, Rachel's can completely slipped out of her hand on a particularly nasty patch of road in Idaho, and she soaked Mom and Dad's suitcase. We'd managed the coffee can maneuver for years and it had become like a tradition to us, but that was it. No more. Dad pulled over to the side of the road if we weren't near a rest stop, and we watered the air.

And after Zach was propositioned by a hooker in Las Vegas, we didn't take any more family vacations at all. Dad had "won" a free vacation to Las Vegas at the Layton Hills mall. To claim his prize, all he had to do was come see a condo up at Powder Mountain[56]. He wasn't interested in condos then, but he was interested in trying his hand in Las Vegas. It's something the Bishop wouldn't have approved of if the Bishop hadn't been running off to Wendover[57] every other Saturday with his wife "to see the shows."

---

[56] Utah's only privately owned ski resort. Located in the mountains near Ogden.

[57] Wendover, Nevada, is a border town about 70 miles from Salt Lake City. Wendover has a few casinos and contracts with several bus companies in the Salt Lake area. These buses run nearly nonstop taking Utahns across the border to gamble and see "Vegas-style" shows. The trip to Wendover from Salt Lake takes the traveler across

There wasn't a lot for the rest of us to do. Mom was adamantly against gambling, and she was nonplussed with the advertisements for the shows. "These showgirls set women back one hundred years. You can't tell me you find this attractive, do you?" she said, pushing a picture of several tall women in sequined bikinis and wearing ceremonial-looking headdresses into my father's face.

"So that's out," he said.

We stayed at Circus-Circus, and we were under strict orders not to leave the second floor where small, swarthy men and women performed high wire acts and swung deliberately from the trapeze. But the show repeated after an hour. The women climbed slowly back up the pole, their shiny rears barely contained by the black mesh of their costumes. The men repeated their furious stares at the rope across from their platforms. We kids deliberated for a few minutes before we decided one of us should go and ask Dad if we could do something else with our evening. Zach was always in Dad's good graces and always the first to volunteer for these missions.

Apparently, as Zach tells it, she was a black woman in her early thirties who just asked him if he wanted a date. Not wanting to be rude, Zach asked her what she meant and Dad just happened

---

the Salt Flats, miles and miles of salt-encrusted land featured in countless westerns and sci-fi movies and home of the Bonneville Salt Flats, where several land-speed records were set in rocket-powered cars. Travelers also drive past the tree of life, a lonely sculpture on the highway of a tree with several large globes, representing its fruit, hanging from its branches and lying broken at its base. The Mormon Church's official position is that it strongly opposes gambling, as do many, many religions, but Mormons are fairly typically American in this way (and many others).

to be moving between the slot machines and the craps when he came suddenly up behind Zach who was listening patiently (but also apparently smiling and nodding) to rates for an around-the-world and a tossed-salad.

I wasn't sure if I was angry at Zach for getting in trouble, which of course meant we were all in trouble, or if I was relieved that we wouldn't be left to our own devices again in Las Vegas. I remember that Dad made sure we knew Jesus was a descendant of David and that David was a descendant of Rabah and Tamar[58], prostitutes from the Bible. This was a random act of a random-seeming world. But he seemed to have made up his mind already. He was clearly shaken, mostly, I think because Zach insisted on acting as if he'd reached some milestone in his manhood simply by negotiating for sex.

---

[58] Before Joshua leads the Israelites on Canaan he sends two spies into Jericho. These spies go directly to the house of the prostitute Rahab, who shelters the spies. Rahab is promised that she and her family will be spared if she will gather her family around her and tie a red cord to her house to identify it. According to Matthew, Rahab begets Boaz, who marries Ruth and is the ancestor of David and Jesus.

Tamar is originally married to Er, who is inexplicably struck dead by God. Her father-in-law, Judah, orders Tamar's brother-in-law, Onan, to sleep with Tamar and raise children for him as was the custom. Onan refuses to raise his brother's heirs and instead chooses to spill his seed on the ground. Rather than receiving a little black star for his calendar, Onan is also struck dead by God for his sin. (It should be noted that although this passage is often cited to curb masturbation in several Christian religions, spilling one's seed

Jaimy told me that her father had been with a prostitute once, when he was in Vietnam and missing her mother. She thought it was a romantic story, at its heart. Her father was such a frail man, the source of all her frailty, I'm sure. He always seemed burdened by something like the story of a prostitute he'd once spent a night with in Vietnam, and by the ghosts of the dead he'd dispatched, and I imagined the hollowness of his house after Jaimy's mother died. Theirs was a passionless-seeming marriage built on the practicalities of raising two girls and getting past the girl they'd lost to a fever when she was three. These kinds of marriages, I think, survive things like an infidelity because an infidelity becomes a misstep instead of a betrayal. It becomes the kind of thing you can tell your children with the regret in your heart still ringing and resonating so vividly that it rings through the souls in the next telling, and the telling after that. "Just imagine that poor girl," Jaimy had said, "lying on the wet mat" (she repeated that detail in each telling) "so full of hate and sadness and

---

actually meant coitus interruptus). Judah then tells Tamar that when his youngest and only remaining son, Shelah, grows up, he will give Tamar children. Judah reneges on his promise, however, and Tamar, desperate for children at this time, plans quite a trick. She dresses as a prostitute and is seduced by Judah. Judah promises this "prostitute" a kid from his flock since he is without money, but Tamar insists that he give her his signet, staff and red cord.

Tamar is pregnant with twins and is brought to Judah to be executed. Tamar presents Judah's signet and is spared. When her twins arrive, one thrusts an arm out of the womb, and a red cord is tied around his arm because he is thought to be the first born. However, the second twin, Perez, is actually delivered first. Perez is another ancestor of David and Jesus.

gratitude. And you're leaving her and your *buddies* are whistling just outside the tin walls and urging you to hurry it up, there's more killing to be done. There's more shots to be fired."

I think of Rhoda and Mr. Mysterious. There's nothing vaguely romantic about Rhoda's reasons to cheat me of her heart in this way. And the multitudinous faces Mr. Mysterious takes as his own race in my mind before me like the rows of green, young corn in the fields. When Rhoda tells me she likes the actor River Phoenix, that there's something so painful in his eyes, I see those eyes on the blank face of Mr. Mysterious. I see Rhoda stare into those eyes, hoping to see something of herself that only those eyes can reflect back.

When she says she likes a cologne that isn't mine in one of my magazines and then goes quiet for one second too long, I smell his musky odor all around her.

I miss her, I think, the smell of her hair. I may even love her, but I know that there is a serpent in our garden and that she has tasted his fruit.

"Amoco's right down there," Randy says. "I gotta call those people, too." He slides back into his arm, buckling it and adjusting it like Rhoda adjusts her brassiere. "That is, if you don't mind."

"I don't mind," I say. What do I care?

As I pump the gas I look out onto the Illinois land. There is a farm whose acreage runs right up to the edge of the gas station. A house and patch of budding trees sit on the blue horizon. The air is clean, bitten only by an updraft of the fuel, the hint of animal smell. There is so much land, and there are so few people here. Their lives, I think, must be deliberate with the kind of deliberation I'll never know. Their loves must be forged instead of forging. A pickup pulls up on the other side of the pump. There are guns in the rack in the rear window, which is something I was used to in

Kaysville. A teenaged boy with skinny legs and tight, dark blue jeans gets out of the truck arguing with the obese girl on the passenger side: "I don't care, Julie! I don't fucking care! I don't give a rat's goddamn, Julie!" He slams the door and I can almost feel her yelling through the glass at him. "Fucking fat bitch," he says, to himself.

Randy comes back as I'm paying the cashier, a short, zitty kid with red hair and freckles the size and color of liver spots. "Get a hold of your Mason friends?" I say. Randy laughs as he digs through his jeans for some money for the gas. He hands me a twenty. "You keep track, Chief."

The skinny kid from outside walks in; his eyes are swollen and he's fighting back crying, trying to make us, himself, believe that he doesn't care about whatever it is Julie's done or said. His eyes, however, give him away with each wipe from the back of his hand. "I don't care," he says, under his breath.

"Fucking mumbler," Randy says to no one in particular.

XVI. In the Beginning

"We'll be to Nauvoo by nightfall, I'll bet," Randy says. "We're chasing the sun now."

I'm secretly pleased with the progress we're making. My mind is on Utah, but I'm intrigued with Nauvoo, as well. "Where do we go?" I say.

"You need to head past Normal about 15 miles and look for 136 and take that west until you see the border."

"Are we staying with your friends there, then? I mean, is it all right if I stay?" I hadn't considered what Randy's friends might be like. I picture a gang of scruffy, grumbling men in baseball caps clacking their way toward me on peg legs, waving hooks in the air, like a home for wayward sailors: "So whose the fucking fuckhead, Fucky?"

"Friends?" Randy says suddenly. "I don't have any friends in Nauvoo. This is business. I want to be in-and-out of that fucking nightmare in about ten seconds."

"Well, where are we going to stay, then?"

"Calm down there, Chompers. Unless they struck oil in Nauvoo since the last time I was there, we'll probably have to head out 218 up to I-somewhere and find a place on the road."

Chompers? I rub my tongue across my teeth, and when I'm sure Randy is looking out the passenger window I snatch a look from the rearview at my mouth. "I wanted to take a look around Nauvoo. I've never been there," I say.

"It's no fucking Disneyland," he says. "The place is soggy with blood, and places like that stay haunted."

"Well, I still want to look around," I say. I can't stop worrying about my teeth. Can they be too big?

"Suit yourself," Randy says. He detaches his arm and turns it around in his lap so that he can scrape at the hook with one of his long fingernails. When he's satisfied, he lays the hook carefully across his chest like it was a teddy bear or a thin child, and leans back into the window to resume his sleep.

Across the sky, still bluish like snow, a hundred geese fly high enough that they cast no shadow on the land, black crows stare at the rabbits and skunks waiting to make their way unsuccessfully through the traffic, and thousands of black starlings clutter the road sides. The land is chocolate brown, and across many of the fields shades of green have begun to make their way out of the soil. It has rained here as well, and I can see the fog lurking in the patches of trees clinging to the creeks and rivers we cross. The green and yellow tractors sit quietly near the shiny tin barns, some tended to while they wait, some lonely. Everywhere I see wooden barns in states of collapse.

These barns are held upright, it seems, only by their original will. The light comes through the roofs of these barns, and even the morning doves prefer the phone lines to the precariousness of the gray wood skeletons. Cows cautiously circle the barns, their noses buried in the green grass.

Jaimy and I visited a farm her cousin worked at down in Layton near Great Salt Lake. The land there flattens like the palm of an upturned hand, in the shadow of the fingers of the mountains. The parcels were small and neat and straight. The farmers here employed mostly illegals who'd come to pick the fruit later in the year. We sat on the hood of my Bronco eating breakfast burritos we'd bought at a stand off Gentile street, sipping coffee from a thermos. The illegals hunched their way down the neat rows, burying onion stems in the crumbling soil. As they worked their way away from us, it looked more and more to me like the onion trail was following them, blurring into conduits of which they were the source. It was a beautiful spring day in Utah, and after I drank my coffee I leaned back against the windshield. I think I'd propped a blanket over the wipers, and put my arm around Jaimy. Her hips were bony and her skinny legs, in the dark denim of her new jeans, flowed down the hood. I thought it might be a nice life. But as we sat there, watching the men in the fields grow smaller and smaller, their conduits like green rays, my back began to hurt.

"When's your cousin going to get here," I said.

"I dunno," Jaimy said. She was so thin and light, her posture rigid, as if she had a helium balloon for a spine. "He said it might be a little while before they get the tomatoes set up." Her cousin was working in the greenhouse setting tomato seeds into seed trays. The greenhouse looked so small, hunched over like the illegals in their white shirts, compared to the long expanse of land, the plowed fields to the right of the onion conduits that would soon hold tomato plants.

"I don't feel so good," Jaimy said. "Do you feel okay?"

"My back hurts a little," I said.

"I think it might be these burritos," she said.

"You think they were bad? I feel okay."

"I don't know," Jaimy said, pulling her legs up near her and then hopping down off the hood suddenly.

"What?"

"I don't know, I feel sick. I think I'm going to be sick."

She was furiously pulling her dark hair back and tying if off, like she didn't want it hanging around her face. "Ohhhh," she said, dropping down to one knee. "I don't know. This is really bad. I need to find a bathroom."

I hopped down off the side of the Bronco and stood beside her, rubbing circles around and around on her small back. "You're shaking," I said.

"I don't just have to throw up," she said. "I need a bathroom."

"I don't know if there's anything out here," I said. "Do you want to try the greenhouse?"

"Oh God, go away," she said. She stood and pushed past me and ran to the other side of the truck. I tried to follow her around the truck, but she turned at me with her watery, death-like eyes and screamed, "Leave me alone!"

"All right, all right," I said. I climbed into the Bronco and stared back out at the illegals in the field, small white dots hunched in the center of the plain, shooting out wave after wave of green stars. When I turned I could see Jaimy clearly in the big outboard mirror on the passenger side. She had her pants pulled down and was squatting near the car. I saw her dig through her pockets for a kleenex, which she always kept to dab at her red and swollen nose, and wipe herself. She stood and braced herself with one hand against the car, angrily kicking dirt over her mess. Then she stopped suddenly, looked into the mirror and saw me, and then kneeled down and vomited where she stood. She vomited once more and spit and climbed weakly into the car.

"Jeez," I said. "We need to get you home."

She began sobbing, which soon turned into full-blown weeping. The tears were coming out so furiously I thought she might dry up, turn to dust before my eyes. "Should we take you to a hospital?"

"No," she summoned. "No."

I tried to rub her leg but she pushed my hand away. "Jaimy," I said. "If it hurts that bad . . ."

"No," she continued to wail between breaths. "I'm embarrassed. You embarrassed me."

"My God!" I said. "Don't be embarrassed. You're sick!"

"Embarrassed," she said. "I'm always so embarrassed."

It had been a year since the sink disaster at my parents' house. I took Jaimy home, stopping a few more times on the way for her to vomit. I nearly had to carry her inside her house when we got there. She was tall, but she was so skinny. I felt I could have lifted her with one hand, like a garden hose. I didn't know what to do after that, so when she shooed me away I left.

When I told my father she'd been so sick all he could say was: "There's something wrong with that girl. She's a nice girl, I'm sure, Brian, but you'll end up being her caretaker if you're not careful."

This was something Dad always resented. He would work an eighty hour week to make sure we all had what we needed: enough groceries for all of us and the larder[59], new clothes, spending money. But if we got sick we needed to leave him out of it. Illness in our house was simply mechanical. We either went into the shop and got repaired, or we found some quiet corner of the house and repaired ourselves. Mom did what she could, but illness was always something I'd dreaded because it was something you had to get through by yourself.

I knew this wasn't how it was treated with other families. I knew that children were cared for tenderly by their parents when they were ill. But when Rhoda got sick last year, running a fever of over 102 and needing someone to make her drink her water, to bring cool towels for her head, I found excuses to stay away.

Out of the corner of my eye, I see Randy stir. He is staring out at the land gushing by. He rubs at the nub of his bird wing and

---

[59] Mormons are generally taught to have enough food on hand for at least two months, usually longer, in case of an emergency. During the Reagan-era, when Brian was growing up, this was especially important because of a general anxiety about the Russians and their nuclear capabilities. Subsequently, when there has been a natural disaster, like the mud-slides in Layton in 1984, community families are quick to respond with food and blankets.

then clutches at his plastic arm. "I know this isn't any of my business," I say. "And if you want to tell me to go to hell, why don't you just say so and we'll let it be water under the bridge and I'll never ask again." Randy stares at me, and I can see his posture has gone defensive. "But how did you lose it?" I'm immediately glad and terrified I was able to ask again.

He relaxes, straightens up in his seat, and when he does I notice that his wing does believe in its phantom arm, pushing down as if his hand had a grip on the seat cushion. "All right, Chief. You really want to know about this?" He waves the wing at me. "This is the source of my troubles," he says. "No," he pauses. "This is the source of my redemption. It's both, really. But don't get your hopes up too much. I'm not about to tell you what kind of thing it was that took my arm away from me. But I will tell you this, and then we're gonna let the rest of it die a dignified death right here on the road: This was something I did to myself and it wasn't anything I'd take back. This didn't open my eyes, but it's part of what keeps them open. I went through some shit, I've seen some shit and done some shit that you wouldn't wish on the most miserable bugfucker in all the world. This is deserved. A few years back I'd have called it God's will, only now I'm not so sure. I think you've got to take responsibility for your own fate and your own mistakes and the things you said and did. And if I get out of this world down just a few pounds of flesh . . . just a little incomplete . . ." He stops and looks out at the farm land, the barns and the houses and the tractors in the distance seem to stand still while the fields rush past us. "Aw, fuck it," he says. "Did I tell you I got a kid out in Moab?"

"A kid?" I say. "And a wife?"

"Just the one wife," he says. "We're not all like that down in Moab."

XVII. Land of My Fathers

Randy's gone quiet again. I want to ask about his kid, but all I get is that his kid is a boy, about seven years old, and that Randy hasn't seen him in five years. That's about enough for me, anyway. When I thought I'd get to know Randy on our trip I didn't really expect him to summon a family out of the thin air. It feels now as if they are with us on our journey together, like Rhoda, like Jaimy. I only wanted to hear stories about his wild times, experiences we could shape a connection by.

We cut through Carthage[60] and take a small highway near Hamilton up toward Nauvoo. I expect something spectacular to

---

[60] Carthage is the city where a mob took Joseph Smith from his jail cell and left the Savior's body, beaten and riddled with bullets, propped against a well. Smith had been struggling to maintain control over some break-away factions of his growing Church of Jesus Christ of Latter Day Saints. Principally, a newspaper called the *Expositor,* put together by two of Smith's former higher-ups, began to publish articles accusing Smith and his inner circle of fostering polygamy, which they secretly practiced, but publicly denied, and also many of the secret negotiations and rituals of Smith's fledgling church. Smith ordered that the new press be destroyed, and the two principal editors of the critical press were informed of murder plots against them. Nearby Warsaw, which had grown increasingly unsympathetic to the rising number of Mormons in their area, began to inflame anti-Mormon sentiment, calling locals to take arms against the "infernal devils." The Governor, whose sympathies had waxed and waned with the general public, and who was at times politically antagonistic to the church, asked Smith to disarm his loyalists,

occur as we drive through Carthage, but nothing happens. I expect the trumpets of angels to herald the arrival or the departure of the town, but they do no such thing. I expect the sky to be more golden, the land to be more profuse with vegetation, the air to be more crisp. It is not.

There is a faded sign into Carthage that Randy carefully watches swoosh by our car announcing: "Come see the death scene of Joseph Smith, founder of the Mormon Church!" There are tours, places to eat, gas to be had. Then it is all gone and we are as we were.

The towns are getting smaller and smaller, the roads less kept. I'm surprised by this. I'd always heard about Nauvoo at church and at home. This is like no pilgrimage I imagined, though, as we chug down unkempt highways, the black slashes of tar covering the cracks in the road are like Band-Aids trying to cover

---

fearing civil war. Smith had fled across the Mississippi, and the governor promised Smith and his compatriots safety if they turned themselves in to Carthage, the country seat, to face charges of violation of property rights.

Smith once said: "A religion that does not require the sacrifice of all things never has power sufficient to produce the faith necessary unto life and salvation." Many historians would note that Smith led the days up to his death with dignity and honor, writing often to his wife and praying. Knowing that he had returned to face certain death: "I am going as the lamb to slaughter." This lamb, however, had a gun smuggled into his cell that he fired into the mob in a last attempt at freedom. He managed to wound three.

Smith's last words, as the angry mob pulled him from his cell were "Oh, Lord, my God . . ." These are the first words of the Masonic cry for help.

gaping wounds. In places there are weeds growing in the middle of the road.

"I'm still confused," I say finally. "How long are we going to be in Nauvoo?"

"We'll be there until we're not there. It won't take me long to do this thing."

"You sound like you're getting set to murder somebody," I say.

Randy doesn't laugh. "It'll be quick," he says. "And then we can get back on the road. We can find a motel somewhere if you like."

"And you don't want to stay in Nauvoo?"

"You don't want to stay in Nauvoo," he says, and then he claws at the radio.

"You'll get electrocuted," I say, swatting the hook away from the radio. It does feel like a block and tackle as I bat at it. There is a new scratch on the face of the radio. "You're dangerous with that thing," I say, feeling braver with Randy again.

It is a pretty short drive into Nauvoo from Carthage. And my first impression is that it is a piece of perfection laid into the otherwise raw landscape. It is like a toy town, a town cut with the cleanness of Leggo plastic blocks. Small and neat and crisp at the edges. Even the grass here looks like a putting green.

"Look-it this crap, will ya?" Randy says, tightening his arm on his shoulder. We drive past the tourist center at the edge of town proclaiming its affiliation with The Church of Jesus Christ of Latter Day Saints. They also lay claim to the Masonic lodge and the Heber C. Kimball[61] house, whose name is familiar to me,

---

[61] Heber C. Kimball, a close friend of Joseph Smith's. Smith once asked Kimball to give his wife, Vilate, to Smith, as it was God's wish. Kimball struggled with this request, but agreed. Smith then told

though I can't think why. We drive by an Amish cart overloaded with tourists leaning out to take pictures of the buildings and signs they pass. "Pull into Grandpa John's Cafe," Randy says. "I've gotta make a phone call there."

Randy goes immediately into the cafe to make his call, but it's a beautiful day. I can hear the Mississippi river whorling in the near distance, and I want to walk around. The town is crowded[62]

Kimball that this was merely a test of his loyalty to the prophet. Smith, however, then asked for Kimball's fourteen-year-old daughter, Helen Mar, the youngest of Smith's brides, who was "sealed" to Smith for eternity. It should be noted that, although polygamy was found then, as it is now, to be a generally repulsive concept, marrying a fourteen-year-old girl was a fairly common practice.

Kimball's great grand-daughter, Winifred "Wink" Shaughnessy, became involved with a Russian dancer named Kosloff in the late 1800s. Wink changed her name to Natacha Rambova and joined the Imperial Russian Ballet Company. Kosloff became insanely jealous of the former Wink and shot her.

Wink survived her wounds and moved to Hollywood to work as a costume designer. There she met and married the very famous Rudolph Valentino who fairly soon thereafter left her a widow. She went on to become a well-known Egyptologist and even bequeathed a tremendous and important collection to the well-regarded Utah Museum of Fine Arts.

[62] Though the town is principally a tourist destination now (in the spirit of Jamestown), in its hey-day, Nauvoo had a militia sworn to Joseph Smith of 4,000 men, almost half the size of the U.S. Army. Nauvoo and the surrounding area were home to nearly 15,000 citizens—rivaling Chicago at the time.

on this warm day, the sidewalks full of families with their children. I see a sign advertising Joseph Smith's burial site and I let myself follow it. I feel pulled there.

The people I pass on the sidewalk are mostly Mormons. I can tell. Athletic couples with their shirts tucked in, some of them struggling to conceal their garments on a day that can't make up its mind whether or not to be hot or pleasant, herding their children, telling the children of the history without any need of the placards and pamphlets. They know this place, and their children are knowing this place. They smile at me and then at each other with the kind of smile that says: "Look honey, he must work here. Wouldn't that be a gas?"

There are missionaries here, their squarish black name plates announcing their presence like hostesses at a Denny's, leading tours and handing out literature to the lost and the found. There is a young black family here, the only one I've seen among these oceans of familiar faces. They are tended to by two sets of missionaries at once. The missionaries lean in carefully to hear every word that comes from their mouths; they all laugh together at a joke the mother makes while singling out her obviously bored son. Maybe it is a funny joke.

I picked cherries when I was about the age of the bored-looking boy. I spent my early summers snatching the bloody fruit from the branches of the orchards up and down the 89 corridor, dropping every red cent into my missionary coffer. And when it didn't add up fast enough I took a job at the Kaysville Pizza Hut, wiping the grease from the walls and floor until 1:30 every school night. Zach had gotten a job as a gopher at the Chevy dealer in town, washing cars occasionally. As far as I could tell, he mostly refilled the coffee pots and sat around listening to the salesmen rating the fuckability of the young mothers looking to replace their sedan with a station wagon with a Suburban. Zach drove a two-year-old Camaro IROC while he was saving money for his mission. And he and Michelle would drive around and around Kaysville on Friday nights, or sometimes they would go up to Ogden and drag the strip.

One time in the early summer, after I'd gotten home from a full day of filling baskets with bing cherries near Fruit Heights, Michelle said: "Brian, why don't you get changed and come with us?"

Michelle practically lived at our house by this time, and she and my mother would spend hours discussing her hope chest, and where they thought Zach might go on his mission. They thought it might be Europe, but Zach couldn't conjugate. Zach whined to my father that there wasn't really room in his car, and that I'd be a big drag on their whole evening.

"You and Michelle see each other enough," Dad said. "Besides, maybe you can help your brother meet someone like Michelle. I think he needs a little help, wouldn't you agree." He put his arm on Zach's shoulder and they both stared down at me like they were deciding whether or not to present me with my manhood.

Michelle never invited me anywhere, and I remember looking at mother, who was looking back at me, nodding encouragement, mouthing the words "It's okay," and "Yes."

"All right," I said. "I'll go."

I had to ride in the back seat, a bench too small for children to sit comfortably on, while Zach, irritated that Michelle and our mother had invited me along, lurched the IROC out of every stop. It was so small I had to ride with my knees tucked up around my chest. The back seat was covered in black vinyl or leather and when he cranked a turn at more than ten miles an hour, I went flying around like a bowling ball, crashing into the sides. When we got to Ogden I realized what kind of hypnotic force

Zach's car had on the throngs of kids dragging the strip. Zach and Michelle were like movie stars. Zach was like a returning hero before he even left.

Dad had always filled us with stories about how he and my uncles used to come to Ogden to drag the strip in his new Ford Fairlane. This was where he met my mother, he said. "Oh, you're awful. That's just a bald-faced lie," my mother said. "He knew me from school already. Your father, he was more shy then, if you dare believe that. But he was always asking to come drive that silly car up and down the street. That was his idea of romance, the big liar." Mom was always calling Dad out on his stories, setting things right.

At every stop light on Washington it seemed the car next to us would rev its engine at us and as soon as the light turned green we'd blast off. My knees would shoot up in the air and my head would slide down into the seat. Zach kept his pole position at the front of the pack up and down Washington most of the night. Finally, we stopped at the 7-11 at the top of the hill where several couples were making out furiously against the brick wall outside the store. Zach and Michelle rolled their windows down and inhaled the compliments, "Nice car," "Cool ride," "Whoo-Hoo."

I was anonymous to all of this, tucked into the back seat like luggage and hidden from view by the small, tinted windows in the back, until a group of girls approached the car on Zach's side. "Who've you got in there with you, Zach?" a girl with bright, white teeth said.

"My little brother Brian," Zach said.

"Is he cute?" she said, and my stomach leapt. She was older than I was, and beautiful in the fluorescent lights from the 7-11 windows.

"I dunno," Zach said. "You cute, Brian?"

I reached out, grabbing the side of Zach's seat and his open window, to birth myself into the conversation. "Hi," I said. "I'm Brian."

"Oh my heck," she said, moving backwards from the car. "What's all over your fingers?"

I looked at my fingers, blotched and stained red from the cherries. "It's from the cherries," I said, but the girls were all laughing by this time, all leaving.

"Smooth move, Ex-lax," Zach said.

"She's a slut," Michelle said. "Don't worry about it."

But I did worry about it. I worried about every day in the orchard, with every drop of cherry juice that fell onto my hands. I worried about it every time I saw Zach pull into the driveway with his immaculately clean IROC. I worried about it until late one night, just after closing at Pizza Hut, when a tall, pale girl came cautiously in with four other kids. "Are you still open?" she said.

She wasn't beautiful in the way a model or a movie star is beautiful. She didn't scatter the heavens before her, as Dad would say. But her ghostly walk and her lilting voice called out to something inside of me. She stayed and talked to me while her friends piled around the Ms. Pacman machine and I made their pizza.

At the end of the street I see again the sign advertising Joseph Smith's grave and his house, and in the upstairs window of the house I see a pale woman's face draw away from the glass and retreat into the shadows. The house, the sign says, is owned and maintained by R.L.D.S.[63] And when I enter the house it feels

---

[63] William Law, formerly second counselor of the L.D.S. Church and another close friend to Joseph Smith, helped found the Reformed Latter Day Saints. On April 11, 1842, the secret Council of Fifty of the L.D.S. Church (formed chiefly as a policy making body) ordained

different, as if I don't belong here somehow. The volunteers are gracious and someone shakes my hand, but I struggle past them to get to the woman in the window.

When I come to the room where she was standing there is a family of four exiting, the father talking excitedly about how much smaller people used to be, and that how much the average Japanese has grown since the introduction of U.S. beef into their diets is clearly related to beef growth hormones. There is no one else in the room.

I walk to the window and look down onto the crowded street and suddenly there is a hand clenching my shoulder. I turn

---

Smith the impressive sounding "King, Priest and Ruler" over the earth. By this time, though, Law was beginning to take issue with many of Smith's ideas. Chiefly, Law was opposed to the idea of polygamy. As tensions between Smith and some of his former friends grew, it has been reported that Smith arranged for spies to keep tabs on Law and other's activities. Law became convinced that Smith, the chief of police and members of the highly secret and secretive Danites, the unrecognized 'enforcer' branch of the growing church, were plotting to kill him, though Smith denied the allegations.

It is also rumored that Smith had propositioned Law's wife. Whatever the case, Law and Smith soon parted ways. Smith made several attempts to reconcile, but Law's conditions were centered on the proviso that Smith would have to publicly apologize for practicing polygamy.

This was obviously out-of-the-question for Smith, and so Law and about 300 others soon formed the Reformed Church of Jesus Christ. Perhaps most significantly, after the Mormon exodus from Illinois to Utah the R.L.D.S., as they were to become known, retained ownership of Smith's grave and two of his houses in Nauvoo.

around and am met with an accusation: "How do you know Sam?" The owner of the raspy voice is a short, wide-bodied old man with a grip like a marine. His face is the face of a farmer, sunburnt, furrowed, serious. His eyes are pale blue, like snow, and he repeats the question: "What's your tie to Sam?"

"I don't know anyone named Sam," I say. "I think you've got me confused with someone else," I say. I try to be polite. He is old and very strong, both of which deserve my respect.

"I followed you from the cafe. No mistake," he says. "You better watch yourself. Both of you. Sampson's not welcome here and neither are his kin."

"Look," I say. "I really don't know anyone named Sam, or Sampson. I'm just passing through. I'm Mormon," I say, thinking it might aid his confusion. "I'm not even R.L.D.S. I'm just seeing the sights."

"You watch your funny mouth," he says, and wags a craggy, withered finger in my face. He holds his pose, staring into my eyes, even though two other families struggle past us into the room.

I get back out to the street, leaving the strange old man standing in the room of Joseph Smith's house like a wax figure, and resume my search for the woman in the glass. It was just a vision, a quick blast of an image, but it seemed so real it still burns in my mind. From this level it is impossible to see anyone. I see only people pushing against people, the din of their voices a wall of sound against the river. I push past them to the cafe and look inside. The cafe is crowded as well, and I can't even see Randy. These bodies, I realize, are muddling the neatness of the town. There is an order here, somewhere, and the countless bodies of the pilgrims and the interlopers and the passers-by sully it with each step, with each voice. There's an anger welling up inside of me I want to turn loose on these crowds, like a superhero who tears open his shirt and unleashes a powerful blast from his chest, scattering these people and their talk of Joseph Smith, of holiness, of beginnings, like flour to the wind.

I turn to the car and I see Randy sitting in the passenger seat, waving me into the car with his hand.

"I was getting really frustrated," I tell him. "Where did all these people come from?"

"They're your brethren, aren't they?" Randy says.

"I can't breathe out there, they're so thick," I say.

"As people go, you wish they would?" Randy says.

"Something like that," I say.

"Just remember ace, no such thing as a perfect stranger."

"You like crowds like this?"

"When you stick out like a sore thumb," Randy says, holding up his hook. "It's good to find a crowd to lose yourself in."

"So you want to get a bite here," I say. I'm tired of Randy's maxims, tired of being in the car with him.

"No," he says. "We've stayed too long already. Better to make hay while the sun is shining."

"Fine, Niota should have a McDonald's or something, right?"

"I like McDonald's," he says. "You better set that clock back," he says, pointing to the clock on the radio with his hook.

"And we can cross the river into Iowa there?"

"We can do any number of things," he says.

"You're chipper," I say.

"Clean conscience, clean slate. I wash my hand of this place," he says. I want to smack him. I want to push him out of the car and drive back home.

XVIII. Stopping for the Night

Randy seems to know these roads like the back of his hand. And our conversation begins to consist more and more of directions and compliances. We're getting hungry. I'm getting hungry. "McDonald's," I say, near some place called Donnellson, Iowa.

We're back on the road in what seems like seconds. "This was quite a bit out of the way," I say, Big Mac in my hand, fries on my tray. "We've still got a couple of hours to get to I-80, don't we?"

"I got the gas for this excursion, Chief," Randy says. "Don't you worry about that."

"That's not it," I say. "I just want to know where we ought to stay. Are you thinking of a motel, or do you know somebody out this way?"

"Motel's fine by me," he says. He stabs at his straw with his metal hook and holds his burger carefully, near the edge, with his pinky finger extended. "What crawled up your ass anyway, smiley?"

"Nothing," I say. "I just want to know where we're going to be staying tonight."

"You've got the reins, Chief." I try to imagine sleeping in the same room with Randy, which seems to be the direction all of this is taking us. I imagine him undressing before getting into his bed, and I wonder if I can not look, can not *know* if his scars have taken anything else from him.

Jaimy took me to a sorority formal once, months before I'd lost my mission calling, our first night in a hotel room together. We roomed with a friend of hers named Sarah and with Sarah's date Jack. Jack was a muscular, funny guy who threw his head backwards when he laughed, like he might swallow swords. Sarah was a big girl, but she was cute and had a tremendous amount of energy. Jaimy envied her, I think. She envied girls who walked heavy and sure-footed through life.

Jack and I became good friends over a night of drinking. We sat at the table, mostly, while Sarah dragged Jaimy out onto the dance floor and twirled her around. When they stood between the table and the lights from the sound system, I could see through Jaimy's dress to her white panties underneath. If I squinted my eyes just a little, Jaimy seemed to become completely translucent, floating in Sarah's big arms like a white dress with no one inside it.

After the dance closed down, we went nervously back to our hotel room. It had a wet bar and two king-sized beds and a hot tub jacuzzi in the bathroom. Jack and I sat down at the table and began drinking shots of whiskey from the bottle he'd poached and camouflaged under his tux while the bartender was closing down. We played quarters and then we drank drink-for-drink until we were half-way through the bottle. Jaimy and Sarah took swigs from the bottle, but mostly they talked and leaned off the balcony together, shouting down to their friends in the moonlight. The moon was so bright I could see through Jaimy's dress again, and I told her this.

"So take it off," Jack said. I thought he was kidding at first, but then Sarah joined him.

"Go ahead, Jaimy, let's do something wild," Sarah said, and she began peeling out of her own dress. She tried to let it graciously fall to the floor, but it held its shape and slipped down her body like a suit of armor that she had to step out of. She was wearing a push-up bra and panties and hose, and her body was solid, like a gymnast's body. She looked fat and she looked strong at the same time. I just stared at Jaimy.

"I think I'll get in the hot tub," she said hurriedly, and moved away from Sarah to her overnight bag on our bed.

Sarah went back to the balcony and began to whoop down to her friends with renewed vigor. "I'll get in, too," I said, and fished my swim trunks out of my own bag. Jack poured himself another shot of whiskey and sipped at it, looking admiringly at Sarah, who was leaning well over the balcony. Her panties disappeared more with every degree.

Jaimy and I shut the bathroom door behind us. "I didn't know it would be like this," Jaimy said.

"It's okay," I said. "They're funny." Jaimy took her dress off and carefully laid it on the sink as I ran the tub. She turned away from me, shyly, to take off her underwear and put on her swimming suit. I reached out to her and stroked her bare back. There were pink welts where her bra had pinched her white skin, and I ran my hand over them like I was caressing a scar.

We sat in the tub for a long while. When the water quit running I could hear Sarah from the other room whooping it up to more friends in the parking lot. I wondered if she might be naked when we got out of the tub.

"You don't think that's how it is, do you, Brian? How it ends?"

"How what is?" I said, lifting my dimpled fingers to my face and turning my hand back and forth in front of my face. I hadn't blown my mission calling yet, and couldn't think to the future like Jaimy was having to. I had two years of time to sit on. Two years where nothing could happen in my life except for me to strengthen my relationship with Jesus and the church, and even that wouldn't happen for another seven months.

"That you just run out of steam with somebody. Like with Jack and Sarah," she whispered. "They suddenly changed into different people."

"I don't really know them," I said. "Should we get out?"

We toweled off and I pulled Jaimy to me and kissed her on the mouth, but her lips were cold and dry, like a body pulled from the water. I didn't push it any farther, and as soon as she had her hair swaddled in a towel we opened the door to the room. The lights were off, but I could clearly see Jack spread-eagled on his bed, nude with a flagging erection. Sarah was beside him, face down on the bed, with her panties pulled down, binding her big thighs. They were passed out. I put my hand over Jaimy's eyes, but she pulled it back down and stared at the two on the bed, maybe the same way I stared at the two on the bed. I pulled the comforter off of our bed and drug it across Jack and Sarah. Jack whispered something to me. A thank you, I thought, until he motioned me closer: "No whiskey-dick here, eh?"

Some time during the night Jack woke up and dumped his contact lenses into a glass of water on the night table between the two beds. And sometime later that morning Sarah woke up and drank Jack's contacts. I opened my eyes just a bit and saw Jaimy looking at me from under a tumble of hair. She was trying not to giggle, and I was relieved, thinking back to the night before. Is this how it ends? Jack was trying unsuccessfully not to yell at Sarah while she got the rest of their undigested things together and we pretended to be asleep. When they left, Jaimy and I made love.

It's early evening in Kalamazoo and Rhoda should be home from her classes, I think. She should be alone, I think. "I'm going to make a phone call," I say. I can't shake the image of Jaimy staring down at me from the Joseph Smith house in Nauvoo.

"Take your sweet time," Randy says, and dabs a paper napkin at the corner of his moustache.

I've got a calling card and I trek through the numbers and instructions until I hear the phone ring. It rings and rings and then Rhoda's machine comes on: "Hi, this is Rhoda. I'm not here right now. You know the drill . . ."

"Rhoda," I say. "It's Brian. I'm in Iowa right now . . ."

"Brian?" Rhoda picks up the phone to the shrill disappointment of the machine. "Brian?"

"Where were you?" I say. I imagine her and Mr. Mysterious locked together in her bed. I hope he still smells my smells in her sheets, I think.

"I was here," she says. "But I was studying. I didn't expect you to call so soon."

"Are you alone?"

"Yes," she says. "Of course." There's hesitation in her voice.

"Hmm," I say. "This Randy guy is driving me out of my friggin' head."

"I told you, Brian," she says. "I don't know what you were thinking. He's not doing anything weird is he?"

"No," I say. "We stopped by Nauvoo."

"Why? Isn't that out of the way?"

"I don't know," I say. "Something Randy had to do. It's where the L.D.S. Church started."

"Oh," Rhoda says, like I've said something wrong or mean-spirited. I wonder if I have to be nearer to her to feel the things I felt last night. Those feelings seem to come and go like a tide under a lunar pull.

"Listen, I better go," I say. "These calling cards cost an arm and a leg."

"Okay," she says. "Will you call me again?"

"I will," I say. There is a long silence on both ends of the phone. "I'll call," I say. She tells me to be careful and that's all. I can't tell if she's alone or not. If she's happy I called or not. If I'm missing anything or not. But only distance has passed between us, no real time.

"Look," I tell Randy. "I was looking at the map on the

wall over there, and I want to stay at Mount Pleasant. If we can get a room there we can probably catch the Jazz game."

"Where're we at?"

"Game three, at Portland. Jazz are up two-zip," I say. "Should be a great game[64]. Those chumps at *USA Today* said we wouldn't get out of the first round."

"From here on out," he says, clicking his hook on the Formica tabletop. "I'm just along for the ride."

---

[64] One game that certainly comes to mind here would have to be the game in which Pistol Pete Maravich set the single-game scoring record for the Jazz. During the 1976-77 season Maravich laid 68 points on the New York Knicks. The Knicks famed trio of Butch Beard, Earl Monroe and Walt Frazier all tried to guard the flashy Maravich, but no one could.

Maravich also played in the first win in franchise history: 102-101 against the Portland Trailblazers, and the first win for the franchise in Utah: 110-109 over San Diego.

Malone has come close to Maravich's record. In 1990, after learning he had not been voted as a starter for the All-Star game in 1990 Malone scored 61 points against the Milwaukee Bucks. Earlier in the season, before a game against the Charlotte Hornets, John Stockton told Malone that he had seen a TV report where a Hornets' player called Malone "overrated." Malone had 52 points, though Stockton later admitted that no one had called Malone "overrated."

We can't forget the game a year prior to Brian's story when John Stockton broke Magic Johnson's all-time assist record. Or when the Jazz came back from a 36 point deficit to beat the Denver Nuggets early the following year. The Jazz claim that game was the turning point for their season, the starting point for a 64 win season.

XIX. The First Night Together

We find a place for the night, called, appropriately, The Starlight Motel. It is dark, even on the highway, and the only light comes from the night sky and from the pink neon of the Starlight's sign. The lamps by the doors of the motel keep their light close, clutching it to the building. This is country dark, as my father would call it. There is no glow on the horizon from a city, and the light of the stars comes almost to the ground.

"How're we gonna work this, then?" I ask Randy. Good grief, I think, I'm beginning to talk like him.

"We can split a room if that's all the same to you," he says. "I don't bite unless bitten." He smiles that bright smile at me, his teeth shiny in the dark of the car, like another gauge on the dash. "In fact, if you do want to share a room, I'll treat."

"You're in an awfully good mood," I say.

"I got a little bit of what was owed to me back there, and in-so-doing I just put the weight of this piece of the world off my shoulders," he says. "And besides, I drug you clear down here. You'd be to Nebraska by now if it wasn't for me."

This is the kind of guy I wanted to be riding with, I think. "All right," I say. "All right." Randy hands me four crisp twenty dollar bills and I leave him and his grin in the green glow of the dash.

The office is small and square. Everything looks as though it were designed to be in a constant state of repair. Including the television, held together with packing tape and secured to the wall with a belt strap and some two-by-fours, sitting in front of a small arm chair with its back to the counter. The first game is winding down, Atlanta is nursing a lead against the Pacers. That puts

Atlanta up two-to-one over the Pacers, but the announcers are quick to point out that the Bulls are still the team to beat in the east. This is Michael Jordan[65]'s first full year back after his

---

[65] Michael Jordan is considered by most to be the best basketball player of all time. Certainly, Jordan was one of the most heavily marketed sports figures of all time. His annual endorsements ran to the hundreds of millions. And his popularity world-wide is largely credited for helping the NBA become the most lucrative league in sports.

After winning three NBA championships in the early nineties, Jordan unexpectedly retired from basketball, saying he had accomplished all he could accomplish with the Bulls. He turned his attentions to major league baseball. And in spite of some obvious physical prowess, he was placed in the minor leagues. Jordan bought a new bus for his team out-of-pocket and quickly became the largest draw in minor league.

There was some speculation in and around Chicago that Jordan's retirement was not entirely his own idea, however. Something the NBA, whose success was clearly linked to Jordan's , refused to comment upon. Jordan had long been known as a risky and flamboyant gambler, risking tens of thousands on a single hole of golf (his other well-publicized passion). Some have suggested that the NBA, fearing a Pete Rose-type situation (the famous Cincinnati Reds baseball player who was banned for life from the league for gambling), asked Jordan to back away from the game until some investigatory heat cooled down.

After a year and a half away from the game, in which the Houston Rockets, led by Hakeem Olajuwan, won consecutive championships—knocking Utah from the playoffs each time—Jordan returned to basketball. Jordan was not in peak basketball condition, however, and the Bulls were eliminated by the Orlando Magic.

mysterious turn as a minor league baseball player, and the Bulls feel more and more like destiny for the Jazz.

There is a bell with a dent in it on the Formica counter with a sign Scotch-taped underneath that reads: RING FOR SERVICE in large, block print. Underneath this someone has scrawled in ballpoint pen: *if you don't know any better.* I gingerly tap on the bell and the knocker inside thuds against the dented, metal dome. I slap it harder and a flat ringing sound escapes the counter.

"You need a room, I s'pose?" a voice says from somewhere in the room.

I look around for the source of the voice, but see only the counter, the bell, and the closed door I just came in.

"Or did you just stop by to ring that bell?"

"I need a room," I say. "Two beds."

"Well speak up then," the voice says. "I don't read minds." A very small man slips from the chair and totters to the counter. His head is normal sized, though his forehead is a bit heavy and knotted. His torso seems to be normal as well, but his limbs are incredibly short and squat—smaller even than children's limbs. He ascends some stairs behind the counter and deftly drags the registry, chained to the desk with the same kind of golden chain that holds the bell secure, onto the countertop. It looks to be almost as big as he is.

"Name?"

"Brian Peterson," I say.

"Patterson?"

"PETERson," I say.

"Speak up," he says. "I can't hear a word you're saying."

He takes my name and address and the make of my car and asks me what's on my license plate, which I have to look out the glass of the door to remember. "Was it a good game?"

"Not bad," he says. "It's a moot point, though."

"Bulls fan?"

"Can't stand the fucking Bulls," he says.

"Who're you pulling for?"

"Rockets," he says. "I'm from Houston, you know?"

"What brings you up here?"

"An exciting life in hotel management. Sometimes," he says, "you don't decide where it is you end up."

I wave the key at Randy, who I can see glowing against the dash lights in the front seat. We park the car and unload our gear. The room smells stale, but looks clean. There are two full size beds with red and blue floral pattern comforters. The carpet is orangeish shag worn thin and flat. There is a television and a phone.

"Which bed do you want?" I ask.

"Which ever one you aren't in," Randy says. He drops his bag onto the bed nearest the door and peers around the room as though it doesn't meet his standards.

"What's the matter?" I say, flopping down on the opposite bed and stretching out.

"I never ever get used to these crappy little rooms," he says. He carefully removes his baseball cap and lays it on the bed stand.

"You stay in a lot of motels?"

"Every day for the last two years, almost," he says. "When I'm not in someplace like this I'm on somebody's couch."

"What have you been doing?"

"Staying out of trouble," he says. "Staying away."

"Oh," I say. I flip on the Jazz game and Randy seems to relax.

"I like basketball," he says. "It's a pure sport. I don't buy all that bitching and bellyaching about how the game's changed[66]. Things that don't change die. There's nothing I believe in more than that, let me tell you: *A state without the means of some change is without the means of its conservation.*"

"Edmund Burke," I say.

"What?"

"*A state without the means of some change is without the means of its conservation.* That's Edmund Burke, isn't it?"

Randy props himself up on his elbow and looks over at me very seriously. "You read Burke?"

"No, my dad is always quoting Burke. He was always quoting everybody when we were growing up. I just remember that quote," I say.

"Good for him. That's always a beginning. *Next to the originator of a good sentence is the first quoter of it.*"

"Emerson?"

───────────────

[66] Self-described basketball purists often decry that the professional game has become more about individual athleticism and showmanship than about a team concept and some of the fundamentals like passing, dribbling, and rebounding. The physical play is also often cited as evidence of the erosion of the game. Karl Malone is often singled out by purists for his consistent improvement in the basics of the game like free throw shooting, passing, and developing more difficult, finesse shots (for a big, power player) like a fade-away jump shot. He is also singled out as one of the players who takes the most liberties with the new rules of the game that put the pressure solely on the defender to establish position. Malone often drives the lane with his knee raised and rebounds with his elbows out. Both techniques are within the letter of the law in the NBA, but potentially dangerous for other players.

"Damn you're good, Chompers. Try this one: *Some, for renown, on scraps of learning dote, And think they grow immortal as they quote.*"

"Edward Young, *Love of Fame.* That's one of Dad's favorites," I feel a thrill at this game, as if I'm plumbing the depths of my own imagination with each line from my memory. "Should you really be quoting that one, though?"

"You're right. *The maxims of men disclose their hearts,*" he says. The game has started, the announcers have said their peace, and the Portland fans seem rabid, drowning out the announcers and creating a minor din in the room. Then there is the tip off and Portland's Arvydas Sabonis knocks it away from Felton Spencer. Two big men known for their light shooting touches, clumsily lunge after a ball, and their going head-to-head seems somehow lamentable.

"I don't know," I say.

"Trick quotation," he says. "Anonymous French proverb. How's this: *By necessity, by proclivity,—and by delight, we all quote?*" Randy is getting seriously wound up, and the mood in our room seems to be taking on slumber party proportions. I remember pressing my ear to the door of Rachel's room when she had her girlfriends over. Instead of two young girls swapping their heart's desires for the boys of their homeroom, we're tossing the words of the dead back and forth. And like it was for Rachel, no doubt, it makes me feel my father is nearby, listening, disapproving.

"Emerson again," I say.

"I can't believe you didn't serve a mission," Randy says.

"What do you mean?"

"The M.T.C. shows you how to do all that. To quote the Bible, to quote *The Book of Mormon.* To quote everything you can get a hold of to keep your foot in the door and your hand in the heart of your prospective convert. Did your dad serve?"

"Of course," I say. "He did his in Ohio in the late sixties. Seems like I get a lot of this stuff vicariously. Fat lot of good it does me."

"*The man who does not read good books has no advantage over the man who can't read them*." Randy says. "All right, so that one doesn't quite work, but you catch my drift."

"Mark Twain[67]," I say. "And no I don't. Not really."

"You've got such a talent there," he says. "You have no idea how dangerous that makes you. God, if I had had a mind like that at your age . . . to just reach out there and find those maxims and their makers . . . But, I guess it's like my friend Bill Shakespeare said, *We cannot all be masters*." Randy sits up on the bed and disconnects his arm. He lays it across the bed like it is an infant.

"You sleep with that on the bed?"

"This baby's all I've got," he says, patting it gently with his good hand. "You'd be surprised what a person's got to go through just to get an arm that fits. It's like finding a wife, in some ways. Closest thing to your completeness. You put a whole lot of energy into it, and you keep putting energy into it."

"What do you mean?"

"There are thousands of models to choose from, and

---

[67] Mark Twain was profoundly disturbed by the Mormon acceptance and encouragement of polygamy. No where was he more critical on his trips westward than he was in *Roughing It*. He likened Brigham Young to a monarch "who received without emotion the news that the august Congress of the United States had enacted a solemn law against polygamy, and then went forth calmly and married twenty-five or thirty more wives."

you've got to decide what kind of arm you want. Do you want to match the shade, or do you want to make sure you can open a door and that kind of jive. I've got this one here," he says, patting the arm again, like it just woke from a slumber and his reassurance returns it to slumbering. "This one is great for opening things and picking things up, but she's not much to look at. And she takes a lot of fumbling around with, to make sure she's comfortable, make sure she opens when I want her to open, swings the way I want her to swing."

"And that's how it's like a wife?" I say. I've heard the old saw about marriage making someone complete, but I've never imagined it like Randy has.

"You know," he says. "A marriage has to have those kinds of adjustments. You pull a strap here, lay down some more tape and gauze there."

"That sounds kind of one-sided," I say.

"I guess that's my fucking problem," Randy says with a laugh.

I want to ask him about his wife, about his kid, but his silence on the subject is profound. We sit and watch the game and Stockton makes an unbelievable pass, through two Trailblazers, to Malone who jams the ball into the basket with one hand and draws a foul. Randy says, "Oh yeah."

There's a break in the action and the game turns to a local commercial for Menards, a kind of lumberyard. Randy stands next to the bed and peels off his shirt. He wipes at his bare chest with the shirt and cautiously digs around in his bag, safely at the end of the bed, careful not to wake the sleeping arm. He procures a bottle of whiskey and deftly tears open the seal with his thumbnail, and spins the cap free with that same thumb. His hand must be twice as strong as a normal human hand, I think. He takes an unbelievably long drink from the bottle. So long that I can see bubbles coming into the syrupy looking liquid, and when he is done the bottle is nearly one fourth empty. He hands it over to me.

"Here you go, Chief," he says.

I take the bottle, overcoming my impulse to wipe the mouth of it before I press it to my lips. The whiskey is hard for me to swallow, but I push into the bottle, one swallow, then two burning swallows, then a third that seems to be meeting the first coming back up my throat like a hot coal. "Well," Randy says. "I'll say this for you: You don't drink like a Mormon."

"Maybe I do," I say, and he laughs. Randy's bare chest is muscular and smooth on the side with the full arm. The hand that holds the whiskey. But on the withered wing side there are craters and canyons into his flesh all along his rib cage. I can't not look at it.

"*Drink no longer water, but use a little wine for thy stomach's sake and thine often infirmities,*" I say.

"Timothy 5:23. *I have taken more good from alcohol than alcohol has taken from me,*" he says. The missing pieces of his body seem to spiral outward from his ribs, and up his wing, across his chest in finer and finer lines and stars, up his neck like a dusting of texture.

"Churchill," I say. "You know . . ."

"Damn, you are so fucking good. We get you to quit your mumbling ways and you could have the world by the balls with a mind like that . . ."

"You never really have told me what your deal is. What were you doing in Kalamazoo? What's with Nauvoo? Where've you been the last few years?"

"*Questioning is not the mode of conversation,*" he says. "*among gentlemen.*" He passes the bottle back to me; the heat, I feel is off of me to take such a measure this time.

"C'mon," I say, wiping my mouth with the back of my

arm. "You can tell me a little something. I mean, you said something about New York. I'm just interested in how you go from a mission in Italy . . . Palermo, did you say? To New York and Kalamazoo."

"And a lot of places a whole-fucking-lot worse than that," he says. There is some silence now.

"All right," he says finally, staring at the television, but clearly not watching the action of the game. I reach for the remote and turn down the volume. "I guess you could say Palermo was a little bit of an eye opener for me. One of my companions, Elder Todd Hinckley was his name, if you're gonna bust my chops about the details, showed me just how fucking fruitless it was to be going door-to-door, trying to get five minutes instead of five knuckles." He stares at the television some more and drinks. And then he stares some more.

"I don't know if we had a bad mission president, or if it's just that damned tough down there, but Hinckley showed me just how forsaken we were. Nobody helped us, and we weren't helping anybody. The fucking guidos from the family in our neighborhood were busting our balls every day of the week except Sunday. Even they rested on Sunday.

"And it didn't take too long for me to fight back. It was against the rules of the mission, you know, but my old man didn't raise me to just stand there and take a beating. Thing is, if you fought one, the next day there'd be two. And if you fought two there'd be three. And those sons-of-bitches fought dirty. They'd grab your fucking nuts and yank 'em off.

"Well Hinckley told me to stop reporting all these ass-beatings. That wasn't getting us anywhere. In fact, the only thing that ever happened was for our fucking mission president to ride our jocks about whether or not we threw any punches back. We were doing God's work, Hinckley said, not the mission's. Not even the church's. I wasn't prepared for that kind of *free thinking*. I'd spent all my time, years of my fucking life, training to believe in the mission and in the people responsible for my mission." Randy's story seems to be a big set-up. I keep waiting for the other shoe to drop, for him to look at me and let me in on the joke, tell me he's making all of this up for the telling. The more he presses into his story, the more I feel I can't trust him.

"There was something about Hinckley. He spoke to me with the kind of authority I must've needed at that time. The guy could've talked the righteous into eating his turds for sacrament, I'll bet. Could've probably talked those guidos into letting us get on with our work if he'd really had a mind to. But the guy wasn't about to genuflect before any one man, he'd said. And let me tell you, he had the brains and brass balls, too. He'd stay up late fabricating a journal of our day each night just to cover our tracks.

"Pretty soon we were waiting for the guidos with baseball bats he pilfered from the chapel. Kicking ass and taking names. Hinckley went off on the guidos, bashing their fucking brains into the cobblestones."

"You could kill somebody," I say, realizing how stupid it sounds only after I say it.

"No shit, Sherlock," Randy says. "Hinckley killed at least two of those fuckers that I know of."

"On his mission?!?"

"Hell yes! But Hinckley got shipped out soon after that and things started escalating with the guidos and the Church. They found a bomb at the chapel one morning, and two missionaries got shot in some lame Italian drive-by. But they both pulled through. Thanks be to God, and all that, you know?"

"Geez," I say. "That's like no mission I've ever heard of." I'm not sure if I should believe Randy or not. He seems serious and I can't think of a reason he'd make all this up, but part of it seems rehearsed, practiced. He's either told this story so many times it plays like a lecture, or he's drunk and having to cling to it as he tells it, or he's full of shit. The whiskey is starting to find its way into the little places now; my toes feel numb, my mouth is watery and wants to keep hanging open.

"Yeah, well. I wasn't done with Hinckley after he left. Or the other way around. So now he had something over me that could get me excommunicated and he made me meet up with him back in the states. It wasn't just the threat of it, the excommunication, that bothered me. Even before Hinckley I was thinking things most missionaries, I'm sure, don't think. It all seemed like some big marketing scam to me. My companions came and went, but I was stuck in Palermo. Palermo, Palermo, Palermo. Sounds funny now: Palermo. But I felt like my sales techniques weren't good enough to get promoted to a more promising area. And the replies that came back were just too fucking predictable. Sure, this was a hard row to hoe, but they were just as fucking sure that I could do it. That even if I never got one single soul into the celestial kingdom, I was doing the Lord's work and I was spreading the good word about the church. But I guess I just wasn't ready to get my ass kicked for Jesus. I busted my balls to get to my mission and it wasn't long before I knew I'd been dealt the shittiest block in the berg, and it didn't seem fair to me at all.

"So when I flew into New York I met up with Hinckley. He introduced me to some friends of his. A couple of R.M.'s like us, but just as many non-L.D.S. We stayed in touch while I was in college, for a while, and then when I was done with school I went back to New York and took them up on their offer to help me along."

"But there were strings attached?" I say.

"There's always fucking strings attached," Randy says, taking another tremendous drink from the bottle and passing it back to me across the chasm between the two beds. Randy's wing is now tracing patterns in the air, like he's conducting an invisible orchestra with an invisible arm. He stares up at the ceiling, which is spray-coated with glittery spackle. The ceiling glistens and shines, like millions of little stars in an eggshell sky.

Randy is just the kind of person Rhoda and Zach would be I-told-you-so's about. But I finally don't feel the least bit bothered by his story. If it's honest, and he was there when Hinckley killed those two Italians, then there's something in his telling that let's me know that's all in the past. That this is something he's moved on from. And if it's a lie, then at least he's an interesting liar. Unlike me.

XX. A New Truth

We watch the end of the game. The Jazz rally and the game goes to overtime, but they don't have enough left in the tank, the Trailblazers feeding off the hostility and the intensity of the crowd, and they go down 94-91[68] in O.T. Randy has finished off the bottle of whiskey; it is tucked under his wing like an egg, and he is fast asleep on top of the bed. I think I should take off his shoes, but that seems too personal. Besides, I'm afraid more than his shoes might come off if I pulled too hard. He looks so harmless

---

[68] Malone led all scorers with 35 points, but the cold-shooting Jazz couldn't get past Arvydas Sabonis' 27 points and a rebound basket by the even older Buck Williams in the final 14.1 seconds. With the game tied 83-83 the Blazers Clifford Robinson made a critical mistake and launched a three-pointer with 5.2 seconds still remaining on the clock. The Jazz rebounded, called a time-out, and David Benoit in-bounded to John Stockton, who dropped the ball into Antoine Carr as he came down the lane. Carr bobbled the ball but managed a ten foot shot that rimmed out. Bryon Russell had a chance to tip the ball, but that also missed, and the game went to over-time.

Antoine Carr, a big-bodied veteran capable of playing at the power forward or the center position, came to the Jazz at the beginning of the 1994–95 season. After watching the Jazz play against the Spurs during the 1994 season, Carr's mother approached Karl Malone and pleaded with him to find a spot on the Jazz' roster for her son.

Carr had been a stand-out at Wichita State in the early 1980s, and, in his prime, was averaging over twenty points per game for the Sacramento Kings.

laid out on the bed like he is. His chest, pock-marked and bitten, rises and falls, falls and rises to its own dreamy rhythms. His jaw hangs open and he moves his tongue as if he is speaking, though no sound escapes his lips.

"Don't mutter so much there, Chompers," I say. I'm disappointed that the Jazz lost the game. I can already see the headlines screaming out from the *USA Today* that the Trailblazers have turned the tide. I want another drink. Just enough so that I can fall asleep. Randy's bag sits on the foot of his still-made bed, its mouth unzipped and falling open. I think I might find another bottle there that I can pin on him in the morning. He won't remember, I think.

When I stand I realize I'm more drunk than I thought, but once I stand it's as if my body is reading from a script. I stand before Randy's bag, a huge duffel bag that must weigh as much as Randy does. It is so full of clothing and books that I can't see into it to where he keeps his stash.

I bury my hand in the bag and work it around like a mole, probing book after book, garment after garment. There are about twenty rolled pairs of socks my hands glide across until I feel the cold neck of a bottle and pull it from the bag.

What comes out of the bag is the cold silver of a handgun. I don't know anything about handguns or their caliber except to know that this one is pointed directly into my face. It is a huge, heavy gun. I've never held a handgun in my palm before, and it is much heavier than I thought it would be. Though it feels good in my palm when I turn it over. It feels like something you want to have in your hand. BANG BANG BANG, I squeeze off three imaginary rounds at the television set before I realize the gun might be loaded.

It's not rocket science to open the gun and check the chamber, and there they are, like six cocoons, or like six wasps waiting to hatch from the nest. I pull them out, carefully, one after the next. They are silver, like the gun, and I think perhaps they are a joke, a souvenir. But they are heavy and stamped ".44" on the bottoms of their casings. Randy stirs, but does not wake. His wing rises from the bed and then falls again, perhaps clutching at something in his dream. Right now, I think, Randy's got his hand back.

I close the chamber and return the gun to Randy's duffel bag, sliding it mindfully past the plastic baggies. I keep the six silver shells in my palm and roll them back and forth with the index finger of my other hand. A simple thing, I think, that Randy can never do. I'm sunk, too loaded to know if this should worry me or not, and I slip the shells into my shaving kit and zip it shut. They are interviewing Cliff Robinson after the game and I turn the television off.

The rest of the night I stare into the stars of the ceiling. They glitter and turn and no dreams will come for me. I think of Rhoda but I'm frustrated that I cannot picture her, that I cannot summon her, until I'm convinced she is resisting me. That I am lying in a motel room in Mt. Pleasant nowhere with a one-armed man and his silver gun and she is lying in a bed with Mr. Mysterious, whose shadowy and sinewy figure I can almost conjure better than Rhoda's. Jaimy comes easier, almost like I can connect the stars on the ceiling into her ghostly figure, floating above me. I'm not even sure I sleep. I don't think I do, yet suddenly the sun is creeping past the leaden drapes of the room, and Randy pushes himself up from the bed and stumbles to the sink where he stands and lets the water run and run and run.

We pass the morning in silence and I keep close note of his ritual. He peels a layer of moldy, white tape from the inside of his arm and refastens new tape from his bag to the inner arm. I watch him closely every time he reaches into the bag.

He removes the gauze sock from his wing, and it is pink and bumpy and frail-looking. He washes it carefully in the sink before he goes into the shower. He is modest when he enters the bathroom, but he comes out nude, rubbing a towel over his head and beard with his hand while the wing flails about, unaware that it does not have hold of the towel.

When it is my turn, I bring my clothes into the shower with me. There are quite a few of Randy's hairs in the sieve at the base of the tub, and I am careful not to step on them. I feel better after the shower, though I still feel a little drunk.

"Little hair of the dog?" Randy says when I come out of the shower. He has another bottle of whiskey opened and takes a small sip from it and this time it affects him. He turns away from the bottle in pain and hands it over to me. The smell is almost enough to make me vomit, but I take a sip anyway. I've never tried the hair of the dog before, but in a few minutes it works its magic and I feel better. I feel strange, out-of-time and out-of-rhythm somehow, but I feel better. "Some game," I say.

"They really could've swept this thing." Randy nods. He hates small talk, I think, and I hate making it, I think, so why do I bother?

It has rained the night before, though I didn't hear anything. The ground is wet and it has cleaned the air. I take it in and drive with the window down, in spite of the chill. Randy doesn't seem to mind. I notice he keeps his bag close, within arm's reach on the floor in the back seat. We don't talk.

The land is rich in shades of green and chocolate browns and we rise up and down on the road like a boat cresting the waves of the earth. Every new hill is a new farm, a new white farm house, a new tin barn, and a new field bursting with new greenery. The sky is blue, not gray like it is in Kalamazoo after a rain, and I can see from horizon to horizon at the top of every hill.

I think I should call my parents and tell them I'm back on course, but the morning seems to slip by. We travel silently through the land; I can hear the meadowlarks perched on the wooden fence posts shooting us their shrill-trill as we coast by.

"You think you've got something over on me, I'll bet," Randy says finally.

"What?"

"After last night. I know I talk too fucking much when I've had something to drink, but don't think you really know all that much. I'm not that stupid," he says. He is sulking down into his seat, turning to face me just enough to spit out his words.

"That's crazy talk," I say. "I have no idea what you're talking about."

"Oh yeah?" he says, and we let that hang in the air between us for several miles. "What's the worst thing you ever did?"

"What do you mean?" I say.

"You heard me, Chompers," he says. "What's the worst thing you ever did?"

"I don't know," I say. I think he's playing at getting me to even the score, but I know I don't have anything close to killing a man, or watching one killed, or whatever his piece of that story was. "I stole some compact discs from Smokey's records once. I always felt terrible about that. They were a nice little store. Smokey was nice to me. You ever go to Smokey's?"

"Are you fucking serious?"

"Look, Randy. I don't know what you want me to say. I never went on a mission. I never had it that tough, I guess."

"Well, what's the worst thing you ever had to do?"

"I accidentally ran over the neighbor's cat, when I was learning how to drive, and I had to go tell the neighbor's kids what happened and then get out there in the street with a bag and bucket and clean up. It felt like the whole neighborhood was watching me scrub that street, but I didn't dare complain, or my dad . . ."

"Would've what?"

"Wouldn't have liked it."

"Well, what's the worst thing you ever saw?"

"I saw a kid slip off of the high dive at the Layton pool and hit his head on the side of the pool right in front of me. Just scream, whack, and down he went into the water trailing a little zig-zag of blood. He died," I say. We come upon a hog farm and the smell is thick and musty. I want to roll up the window, but I can tell it's fading already.

"Not bad," he says, like this has become a contest.

"Well what's the worst thing you ever saw," I say.

"You really want to know?"

"Yes," I say. "I told you mine."

"You really want me to tell you this?"

"Yes, of course I do," I say. I think he's already spilled his beans.

"You wanted to know how I ended up in Kalamazoo, right?"

"Yes," I say.

"Remember Hinckley?"

"Your companion in Palermo?"

"I went and stayed with Hinckley in New York," he says. His stories seem so rehearsed I just can't make heads or tails of them, but they calm him down in the telling and they pass the time. By my estimation, if we drive all day today we can get well into Nebraska. And then if we don't have another night like last night, we can leave early in the morning, and I can catch the tail end of game four back in Kaysville. The mountains seem nearer to me, though I know Nebraska and Wyoming are still far away. "He introduced me to some people and I made some friends with those people. Those people introduced to me some more people. Some important people in certain circles."

I can't imagine Randy with anyone important. I assume his idea of important and my own are worlds apart. "I was back and forth between New York and Utah for a long time there. And some of these people paid me for my education and never asked me for anything in return. But I did things for these people. I did things for these people because they showed me certain . . . problems . . . ah, problems with the world that they were trying to . . . fix." So much for interesting stories, I think. This is not the same Randy from yesterday, and I think he must have blown an amp or two last night.

"You know what a Danite[69] is?" he says.

"No," I say, but he doesn't bother to explain.

"I bought what these fuckers were selling, man. Hook, line, and sinker. If they'd told me that Orrin Hatch was the devil incarnate I'd have believed them. And if they'd told me to do something about it, I would've."

_____

[69] The Danites were formed by one of Smith's renegade devout, Sampson Avard, as a secret retributionary society against internal trouble-makers and dissenters. It later carried out retaliatory strikes against the anti-Mormon mobs and more, such as those at Haun's Mill where seventeen men, women and children were massacred. Missouri governor Lilburn Bogs, acting on panicked reports of Danite plundering, ordered 200 militia to attack the Haun's Mill settlement in 1838, treating the settlers as "enemies" who "must be exterminated or driven from the state." The early church's ultimate relationship to the Danites has never been known, and their eventual fate never fully documented.

"You make this sound like some sort of militia group," I say.

"Why don't you just let me finish?"

"Fine," I say.

"Well Hinckley was a powerful presence among these people. He could talk circles around most of them. And like most young prophets he had as many enemies as he had friends."

"Prophet?" I say.

"There's nothing I wouldn't have done for Hinckley," he says.

"I don't think I've ever known anybody like that," I say.

"Well," he says. "Not everybody liked Hinckley's ideas. And one somebody in particular took real offense when Hinckley started slowly coming back around. Started denying things he himself had stood behind for years. Started trying to make amends for some of the things he'd done. It takes a strong man to do that. To admit when you've been wrong and to try to right those wrongs."

"I know what you mean," I say.

"Bullshit," he says. "You don't know shit about shit."

"Then why tell me all this?" I say.

"You're right," Randy says. "I'm sorry. I really, truly am sorry. I wouldn't be telling you any of this if I didn't respect you."

I'm getting tired of these games. I can't tell what's sincere with him and what's not. "We were on the platform, you know," he continues. "We were just standing there, waiting for the subway to take us uptown to see this Mexican speaker talk about the revolution. They've got armed conflict down there, you know?" Randy seems to have gone all sentimental now. "Anyway, we were just standing there waiting on the train, talking about how things were going to change. Hinckley was going to leave New York in a couple more months and move back to Denver where he was from.

"We're just standing there on the platform with the train coming in and one of these old friends of his comes up behind and gives him a little push. Just a little push."

"Jesus," I say. This sounds suspiciously like something I've seen on TV before, but I can't place it in a show or some news report. But I don't think he's lying now, and if he is, he's lying to himself as well. His pain seems real enough.

"Just a little push," he says again. "He grabbed my arm," he says, laughing a crazy little laugh while he pulls his arm free and waves it in front of the windshield. "Nothing I could do," he says. "It happened so fast, that first part."

"First part?" I say.

"Yeah," he says. "You don't get run down by the train if they push right between the train and curb."

"What do you mean?" I say. I feel as though I should pull the car over. I let our speed drop to 55.

"You fall between, when they push like that. And that motherfucker knew just how to push. He'd done it before, I think. That'd be my guess, that he'd done it before to get it just right like that.

"He pushed Hinckley and Hinckley nearly grabbed my arm off, slapping me to the ground like a wet bag, and he went twisting around and around down the platform, knocking people over and spinning like a top. Women were screaming all over the fucking place. And a couple of times the watch on his hand struck the ground and I saw sparks fly."

"Jesus," I say.

"That ain't it," he says. "That ain't the half of it. You don't die when that happens."

"Really," I say, thinking this might turn out okay after all, like in a television show.

"No, the train twists you up from the waist down like a

plastic bag. Like a bag you fill with water and twist shut and then turn upside down. It'll hold as long as you keep that bag pinched shut at the bottom.

"That was Hinckley. He was pressed into the train and I don't think he even knew how bad he was hurt at first. But I ran down there, into the a crowd of people around him now. This one old woman was trying to pull him out from under the train before anyone else got down there. Oh, there was a crowd. Let me tell you, there was a fucking crowd. And when the word got out, there was a bigger and bigger crowd.

"The cops came and shooed everyone back. And then they let me through and Hinckley just apologized for grabbing my arm, like the only thing to worry about right then was whether or not I'd be mad I got knocked down, you know?"

"He just put his hand on my arm and he told me he didn't feel so good. I stayed and I held his hand while the cops cleared everybody out. And then this one cop, a real nice fat fellow with red hair and a moustache, asked to talk to me.

"He said they were going to have to pull the train off of him. And when they did, his guts were gonna spill out of him and he was going to be dead."

"There wasn't any other way?"

"No. There was no other way. The nice cop gave me a cell phone. They were new then, and I'd never used a cell phone before. Never seen one. I called Hinckley's girl at her work and she came right down. I had to go over and tell Hinckley, but he already knew. Jesus, he was so pale. His face looked like white rubber. Like a cheap mask of Hinckley.

"He said it didn't take Einstein to know that he was a chest and a head. Still trying to joke, you know? He could feel himself dying. So he just wanted to say a couple of goodbyes. He called his parents in Denver, but they didn't understand what was going to happen, and then he said goodbye to his girl. She didn't stay. Hinckley told her to leave and she did. And I held his hand there until he died. And when they pulled the train away there was the worst sucking noise I've ever heard in my life and everything that was in him was on the tracks."

"Good God," I say. "That's the worst thing I've ever heard in my life!"

"A paramedic and a cop helped me hold his body from falling down and then we hoisted him onto the platform," Randy's voice is getting caught in his throat. "Do you believe people can change?" Randy says.

"Like Hinckley?" I say. "Nobody deserves that. Nobody deserves to die like that." We're past it now, and I let our speed wander up the arc.

"But do you think people can change? I wouldn't have believed it if it weren't for Hinckley. He was a good man at heart. He believed in things, and he had a passion for what was right. I never met anyone before or since who could prove to me that they had a passion for what was right. Even when he was all about hate. Even when he was going after those Italians, he was doing it because he thought he was there to save the others. That sometimes you have to give up a few to save the lot, you know. That's basic mission training.

"But I think people can change. I really do," he says. "I think people make their own salvation. Fill in what's missing. That's something I've got in my heart." Randy's a sappy drunk, I thought after the night before, but now I think he's just a sentimentalist.

XXI. The Long, Clear Road Ahead

There isn't much to say after Randy's outburst, and his story leaves both us looking out on the beautiful Iowa landscape with new sets of eyes. We drive silently that way until we reach Iowa City, and I stop the car for gas and to stretch my legs. Randy demands a certain Amoco again, which is fine because it is on the right side of the road and looks clean and well kept. The hair of the dog is long gone, and a tremendous headache is laying claim to my skull.

For the first time, Randy doesn't offer to pay for the gas. I have gotten used to it, and I wonder how we'll work the sleeping arrangements tonight. His terrible story will surely color the night.

Randy goes into the convenience store and disappears for a long time. I pay for the gas and then have to park the car in front of the store. Still no Randy.

I start to worry that he has left me, though I'm not sure why that would worry me. Some separation anxiety that tells me I'm already used to his company. I decide I should call my parents now that we are so close to I-80. It will be a straight shot across Iowa, Nebraska and Wyoming into Utah[70].

---

[70] On October 1, 1845, the Quorum of the Twelve Apostles were ready to leave Nauvoo and head west with the rest of their eager and devoted flock. They would leave in the following spring when the grasses could provide for their animals on the long trek across the prairie.

The faithful had spent much of their time completing work on the Nauvoo temple in December of that year, but soon after they left it would be destroyed by arson. The rest of their time in Nauvoo was devoted to prayer and preparation for the long journey west.

These acts of preparation would become an important substantiation of their faith.

The Council of Fifty ultimately decided on the Salt Lake Valley, owned by Mexico at the time, largely because it was the most secluded spot for the Mormons. By this time they all were suffering from marauding gangs of anti-Mormon radicals who raped, murdered and burned their homes.

Brigham Young was chosen to lead the more than 3,200 families west. They had more than 4,000 wagons, and by 1846 there were close to 16,000 faithful converts on the trail. Young was a strict disciplinarian on the journey, doling out punishments for transactions as slight as swearing. But his greatest leadership skill was his ability as a powerful orator and he quickly received the trust of his people.

Their first stop was Winter Quarters, near what is now Omaha. Winter Quarters became an important stop over for the thousands of faithful who would follow the initial trek. While at Winter Quarters Young shrewdly helped finance the journey by lending a battalion of more than 500 Mormons to the fight with Mexico.

Young's difficult journey into Utah, which culminated with his famous "This is the place" declaration upon entering Salt Lake Valley, is celebrated every year on July 24. Though the non-denominational name of "Pioneer Day" was given to July 24, the celebration clearly continues to lionize the struggles of the Mormon faithful and their formidable exodus into the desert.

Karl Malone, whose birthday happens to be on July 24, first came to Utah in late July after being drafted by the Jazz. He says his first reaction, on seeing all the people lining the streets of Salt Lake and the parades, was that the city had come out to celebrate his birthday.

When I enter the convenience store again, I don't see Randy anywhere, though the store is so overwrought with Iowa Hawkeyes merchandise it would be easy enough for him not to be seen. However, when I find the pay phones near the rest rooms, I see Randy coming out of the men's room writing on a piece of paper laid across his plastic arm. He uses the arm as if it were a desk top.

He doesn't see me, and he doesn't hear me when I say his name. Instead, he turns to the phone, looking down at the scrap of paper resting on his plastic arm, and dials a number. He turns away from the store and from me, cradling the phone under his chin. I can't hear him, but he's speaking vigorously, nodding his head and growing more and more irate with every gesture. Finally, he slaps the phone back into its cradle and crumples the paper he was tending so carefully into his fist. "Fuck," he says. I hear that.

"Fuck!" He picks up the phone again and pauses before turning around. He looks at me as if he'd been waiting to see me standing there. "What the fuck are you doing there, Chompers? You spying on me?"

"No," I say. "I've got to use the bathroom."

"Well hurry it up, we've got to get out of here ASAP."

"Why?"

"Why what?" he says, snapping at me as puts the phone back.

"Why do we have to get out of here?"

"Make some hay while the sun still shines," he says. "Hurry up." He brushes past me and walks outside to the car. I pat my pocket to make sure my car keys are safely there before I walk into the small, stinking rest room.

It smells like old urine and air freshener. Maybe, I think, someone's come up with an air freshener that smells like old urine. My urine is hot and dark gold from all the whiskey last night. I read the signs and symbols and slogans on the wall: *How many dead Niggers and Mexicans does it take to fill up the Grand Canyon? Let's find out. Metallica rules! Incest is best, put your sister to the test!* It seems the farther west we travel, the less original the toilet banter becomes. Then, as I zip my pants and step on the silver flushing handle, I see the letters Z.O.G. again. They are written carefully, and in the same stylized hand from back in Michigan. Very distinctive, gothic print. And on the opposite wall, written in the same thick ink, Cindy is advertising her services again.

I call my parents and leave a message with them that we're about to get onto I-80 and that I should be there in two days, if the weather holds up. When I get to the car, Randy is sitting in the passenger seat with his seat belt pulled tight. "Let's get a move-on, Jehosaphat," he says. He seems to be in a better mood, but now he's acting nervous. I don't dare ask him about Z.O.G.

When we find the interstate I ask him a simple question: "Did you call your wife and tell her you're on your way?"

"My wife?" he says, incredulously.

"To let her know you're coming," I say.

"Jesus H. Christ, you're a buggy little s.o.b., aren't you? You always stick your nose into other people's business like this?" he asks. It doesn't seem like a rhetorical question.

"I called my parents, that's all. And told them we'd probably get in the day after tomorrow at the latest."

"You ask them if you can wipe your own ass?"

"Man," I say.

"What's that, Chief?" he says.

"Nothing," I say. "Why don't you take a nap or something?"

Randy doesn't say anything. He just stares out his window for a while, and then when we separate from the traffic of big rigs and sedans, he unslings his plastic arm and leans his head back onto the greasy glass like a giant specimen slide of himself for all the plains to see. It's prettier across this part of Iowa than I know it will be across Nebraska and Wyoming, but the hills already seem to flatten out, the streams and rivers straighten their backs, and farm houses move farther and farther from the interstate. We're in the commerce traffic now, anonymous and distant from the people and the country, blips on someone's horizon.

"I can't tell my wife I'm coming," Randy says. I look over at him and his eyes are closed and he seems to be sleeping. I wonder if he actually said anything at all, or if I'm imagining his voice. When I turn back to the road he speaks again: "There's a fucking good chance she'll take our son and hide out until she knows I'm gone again. And who's to blame her?" I still can't be certain he's speaking.

"She's mad at you?"

"You could say that," the voice says. "I know in my heart that I've changed, but there's no way she can know how deep those changes are."

"What do you mean?" I say. The traffic picks up and I can't afford to look over at Randy.

"I'll tell you, when our son was born, I couldn't handle it. He had some problems, that they knew before too long. He was what you call autistic, and to me that just meant plain old retarded. You know, like those knuckle-dragging monkey-boys you'd see in school always chasing after some pretty girl. That's all it meant to me. Retarded. I couldn't take it."

"So you left?"

"What a prick. I was already gone, really. I'd had that standing offer in New York, and it sure beat anything going on in Moab. Fucking Moab. So I went to New York and told her I'd send some money and when things settled down for me I'd have her come up to New York if she wanted."

"And you didn't send for her?" I say.

"The group I was with at the time . . . It couldn't happen. And then after Hinckley. Well, you know the first thing I'd do if I had my hand back?"

"No," I say.

"I'd drive a nail through it, just so I'd know it was real."

I shoot a quick look over at Randy, but his face is turned toward the glass, and I can't tell if he's really in this conversation or not.

"I left somebody once," I say. Randy doesn't say anything and it makes me feel like I should explain so it won't sound condescending, like I'm patronizing him about his son and his wife. "The worst thing I remember was the feeling I had that it *might* be permanent. Not that it was permanent, but that it just *might* be permanent. I hated that about it."

"Nothing's *permanent*," Randy says.

"Death?" I say.

"Don't pretend for a minute you know anything more about death than anybody else. You can't use something for an example when you don't even fucking know how it works or what it does." Randy doesn't say anything while I pass a big rig. It's a Simon rig out of Utah, and though I don't know any truckers, I feel a kind of kinship with the truck. I try to watch it grow smaller in the rearview. "Is she dead, then?" Randy says finally.

"No," I say. "I don't think so. She's dead to me, though. I haven't spoken to her in a couple of years. We dated for quite a while there in high school and a bit into college, but then I knew it was time for both of us to move on." I don't typically remember how someone looks when I remember an event, when I can recall something with other people involved. But I remember Jaimy's face when I told her I needed a break. Jaimy would cry when we passed road kill on the highway, but she just sat on the bed in my dorm room like I was delivering a lecture, or a sermon. She thought about what I'd said, I could tell, but she didn't say anything. Not one thing. Jaimy wasn't the type to blow up, but I thought she might cry or something. She just sat on the bed and looked at me like a student looks at a teacher who's just told them they're failing a class. That's how I saw our relationship, I suppose.

"She just looked at me when I told her," I say. "Just stared at me for the longest time. And then all she would say to me was, *I didn't know you felt that way,* and she stood up and looked around my dorm room, like she was trying to remember if there was anything she needed to take with her. Like maybe it was the kind of situation where she was supposed to take something with her. And she left and I didn't hear from her for a long, long time. I didn't even see her around campus for almost a year, and I had to keep tabs on her through a mutual friend who said she took it really hard, but you wouldn't know that from where I stood. She just looked around like she was supposed to take something with her, and she walked right out the door without shedding a tear." I look over at Randy, who's being conspicuously quiet. He breathes a deep, hard breath that could mean he's drifting off into sleep again, or that he's simply making his disapproval known. And then I have to think maybe he's been asleep this whole time and I've only imagined we've been speaking.

"I'm going to look her up, I think," I say, only this time it doesn't matter if he's awake to hear me or not. It doesn't matter if I actually say anything or not. I'm moving at more than sixty miles per hour across the funeral silence of the Iowa countryside, and my words may be falling like highway litter from my mouth. They may be not be words at all.

XXII. Winter Quarters

Iowa is longer and more silent than I recalled. And it is later afternoon before we reach Omaha[71]. The earth seems to be moving against us. As we cross the Missouri River, I can see several riverboat casinos moored to their stations. Their lights are on,

---

[71] As Brigham Young and the Mormons made themselves at home in the Salt Lake Valley, they encouraged overseas converts to join them in Utah via the Perpetual Emigrating Fund, which specifically began their exodus from Liverpool, England. The P.E.F., as it was known, tried to maximize their investments and decided that handcarts, instead of the slower, more expensive ox carts, would be a more economical method of bringing converts from Winter Quarters to Salt Lake City.

Given ideal conditions, these carts (oversized wheelbarrows) could carry several hundred pounds of supplies and food for able-bodied pioneers. Nearly 4,000 converts relied on this arduous method of travel before 1860. And indeed, the method proved highly successful until the Willie and Martin expedition of 1856. This group of more than 1,000 pioneers had been outfitted with shoddy carts constructed of green wood that fell apart as the group sojourned through one of the worst blizzards in the history of the Rockies. Word came to Brigham Young of their travails, and though help was sent, the trail was marked with the graves of hundreds of the pioneers, and the dozens of babies who died of exposure that trip. Many of the survivors who arrived in Salt Lake City had a meeting with the surgeon's knife as their flesh, rotted away by frost bite and gangrene, had to be amputated. But the pioneers continued to use these handcarts continued until 1869, when the Transcontinental Railroad delivered its golden spike into the heart of Utah.

though they're probably on all day long, and in the shadow of the cliffs above the river they have a mellow, hypnotic pull to them. Their glow seems more intense and more enticing than the sun setting almost directly in front of us.

There aren't many bugs out this time of year, but the ones I have hit seem to be filled with their buggy gelatin, and they splay their guts across my windshield like brush strokes on a canvas. I feel, looking directly into the sun, as though I am inside of a painting in progress, being rendered by the light and by the heat and by the bugs and dust of the land.

Randy has come out of his slumber on occasion to tell me that my driving is affecting his nerves, but he doesn't offer anything else about his wife or his son. I can't imagine Randy with an autistic child when he's awake, but I notice that he cradles his arm across his lap, careful never to let it drop onto the floor, no matter how often I swerve or how many potholes I bang into. There's affection in those actions, my dad might say. He loves to scrutinize the smallest, most quotidian action and draw it into a psychological study. "People always betray themselves," he says. "They're usually doing it from the moment you meet them."

I have to pull over for gas, and the Omaha entry point to Nebraska seems as good a place as any. There is a twilight life to Omaha, the sparkle and blaze of the thousands of homes turning on all-at-once-like as the sun finally drops behind the flat and wide horizon. I take my sunglasses off and squinch my eyes, trying to muster some tears. They feel dry and I realize I can't really see very well in the dusk. This is the part of the day where dogs and wolves can see so much better than humans. Rhoda says it has to do with the elliptical way their eyes take in light that cuts the murk of the evening.

Randy does not budge as I pull off of I-80 and slowly squeal to a stop at the end of the ramp. He doesn't wake as I pull into the Flying J, whose greasy menu beckons truckers and families from a huge stadium-like jumbo-tron leering out over the highway. And he still hugs the cold glass of the window as I come to a stop in front of one of the dozens of orange pumps hunching like tombstones in the enormous cement lot. I slide the pump in and let the catch feed the tank while I go find the rest room. I see Randy beginning to stir, but standing up has made my needs more pressing than whatever coded toilet Randy would've demanded we find, someplace farther down the road.

I walk into the Flying J, past the racks and shelves of sugar-foods, foods the Snack-Machines would love, I think. I haven't thought of them in so long now, I suddenly realize that this trip is taking me farther from my life in Kalamazoo than just Utah. Rhoda, I think, Rhoda. I try to conjure her face, and I can see her in bits and pieces: in my mind I can see her hair, and her teeth, her strong, white teeth coming together, but I can't put a frame around the pieces; they're just pieces.

The Flying J bathroom is dingy, yet the walls above the urinal appear to be clean of graffiti. But as I lean into the urinal I can see that the names of cities and towns have been penned into the grout: *Buffalo, Cody, Sioux City.*

Someone comes in behind me. There are nearly a dozen urinals against one wall at the Flying J, and yet two men come in and take up stations on either side of me. Something is wrong with this, I think.

"You're from Michigan, huh?" the man on my right says. He wears a baseball cap with the number three stitched on the front. He needs a shave, but otherwise he looks well kept. He stares straight into the tiles above the urinals as if he were reading a map.

"Excuse me?" I say.

"He said you're from Michigan," the man on my left says.

"That right?" He's less groomed than his friend, and his ball cap barely contains a mass of greasy, dark hair. He's a tall man, maybe six foot four, and his beer gut hangs into the urinal like a cello into its case. He stares into the tile as well, and I start to think maybe I'm losing my mind.

"Michigan? Yeah," I say. "Kalamazoo. How'd you know?" I finish my business. The door opens behind me and the two men look as though they're considering this.

"Well, this here bathroom's a men's room, see," The Cello says. His voice vibrates off the wall in front of him, only this time I see his lips move and I know he's speaking. "For men."

"Well it looks like they've got an open door policy on assholes then, don't it." It's Randy, and he's holding the door open with his good hand. "Go on out and pay for the gas," he says to me.

"What are you going to do?" I ask.

"I think these gentlemen and I need to have a little talk. You go on out, pay for the gas, and wait for me in the car," he says.

"I thought we'd get something to eat," I say.

"Jesus fucking Christ!" Randy says, and he shoots me a look that's both furious and embarrassed. The two men move away from the urinals and stand facing Randy, and suddenly I feel as though I'm standing in the middle of a showdown.

"Looks like your friend wants to stay, Sam," The Cello says.

"He's not my friend," Randy says. "He's my ride."

I'm not sure I should leave, even with Randy's dismissal, but he motions with his head for me to go on out. I walk to the door. Outside I find a highway patrolman leaning against a wall and talking to an obese trucker. "There's some weird guys in the bathroom," I say.

"What do you mean?" he asks, and I can feel the eyes of the fat trucker on me.

"I don't know," I say. "I think they're trying to pick up men." I hate to play on homophobia, but I can tell it's a safe bet with this guy.

"Wait right here," he tells me. He hikes up his belt and speaks into a call box on his shoulder as he walks toward the bathroom door.

"Faggots?" the obese trucker says.

"Could be," I say.

The trucker is leaning against a couple of newspaper machines, and I see Chris Dudley's[72] face in the upper corner of the front page as the teaser. Dudley's a scrub, so I'm surprised, until I see that he's won the Walter Kennedy award. It still points to a Portland bias, I think. I wait and I wait for Randy to come out

---

[72] Dudley, the Blazer's back-up center, was named the 1995–96 J. Walter Kennedy Citizenship Award recipient. The award recognizes players, coaches, or trainers for outstanding community service and charitable works.

Dudley was diagnosed as a diabetic when he was a sophomore in high school. He donated $150,000 for construction projects at Gates Creek Camp, a rec facility for children dealing with diabetes. Dudley also held the first Chris Dudley Basketball Camp for kids with the disease.

Dudley also donated $300,000 to the Oregon chapter of the "I Have a Dream" foundation. Though to many NBA players these donations might not seem like much, a reserve center is not particularly well-paid by comparison, and so Dudley's gifts were indeed generous.

Utah's Thurl Bailey (1988–89) and Frank Layden (1983–84) were among the previous twenty winners of the prestigious award.

of the rest room and he never does. I know the patrolman is in there, and so I decide I'd better not intrude as he sorts things out.

I remember that The Cello called Randy "Sam," and I think back to Nauvoo and the old man in the Joseph Smith house. I know I need to just get out to Utah and get some distance between Randy and me. I decide to pay for the gas while I'm waiting, and the obese trucker gives me a look of disapproval, but then leaves himself and heads toward the cafeteria.

As I'm handing over my cash Randy comes up behind me and breathes into my ear: "You send that cop in there?"

"No," I say. "What cop?"

"Uh huh," Randy says. "Let's get going." He walks quickly out to the Bronco and gets back into the passenger side.

When I get into the truck he's already taken his arm off and is working at the hook with his good hand. Pulling on it, making adjustments. "What happened in there?" I say.

"Let's get going and get going right now," Randy says.

"Look, are you in some kind of trouble with those guys?"

"C'mon, Chief, hit the gas and get us back on the fucking interstate, will you?"

I don't care for Randy's tone, but I don't want a scene if the two yahoos from the bathroom come back outside. "Did the cop take care of those guys?"

"So you did send the fucking cop in there!" Randy says, putting his arm down for a moment and looking back toward the Flying J. "Fuck!"

"Calm down," I say. "I didn't know what was going on. You don't tell me anything and then all of a sudden I've got these two big guys asking me if I'm from Michigan, and I'm just standing there . . . "

"With your dick in your hand? Yeah, I know, I know. But that should be a familiar position for someone like you." Satisfied with his repair job, he reattaches his arm to his shoulder.

"Look, I don't know if I can drive two more days like this," I say. "I mean, no offense, but it seems like you're involved in some things that you don't want me to know about, and yet they keep coming around. It's very stressful."

"You might be right, Chief. Why don't you just stop on the other side of Omaha there. There's a Perkins we can catch some food at and we'll get this sorted out. I might be able to catch a break out there. I know a few folks out to Swedeburg who might put up with me until things cool down. Until I can catch another ride."

"I'm not throwing you out," I say.

"Oh, I know that all right, Chief," he says. "But you're probably right. You don't need to worry about all the other shit that follows me around, and I don't need to worry about you running to the cops every time something like this comes up."

"If I'd have known that you didn't want the cops . . . "

"I'm not blaming you, Chief. You didn't know, now, did you?"

"Look, I'm not throwing you out," I say. "I really don't have a problem with you, and I'd be happy to keep on going until we get to Utah. I just think we need a few ground rules, or something."

"You get me to the Perkins and I'll bet I can cut you loose from this," Randy says. I feel a terrible anxiety about all of this, and something keeps telling me I should be talking him out of leaving me. I don't like the idea of Randy out there by himself, though I'm sure he'll do just fine. Unlike me, and in spite of his arm, and his run-down, hang-dog looks, he's the kind of person who's just fine on his own.

XXIII. Unchained Again

The Perkins is just where Randy says it will be, impossible to see coming in from the east, but the call of its green light ready and waiting for all the western traffic. And perhaps best of all, it is mostly empty.

"Give us a booth," Randy says. "Honey."

We sit down and both of us unfold our ridiculously large menus. The slippery booth and the large menus make me feel like a child, making his own choices for the first time.

"Keep the coffee coming, Honey," Randy says after we order. He holds his cup with his pinkie finger crooked and extended. I drink cold water. "I'll make a couple of phone calls and things should take care of themselves," he says after the waitress leaves.

"How far is Swedeburg?" I say.

"It's not far now. You can probably drop me there, spend the night, and by tomorrow night, if you really pushed it across Wyoming, you could be back in Kaysville by midnight."

"I'm not kicking you out," I say.

"Nobody's kicking anybody anywhere," Randy says. "Some ideas just don't play through."

I run my finger around the edge of my water glass. There's only ice in there now, fused together in a white and opaque lump at the bottom of my glass. "What happened back there at the Flying J?"

"Why?" Randy says. I don't know why, but I know that something more happened than Randy just walking out of that bathroom.

"Did you do anything to those guys? To that cop?"

"Why'd you send that cop in there, Chief? What made you think there was some kind of problem I couldn't take care of?"

"I know you can take care of yourself. But I don't call two against one fair odds," I say.

"For who?" Randy says with a laugh, and tap-tap-taps his hook on the tabletop. "What'd you tell that cop, anyway?"

"I told him there were some gay guys in there trying to pick up," I say.

Randy laughs. A loud Ha-Ha-Haaaa that seems to echo out of the restaurant. So loud that I feel they're watching us from I-80, those slow-moving, yellow-eyed pack horses and their riders. "I'd have never thought it," he says. "You are an evil little one, aren't you?"

"Depends on who you ask, I guess," I say.

"Ho-mo-sex-you-alls, officer. Dirty toilet-lovin' ho-mo-sex-you-alls," Randy says in a phony southern accent. "That's great! That's fucking great!"

"So nothing happened?" I say.

Randy stops laughing and lays his menu flat against the table. "You wouldn't know what happened to my silver bullets, now would you?" Randy says. He's not angry, I don't think, and he stares back into his giant menu.

I can't answer for a moment. I want to lie, but I know I'm found out already. "They're in my shave kit," I say finally.

"You think I can get those back from you before we part company?"

"Are they real silver?" I say.

"They were a gift," Randy says. "As was the gun. And if it's all the same to you, I'd like to have them back. They're a matching set, and I'd hate to lose any of them." He said "lose," but I know I heard "use" and I'm not giving them back, I decide, until I'm pulling away from Swedeburg.

Our food comes and we pass dinner in silence. Randy doesn't seem mad at all about parting ways, about the cop, or about the bullets. In fact, he seems as if he can take me or leave me now that everything's been decided. Part of me is glad to be rid of him, his dark stories and the especially darker ones he's not telling me. But another part of me thought we'd become friends.

I think of Rhoda now, and I feel like I need her more than I ever did before. I wish I had brought her on the trip instead of Randy. But I'm glad, at least and in spite of everything, that I haven't come this far alone. There's still Dee Dee to consider, and she would've been weighing on me the whole way, I think, if I'd been alone. It would have been, I'm sure now, like driving across the country with a baby lying on the back seat.

It's evening here, and the day has settled down for Omaha. The sunset feels sudden and intensely black, as if the day stumbled to a close and fell onto the horizon. Back in Kalamazoo it will have been dark for hours, probably, and Rhoda will be finishing up her homework. Even if Mr. Mysterious is there, he will have to wait. I know this about Rhoda, and it's something I can respect and admire. She prioritizes and then she gets things done in the order of most importance.

What would I have done with Rhoda in Utah? Though I want her near me now, I feel that Omaha is as far as I could've possibly gone with Rhoda, as well. My family, I think, would be outwardly gracious, but quietly hostile to another Catholic girlfriend in the house. And what of that house? They're leaving that place now, even as I try to assemble the rooms in my mind. Maybe it's because of Zach, but I can only think of the rooms in terms of the furniture now. The floral couch and love seat and the knickknack cabinets from my mother's mother in the living room. The austere hand-turned oak furniture of my parents' bedroom. The stain of the enormous bedposts and the towering wardrobe a rich, dusky mahogany that seemed to resonate through the rest of the house.

I think of the enormous projection television set we bought for them several years ago, how it roosted like a giant monolithic temple-piece two feet in front of the wall so that it wouldn't overheat or scorch the ivy trim in the living room. It was Zach's idea, of course, and Rachel and Luke and I kicked in nearly four hundred dollars each.

I couldn't really afford to contribute to the television, but then I couldn't really afford not to. I'd just blown my mission calling, and the money I'd set aside for the calling was going to pay my way through college. Things had been very carefully budgeted for my windfall, as if attention to these details might recoup some of the humility and pain I'd been squandering. But Zach's Christmas fugue meant I had orchard flashbacks, meant I had to cut back on my already frugal dating with Jaimy.

Jaimy and I had fallen into familiarity even before my mission calling fell apart, and she knew I needed to save money and so she was understanding when I told her we'd have to watch a movie at home, or we'd have to play another game of Trivial Pursuit with my parents and Jessica. I was never a very good boyfriend to her, I think. Part of it was that I was new to dating, new to a real girlfriend, but part of it was I saw the way my father treated my mother as his waitress rather than his wife.

My parents made no secret of their dislike for Jaimy after I blew my mission calling, and when my father got four Jazz tickets from work one week it was assumed that Luke and Jessica would go rather than Jaimy and me. The tickets weren't that expensive then, Frank Layden[73] was still the coach and the Jazz were

---

[73] The Jazz suffered through several years of mismanagement tied, most felt, to the fact that the organization relied heavily on "non-basketball people" to make basketball decisions. While still in New Orleans, for example, the Jazz brokered a trade with the Los Angeles

struggling to stay above 500. But it was a big game against the Lakers, who were the top team in the league. Tickets were hard to come by, and these were fantastic tickets.

Jaimy and I watched the game at my parents' house, the lights turned down, the giant television pulsating its images into the darkened room. We had trouble finding something to talk about, and the game seemed to relieve some of the tension between us. And I remember Jaimy finding my family on the television, as the camera hovered around the Laker bench during a time-out. We sat there quietly, I remember, in the blue glow of the television, and looked on as my parents and Luke and Jessica sat like extras in their seats, waiting for the director to tell them to cheer or boo.

Lakers for Gail Goodrich, a fine player in his prime who might bring some veteran savvy and experience to a struggling team, but a player whose best years were clearly behind him. The Jazz gave up their first round pick that year and the Lakers selected Earvin "Magic" Johnson out of Michigan State. Even most non-basketball people understand what Magic Johnson meant to the NBA.

Frank Layden was brought into the Jazz organization as general manager in 1980. He was a little-known commodity at the time, and many around the league questioned the move. But one thing was clear, Layden, who had grown up in Brooklyn, New York, was emerging as a great motivator and evaluator of talent in the league. And as a caustic wit. On his tough high school days in Brooklyn, Layden said: "We had a lot of nicknames—Scarface, Blackie, Toothless. And those were just the cheerleaders."

Not long after he assumed his G.M. Duties, Layden brought in his son, Scott; a move criticized by many outside the front offices as nepotism, to which Layden simply responded: "I didn't hire Scott because he's my son. I hired him because I'm married to his mother."

The Jazz were becoming more and more like a family than a sports organization, only they were a family whose finances and internal troubles were very much in the public eye.

Layden was known as much for his girth and shabby dress as he was for his intense drive and outlandish sense of humor. This sense of humor helped him through several of the rough, early years with the Jazz. "We formed a booster club in Utah," Layden said. "But by the end of the season it had turned into a terrorist group." And his wit began to draw more and more national attention to the Jazz.

Layden eschewed personal fitness, and turned his physique into a sounding board for his self-effacing wit. When asked if he lifted weights, Layden responded: "I get a lot of practice just lifting myself out of bed everyday." Layden weighed nearly 300 pounds when he came to the Jazz, and didn't show any signs of letting his weight slow him down. "I have a great body," he once said. "It's just hidden under this one."

But he wasn't just known for using his wit to poke fun at his own shortcomings. Layden was even known to stand outside the old Salt Palace and try to lure passers-by into the games like a carnival barker. The Jazz were still having a difficult time filling the Salt Palace, the second smallest NBA venue at the time, two years after Layden's arrival. He claims that in the early years a fan phoned him in his office asking what time the game would start that night, to which Layden replied: "What time can you be here?" His wit made him a star, and soon he was as much in demand off the court as on. After speaking at Harvard Law School he said: "It was awful. Everybody knew I was the dumbest one in the room." But word was getting out about the Jazz and their peculiar ring-leader.

When the Jazz were to play the Lakers and Magic Johnson, clearly the class of the league at the time, the marquee at the Forum was said to read: Lakers vs. Jazz, Featuring Frank Layden. He spent his camera time mocking Lakers' coach Pat Riley by slicking back his hair and mugging for the fans at the Forum. 'He spends more on his haircut than I do on a sports jacket," Layden quipped. And later, comparing his coaching style to Riley's, "We're both Irish and we're both from New York and we're both good looking. The only difference is that he has his clothes tailored and I find mine." In the fourth quarter, as the Lakers were up by over twenty points against the lack-luster Jazz, Layden abruptly left the arena before the end. His explanation? "The restaurant in the hotel doesn't stay open after the game."

Layden, responding to the idea that the Jazz would always struggle because of their fragile financial situation (it was so bad at one time that the team had to pull out of the annual Pioneer Days parade when they couldn't afford the $1,500 cost of the float), said he had a "Catholic School Philosophy—that we'll win because we're the good guys . . . If we do everything the right way, and I work hard and the players are good people, we'll win our share." He insisted on finding good players and good people for his team. Good players like John Stockton and Karl Malone and Jeff Hornacek: "If you gave Michelangelo bad marble, he couldn't make a great statue. You've got to have good material. We're America's team," he claimed, "But nobody knows it."

And Layden finally turned the Jazz onto winning when Woody Paige, of *The Denver Post,* wrote in his column that the Nuggets would finish out their play-off series with the Jazz that very night because the Jazz didn't have the heart to come back. Layden sprung into action. He called on some friends at the University of Utah artificial heart research labs to bring their staff into the Jazz locker room. Layden held aloft an artificial heart like the one that maintained Barney Clark for nearly one year, and said: "Here's your fucking heart, right here, baby."

He passed the heart around the locker room, demanding that each player hold and examine it as he read from Paige's column.

And he said to his players: "Now go shove that heart up Denver's ass!" They beat Denver that night and again two nights later to begin their long-running play-off streak.

Layden would eventually win coach of the year honors, to which he responded: "After I got the call from New York, five minutes later my wife had me take the garbage out." After Layden retired as coach of the Jazz, passing the torch to Jerry Sloan in December of 1988, the Jazz retired a jersey with the number one to the rafters of the Delta Center in honor of Layden's hard work and determination in bringing the sagging Jazz organization to respectability. As his friend Pat Williams once said: "When the list of great coaches is finally read—I believe Frank Layden will be there listening."

XXIV. One Last Night Together

Randy makes his secret phone call after we've finished our dinners. When he comes back he's smiling and I think this will be it, then. A drive over to Swedeburg, the silver bullet exchange, and Randy getting smaller in the dark of my rearview mirror. "It's all good," he says as he approaches. "We're all good to go."

As we get into the Bronco Randy asks me, "You're spending the night out there, aren't you?"

"I think I really ought to get going a little farther down the road tonight. That's a long trek still across Nebraska and Wyoming tomorrow."

"It's sixteen hours, tops," Randy says. "You should stay. These are good people."

"I'm sure they are," I say. "But I don't know them." It goes far beyond me not wanting to impose. I really don't like the idea of staying the night in a strange house, in a strange town. Strange state, strange planet. Dad loved to beat home that old Ben Franklin maxim, *Neither a borrower nor a lender be . . .* "You never escape from debt," Dad would say. "It's part of our belief system. You'll always be indebted to Christ and Joseph Smith and to anyone whose charity you rely upon. Regardless the reason. It's better to go hungry for one night, than to take on the interest of a warm meal." But here was Randy, who seemed to be the most self-reliant person I'd ever met, knocking on doors and running up tabs all the way from New York to Moab.

He guides me out of the city and back into the country north west of Omaha. The hills are leveling off; though it is still quite beautiful, we are leaving the surprises of the Iowa hills for the open-handed expanse of Nebraska. Even in the pitch dark I can see the farms lay themselves out like sheets on a bed. The lights from the windows of the houses keep furious watch over the land and her nubile crops squirming their way out of the earth in the cool and breezy moonlight like millions of invisible teenagers escaping through bedroom windows and into the night.

Swedeburg is a small town with few options and we are past it and back into the country veil in minutes. Even the infantile glow of a city like Swedeburg is still enough that it occludes the stars from the sky for miles and miles. It's as if we are driving toward the stars, driving into the night sky the farther we get from Swedeburg and from Omaha and Chicago and Kalamazoo. The roads are straight and Randy is quiet except to occasionally tell me to turn or to slow so that he can get his bearings. He leans forward into the dash and it seems almost as though he is finding his way by the stars in the night sky. The incandescent green from the dash on his face is like the mythical sea phosphor I've read about, I think.

I feel a nervousness in the pit of my stomach as I know we are drawing nearer and nearer to the farm of Randy's friends. The idea of saying goodbye to Randy in the presence of these people I don't know makes me certain I'm doomed to slink away from the scene like the helping hand whose only purpose is to offer a blanket to someone rescued from an icy lake.

"You gonna remember how to get back out of here, Chief?" Randy says.

"Straight shot, pretty much," I say. Though, now that he mentions it, I'm not that confident I won't end up in South Dakota by morning.

"Yeah, well you make sure we get you some decent directions before you get back to the road. I been doing all this by touch, and there might be a quicker way back to I-80. This is the one right here," Randy says as we approach a gravel driveway and a farmhouse about two hundred yards off the road. The house is surrounded by trees, pines from the looks of things, nearly hidden

216

away in the night, but the fields extend for miles on both sides, and the moon shines down on them like on water. The glow from the moon captured by the million foundling sprigs creeping up at this late hour.

"How do you know these folks?" I say. "Or is that something I'm not supposed to ask?"

"You're gonna get smart-mouthed on me right now, Chief?" Randy says. "They're some friends of some friends I met in New York."

"Mormon?" I say.

"Noooooooooo!" Randy says with a laugh. "Good fucking people, though. Salt of the fucking earth[74]."

---

[74] Matthew 5:13. This worn-out cliche is taken from Jesus' Sermon on the Mount, which includes many of His most familiar teachings, including the Lord's Prayer. The book of Matthew also goes to great lengths to make clear that Mary was indeed a virgin when she was pregnant with Jesus. The term virgin, as used in the Old Testament, would have been translated into Greek by the author of the book. This is problematic in that the term 'virgin' refers to a young woman as well as to someone who has never had intercourse. There is also frequent mention of Jesus' siblings in the gospels, though these have often been explained away as cousins, or children from a previous, though not Biblically cited, marriage of Joseph's. Another eyebrow raising incident happens when the angel warns Joseph to take Mary away because Herod is planning to kill all the children. But since Joseph and Mary are not yet married, Joseph's plan is to simply "dismiss" her. The angel, obviously, helps Joseph come to his senses and he and Mary are married and leave for Egypt after Jesus is born to await another sign that they may return to Bethlehem. Matthew also somewhat problematically traces Jesus' lineage back to David through Joseph.

There is a tremendous gravel driveway next to the house that looks more like a salvage yard than a private residence. Cars of all makes and years are scattered through the yard and piled in pieces in the drive. In the fuzzy glow of the hanging lights I can see that most of the cars are rusted through. Inside the garage two cars are raised onto platforms, their wheels hanging loose like the limbs of two fat cats sleeping on tree branches.

"C'mon," Randy says as I slide to a stop near the outer edge of the salvage yard.

"Maybe I ought to just say goodbye right here," I say.

"Look, if you're going to leave out here in Nebraska, the least you can do is to come inside and say a quick hello to my friends. You don't have to stay if you don't want to, I understand that. But the least you can do is go on into that house over there and say hello." Randy grabs his bag from between the seats, adjusts his arm, opens the door and holds it open with his hook while he stares in at me. "Plus you owe me six silver bullets."

I turn the engine off and let it sputter down. "All right," I say. My kit is buried in my own bag and the bullets have rolled all over inside of it. It takes me a few minutes to retrieve them all, and when I do they are warm from being on the floor of the Bronco and they are covered in something shiny and slick, like hair shampoo. My entire kit is covered in it, and though it has no smell to it, it is very hard to wipe away from Randy's bullets. I hand them over to him one at a time.

"You lube these guys up?" he says, rolling them between his fingers before he slips them back into the chambers of his pistol. He holds the butt of the pistol between the two hooks of his plastic arm, and though I know he can't possibly fire the gun like that, I worry that he may drop it and discharge it accidentally. But Randy acts as though he has done this hundreds of times, and when I hand him the last bullet he even manages to flip the chamber closed with his plastic arm. He switches hands with the gun and aims it at one of the lights in the yard, studying it. The gun glints like a flashlight in his hand and he says: "Hope these greasy bullets still fly right, Chief."

"You don't really shoot that thing, do you?" I say, coming around to his side of the car and staring down his arm at the spot of light in his hand.

"What's the point in hanging onto something you can't ever use? I'm no collector and I'm no shootist, but when I accepted this gun I knew I'd have to use it someday or sell it off. I don't have any need for a gun of no real caliber." He pulls the gun back out of the air and takes one more solid look at it before he slips it back into his bag. "C'mon," he says. "They're good people and you're going to like them."

As we walk up to the house I see that it is in desperate need of a coat of paint, the gray boards only speckled with whorls and petals of white. The windows still have sheets of plastic stapled around them, casting a fish tank glow. The silhouette of a woman standing behind the screen door whose giant, gothic 'S' seems to hover over her hips, is watching us approach. She calls out: "Did you get lost? I didn't think you two would ever get here." Then she lets out a little gasp, "Oh my goodness, look at your arm! Oh my, oh my."

"It's been a while, that's all," Randy says, and he pulls open the door with his good hand and reaches inside to draw her out. She's a very pretty woman, in her late thirties, I'd say, maybe older against real light. Her dark hair is pulled back on her head, and I can see her clavicles poking out from her black tank top. She hugs Randy long and hard and looks me in the eye over his shoulder as she does.

"So who's your friend here?" she says, standing back and dividing her attention between me and Randy's plastic arm.

"This is Brian. And I want you guys to be extra nice to him because he's from Utah."

"Oh," she says, impressed. "And you'd be a Mormon, I'm guessing, Brian?" Her voice is older than she is, and she coos like an elementary school teacher.

"Yes," I say, and I reach my hand out. She takes my hand into her own and shakes it slowly. Her hand is rough and stony, but there is a smoothness and comfort to it, like an old leather coat. "I'm Suzanne," she tells me.

"Well you two come on in. Come right on in," Suzanne says, and she retreats into the house. The inside of the house is clean and orderly, though there is a smell of mold that greets me at the door. We pass a long hallway with dark, empty-feeling rooms on either side, and find our way toward a bright, large kitchen where two men in flannel shirts sit hunched at a table in front of the remains of some dessert and coffee. "This is Bailey," Suzanne says, pointing me toward the older of the two men. He has gigantic jug ears that peel away from his white skull like his head might take flight. Though that seems entirely impossible, given that his head seems connected directly to his body without the hindrance of a neck. His body is round and he moves slowly and clumsily to rise. His hand comes to meet me and I see that he is a hard-working man. The fingernails on his hand are brittle and yellow and several are deeply bruised at the tips. "How're you?" he says.

"And this is Randy," she says of the other man at the table. He is tall, I can tell, though he doesn't rise to greet me. His hands are bruised and a road map of grease and veins. He looks like a very powerful man, and all he is willing to give me is a nod of his head before he returns his attention to his coffee, which disappears in the grasp of his two mammoth hands.

"Randy's all around, I guess," I say. This is met with blank stares by Bailey and Suzanne.

"Yeah, well I'd like you boys to meet my friend, Brian," one-armed Randy says.

"Welcome, welcome," Bailey says and kicks a chair out from in front of the table. "Have a seat, why don't you?"

I sit quietly while Suzanne and Bailey ask Randy about our trip, about Kalamazoo and New York, and something in the circumlocutory way that Randy answers strikes me that I might know more about his recent history than his friends do.

"So how do you guys know Randy?" I say finally. Randy gives me a dirty look. Both Randys give me dirty looks, but Suzanne seems to come out of the confusion and tension and has the grace to answer.

"My second husband was, ahh, Randy's," and she lays her long, pretty arm across the back of his chair, "missionary companion for a while."

"Hinckley?" I say, and this is met with even stonier silence. Even Bailey seems uncomfortable, though to help him through the moment he seizes upon a piece of pie left in a tin at the far end of the table.

"Did you know Todd?" Suzanne says.

"No, just what Randy told me on the way out here."

"Just simple road talk," Randy says. "Brian here was all set to go on a mission himself, and we got to talking about my mission and my Mormon years. That's all," Randy says.

"Well, I got to get," Tall Randy says and pushes away from the table. He's taller than I'd even expected, at least six foot six. He nods to me. "Good seeing you," he says to Randy. "You come by tomorrow and we'll have a beer."

"I'd like that, Randy," my Randy says.

"Bailey. Suzanne, thanks for the pie." He puts his hand gently on Suzanne's shoulder and gives it a squeeze, and then he saunters down the long hall way and out the door.

"I should probably be going, too," I say. It seems like a good time to leave.

"You'll do no such thing," Suzanne says. She reminds me of someone, though I can't think of who. It's a good, comforting resonance, like an echo of an aunt I'd never known[75]. "You can stay in Connie's room tonight, and in the morning, if you've got to get going, you can do it then. You won't make up much time at this hour, I don't care what you think right now."

---

[75] Brian's mother's sister, Janice, was excommunicated by the Mormon church for refusing to denounce her polygamous relationship with a man she met and married in St. George, Utah. Brian's family excommunicated her as well, though Brian suspects his mother was more forgiving than she let on at the time.

The specter of polygamy still hangs over Utah and the L.D.S. Church—a specter whose roots are bound inextricably with the roots of the church. As a child Joseph Smith was at least partially influenced by the Swedish scientist/spiritualist Emanuel Swedenborg who believed in a spiritual marriage that was eternal. Smith's revelations were Swedenborg with a bit of Islam thrown in with a new twist, all his own, that tied polygamy directly to salvation.

The deep social and psychological inequities of polygamy would fill a library, but the fact of the matter is it continues to thrive in Utah and the West. Conservative estimates place the number of polygamists in the inter-mountain area at at least 30,000, though some say the number is actually many times that.

In spite of nearly being castrated by the angry mob who tarred and feathered Smith in Kirtland, Ohio (he was only saved when the doctor brought along to perform the "surgery" refused), and the deep hurt and jealousy it caused his first wife Emma, Smith continued to take new wives. Emma was eventually given the right of approval, but Smith didn't adhere to this rule very often, and indeed at least one time Emma "approved" a pair of sisters (Eliza and Emily Partridge) who were already secretly married to Joseph.

Fawn Brodie, daughter of church president David O. McKay, who was eventually excommunicated from the church in 1946 for her inflammatory biography of Joseph Smith, estimated the final tally for Smith at 48 wives. The majority of these wives were very young teenagers. And indeed it was legal until the last year of the twentieth century to marry at fourteen years of age in Utah (the legal age was then raised to sixteen, or fifteen with parental permission). Some of Smith's wives were involved in polyandrous relationships, further complicating an already complex genealogy.

Even Brigham Young was initially repulsed by the idea of Smith's secret commandment of polygamy, saying it left him lusting only for the grave, envious of every corpse at every funeral he saw. But he obviously overcame these objections, marrying twenty wives and fathering over 50 children. Mark Twain, again in *Roughing It,* wrote, "The man that marries one of them has done an act of Christian charity which entitles him to the kindly applause of mankind, not their harsh censure." While Twain mocked the homely brides of Young, he simultaneously attacked Brigham Young as the only law in the land, a self-supreme monarch defying our president.

And Twain wasn't alone. The Edmunds-Tucker Act of 1887 was aimed solely at eliminating polygamy, even encouraging and authorizing hunts for those guilty of the crime. The law provided for seizure of church properties and put tremendous pressure on the church to abandon its polygamous stance.

Ironically, Utah (still a territory at this time) was the first governing body in the nation to give women the vote (1870). And outspoken pro-polygamists, like Martha Hughes Cannon, began publishing and speaking out. Hughes Cannon graduated with a medical degree from the University of Michigan, on the other side of the state from Brian, and went on to defeat her Republican husband for a seat on the first state senate. The church continued to outwardly

"Connie?" I said.

"My daughter," Suzanne laughed. "You know the old joke: traveling salesman arrives at a farmhouse late at night, and the farmer says *You can spend the night, but you've got to sleep with one of my daughters . . .*" She and Randy and Bailey think this is absolutely hysterical.

"How old is Connie, now?" Randy says.

"Sixteen and heck on wheels," Suzanne tells him. "She's out to Omaha tonight with her weird friends and won't be back until really late. I just did the sheets on her bed, and you can take that room."

"I don't want to take anybody's bed," I protest. "Maybe I should just head on out. I can find a motel somewhere and be that much closer tomorrow."

Suzanne won't take no for an answer, and I can tell I'm getting her ire up, that she's used to getting what she wants from men, I think. She is very pretty, in fact, in the light of the kitchen, and I am haunted by the idea that she reminds me of someone, but I can't quite place who it might be.

"Sixteen," Randy says again. "I don't know, Suzanne. This one here's still a little wet behind the ears, himself. Maybe you want to worry about him slipping Connie the Latter Day Salami."

"That's it," Suzanne says, moving to the cupboard and bringing out a dented old red and yellow tobacco tin. "It's been a

oppose polygamy, but secretly persisted in granting polygamous marriages temple sealings into the twentieth century. It's easy to see, given the harsh and immediate government reaction against polygamy in the late 1800s, why the principle community for polygamy still existing in the United States seems directly tied to anti-government fundamentalists.

while, but you still know the house rules." She sticks the tin out, under Randy's nose. Her arms are thin and muscular.

"How is Latter Day Salami a swear word?"

My mother had the same rule, and Jaimy's mother had the same rule, and Jaimy eventually tried to have the same rule with me, though neither of us swore enough to change a five. "Brian?" Suzanne says. "Is that a curse?"

"Against Connie, maybe," I say. "I dunno."

"Well fuck it, then," Randy says, drawing his wallet out of his back pocket. "Here's a twenty. Run me a tab."

"Speaking of running a tab," Bailey says. "Anybody want to go down to Wagon Wheel?"

"We've got beer here," Suzanne says, clipping the twenty from Randy's fingers and putting it in the tin. "Smart ass," she says. "I'm putting that one on your tab, too. Do you want a beer, Brian?"

"Yeah," I say. "I think I would." I guess I'm staying then, I think. "You sure Connie's not going to be upset? I know I wouldn't be happy about somebody crashed out in my bed when I was her age."

"Connie's not the kind of girl to mind sharing her bed," Suzanne says, plucking beers from the bottom shelf of the refrigerator.

"I can't believe that girl's sixteen years old," Randy says.

"Just so long as your buddy don't try that excuse in the morning," Bailey says, and he cracks his beer open. Everybody laughs.

XXV. Moved by the Spirit

We have a beer together. The beer is Coors, a beer I haven't had in ages. The Coors company had some kind of covert operation to fund the Contras when I was in college, and the word around campus was that if you drank Coors you were a Reaganite. It fell out of favor. They even stopped carrying it at the 7-11 between 1st and 2nd street.

And then we have another, each time drinking them out of the cans. When we get to our third beer, Suzanne asks Bailey to get another case out of the basement. He totters down the stairs like he's tottered down the stairs of her basement a thousand times. He looks like a young child when he walks, and like a young child he defies the seeming certainty that he will fall down. Even more amazing is the relative ease with which he carries the case of beer up the stairs. He has superhuman farmer strength, I think. I've seen it before with some of Jaimy's relatives.

"I'm just going to get me a roadie," Bailey says, wiping his brow with a red handkerchief from his back pocket. "Lucy will have my ass if I stay around here any longer."

"You bring Lucy by in the morning," Randy says.

"She'll sure be glad to see you standing here," Bailey says. "Welcome to Nebraska," he says, patting me on the shoulder.

"Not too early," Suzanne says and gives Randy a flirtatious smile.

"Now, now, you two. You've got a young, impressionable boy here . . ." Bailey waits for Randy and Suzanne to laugh before he totters his way down the long, dark hallway.

Randy pulls his shirt off and carefully slides it over his plastic arm, letting it fall to the floor. I had nearly forgotten about his arm, but now it is as if its absence was invited back into the room. I feel embarrassed for him, though I don't approve of whatever's going on between him and Suzanne. Part of me, I think, may be jealous.

"Oh, your poor arm," Suzanne says, moving over to Randy and taking his plastic arm in her strong, rough hands. She handles it as though it were alive but dying. She strokes it, and bends it at the elbow joints, making the hooks snap open and closed again.

"You know, Suzanne," Randy says. "The great thing here is that my ghost hand is free to motor all over your body right now. And nobody's the wiser." He winks at me before looking back at Suzanne.

"It's getting late," she says suddenly, drawing back from Randy. "I think I'm going to get ready for bed." She runs her fingers through Randy's hair, and I know this is when I should've been gone. "You'll show him Connie's room?"

"Yeah," Randy says, giving her hand a squeeze with his good hand. "Good night."

"It was nice to meet you, Brian. And I'll leave a note for Connie so she doesn't wake you when she comes home."

"It's really no problem for me to grab a motel," I say.

Suzanne looks plainly irritated at this. "You will not," she says, emphatically before walking away down the long, dark hall.

"C'mon outside with me," Randy says, and he reaches into the refrigerator for two more beers before going out a door at the back of the kitchen.

It's nice outside. A bit chilly, but not cold. The moon is high in the sky by this time, and the blue clouds are moving quickly across its face. The stars are mostly gone, and the horizon melds the ground and sky into a deep, dark void. The light from the house stumbles into the field in front of us, and I can see a thousand green furrows extending into that void.

"Suzanne and I have an agreement," Randy says. "I know what you're thinking." He nods toward the side of the house where I can see Suzanne through a thin drape in her bedroom. She seems to be straightening the room. "She's a wonderful woman," Randy says. "And I have no idea what's waiting for me out in Utah. In some ways, Suzanne and Connie are more like my wife and kid than my own wife and kid. There's no better explanation than that, and there's no better reason."

"She's really great. But you don't have to . . ." Suzanne takes one last survey of the room and then unbuttons her jeans and takes them off. I'm embarrassed by this, by her blue, floral underwear, but Randy just stares toward the window like this is something we should be seeing to help him make his point.

"I know I don't," Randy says. "But maybe part of me feels bad about it and wants to tell you that." Suzanne turns off the bedroom light and I am relieved that there's no more for us to see. She's very beautiful, and through the gauze of her window, almost mystic. But she also haunts me enough that I don't feel any sexual attraction to her.

I automatically want to say, "You want to talk about it then?" But I think the only thing that comes out of my mouth is, "Hmm."

"Yeah. I suppose . . ." Randy says. "I'm done with that part of it. I just wanted you to know that there's no hard feelings about the bullets and about those goons back there a ways."

"No, I'm the one who should feel bad. You know I'm not kicking you out. If you want, we can leave tomorrow. You can still come along."

"I don't think that'd be right. I wasn't planning on stopping over here, because I knew this might happen. Fuck!" he says, and he takes a long drink out of his beer can.

"Well, I'll leave the option open. How's that?"

"That's good, but I think I'm going to be out here a little longer. It might be a good thing, anyway, for me not to be such a straight shot into Moab now that a little dust has been kicked up." Randy hands me his beer can and unzips his pants. He urinates in loud, splattery bursts into the dirt of the yard.

"I'll leave the option open and you can tell me in the morning. But I think I'm going to try to get going pretty early and push into Kaysville by midnight."

"Ah, Sun-flower!" Randy says, cutting golden arcs in the air with his piss. "Weary of time, who countest the steps of the Sun; Seeking after that sweet golden clime, Where the traveler's journey is done . . ."

"I don't know that one," I say.

"Guess you are human, then. Thought I was going to have to take you apart to find out."

"Blake?" I say, thinking it sounds like something from Blake.

"Oh you motherfucker," Randy says, finishing and zipping his pants. He snatches his beer from my hand and finishes it in one shot. "I'll catch you up before you leave, or I'll cut you open and see what makes you tick."

"Our meddling intellect misshapes the beauteous forms of things—We murder to dissect."

"All right, now you're just creeping me out," Randy says. He throws his empty can as hard as he can out toward the field, but it drops about ten feet short, and when he comes back to his pitcher's stance, his arm comes loose and dangles off his shoulder. "Fuck!" Randy says. "That ought to round out that twenty-spot, huh?" The sound of his voice echoes across the fields, but doesn't come back. If I didn't know any better, I'd think he was drunk already. "Don't worry, Quote-tidian. I'm going to fucking call you Quote-tidian, I think," he says, picking up his arm and simply cradling it against his stomach like a watermelon. "I don't need any more ghosts haunting me. I could plant a ghost in every foot of this fucking field out here," he says, swinging his plastic arm out wildly. "And have a bumper crop of bad memories for a thousand years."

"I'm sorry," I say.

"Guess I better go drop another coin in the fucking tin, huh?" He turns back toward the house, holding his arm back against his body now.

"Which one is Connie's room?" I say.

"That one," Randy says, pointing at the window on the other side of the house from where we watched Suzanne. And he leaves me with my beer.

I think of Randy's image, of a field of ghosts, and I wonder why it is that I couldn't even plant a garden. Sure, I think, Dee Dee might take a few extra feet, and I don't mean that meanly, I think, I don't mean that as disrespectful. That was Dee Dee. She was fat, and there's nothing wrong with me thinking of her as fat. Randy turns the light on in Suzanne's room and I can see him talking to her. He's found another beer on the way to the bedroom, and he sets it carefully on the dresser. I can tell that Suzanne chastises him about it because he very hurriedly moves it again. His arm is mostly unslung already, and I can see him working his mouth as he finishes the job. When he is free of the arm he holds it up and inspects it before he lays it on the dresser next to his beer.

I shouldn't watch, I think. But I'm not really seeing anything, not really hearing anything. Randy keeps talking, taking sips of his beer. He points to his arm, and then raises his shoulders to show he doesn't understand something. The wing rises up too, showing even less understanding, I think. Then he peels his shirt off, and his pants, and his underwear. I can see him now, naked to his knees, looking down at the place I imagine Suzanne must be.

Then he looks out the window. At first I'm scared, because he I think he might see me, but I know it's too dark out here for him to see anything. He stares for a moment, then shuts the door and turns out the light.

I wonder what it is like for Suzanne. This is something they've done before, obviously, but does she believe in the phantom arm and hand, as well? I have to urinate, and like Randy I just let it go. Only I face the window, and I lower my pants even farther than I need to so that I am completely exposed. I know that with the lights turned down there is a better chance that they can see me. If they just stop what they're doing and look out their window, there's a chance they might actually see me out here, against the field of ghosts. My own ghosts, though, are nothing more than weeds in this place.

XXVI. The Night Visitor

The house is quiet when I come back in, and I feel like a burglar, a prowler. In the hallway I linger, hoping to hear something from Randy and Suzanne, some rustling of sheets, some deep breathing, that will let me know I'm not alone in this house.

Connie's room seems overly Spartan to be the room of a teenage girl. I expected *Tigerbeat* photos on the walls, unicorns or cupids or some other nonsense. Instead I feel as though I've come to a monk's cell, complete with a colossal ginger-colored cross hanging over the headboard.

There is nothing but the moon and its fractured twin on the field out the window, the swarthy blue night sky, and the shadowy pines hovering over the house. My breath fogs at the window glass, and I trace my name in the wet, then frost it over with my breath again.

The cross above Connie's bed casts a dark shadow sideways onto the wall from the pale moonlight. When I lie down, there are the peaked phantoms of the pine shadows swaying across the ceiling of Connie's bedroom. When I close my eyes, they are still there.

The hems of Connie's sheets are hand embroidered with small flowers, roses, I think. As soon as my head hits her pillow, I know that I'm in a girl's bed. The bouquet of her hair still remains in the fabric of her pillow and her sheets. She smells, I think, a little like Rhoda, a little like the farm, a little like rose petals. Outside, a coyote howls and is answered. The coyote sounds close to the window, and so I go to look back outside, at the farm. I've never seen a coyote, and part of me, I think, worries they are like wolves circling a cottage.

I stare at the ceiling this way, with my eyes closed and open, for what seems like hours, until I hear the creak of floorboards in the room, and I slowly pull myself upright in the bed. A tall, thin figure, arms hunched and shoulders stooped, moves across the room to the bureau. She has a mass of hair blackened into shadow, and hiding her face, but her skin is ashen in the wan light of the room.

She carefully slides a drawer open in the bureau, turning her dark head to look at me with every squeak and whine of the wood. Her long, slim arms slide into the drawer and pull out some white material. She begins to work the drawer slowly closed again. She can't see me, I think. I'm invisible to her.

The phantom unbuttons her pants, still facing me, and they drop to the floor in a thump. Her legs are so white and thin. So frail and long. She slides her hands up into her shirt and fumbles with her bra underneath, then turns her back to me and pulls the shirt over her head. Her back is long and slender and as white as the moon, and then it is gone under a nightgown. She drops the shirt to the floor and pauses at the foot of my bed. I still can't make out her face, but I know it is her.

"Jaimy?" I whisper.

She comes around to the side of the bed. Her face is near me now, but it is impossible to see with that hair hanging over it. She leans closer, "Who are you?" she whispers. Her breath is sweet with alcohol and smoke, and like smoke it hangs in the air near my face.

"Jaimy?" I whisper again, only I know better as soon as I hear the name escape from my mouth.

"Go to sleep," she says. "Just go to sleep, now." Her voice is soothing and I lie back into the pillow and feel the pull of a dream come over me.

I am awakened by a terrible dream. The sun has come into the room, and I'm not sure where I am for a moment. The bed smells familiar, and the light of the room is familiar, like the morning I left Rhoda.

I sit at the side of the bed and pull my pants on. The house is quiet, and I see a clock near the bed whose bright, red numbers read 6:30 exactly. I find the hallway and I'm hungry, though I don't know how much I should make myself at home. I'm hoping no one is awake yet. My dream still has its claws in me.

I walk by the living room, a dark and empty room the night before, and there is Connie, asleep on the couch, curled with her back to me in her nightgown. The bottoms of her pink feet are cupped toward me, and I think she does look like I remember Jaimy looking. There is a phone in the kitchen and I decide I have to call Rhoda. It's early for her, or anyone, really, but I have to tell her about my dream.

She answers the phone with some alarm. "Hello?"

"Rhoda?" I say.

"Brian?"

"Are you busy," I say. I mean, is she alone.

"Busy sleeping," she says, and her voice calms and drifts into a sleepy mumble. "Where are you?"

"Nebraska-somewhere," I say. "I'm going to leave here in a bit and I should be there late tonight."

"How's it going with that guy?" she says, and I can tell she's fading.

"I had a terrible dream," I say. "I just wanted to hear your voice."

"What kind of dream?" she says, though I know she's barely listening.

"I dreamed we were walking along a beach at the bottom of a sea cliff together, somewhere," I say. "We were holding hands and looking out at the ocean."

"Mmmm, that sounds nice," she says.

"Only we stepped on a land mine, or something like that," I say. "And it exploded and we both went flying."

"That's terrible."

"You were okay, but you were blown out into the ocean and had to swim back to shore."

"Where were you?" she says.

"I got blown up onto the cliffs, and my guts, my guts," I say. "Were blown out. They were hanging out of my body and I was dying."

"That's terrible," she says.

"And when you got back to the shore you couldn't get back up the cliffs to see me before I died," I say. "And so I had to sling my intestines down, over the side of the cliff, and you had to tie them around your waist. No, first you had to rub sand all over them so they wouldn't be so slippery, then you had to tie them to your waist, and I had to pull you up the side of the cliff."

"That's really sweet," she says.

"I feel exhausted," I say. "I must have slept clenched into a little ball." I hear footsteps behind me.

"You ready for some breakfast?" Suzanne says.

"Who's that?" Rhoda says.

"That's Suzanne, Randy's friend." I say, and I nod at her.

"Connie keep you up last night, did she?" Suzanne says.

"No," I say.

"Who's Connie?" Rhoda asks.

"Suzanne's daughter. She's just a kid. Don't worry. I had to sleep in her bed last night."

"What's going on?" Rhoda demands.

"Morning!" Randy says as he comes into the kitchen too. His shirt is off and he is just wearing a baggy pair of boxers. He comes up behind Suzanne who is working some eggs on the stove and hugs her with his arm and his wing.

"Will you put some clothes on, please," Suzanne says.

"Who's she talking to?" Rhoda asks.

"To Randy," I say. "Listen. I'd better go. Don't worry about anything. I didn't mean to wake you up. I didn't mean to wake anybody up. I'll call you from the road today, okay?"

"Do what you want," Rhoda says and hangs up the phone. I say her name anyway. Rhoda.

"Do you know whose truck that is out there?" Connie says. She's come into the kitchen too, pulling a robe around herself.

"Oh, Jesus," Randy says, and he tries to cover his boxers with his hand. His ghost hand, I can tell, tries to cover, as well. He backs out of the kitchen, and it's the first time I've seen him embarrassed about anything.

"Go get some clothes on!" Suzanne says, turning her attention to the toast. The breakfast smells terrific. "Did you meet Brian?"

"No," Connie says, dropping down into a chair at the kitchen table.

"Hi," I say. "Do you mean the Bronco out there? That's mine."

"No," Connie says. "There was a rig parked out on the road about a hundred yards from the drive. Had its parking lights on."

"I don't know, honey," Suzanne says. "Hey!" She calls into the other room, "Was there a truck out there when you two came in last night?"

"I don't think so," Randy says, coming back into the room in a pair of jeans, but still without a shirt.

"Did you sleep okay," Suzanne says to me, and she hands me a plate heaped with eggs and toast.

"Terrific," I say. "Listen," turning to Connie who seems as

if she can barely tolerate the lot of us, "thanks for the bed. I wasn't really planning on staying last night, but your mom and Randy talked me into it."

"Randy was here?" she says.

"Right here," Randy says, and nods at her.

"Oh," Connie says. "Well, that's kind of par for the course around this place. You don't get into bed before nine o'clock and you run the risk that someone else might be sleeping there in your place." She gives Randy a sour look. "I'm going to take a shower before all the hot water is gone."

"A rig, huh?" Randy says after her.

"It was there when I came home last night. About three o'clock, I guess," Connie says, and she is gone.

"Well, we'd better go see about that," Randy says. "We'd better see."

XXVII. A Long, Hard Sleep

After breakfast and a shower I think it's time to say my goodbyes. In spite of my dreams, I feel well rested. I feel better, I think, than I would if I'd spent the night in a motel out on the highway. Suzanne gives me a hug. Randy walks me out to the front step and leans against the screen door.

"Randy," I say. "There's still a chance. I'm not kicking you out."

"I couldn't go right now if I had to," he says. "And I'm pretty fucking sure there might be some more things I need to take care of before I venture back into Moab."

"Suzanne?" I say.

"Among others," he says. He looks out over my shoulder toward the road, studying something. "You know what, though. Would you mind just giving me one more ride. There's a Shop-Quik about five miles down the road. I'd like to get some beers and some smokes for Suzanne."

"Oh yeah," I say. "Let me get the beers. It's the least I can do. In fact, why don't you just kick back here, and let me go and get the beers and the smokes. I've never bought cigarettes before, so this will be my treat."

"No, you just wait here a minute and I'm going to put on a shirt," Randy says, still looking past me and out toward the road. "I'll be right back."

Randy comes back wearing a jean jacket over a dirty white T-shirt. His arm is on, and he keeps tucking and retucking his shirt tails beneath the jacket all the way to the car. "Well," I say. "You think about coming along with me to Utah. Maybe you could spend the night at my folks' house, if they haven't taken all the furniture up to Park City yet." The idea of Randy meeting my parents strikes me as particularly funny.

"Hmm," Randy says. I can tell he's not listening to me.

We pull out onto the road, and I can see the truck that Connie was talking about. Randy leans forward, into the dash, trying to get a better look. "Can you make out the name on the door up there?"

The truck is on my side. It looks strange, I think, a rig sitting out here without any trailer. It's painted pale blue and white, with red script letters on the door. "It's catching too much glare from the sun," I say, and I slow down as we pass it. I can see the trucker up inside looking back down at me from behind reflective sun glasses. He's a fat-faced man with wisps of greasy hair escaping from beneath his baseball cap. "Hey," I say suddenly. "I know that guy! That's The Cello from the Flying J."

"Get the fuck out of here!" Randy says.

"No, really. I think it's him," I say.

"NO, I MEAN GET THE FUCK OUT OF HERE!" Randy says, and he tries to reach his leg around to the gas pedal on the floor. Our feet get tangled up, and in that moment I can hear the big rig rumble on, can hear the belch of its exhaust, and the wheels begin to spin and spray gravel all over the road and against my car.

"That mother . . ." I say, pissed off that my car is getting sand-blasted from the rig.

"JUST FUCKING GO!" Randy says, and he reaches around behind him and brings out his silver gun.

"What's going on, Randy?" I say. My foot finds the gas, and we slide sideways as we move forward on the gravel road. I can see the rig in the rearview furiously attempting a Y-turn. We start to pull away from the rig, but it comes out of the Y with incredible acceleration, as if it's just come through the wings of a slingshot.

"Can this go any faster?" Randy says. He's watching the rig gain on us in the outboard mirror.

"I've got it floored!" I say. The rig is closing and picking up speed as it does so. There's nothing out on this road. No place to turn except into the fields.

"Look, pop it into four-by and get us off the road. They can't follow us into the fields," Randy says.

"Are you sure?" The rig is nearly on us, and I don't wait for an answer. I pop the turn signal out of habit and slow down so that I can pull into the irrigation ditch by the road without flipping the car over. The rig keeps coming, and I think they're going to speed by us, but I keep turning, slightly, into the ditch; our speed, I think, might flip us over, but I pull it in there, a little at a time, still going too fast, and the rig is almost to us, and then I feel the Bronco take the hit from the rig and I know all four wheels have left the earth and we are thrown sideways. I can see the field head-on, and then the wheels catch again, and the rig smashes into us again, and we go spinning sideways through the ditch. I shut my eyes, and I feel at least three full revolutions and I'm screaming and something, the roof? Comes down hard onto my head. When I open my eyes, we're upside down, and I can see Randy's silver gun lying in the dirt right in front of me. Randy's hand reaches out to snatch it away. "Randy?" I say, and the pain starts to come. My head is cracked open, I can feel the light escaping, and I feel myself choking, and my arm, my arm won't move. I can hear Randy moving around. He's cursing, and then he thumps out of his seat and I can see his plastic arm, the silver hooks, right near my face. "Randy," I say. I hear the rig coming back, and I try to find my seat belt, but I can't feel my arm, and the belt is pinching my throat, making it hard to breathe, and there's a stinging in my eyes— blood—and I'm upside down and my arm is coming back to me now. There's the belch of the rig. There's the silver button for the belt release. There's the sound of a gun being fired and Randy's voice, cursing and proclaiming. I find the button, and I feel the weight of my body coming down, spilling down, like water over a cliff.

XXVIII Several Different Kinds of Comas⁷⁶

76 There are several different kinds of comas. The one constant is that there really is no treatment. The brain turns itself off so that the body can better focus its energies on healing the victim. An old remedy for such unconsciousness, whether or not there is any basis for the effectiveness of such treatments, is for someone close to the victim to hold their hand or speak to them or otherwise kindle memories of warmth and safety to try to lure the brain back into consciousness.

Randy and Bailey take Brian to Bailey's house to wait for the doctor to arrive. And Connie is enlisted to treat Brian's wounds and keep watch over him while Randy and Bailey use Suzanne's tractor to pull the rig and Brian's Bronco off the road. Connie asks that Randy retrieve some of Brian's cassettes from the Bronco for her, and a television is put into the room with Brian so that he can "hear" the game. But that very night, the Jazz lose another game at Portland, evening the series at two games apiece, and Connie turns the television off during a break in the fourth quarter action.

The Jazz have a new concern with the Trailblazers. Portland coach P.J. Carlesimo started veteran guard Aaron McKie in the first game, replaced him in game two, and went back to him in the Blazers' overtime victory over the Jazz. While McKie was held scoreless through the first two games, and gave up 48 points to Jeff Hornacek[1] over that stretch, he finished with 16 points in the Blazers' victory, holding Hornacek to nine points on 4-13 shooting.

Rod Strickland (who demanded a trade as soon as the season ended) scored 27 and Arvydas Sabonis, playing younger and younger as the playoffs progress, added 25 points. Hornacek roared back for 30 points, but Malone continued to struggle, scoring 15 points on 4-16 shooting. "Portland waxed our butts from the start," Coach Jerry Sloan said. "We just couldn't get back into the game. Portland was

243

just too tough for us. We didn't stand up to them. We let them dictate what we did, and you aren't going to shoot well when that happens. We couldn't get any life. We didn't come in with the attitude that we had to do anything special here . . ."

Malone admitted he was frustrated by some non-calls when he drove into the lane. After he was given a technical foul by referee Joe Forte, Malone moved his game from the interior to the perimeter, missing twelve of his last thirteen shots. "I wasn't as aggressive as I've been in the past," Malone said. "I'm a professional athlete. I'm supposed to adjust to things like officiating."

And so it came down to a do-or-die game five back at the Delta Center on May 5. *The Salt Lake Tribune* began questioning whether or not the Stockton-Malone era was coming to an end in Utah, and *USA Today* began to throw around words like "Fade" and "Choke." The Jazz had a short history of failure in the first round of the playoffs: in 1992 John Stockton nearly had his eye knocked out in a playoff loss against these same Trailblazers, in 1993 they blew a 2-1 lead over the Seattle Supersonics, and in 1994 Malone struggled to play with the flu, but the Jazz were sent home by the Houston Rockets. The following year the Jazz won a club record 60 games and faced a sixth seeded Houston Rockets team. The Jazz blew a lead in the final five minutes, and the Rockets went on to become the first team to win an NBA championship without the benefit of home court in any round of the playoffs.

Arvydas Sabonis, whose wife Ingrida gave birth to their third child, a son, the Saturday before game five, continues to be a problem for the Jazz. The Jazz tried throwing 290 pound Felton Spencer, 280 pound Greg Ostertag, and 265 pound Antoine Carr at him in the lane, but the 7'3" Lithuanian has been undaunted. The play of Sabonis has helped the Trailblazers take a commanding lead in rebounding in the first four games.

But game five would prove to be a different story on the boards.

Utah outrebounded Portland 54-33 and won in decisive fashion: 102-64. Portland's 24 first half points and 64 total points were both all-time league playoff lows. Chris Dudley surmised the Jazz actually won the series in the regular season when they won home court advantage for round one. "They are a different team in this building," he said. "As different at home as any team in the league."

One possible downside? Stockton limped off the court in the final minute of the second quarter. He had pulled a hamstring and, during intermission, it was unclear whether or not he would be able to play in the second half. Malone stated, after the game: "If Stock can play, he will play. You won't see him make any excuses. You media guys have been making more excuses for him than he's made in this series."

Even with a Jazz victory, however, they are still slow to warm the country, and the people at NBC, to their side. Because the Jazz are seen as a small market team, NBC hasn't aired a single Jazz game all season long. And even when they were the featured team on Sunday the network devoted their pre-game "NBA Showtime" program to Michael Jordan and the Chicago Bulls. Karl Malone has been upset all season long at NBC for not showcasing the Jazz and has threatened to refuse interviews with the network and its affiliates, a disaster for a network already concerned about the relative low profile of their feature. NBC has clearly profited from the interest generated by the league's marquee superstars. Every post and pre-game interview helps shape the soap opera that each series generates. It helps the studios teach its viewers how to watch the games, and if the superstar isn't talking it makes it that much more difficult for the league to attach significance and purpose to each series.

The Unibomber is in the news, and the Olympic torch leaves Los Angeles on its way to Atlanta, GA, site of another bombing. Utah has had its own trouble with bombings, including at least one tied to Ted Kaczynski, in the past. In the mid eighties, former med student Mark

Hofmann claimed to have uncovered a letter from Joseph Smith in which Smith confessed that he received his divine prophesies and revelations from a giant white salamander instead of the angel Moroni.

In 1984 the church had a sticky situation on its hands when a biography of Emma Smith appeared, written by Valeen Tippetts Avery and Linda King Newell. It presented a mostly sympathetic portrait of Smith and seemed critical of her husband's chicanery and duplicity concerning polygamy. The church had long held a dim view of Emma, who eventually rifted with Brigham Young and lent her support to the R.L.D.S. The church's censure of Avery and Newell came at a time when private collectors had created a boom in historical church documents that engaged these disagreements.

And Mark Hofmann, a returned missionary, husband and father, was a master at producing (rather than procuring) these documents. The church, trying to avoid the embarrassment of a white salamander revelation, began buying documents from Hofmann. The church paid an estimated $30,000 for the Lucy Mack Smith letter, and later paid $40,000 through collector Steve Christiensen for the white salamander letter. They would eventually purchase at least 48 documents from Hofmann directly or indirectly through collectors.

When Hofmann's forgeries began to catch up with him he killed Christiensen and one other innocent victim with a car bomb outside the Desert Gym at the top of Main Street in Salt Lake. Hofmann apparently saw these murders as a potential decoy, but when he ended up injuring himself with a pipe bomb he was finally arrested and is currently at the Point of the Mountain serving life without parole.

And as the federal government began tearing apart Kaczynski's cabin in Montana searching for clues to tie him to the bombing in Salt Lake and the others through out the United States, the Jazz had only one day's rest before their next test against the San Antonio Spurs and their all-star center David Robinson. Robinson, nicknamed "The

Admiral" for his time in the Naval Academy, is another one of "the good guys" as Frank Layden would have it. The Jazz centers know they will have their problems trying to wear down Robinson, and this time they won't have the benefit of home court. On top of this, San Antonio won three of four games against the Jazz during the regular season. *USA Today*'s David DuPree made a pointed attack against the Jazz' chances, saying that they are simply "awful" away from the Delta Center. DuPree and others give the Jazz little chance in the series.

But hold on. Home court is hard to establish without a loud, raucous crowd to support the home team. And for the first game of the series only 15,112 fans showed up in the cavernous Alamodome. This clearly pales in comparison to the more than 35,000 who showed up for the Spurs-Rockets conference finals a year ago. And home court goes back to the Jazz, who embarrassed the Spurs 95-75.

John Stockton[2], who was plagued by rumors about the demise of his all around game all season long, scored 13 points and dealt out 19 assists in only 39 minutes. Malone scored a workman-like 23 and Hornacek added 17. But the biggest surprise was the play of Chris Morris who started in place of David Benoit, who did not play due to a bruised knee. Morris finished with 13 points, five boards, and one steal and blocked shot. More importantly, perhaps, he helped limit Sean Elliot to 14 points on 2-7 shooting. For the season Elliot had averaged more than 24 points per game.

Connie, seeing the Jazz blow out the Spurs, brought the television back into Brian's room and turned it on just as Chris Morris hit a three point shot. After the game Morris, who came to the Jazz as a free agent from the New Jersey Nets, said: "I'm just glad to be in a situation like this. I could be at home, watching the playoffs on TV. That's where I usually was at this time of year in New Jersey."

The consensus here was that the Jazz were playing great defense in their last two games. Karl Malone compared their defensive effort in the first game against San Antonio to the kind of defensive stands made famous by Jerry Sloan[3] when he played for the Bulls "in the '50s and '60s." The reporter quickly reminded Malone that Sloan played from 1965–76, to which Malone replied: "Oops."

And while the Jazz maintained some defensive intensity in game two, the Admiral scored 24 points and helped sink the Jazz 88-77. Connie, still hoping for Brian to awaken from his coma, left the entire game on for him, and then played one of his favorite tapes by the Replacements three times straight through.

While the Jazz clearly struggled in game two, one bright spot had to be the emergence of their bench, which has been steadily improving throughout the playoffs. Antoine Carr and Adam Keefe contributed twenty points, and Bryon Russell[4], the second round pick out of Long Beach State, scored 16 points.

The Jazz would have little trouble in games three and four, thanks again to strong contributions from the bench, especially at the three spot. Chris Morris, called into action once more due to Benoit's nagging knee bruise, lit up the Spurs for 25 points in the first thirty minutes of game four. "Once I was in the phase, I couldn't be stopped," Morris said after the game. Morris' game was a real departure for the methodical, pick-and-role Jazz. Morris was flipping passes, one-arming rebounds, and clowning in the stands by propping his feet up after chasing a loose ball out of bounds. It seemed more like the days of Maravich than Malone.

The Spurs were down 3-1 heading into a game five showdown at the Alamodome. The Sonics, meanwhile, eliminated the Rockets and were waiting the winner of this series for the western conference championship. And the Chicago Bulls and Michael Jordan were awaiting a rematch with the Orlando Magic in the east.

The Spurs took game five, stifling Utah's hot-shooting bench (seven players combined for just 21 points and a ridiculous 7 rebounds). The San Antonio fans showed up again (34,215), as well, thanks largely to reduced ticket prices ($5 a piece). "If we had that kind of crowd all the time, we'd have a huge homecourt advantage," the Admiral said after the game.

But game six would be played back in Utah at the cacophonous Delta Center. Much to coach Sloan's chagrin Bryon Russell began declaring to the Utah press: "There's no way the Spurs can beat us three games in a row!" And he would be right, led by the bench, who scored 51 points to the Spurs' 16.

The Mailman held the Admiral scoreless in the first half, helping himself to 25 points, 13 boards, and six assists. Malone even bounced back from a hard foul that left him writhing in pain on the Delta Center floor, complaining of a tingling in his shoulder. On the next play he would get one of his six assists to Adam Keefe who, in the words of Jazz announcer Hot Rod Hundley, "softly laid that baby to bed." The Jazz said goodnight to the Spurs, 108-81, and hello to the Seattle Supersonics in the conference finals. "To hell with all the demons," the Salt Lake Tribune declared. "For all of Jazzdom, this is hoop heaven."

The Tribune, interestingly enough, was founded by a group known as the Godbeites, after William Godbe, a successful merchant and close friend of Brigham Young. When Young began to encourage Mormons to boycott Gentile merchants (the impetus for the still successful Z.C.M.I. , Zion's Cooperative Mercantile Institution, mall and department store chain), Godbe and other Salt Lake intellectuals wanted an end to the insulatory policies they felt were a threat to more than the budding state's free enterprise. They founded *Utah Magazine* to help argue their ideas, and this eventually became *The Salt Lake Tribune* not long before the Godbeites were all excommunicated. The Tribune has softened its anti-Mormon rhetoric in favor of being a secular alternative to *The Deseret News*.

Young wasn't content with mere economic isolationism, and in fact tried to create his own language. In 1852, in his address to the L.D.S. General Conference, Young asked the board of regents "to cast out from their system of education the present orthography and written form of our language, that when my children are taught the graphic sign for A, it may always represent that individual sound." And thus was born the Deseret Alphabet. A book on Young's overly complex phonetic alphabet was published in 1869, and *The Deseret News* printed a few articles in the new alphabet, but like Esperanto and other contemporary attempts to create a new language, it soon died.

The core of Young's isolationist policies, however, still find favor with a small, but fervent group of Mormons. Most notable among these isolationists, perhaps, is character actor Wilford Brimley (see the Ron Howard movie *Cocoon*). Brimley, a long time Jazz fan who can be seen in the front rows at most home games (he and Steve Young and the occasional Osmond are Utah's equivalent to the New York Knicks' Spike Lee and Woody Allen, or the L.A. Lakers' Jack Nicholson and Dyan Cannon), suggested that all Gentiles pack their things and get out of Utah, leaving it to the Mormons who were intended by God to be there. The church, of course, does not endorse Brimley's view.

Conversely, the name *Utah* was used to cultivate a larger base of allegiance when the Jazz franchise moved to Salt Lake City in 1979. Salt Lake was clearly a very small market for a professional sports franchise; that's why the Jazz employed all their marketing tools to help build a larger regional fan base. This includes everything from running basketball clinics and pre-season games in Idaho to assembling network affiliates in several states including Idaho, Wyoming, Montana, and Nevada. The series with the Sonics will engage most of the West coast, and nowhere are the split loyalties more apparent than at Jack and Dan's tavern in Gonzaga, where even Sonics fans still pull for John Stockton and keep close tabs on his assists and steals.

[1]Hornacek was widely dismissed by most college recruiters when he came out of high school. In fact, Hornacek's first passion, growing up in the Chicago area, had always been hockey. His dream had been to play professional hockey, but though he is often considered one of the smaller shooting guards in the league, Hornacek grew too tall for hockey, where a low center of gravity is sometimes the only thing to keep you from getting your head checked into the boards.

Hornacek, certain he was not going to become an athletic superstar, chose to try his luck as a walk-on at Iowa State. Hornacek, skinny, suffering from bad ankles and later from bad knees, concentrated on getting his degree in accounting. But it soon became apparent that his shooting touch was nothing short of remarkable. He had developed an extremely high arc shooting over electrical wires in his driveway as kid, and he was deadly from the charity stripe. He became a starter for the Iowa State Cyclones after just four games.

After college he was taken, safely, in the second round of the NBA draft by the Phoenix Suns in 1986. Hornacek was traded to Philadelphia as part of the Charles Barkley deal in 1992, and two and half years later traded to the Jazz for Jeff Malone (no relation to Karl). It turned out that Hornacek would be one of four players (including Howard Eisley, Greg Foster, and Bryon Russell) to make it out of the second round of the draft and onto the Jazz roster. But more importantly, Hornacek addressed Layden's Catholic School Philosophy, bringing his affable, easygoing and charitable personality along with the kind of intense work ethic Jerry Sloan demanded.

[2] Stockton came aboard in the 1984 draft. Because the Jazz had made the playoffs that year, their draft pick was at number sixteen—not usually the place to find superstars. Stockton's play

for tiny Gonzaga University in Washington momentarily stunned the thousands of fans who had gathered in the Salt Palace. They had come to watch the draft on closed circuit television, and their subsequent furious flipping through the draft guides a few moments after Stockton's name was called could reportedly be heard across the street in the Crossroads Mall. Who was this kid? His grandfather had been an All-American running back, and his father owned a pub, the famous Jack and Dan's, near the Spokane college campus. "He has a lot of things going for him," joked Frank Layden. "He's Irish Catholic, he laughs at my jokes, and his dad owns a bar."

While Stockton would emerge as one of the all-time best at his position, holding the records for career steals and assists, he came to the Jazz primarily as a soft-spoken scorer. As a rookie he played only eighteen minutes per game. His quiet demeanor, though, was probably a blessing that year since All-Star Dantley held out for more money (playing only 55 out of 82 games that season), and John Drew (who the Jazz received in a trade for Dominique Wilkins, one of the best individual talents the league has seen) was battling with drug problems which kept him out of all but nineteen games. On top of those troubles the team was struggling financially and considering a buy-out from a group hoping to bring an NBA team to Minnesota. But Stockton was another piece of the Catholic School Philosophy.

Even as his game took off, he remained shy of reporters and the fame brought by a highly successful NBA career. Stockton has never used an agent, negotiating his deals with the Jazz with a handshake. And though he did foray into the lucrative world of endorsements for a Coca-Cola ad in the late eighties, the experience would be his last. He even married his high school sweetheart, Nada Stepovich, and they continue to try to live as far from the glare of the NBA as they can.

Playing on his perceived anonymity, NBC asked John and Nada to take a camcorder with them to record their day excursions at the Barcelona Olympics. Stockton had been named to the Olympic team, but had broken his leg during practices, and though he traveled with the team and sat on the bench, he obviously could not play. Charles Barkley, never shy of the camera himself, said: "We call him Chevy Chase. He's over here on a European Vacation." While John and Nada were enjoying the sights of Barcelona on their European Vacation they ran into another American tourist who had come to watch the Olympics. She was wearing a Dream Team T-shirt featuring the likenesses of all the members of basketball team. Nada filmed away while John asked her if she liked professional basketball. She did. They were, in fact, the main reason she had come to Barcelona. John then asked if she knew the team. She did, Michael Jordan was her favorite. And Stockton pointed at the other faces on her shirt. Did she know who that was? The Admiral. Who that was? Charles Barkley. And who's that guy down here in the corner, Stockton said, pointing to his own likeness. Oh, I don't know who that guy is.

Stockton's avoidance of the press is legendary. He would wait for a half hour after games in the off-limits area of the locker rooms until he was certain the press had gone home or were all engaged in interviews with other players. And though his discomfort at being in the public eye was well known, his sense of humor and his competitiveness were slower to emerge.

During a Jazz dinner when hall-of-famer Bob Lanier was praising Karl Malone's rise to the elite ranks of the NBA, he pointed to Stockton and said: "You ought to give a couple of hundred thousand to that little white boy over there." Stockton gave Lanier a one-man ovation. Lanier was right, though, a great number of those record-setting assists and vicious picks were set for Malone. Stockton, as noted in his lone Coca-Cola commercial, where he encourages a young boy who is being left out of a game with some older boys because he is too short, was one of the smallest players in the league. Not many games went by where Stockton wasn't sent sprawling to the floor trying to set picks on the larger players. But Stockton would simply pick himself up, dust himself off, dish out a few high fives, and step to the line for another free throw.

3 Jerry Sloan took the reins from Frank Layden halfway through the 1988 season. Sloan grew up on a poor Illinois farm. His father had died in an accident on the farm when Jerry was just four years old. Sloan was the youngest of ten children and learned early to work hard and to sacrifice just to avoid going hungry. He worked the farm until he was old enough to tackle the oil fields in nearby McLeansboro where he would go to high school. McLeansboro must have seemed like the big time to Sloan who had spent the first eight years of school in a one room school house. And as the old saw goes, he walked sixteen miles a day for the privilege of attending McLeansboro.

He was only 5'6" tall as a freshman at McLeansboro. And it was there that he met Bobbye Irvin (three inches taller than he at the time). She was class president and he the vice president. She refused his first date, and when she did acquiesce, she told her mother: "I'll never go out with him again. He didn't speak two words the whole night."

Sloan grew (to 6'5" tall) and grew on Irvin before he left to enroll at Evansville College in Indiana. He married Bobbye at the end of that year. Sloan sat out his first year as a transfer student, but came on strong his last three years, averaging more than 15 points and 12 boards per game and leading his team to the Division II national championship. He was drafted by the

Baltimore Bullets and played one season before going to Chicago in the expansion draft. And in Chicago he really took off.

He always arrived hours early for every game, taping and retaping his ankles, and refusing to go onto the court to warm up because he didn't want to let the other team get friendly with him. He was going to war every time he stepped onto the court. "He'd just sit in the corner and smoke a cigarette," his coach, Dick Motta said. "I sure as hell wasn't going to mess with him."

His intensity on the court was legendary, and opponents grew to fear him as much as respect him. But after a ten year career with the Bulls, named to the All Defensive team six times, he retired after a particularly severe groin injury in 1976. He took a job as head coach of his alma mater at Evansville, but unexpectedly and mysteriously quit several days later. A few months later the Evansville Aces and their new coach, Bobby Watson, boarded a flight from Evansville to Nashville, Tennessee. Five minutes after take off the plane plunged out of the fog into some rail tracks near the airport killing everyone on board.

Sloan brought his intensity to coaching, but it was always tempered with the sense, after the horrible crash, that this was only a game. He continued to run many of the same schemes Frank Layden developed, but with Malone and Stockton the staple clearly was the pick and roll, a seemingly easy play to defend, but not if it's run to perfection. And that's what Sloan demanded of his players. Mental toughness and a simple approach to the game. No one wanted to argue. "Nobody fights with Jerry," Layden said. "Because you know the price would be too high. You might come out the winner, at his age. You might even lick him. But you'd lose an eye, an arm, your testicles in the process."

4 Bryon Russell, the second round pick out of Long Beach State,

had nearly been cut during this season. In fact, announcers had no end of trouble calling him BRY-ON, instead of BY-RON Russell, after the comedian of the latter name. But because of injuries to other players saw himself not only staying with the team, but playing extended minutes in the playoffs because of Benoit's injury and Sloan's distrust that Morris wouldn't just start shooting every time he had the ball in his hands. During the season Russell had been blasted by Malone (indeed, Malone had come down like a ton of bricks on most of his team mates early in the season) for a seeming indifference to playing. But during the playoffs, inspired by Malone to make more of an effort, Russell was diving for loose balls, playing tenacious defense on the perimeter, and sinking his long shots that kept defenders from playing two on one against Malone in the post. At this time he is considered one of the best defenders in the league, but Russell owes his work ethic and scrappiness to the examples of Malone and Sloan.

Our own Brian, however, has found his way back to Randy, Suzanne, Bailey, and Connie.

XXIX Recovery and Reformation

"You see, he's moving."

"How do you know that's not just twitching," Randy says.

"They don't twitch like that if there's no brain activity," Connie says. "That's a very good sign."

"Should you run some more of that music by him again?"

"Let's let him rest," she says, and I can feel her hand on my arm, but I'm so tired.

The ceiling has cracks and I thank God that they are there, that it isn't a wash of white for me to struggle against. There is something on my face, some materials, and I have the urgent need to urinate. I try to sit up, but my back and my arms and my legs have to be remembered, as if I have to coach them into action for the very first time. There is a jingling sound coming from somewhere on my body and it acts as a signal, a beacon to the pain. The pain is a dull pain that seems to come shooting back from every part of my body straight into my skull like an avalanche coming through a small house. I expect the sides of my head to explode, and even moaning hurts.

"He's up," Connie says. "Now you just lay right there. Just lay back and relax."

I hear Randy speaking, reciting one of the Psalms, "Blessed be the Lord, my rock, / who trains my hands for war, / and my fingers for battle; / my rock and my fortress, / my stronghold and my / deliverer," he says.

I try to speak, to say his name.

"Hush up, now," Connie says. Her voice is familiar and commanding. It has the same timorous fragility Jaimy's voice had, but she wields it with the conviction of a full grown woman.

"My shield, in whom I take refuge, / who subdues the peoples / under me," I try to speak again, but the sound is like the seal breaking on a jar of preserves[77].

"Hush!" Connie says, and I still can't see her, can't see Randy, can only see the cracks shooting through the ceiling like the pain shoots through my head.

"O Lord, what are human beings / that you regard them, / or mortals that you think of them?"

I try to sit up. "I'm not going to keep telling you," Connie says.

---

[77] Church President Ezra Taft Benson, in an address to the church in the early '70s, said: "The Lord has warned us of famines, but the righteous will have listened to prophets and stored at least a year's supply of survival food." He was speaking to what is generally perceived to be a Mormon concern with apocalyptic prophesy.

In fact, largely due to Y2K fears, stores all along the Salt Lake valley began to advertise and stock emergency survival kits. But most L.D.S. are encouraged to be better prepared than this. Young couples are often referred to *Achieving a Celestial Marriage,* a book addressing the needs and concerns facing new families, and practical solutions and approaches to these troubles. The book suggests young couples set aside up to 50 percent of their Christmas budget to prepare their first storage program.

These storage programs are similar to 1950s fallout shelters, but L.D.S. are encouraged to rotate their foods and to keep at least a two week supply of fresh water on hand. All apocalypses aside, one very practical application of these programs has been in the case of natural disaster, like the mud slides in Brian's hometown in the spring of 1984. L.D.S. were able to dip into their larders and assist their devastated neighbors with clothing and food.

"They are like a breath; / their days are like a passing / shadow . . ."

"You just shut your mouth, *Randy*. Or you get on out of here, I don't care which. But you just hush with all that. It's not funny, I don't care what you say. He's not out of the woods yet. Not by a long shot." I can hear Randy chuckling to himself and protesting to Connie as she moves him farther away from me, and then I feel I am alone in the room, the cracks in the ceiling reach their lightning into my skull like grounding wires sapping the spark of my pain, and I feel as though sleep is going to find me.

I have to urinate, and as soon as I realize this, the pain returns. I can feel my arms now, though, and they feel weak, as though I've been carrying bags of sand all day. I can lift my head, and there is the blue glow of the television past the foot of my bed. There is another cross, like the one in Connie's room, carrying all the weight of the white room in its dark heaviness, and there is Connie, chin down, looking at a magazine in her lap. Her hair is down over her face, and if not for her sanguine posture I could swear it was Jaimy. "Oh," she says. "You're back with me now."

"I have to . . ." My voice is still hollow and quiet. "I need to," I say. My voice seems to improve with every word.

"Do you have to pee again?" Connie says. I nod. "Do you think you can hold the pan?"

"The pan?" I say.

"We tried a catheter, but it wasn't very successful. You may be a little sore down there." She hands me a dirty plastic hospital bed pan. "It was just easier to put some towels down and clean you up. You didn't go too much after the first couple of days, even with the I.V."

I look down at my arms. My left arm is bruised and bandaged, and a bright red cord and silver bell is tied to my wrist.

It looks like a cat collar. I think it is a cat collar. My right arm is stitched closed from the elbow to the knuckles and I have an I.V. cord extending from some bandaging to an empty bag hung on a nail near my head. I want Connie to leave, but I'm scared to be alone just yet.

"No need to be shy now," she says. "I've been cleaning up after you for nearly two weeks now."

I slide the bed pan under the covers with my left hand, and she is right, I'm naked from the waist down and sitting on a pile of old towels and I can tell I've urinated on myself recently. "Where am I?" Why would they let a sixteen-year-old-girl see me naked, I wonder.

"You're at Bailey's," she says. "They brought you here since the accident. I'm not supposed to talk about it, but everybody's gone right now. Bailey's at our house with Randy and—and your Randy too, I guess—dropping the engine back in. I've been here watching after you almost the whole time," she says.

"Have the cops been here?" Connie looks down at the sheets coming loose at my feet and reaches to tuck them back in, but I know that's supposed to pass for an answer. "Why didn't I go to a hospital?"

"You know why," she says.

"I need a phone," I say.

"No," Connie says. She's very sure of this, and I know I can't even get out of the bed yet. I hand her back the pan, and it's incredibly difficult for me not to spill any of it on the bedsheets. "Can you swallow something now?"

"I think so," I say, and she puts the pan down and hands me a glass of warm water and a couple of yellow pills.

"They'll help you to sleep," she says, and she rubs her hand across my forehead. Her hand is soft and warm and smells like soap.

When I wake Randy and Bailey and Suzanne are standing over me. My I.V. is gone and I feel like I can move my arm now that it is untethered, but it still gets away from me a bit.

"I wasn't sure you'd make it," Randy says. He is clean-shaven, his hair is clean and cut short and he is wearing a nice shirt. His hooks are gone as well, and at the end of his sleeve is a rubber hand that looks dead, but certainly more human than its alternative.

"You clean up nice," I say.

"Suzanne's got some rules," he says, nodding to her as if I didn't know she was in the room. "See, he's making jokes."

"You think you can eat something today?" Bailey says. "I got some soup on."

"Yeah," I say. "I think I can." I start to swing my legs over the side of the bed, but I can't do it. Everything is so heavy and hurts.

"Can we be alone for a minute?" Randy says, and the other two say how relieved they are that I've come through and shut the door behind them on their way out. "There was a bit of trouble," Randy says. "I don't know what all you remember."

"I remember the car wreck, if that's what you mean. Can I get some pants on?"

"Sure, sure," Randy says, and he searches the room for a pair of boxer shorts. He has to help me from the bed, and when he has me standing, naked from the waist down, the cold, crusty feel of the pee clinging to my backside, I know that I can't put the pants on by myself. Randy is gentle with me, letting me lean onto his back while he slips one of my feet into the boxer shorts, then the next. I feel strange having a man brush up against my genitals and pull my underpants up like this, but I'm relieved to have something to cover up with. Randy pulls the towels off the bed behind me and they land with a thump in the plastic clothes basket against the wall. "You look like you came out of this just fine. The girls were a little worried there might be some lasting problems," he says, pointing to his forehead with his index finger. "You know . . .?"

There's a full length mirror on the back of the bedroom door, and I can see that I haven't come out of anything. My face is swollen and both eyes are black. The white of my right eye is a mass of crimson, and my arms and legs are bruised, the right arm having been open at one time and now held shut with hundreds of black threads. I sit back on the bed.

"What happened to The Cello?" I say.

"The cello?" Randy says. "What cello?"

"The trucker! The fucking trucker! Where'd he go?"

"He's taken care of," Randy says. "You still need to rest."

"What did you do?" I say.

"Nothing I didn't have to do," he says. "I wouldn't have let you spend the night that night if I ever knew. You gotta believe me," Randy says. "Stupid mother fuckers like that," he says. "Stupid, tragic mother fuckers."

"What happened?" I say. "What was that all about?"

"Some people and some ideas don't leave you just because you leave them, you know?" Randy says. "Look, I told you I got involved in some things, I believed in some things I never should have. Things I can't believe I believed in. People I can't believe I believed in. They had some ideas I thought made sense when I was open to that kind of talk."

"You're not telling me anything," I say. I want to be angry at Randy, but I'm too tired to be angry. It's something that will have to wait. "I don't care about all that."

"You know my son? My little boy out in Moab?" I nod. "These people are pretty fucking sure there's no place in the world for kids like that. There's no place in the world for a lot of people, and here I was buying into all that until it hit too close to home."

"So they didn't have any place for you?" I say. "Is that what you're saying? I don't know what you're saying, Randy. What happened to the trucker? Why didn't you call the cops? I could've been killed. I could be dead right now."

"That's right," Randy says seriously. "You might be dead right now." He moves away from me, but studies me, watches my face, which doesn't feel like my face right now. "You know your Psalms?" he says. "*A blessing on him who seizes your babies and dashes them against the rocks.* That's nobody I want any part of. That's no God I want any part of. I barely even know this kid, but he's my kid, you know?" Randy's eyes are wet. "There's a responsibility there. He's got such sweetness in him, that kid. And it's got nothing to do with the kid being a retard, if that's what you're thinking. I've done some things in my life I'm sure I need to pay for, but every time I try to pay for them somebody else ends up getting hurt."

"So go to the cops," I say. "What does that have to do with me?" I say. Randy is carrying on, not making sense, which doesn't seem like something he'd do at all, but there's something insincere about it all too. I can't tell if he's just not used to feeling anything or if he's feeding me a line.

"It's got nothing to do with you, Chief," Randy says. "And it won't. Not ever again. You're going to get better, and you're going to get out of here and go back to Utah, or go back to Michigan, and things are going to be just fine for you. I'll see what I can do to make things right for you before you leave, but that's all I can do. What's done is done is fucking done!"

I want to be gone more than I want to actually go. Everything seems so tiring. I want to be in both places at one time. I want to be in Michigan, in my apartment with Rhoda, and I want to be in Utah, with my family. "So I'm supposed to just leave then, and not say anything about this? Is that what I'm supposed to do? How is that even possible?"

"You were in a car wreck and these people here took care of you. They took *good* care of you. They looked after you," he says. "That's all you need to say." Randy's serious now. "That's all there is to say." He wipes his eyes with the back of his sleeve and helps me up from the bed. His fingers are very tight on my arm, and I can't tell if he's trying to hurt me or help me. I see us in the mirror behind the door, side by side, and then he opens the door, one of those many miracles he must perform every day without the assistance of a real hand, and our image slides sideways out of sight.

XXX. Goodbye to a Young Girl of My Dreams

In a couple of days, I'm back on solid foods, and I'm getting around much better. Bailey won't let me use his phone, though. And they insist I keep the red cord and bell on my arm, in case I need some help. But aside from that, they are all so helpful with me, especially Connie, who acts like an indentured servant as often as she acts like my prison guard, bringing me food when I ask for it, tending my wounds, reading to me from her school work. It helps her study, she says. She also reads to me from some of her favorite classics. We read *Heart of Darkness* and *My Antonia,* neither of which we finish, but both of which I've read before, and it takes me back to my own school days.

"When do you think I can go?" I say. In spite of Connie's good company, I'm starting to feel like aprisoner in Bailey's house. I can walk now, and I have begun to peel the stitches away from my wound with my fingernails. That's one thing Connie hasn't tended to.

"That is so gross," she says. "As soon as the vet can take one more look at you, I'd guess," Connie says. She's a very nonplussed warden. The vet, it turns out, is the veterinarian who stitched up my arm and who put the I.V. into my arm while I was out. Apparently, a doctor was out of the question and the general feel I'm getting is that if my injuries *had* been life threatening it wouldn't have made any difference. I picture Randy and Bailey dumping my body onto the cold sidewalk in front of an emergency bay somewhere in Omaha.

Randy was apparently pretty beat up as well, but he recovered much faster. Connie thinks that when his arm flew off it must have smashed into the back of my head, and I don't really have anything better to offer up than that. I'd like to think they'd at least have dropped me at that emergency room at the Swedeburg hospital, if there even is a Swedeburg hospital, if my pulse had stopped or if I had gone into convulsions, but I clearly have no idea about what is really going on. I still have the littlest bit of faith in Randy, though by now every cell in my body is telling me to reject that faith and think about breaking out of Bailey's house and finding a phone.

The television has been at my disposal the entire time, and what bothers me most, I think, is the feeling that I'm watching the world continue without me in it. My parents don't know about me, Rhoda doesn't know about me, my job doesn't know, though that's hardly a concern any more. And yet the sitcoms keep coming, the news keeps rolling, the NBA playoffs keep playing. I wonder if my disappearance is any more of a shock to L.T. and Geoff and Kitty than Dee Dee's.

After dinner I ask Connie if we can get outside. I can see from the window that it's a warm day and fields have grown taller since I first came here.

The sun is going down and Connie walks me to the edge of the field and then brings out some lawn chairs and we sit down and stare out at the curvature of the earth. The sun is a rich, hot egg yolk and it slides down into the west, rolling over the mountains on the other side of the horizon. I close my eyes and the sun is still there. I can feel it with both eyes, burning like two suns and warming my face, warming the fields. I remember Randy likening the field to a ghost yard, and looking around, I wonder how many have died out here, on halcyon nights like this. And if the fields receive them. The sky is silent, the road is empty, the shadows are long and dark. "This is really beautiful," I say. "I'm going to miss it." I want to tell Connie I'm going to miss her, too, but I don't know how much of that is true, or to what degree. She's so young.

Connie and I sit and we don't say much. It's like we're an old couple, and I imagine this is what it would have been like if Jaimy and I had lasted: quiet, warm, with perhaps this kind of loneliness between us. Only I think this is something Connie's used to. When the sun is gone, the shadows seem to spread out like dark blood into fresh water, and then the crickets[78] begin to call. They are singing to each other in the warm grass. Their song is like the rhythm of a million tiny hearts beating out in the fields.

"Do you know why it's so windy in Nebraska?" Connie says. "Because South Dakota sucks and Kansas blows."

"You don't like it here?" I say.

---

[78] In the spring of 1848, after a very rough winter where stored food was already running scarce all along the Salt Valley, the early spring crops were coming in already bitten by frost and afflicted by irrigation problems. The arrival of a swarm of crickets was understandably seen as a plague of biblical proportions. The conditions must have been absolutely perfect for an outbreak of cricket pestilence. And the crickets continued to come and come. Families tried everything from smoking them out to simply stomping them, but they just kept coming and coming, eating every stock and piece of greenery in the land.

And then, almost as suddenly as the crickets, storms of California Gulls from Great Salt Lake came in and began gorging themselves on the crickets. Diaries of the times report the birds regurgitating the indigestible pieces and then continuing to eat more and more of the crickets. And while the arrival of the gulls has been turned into a Great Salt Lake legend it was not quite "The Miracle of the Gulls" the Salt Lake Temple shows to its tourists. In fact, many diaries of the times refer quite often to the crickets, but make no mention of the gulls.

Connie sighs and looks out into the darkening field. She takes out a package of cigarettes and lights one. I know she is not supposed to be smoking, but the smell seems like it kindles the perfect evening. "Can I try one of those?" I say.

Connie expertly frees a cigarette from the pack, Camel Lights, and hands it over to me with the lighter. My bell jingles as I take the cigarette from her soft little fingers. I don't know why I haven't taken it off yet. It reminds me that I have an arm, I suppose.

Connie is young and it doesn't seem like I *wouldn't* smoke, to her. When you're her age, I remember, it doesn't seem like there should be new experiences out of your teens. There's something intimate between us, I think, now that she's seen me naked and paralyzed, now that she's washed my body with her bare hands. She's nearly half my age, but I find I feel shy around her. Shy and inexperienced.

I cough up a little bit of the smoke at first, but it gets easier as I get higher. It hits me faster than the caffeine, and I can see why people smoke these things. It's immediate and I feel as though I'm floating above my body.

"It was okay," Connie says, taking up the conversation again. "Until they brought in all the niggers and gooks at the meat plant," she says. "That used to be Omaha, and now it's out here too."

"What?" I say. "Niggers and gooks?" The words feel ugly and awkward in my mouth, as if I need to spit them out. I can't believe these things can come from her beautiful young mouth too.

"The meat plant opened up and they came running out here by the dozens," she says. "I've got niggers in my home room, niggers in my gym class, niggers eating in my cafeteria. It makes me sick to my stomach to see them."

"Jesus," I say. "I think I need to go back in, Connie."

"Oh, I'm sorry," she says. "I didn't mean to upset you. It just makes me sick, you know?"

Connie helps me back into the house. I feel more clumsy since the cigarette and since Connie let loose with her world view. She steers me into my room, a room so white and empty it seems like Bailey might run this kind of recuperative bed and breakfast all the time. The towels are gone and Connie's put fresh sheets on the bed today, but I can still smell a little urine when I sit down on the bed. She turns on the television, as though it's one more thing that has to be done, and finds the Jazz game. She's already told me she won't watch professional sports, and when I see Karl Malone[79] during the shoot around, I think I know why. It sickens me to think we could be both looking at the same thing and I'd find beauty there and Connie could only find fault. I'd like to think that this is something I could talk Connie down from, that I could make her see how wrong she is to harbor these beliefs at her age. But she's so certain, so confident in her small voice that I know there's nothing I could offer her wise enough or impressive enough to convert her thinking.

---

[79] The Jazz came into the first game of the Seattle series looking completely unprepared and they lost by thirty points: 102-72. The blowout was so bad that Karl Malone was benched for the last ten minutes of the game. Stockton was held to 2-10 shooting by Seattle point guard Gary Payton. The Jazz could not even muster any Divine help in this game, as one Seattle newspaper taunted: "The Supreme Being is on Utah's side; who would you pick, Payton and his bandits, or Stockton and his choirboys?"

Things got worse for the Jazz, too. In a pre-series interview Seattle coach George Karl cried that Karl Malone took too long on each free throw. The league rule, seldom-if-ever enforced, calls for a player to shoot his free throw within ten seconds of receiving the ball.

Karl charged that Malone takes upwards of 25 seconds every time he shoots his free throws, prompting the Seattle crowd to roar out a count every time Malone stepped to the charity line. Impressive though he may have thought it was that so many in Seattle fans could count past ten, the Mailman was obviously bothered by the thunderous chant, going only 1-6 from the line.

A bit later in the game the crowd really turned it on when Coach Sloan benched Chris Morris for throwing a white towel onto the floor. The crowd erupted as Sloan turned on his surrenderous player and openly chastised him on national television. Speaking from experience Sloan knows that many excellent teams don't win an NBA championship. "You have to have everything go perfect. Every little thing can throw you off."

At the start of the series Malone received word that a young boy he and wife Kay had befriended the summer before during a visit to Primary Children's Medical Center, had taken a turn for the worse with his leukemia. Malone, like his coach, was raised without a father and had always responded to meetings with kids as most professional athletes do (kids seldom view with the antagonism and commercialism adults often do, in spite of the ubiquitous corporate hand in professional sports). Malone's father commited suicide when Karl was only three years old. And he is known for his efforts to help the needy, including dropping a hundred-dollar bill into the cup of a transient at the Atlanta airport with the warning to keep it out of the cup so it wouldn't be stolen. He gives his shoes and wristbands away after every game (something many professional athletes don't do, choosing instead to broker their wares through an agent for sale on the lucrative memorabilia market), and he and Kay started The Karl Malone Foundation for Kids after the 1996 season.

But Malone wasn't always so generous with his time or money. In addition to his and Kay's children, Malone settled paternity suits involving three children born before he and Kay were married. He not only resisted helping to pay for his children, but once when he chanced to cross paths with them in Louisiana Malone refused to acknowledge or even speak to them. Only now, after the events of the 1996 season, has Malone made some overtures to the children, amid no small amount of criticism and scrutiny from the press.

In the next game of the Seattle series Malone continued to struggle to contain Seattle's center/power forward Shawn Kemp. The Jazz led by eight early in the fourth quarter, and were tied with 90 seconds left in the game. The Jazz seemed out of sync on their next possession, with Hornacek throwing up a wild three point attempt as the 24 second clock expired. And then Kemp scored over Malone to put the Sonics ahead by two. "We've got to help a little on Kemp," coach Sloan said. "We've got to make him kick the ball out and make them hit the perimeter shot." Antoine Carr tapped in David Benoit's miss to tie the game again, but on the next possession the ball went in to Kemp again. He knocked Malone out of the way with his left arm and made an easy score. On the next possession Stockton drove into the lane looking to dish out of the pick and roll, but the Sonics defended it perfectly, with Kemp intercepting Stockton's pass. For all intents and purposes, the game was over. And the Jazz return to the Delta Center down 2-0 in the best of seven western conference finals.

"They think we're not the same caliber of team as them," Malone said. "Nobody does right now. Since the series started, you could they think they're head and shoulders above us. I don't think they've given us any respect. Nobody gives us any respect." But Malone acknowledges it's the Jazz who must earn that respect. "You earn it by winning, and we haven't done that."

XXXI. The Apologists

Another day goes before the vet comes to look at my wounds. He's a skinny old guy with eyebrows that jet out from his face like bull horns on the face of a '50s Cadillac. He pulls my eyelids open with his crusty fingers and shines a light into my skull. He mutters to himself when he gets to my red eye, "Not detached, that's good. Responsive. Hmmm. You can see, can't-cha?"

"Yes," I say.

"Well let's have a look at this arm, then." He takes my arm and turns it over and back and then up toward my chest. "Make a fist around my finger," he says. "C'mon, tighter. Tighter! Don't be a girl about it."

He pulls his finger loose and listens to my chest. "Any more blood in the urine?"

"No," I say. "I didn't know there had been."

"You're one lucky sonuvabitch," he says.

"I don't feel lucky," I say.

"Well, you are. Good Mormon living, I'll betcha," he says, and he goes out of the room with Randy and Bailey and Connie in tow. They close the door behind them and I'm left to look at myself in the mirror. My eye still looks bad, bloodied and swollen, and my face is pocked with scabs from the windshield's implosion. I will have, everyone has assured me, a nice, thick scar the length of my arm. It will look, Connie said, like a giant earthworm crawling under my skin.

Randy comes back into the room as I'm pulling my shirt back over my head. The silver bell catches on the inside of the shirt and I have to work myself free of the material. "Doc says you're good to go."

"So I can go, then?" I say.

"You can go whenever you like," Randy says. "Just say the magic word and you're out of here." He seems disapproving.

"Then why can't I make a phone call?"

"Bailey's house," Randy says. "Bailey's rules. He doesn't want anything tracing you back to here. But I told him you wouldn't do that to him, anyway. If you want to make a call I can drive you into town."

"You're just going to let me go, then?"

"You're not a prisoner, goddamnit. We just had to make sure you were well enough to travel. There's no cloak-and-dagger bullshit here. What happened out on that road was personal. It was between me and him and nobody else. Not you, not Suzanne, not Bailey, not anybody, understand?"

"No," I say. "I don't understand. What is going on here? Why haven't there been any police? Any sheriff?"

"These are good people," Randy says. He's a different person from the one I came out here with. He's clean shaven, dressing in button-down shirts, his hair is combed and cut. "You owe them your fucking life, all right?"

"And what's the deal with Connie," I say, lowering my voice. I don't believe in his good people. "She's all sweet and innocent one minute, and the next minute she's spouting off 'nigger-this' and 'nigger-that'."

"They're good people," Randy says. "They're just a bit lost on some things. Let me tell you something, I've been a lot farther down than that, and I'm still coming back. I'm fighting my way back. Every fucking day." He leans over the bed and looks me right in the eye. "Understand? You and me," he says, sticking his finger in my chest. "We come from the same stock, the same history. Are you going to tell me you've never had somebody look down on you because you're L.D.S.?"

"Oh come on, Randy! You know that's different," I say. "You can choose a religion."

"But you can't choose a faith," he says. "I'm not saying what Connie thinks is right. It's not. Any fool can see that. But do you believe in revelations? You believe in the Pearl of Great Price[80]? You believe . . ." He stops, looks over his shoulder at the door and exhales long and deep. "Fuck all that. Fuck all of that. I know you. And I know you've been lost before too, so don't get all fucking pious with me. Or with Connie. She's a fucking kid for God's sake."

---

[80] The Pearl of Great Price refers to Smith's revelations that are a part of the Book of Moses and the Book of Abraham. Refering to the rebellious American Lamanites, in 2 Nephi 5 of *The Book of Mormon*, the Lord has caused "cursing to come upon them, yea, even a sore cursing . . . the Lord God did cause a skin of blackness to come upon them. And thus saith the Lord God: I will cause that they shall be loathsome unto thy people, save they shall repent of their iniquities" (21-22). The book further describes how those who "mixeth with their seed" shall also be cursed.

These works were directly responsible for blacks being denied the priesthood in the L.D.S. Church until 1978, but the Old Testament clearly offers similar problems. For hundreds of years, God's curse on Cain in Genesis was interpreted as a condemnation of dark skinned peoples. Enraged that God had rejected his offering in favor of his brother Abel's, Cain, the first born son of the first couple, killed Abel. Afterwards, God asked Cain where his brother Abel was, and Cain gave his famous, cynical reply: "Am I my brother's keeper?" God cursed Cain and marked him with an unspecified sign, often conveniently and wrongly interpreted to justify everything from slavery to ubiquitous prejudice. In actuality, God's sign was a divinely protective symbol aimed at preventing anyone from murdering Cain.

"What are you talking about?" I say.

"I know a thing or two about you and your mission calling," Randy says.

"You don't know anything," I say.

"I know there was a little funny business with a Gentile girl just before you were going to go on your mission."

I feel my blood coming hot into my neck and then back out, like my body is a thermos turned one way and then the other. "You," I say. "You don't know."

"You want to know where you'd been pegged to go before Little Brian got other ideas? I can even tell you that," Randy says. I hate him.

"You don't know these things. You couldn't know these things."

"I know all about you and your little Gentile girl. I still know some people back in Utah. You just say the word and I can tell you where you were going to be sent on your mission calling. Maybe you can go straight there from here and help some of those people not talk about niggers," he says the word sideways, like it's not a real word, like it's something I'm making up. "Or whatever it is you think you ought to do. You can get going tomorrow if you like. But I want you to know one thing before you go. These people saved your fucking life. Regardless of how it got put in jeopardy, and you owe for that. The one thing in your life you fucking owe for is when it's saved for you. So you just remember that," he says. He turns to leave. "And don't think I don't see you making those fuck-fuck eyes at Connie."

"Fuck you," I say. "Just leave me alone, and I'll be gone in the morning. I'll *walk* to the bus station if I have to . . ."

"Oh yeah," Randy says. "Sure you will. I know you," he says. "I know all about you." And I hate him.

XXXII. A Little Blood

The next morning Connie brings me a grapefruit she has peeled. Her fingers are wet with it and she sits at the foot of my bed and tears the pieces apart and hands them to me one at a time. "You'll want to stay until tomorrow," she says. "Bailey's taking a steer this afternoon and we're going to have fresh steaks tonight." The grapefruit sections look larval, and they seem to wriggle in her fingers as she tears them one from the other.

"I need to leave, Connie," I say. "My family doesn't know where I am. Nobody does."

"Who else?"

"Who else what?" I say. "Isn't that enough?"

"Who else are you worried about?"

Probably Connie's wishing I would divulge something about Rhoda. I'll bet she knows everything I've already told Randy. Maybe more. I worry I've said things in my sleep. There's no way I can trust her now, and I feel betrayed. "You know what I mean, Connie. I mean, c'mon. I've got a job back in Michigan. They haven't heard from me in almost two weeks. They don't know if I'm alive or if I'm dead."

"So they've probably hired somebody else, right?"

That's something I hadn't considered, but it makes perfect sense. My God, I think, if I worked in Zach's office he'd probably have done the interviews himself. "I can get my job back," I say. "But there's a lot of people who'll be worried about me."

Connie takes one of the grapefruit sections into her mouth and turns it over with her tongue several times before biting it in half. "You can stay one more night," she says.

"Connie," I say. "I need to go. I've got to let my family

know that I'm okay. Don't you understand that? Can't you understand that?" It's hard for me to be patient with her now, to explain things to her.

"The meat's only that good once," she says. "You'll want to have some before you go."

"Look, Connie," I say. "I know you want things to turn out differently here. You want something to happen here and you probably think that I'm the catalyst for it to happen. I mean, I can understand that. I just kind of dropped myself in your lap and suddenly there are all these . . . these things happening." Connie just looks at me like I'm talking about refund procedure. "You took care of me when I was hurt," I say. And for the first time I look at her, at her wet little fingers, her soft, childish features, and I picture her moving her hands over my body, over my wounds. The fact that she healed me seems much more personal than the idea of her seeing me naked, of her putting her hands all over my body and cleaning up after me: washing me down. Healing reminds us that we're human, my father used to say, and the healer is the most human of all.

After Jaimy and I found out, but before we went to Wendover, she wanted to take a trip to see the Crying Virgin[81] in Salt Lake City. The irony of the two of us seeing a sacred virgin

---

[81] Near 10th South Street in Salt Lake City there is a large, beautiful park full of hundred year oaks. The exposed limb of one of these trees shows a likeness of the Virgin Mary in its rings, and the sap that runs out of the tree seems to come through the eyes of the Virgin, making it appear as if she is crying. The large Catholic/Mexican-American population of Salt Lake took this to be a miracle and a staging area was erected for the faithful to place candles and leave donations for the Catholic diocese of Salt Lake. There have been several reports of miraculous healings associated with the tree and

278

wasn't lost on us, either, I remember, and it buoyed the trip into Salt Lake. It was almost something we could make jokes about.

She touched the sap when we got there and lit a candle and said a prayer, crossing herself several times and engaging in other rituals that made me feel as though I was watching primitive rites. Jaimy was desperate, though, and I was desperate enough to try this too. I'd just achieved the Melchizedek priesthood[82] a few months earlier, and technically, I was supposed to be able to pronounce blessings and do a laying on of the hands, though Jaimy had said that was what got us there in the first place.

---

the tears of the Virgin. Tracey Aviary lies at one end of Liberty park: a wonderful collection of unique bird species from around the world that is a big draw for the area. However, one night in the late eighties the park made national news again when a man high on L.S.D. broke into the park and raped a stork to death.

[82] Young Mormon boys are ordained into two lower levels of priesthood. The Aaronic priesthood takes place at age twelve and involves three sub-levels. As a deacon of the Aaronic priesthood he distributes the sacrament and generally abides by the Boy Scout codes. The L.D.S. church has long sponsered Boy Scout troops and ties the principles learned in the Scouts (assisting the elderly, community and church restoration, etc.) firmly to the priesthood.

As a teacher of the Aaronic priesthood Brian was able to ordain deacons and occaisonly speak at church meetings. And though he was encouraged to do so, he rarely participated in home teachings (monthly visits to ward houses that act as kind of a dry run for the missionaries). As a priest of the Aaronic priesthood Brian baptized the dead, ordained deacons and teachers, and administered the sacrament. He had just reached the title of elder of the Melchizedek priesthood when he and Jaimy found out they were pregnant.

There was no miraculous *cure,* no *healing* to be done, naturally, which is what I'd hoped the Virgin would bring. But then I couldn't really see the face of the Virgin like Jaimy claimed to. I thought there was something of a shrouded figure to the shape, and the sap did come from where the face should be, but there was no face—just concentric lines tracing out the years of that tree before it became Catholic. And a long line of faithful waiting to unburden themselves in its presence.

All around the park there were people lying in the sun in their swimming suits, playing Frisbee or Hacky Sack, jogging and rollerblading (which I remember being new and strange then, maybe it was the first time I'd seen someone on rollerblades). One guy I remember was playing Frisbee with his dog. I remember the dog was gray and white with black spots, but I can't remember what the man looked like.

"How poor are they that have not patience! What wound did ever heal but by degrees," I say to Connie, though I know I'm not the salesman my father is. Not the artist with words that he is, and Connie looks at me like I'm from Mars. "You're young, Connie. And you'll forget about all this." Connie is young, she seems younger to me every time I look at her, but she's not the most malleable of all. I don't wonder that the healer can corrupt the convalescing, but I wonder if it goes both ways?

"I don't know what you're talking about," Connie says, petulantly. "Bailey's taking a steer this afternoon, and you're going to want to stay for that." She wants to leave the room, and she looks toward the door, but she doesn't go anywhere. "Nobody's keeping you here."

"Nobody's keeping me here?" I say. "All right."

"Your eye is still bloody. Your stitches aren't out."

"I'm plucking these things out," I say, and I hold up my arm and free another stitch with my fingernails. The thick, black thread comes loose and slides out of the loop in my skin, leaving a perfectly round and small hole in its wake and dragging a whitish goo. Inside the hole there is a speck of blood.

"Do you want me to read to you some more?" Connie starts to dig through her school bag, pulling out *Heart of Darkness* and *My Antonia*. She holds both of them up for me to choose.

I let out a sigh. I can't tell if Connie's been told to keep me occupied or if she's really that desperate for the company, but I *can* tell from her body language and her agitation that I'm not going anywhere. "Conrad," I say.

Connie begins: "The *Nellie,* a cruising yawl, swung to her anchor without a flutter of the sails, and was at rest. The flood had made, the wind was nearly calm, and being bound down the river, the only thing for it was to come to and wait for the turn of the tide . . ."

"You know Connie," I say. "When we were little kids my father used to read to us, my brothers and my sister and me. We'd have family home evening and we'd almost always get through a whole book then, but every other night he'd try to read to us, as well."

Connie puts the book down and slowly raises her head as if she's following the text of the novel right into my own story. "But one time Dad started reading to us out of *Moby Dick* and I couldn't stomach the whale sections, so in the morning, when my brothers were at breakfast, I moved the bookmark forward a little bit." I see I still have Connie's attention, so I continue. "A couple of times after this happened, Dad seemed confused, like he might catch on. But he read so much, I could tell he just thought the pieces were swimming together in his head. My brothers had such an implicit trust in my dad that they didn't dare ask a question if something seemed out of place. We were there to listen and appreciate, he'd always say.

"But then I started to feel sorry for the whale, and I started to hate Ahab, and one night I got brave and moved the bookmark nearly to the end of the book. Again, no one said anything, and we finished *Moby Dick* in leaps and bounds.

"And as we worked our way through the other books, when we read something I didn't like, or when we read something like *Frankenstein,* which made me sad, I moved the bookmark.

"And one day, when we began to read *The Return of the Native,* I took the book and hid it behind a stack of other books in the library. That heath, I remember, weighed on me like nothing I'd ever heard of before, and I knew, from Hardy's telling, that the story held nothing but doom. I knew it couldn't end well for anyone, and I took it and hid it and let my father think he'd misplaced it. But I'm thinking now, now that they're moving out of their house and they're packing things up and putting them into boxes, my father is going to go into the library and move that stack of old medical books he got from his grandfather, and he's going to find *The Return of the Native.* He's already found it, I'm sure."

Connie starts to say something, but there's two loud raps at the door and Randy comes into the room. He looks better and better every time I see him. Not just healed from the wreck, but healed from everything else as well. Healed from his life. He looks younger, and his fake hand seems to fit him better, like it's turning into real flesh.

"Here you go, Chief," he says, and he tosses something at me.

It's a cellular phone. "What?" I say, turning the phone over in my hand. It's as if I'd never seen one before.

"Make your calls, if you want. This won't go onto Bailey's bill."

Connie looks down at her book and then clutches her bookmark against the outside of the cover and shoves them both into her backpack and storms out of the room. Randy stays and stares down at me, waiting for me to use the phone. "Go ahead, Chief," he says. "Won't bite you."

XXXIII. A Lot of Blood

"Why don't you call your folks and tell them you should be back on the road by tomorrow morning, if you want."

"Tomorrow?" I say.

"We're having a little trouble with the rotor, but Bailey thinks he can get it cleaned up this evening after he takes the steer. Plus, then you can get in on some of the bar-b-que."

"Rotor?" I say.

"Yeah," Randy says. "I wanted it to be a surprise, but we got your car all fixed up. It's a new color, and there's a lot more parts on it now that weren't there when you came, but I think it looks a damn sight better than that bucket of fuck you drove us down here with. Shit, not a spot of rust on that mother fucker now. Randy and Bailey've worked their asses off. Randy's a fucking artist with cars, you know. Had to tear the whole fucking frame apart, but the engine and the transmission and the chassis, and I can't fucking believe this, the chassis was fine. So we'll get that rotor problem figured out and you'll be on your way in the morning."

I stare at the phone, and at the cat collar on my wrist. Connie is wrong, the scar on my arm doesn't look like an earthworm at all, it looks like a cable's been buried in my arm. Randy lingers by the door, but I know he won't leave me alone with the phone.

He says again that I should call my parents, but I can't. I'm troubled by the same feeling I've had since before we left Michigan that I've done something wrong, and now I'm even more afraid to come clean with my parents about where I am, who I'm with. The feeling is hauntingly similar to the moment I picked up the phone to call my parents about Jaimy from the clinic in Wendover. I dial Rhoda, hoping somehow she won't be home.

A man's voice answers and I hang up.

"What are you doing?" Randy says.

"Wrong number, I guess," I say.

"Say. Maybe you did come out of this a little fuzzy," he says with a laugh, and I still hate him. Even his teeth seem whiter since we've been here, but maybe they were always that white.

I redial Rhoda's number, careful to summon each number as though it were leading me back to her through Swedeburg, Omaha, Mount Pleasant, Donallson, Nauvoo, Chicago, Kalamazoo. "Hello?" It is the man's voice again. Mr. Mysterious, I think. Of all the times I would've relished the chance to confront him, this just isn't it. I can practically feel Randy staring at me.

"I . . . Is . . ." I feel the blood rushing to my face and I don't know if it's jealousy or fear or just raw excitement.

Randy interrupts, "Speak up there, Chompers, you're not that damaged."

"Is Rhoda there?" I say.

"Yeah," Mysterious says, and I hear him call out into the air of Rhoda's apartment. At least she's not consoling herself under his arm, I think, but I don't like it that he's familiar enough to wander away from her in the vanishing sanctity of her apartment. I imagine his fingers passing over the many things I've given to her, brushing aside astrological guides and the copy of the Neruda poems with the woman and the stars on the cover, fidgeting with the crusty starfish I picked out of a junk pile near my apartment, rolling the Petoskey stone around in the palm of his hand. And he has the gall to pick up her phone when it rings.

"Hello?" Her voice is like deja vu. "Hello?"

"Rhoda," I say.

"Attaboy, Chief. One word at a time. Take it slow."

"Who is this?"

"It's Brian, Rhoda," I say. She can't have forgotten.

"Brian?" she says, her voice is excited now. "Oh my God! Is this a joke? Brian?"

"Rhoda? I'm okay," I say, but I don't sound like I'd believe myself.

"Brian? Where are you? Where have you been?"

"I'm in Nebraska. There was . . . There was a car accident. But I'm all right now. I'm okay."

"Oh my God. Brian?" she says. "Brian?"

"It's all right, Rhoda. I'm okay." I can hear Mysterious asking over and over in the background, "What? What?"

"Brian?"

"I'm all right, Rhoda. Who's that there with you?"

"That's my brother. That's Stan," she says, as if I should know that he'd be there. "Brian, the cops were here. Your brother was here. I thought . . . We thought . . . What happened? Why didn't you call? Why didn't you call anybody?"

"I was unconscious. It was a terrible accident," I say. I can hear Rhoda's hair against the receiver like a whisk against a drum kit. It's always like that when we talk on the phone and I want to be there with her. I want to be back in her bed on the night before we left and I want her to tell about the falling light of stars and their impossible names and the way any number of greater things in the universe have died out but that we're still seeing them burn on, their names are still on her lips.

"You're in Nebraska?"

"Yes," I say. "But I'm leaving tomorrow?" I look over at Randy. He smiles and shrugs his shoulders at me as if to say it's all my decision. "I'm pretty beat up."

"Oh my God!" Rhoda says, and we laugh. She's crying, but she's laughing too, and I actually feel as though I might cry as well. It doesn't feel like I've been gone for weeks, and yet the fierce way the world has carried on without me makes me think every day was a lifetime. Enough time, Rhoda would say, for a million stars to extinguish their diminished light.

"Just remember," Randy says. "This ain't on your dime."

"I think I have to go," I say. "But I'll call you tomorrow. I promise."

"Are you coming back tomorrow? Should we come get you?"

"No," I say. "I think I've got to go on out to Utah."

"No, Brian. Don't go there. Don't do that," Rhoda says. "Come back. Come back here. You don't need to do that." She sounds like she's afraid she might lose me out there, but I know now that she won't.

"Can you meet me out there in about a week?" I say. "Can you get a flight out?"

"Come home, Brian. Come back," she says.

"Look Chief, you can call her back on your own dime, if you want to."

"I've got to go, but I'll call you tomorrow. Will you call Zach for me? Will you wait for me to call you tomorrow?"

"Oh Brian," she says. "Come back."

"I love you, Rhoda," I say. This is something I would never have said in front of someone like Randy before. The wreck has changed me that way at least.

"Don't hang up, please. Please," she says.

She asks me for a phone number that I can't give her, and when I hang up Randy takes the phone from my hands. "I thought you were going to call your folks," he says accusingly.

"I just couldn't do that," I say.

"C'mon," Randy says, pulling me from the bed by the arm. The blood rushes to my head and I feel for a moment like I might fall down. He takes the phone from my hand and lays it on the dresser. "You're going to want to see this, city boy."

Bailey's house is quiet and the spring air is coming in through the open windows. Randy doesn't assist me on our walk and as soon as we're outside, he brings out his silver gun and examines it in the clear sunlight. "What's going on," I say, backing toward the house.

"Oh, don't be such a pussy. This is for the steer," he says. "Bailey's out of ammo." He continues walking to the barn, and I can see that Bailey is out there and an old light blue pickup truck with a rusty metal cage welded to the bed is backed into the barn.

"There he is," Bailey says as I round the front of the truck. "Getting some air in you before you head on out, I guess." There is a steer tethered to a pole in the barn, and I know I don't want to see it put down. Its stupid round eye rolls around in its head to take a look at me and then it returns to its dull, interminable stare. My own eye, I think, must look as inhuman and lifeless. Bailey takes the tether and leads it into a small stall with several block-and-tackles dangling ominously above it.

Randy locks the chamber and looks over at me. He walks to the front of the stall, and as soon as Bailey has raised a chain gate across the back of the steer's butt Randy says, "Know where you get your meat from?"

"Hold on," Bailey says, and the steer lifts its tail and I watch it push an enormous amount of poop out of its butt. Bailey takes a shovel to the wet pile and flings it into an adjoining stall. That's the last bit of pleasure in the dumb beast's life. "All right."

Randy lifts the gun over the side of the stall and puts it against the steer's head. The gun shot is loud and startling and seems like something you know can never be taken back. The steer collapses in a sad, thunderous heap on the floor of the barn and Randy comes back to me.

"You wanted me to see that?" I say.

"Not just that, Chief," he says. And he fishes a smoking, silver cartridge out of the chamber and passes it to me. He does this with one hand, and I am so amazed by his deft control of the gun with only one working hand I don't realize how hot the bullet is until it has burned my palm. "Real silver," he says. "A gift. And something to remember us by."

XXXIV. Flesh of My Flesh

I stay and watch as Randy and Bailey hoist the steer with the help of the truck and unload its offal onto the ground. There's a wash of blood when they begin and it pours over the ground, kicking up a froth with the loose dirt before settling down into the soil as I know thousands of others probably have in this very spot. The smell is terrible, like the sulfuric smell off Great Salt Lake that would blow into our classrooms in the spring.

I see the barn cats come creeping out of the hay and the empty stalls and around the shadowy edges of the barn. They sit and watch and lick at their feet, unimpressed by the playlessness of the kill, and yet borne there by the scent of the blood and the offal.

They use two shovels to sling this into a large blue plastic barrel near the door. The guts are slippery and full of blues and whites and reds, and Randy and Bailey have to work in tandem, pushing the piles together, lifting together, and letting go all at once. It's amazing to watch Randy work his shovel, as if his arm has regenerated since we've been marooned here. Then they take the hide from the steer. This takes a long time, and slowly the steer begins to resemble meat and skin more than the animal it was yesterday.

The skin lies on the dirty ground while they finish with the steer. Randy reaches down with his good hand and takes hold of one of the ears, dragging the head and neck upwards like some bloody mask, and in one swoosh a blade or a knife in his bad hand slings down and frees the ear from the rest. "Here you go, Chief," he says, and he tosses the ear at me. My first impulse is to move out of its trajectory, but I manage to catch it. The bell on my wrist jingles on the way up. For the first time there is blood and dirt on my hands and I feel how useless I am in the whole process.

"They're good luck," Randy says, and goes about dragging the husk of the steer back over to the side of the pen that held it still for his gun.

"Good luck?" I say.

"I think you'd better keep it under your pillow," Bailey says, and he and Randy think this is a gas.

I wander out into the yard between the barn and the field and the house and the road. The air is better there, and though I can still smell the steer—maybe the ear has something to do with this, and the hint of a feed lot somewhere down the road—it's intoxicating. I want to lie in the grass, on my back, and bust the clouds like we did when I was a child. My father would take Zach and me up the mountain near Layton and we'd lie on our backs on the plateau overlooking Gentile street, the street dividing Layton from Kaysville, that ran from the mountain all the way out to Great Salt Lake like a tether. It was something my dad would do with the two of us. Zach always saw it as competition, and he would scuttle down the broken sandstone back to the car proclaiming himself the emperor of the clouds, the Genghis Khan of the Four Winds. It gave Dad and me time to talk on the half hour walk back to the car, but I'm not sure I ever really had anything to talk about. My dad always asked the questions, about school, about girls, about what I thought of the Jazz. I never asked him any of the same questions, which, I admit, would seem weird from a kid of twelve or so. But at what age was I supposed to ask those questions, I wonder? Maybe, at one time in his life, he'd been kidnapped by a one-armed R.M. and stood on the great prairie with a steer's bloody ear in his fist, sniffing at the air, wondering which way and how far to keep wandering.

Randy and Bailey work through the afternoon breaking the carcass into smaller and smaller pieces, until a hefty section of one side is left on a hook. The foot is still ringed with hair and the toes are muddy. This they take around the barn and skewer with a long black metal spear that they make into a spit over a giant brick cavity filled with black ash. Connie and Suzanne keep busy in the barn wrapping the smaller portions in brown paper that they tie off with twine and lay in the back of the pickup truck. I haven't seen much of Suzanne since I looked at her through her bedroom window that night before the accident. I think there's something Diana-like about her, the way her fingers gouge out the red meat and work against the paper and twine.

Bailey constructs a fire that I can feel from twenty feet away, and the ash falls across the lawn and the fields like snow. While the sun slips under the horizon, his fire gets bigger, claiming all the golds and reds of the dying heat of the day for itself. The shadows take care of the blood, and Randy hands me a beer, amazingly with his fake hand. For the first time I see that it has fingernails etched into the flesh, and I don't know why, but this surprises me. And for the first time I also realize I have a cigarette hanging from my lip. I flick the butt into the blaze and, magically, there is another one in my mouth.

Randy toasts me in front of Bailey's fire, "To your trip."

"To my trip," I say, though something in the sinister shadows on Randy's face makes me doubt I'll ever leave. Maybe I imagined the phone call to Rhoda, I think. Maybe I'm not here at all. I know the heat of the fire, but it seems to die with each turn of the black meat, each ladle of Bailey's special sauce that looks just like blood in the firelight. Bailey works the fire like Vulcan. I try to think of him as Vulcan, and it's not hard.

As the night comes in, new faces step out of the dark. Friends of Bailey's and Suzanne's who've come for some of the bar-b-que. Who've come, it seems, to stare at me from the corners of the fire. There are at least a lucky dozen of them keeping their distance from me.

Connie brings me a fresh beer and a plate of meat carved from the spit and drowning in Bailey's bloody sauce. She's keeping her distance too, and though something in me wants to act out a scene from a sappy movie where the hero, me, has to explain to the young girl, her, that it's time for him to move along, I know there's no dialogue that will take me past the first line. And everything she's got to say, I think, probably needs a little editing.

A little too much editing, I think, and she could become Jaimy. Or at least the spirit of Jaimy, especially in the dark, with the flicker poking at her face, making it look one way and then another. She could be Jaimy, if she wanted to, I think, if she wasn't careful, so guarded, so young, and so difficult. I try to summon something of Jaimy into the hasty firelight, but just as I sense her spirit nearby my heart feels like it runs out of gas. So we stand, several feet apart from each other, and eat from our plates until Bailey decides we need to say grace.

"Dear Father," he begins, and faces in the dark are almost gone by now, lit only by the embers of the pit. "We thank you for this bountiful feast. As your only son, Jesus Christ, told his disciples," I can tell Bailey's unsteady now, "take this flesh of my flesh. For it is my flesh." Bailey's drunk or exhausted or both. "And take this wine," Bailey says, raising his shiny can of beer into the night air. It's met by a chorus of "Here-here!" and Bailey nods several times and takes a drink between each nod before he continues. "For it is my blood. And we thank You for taking our sins, and we thank You for giving us the light," he says. "Amen." Bailey's grace is met with another chorus and he throws his empty can into the fire. Bailey's given us the sacrament[83] and grace and absolution all at once.

---

[83] What many Christian churches think of as communion, the Mormons traditionally call "sacrament." Rather than a ritual

designed to bestow grace on the faithful who partake, it is seen more as a physical reminder of Christ's body. The more traditional invitation from Luke 22:19, which recalls Christ's invitation at the last supper to take the bread as his body and to take the wine that is his blood, is never mentioned in the Mormon sacrament. Instead, two prayers are given while, typically, bits of Wonder bread and cups of water are distributed. These prayers are taken from the Native American Christianity Joseph Smith reported in *The Book of Mormon*, and if any mistake, even the slightest misutterance, is made during the prayers they must be repeated by the officiating member.

XXXV. Strong Good Wagon, Well Covered[84]

Night overtakes the fire and the faces fade until they disappear completely into the sound of engines turning over and the crunching of gravel. Connie looks at me once, as if to say what a shame I have been. She knows me from head to toe, and something about that won't dissolve in the distance out of Nebraska, or the years from this time. I slip away myself, smelling of the fire, of the things burned there. I am so very drunk on this night spent drinking and on all things burned away.

My last night in Nebraska, I think. Though it strikes me that there must be a return trip to Michigan. A way back into my own life. Maybe I can take I-70, I think. Maybe I can fly.

And for some time I feel that I'm flying already. I lie on my back in my bed and stare so long and so far into the ceiling I feel as though I'm losing my body by degrees. The only thing holding me to my consciousness and holding my consciousness to the world is a litany of sensations. The heat of the room on my face, the smell of char on my body, the sound of the fire outside and the primal murmurs of steadfast drunks biting off the last of their meat against the crackle of embers. All above me the ceiling so gray and pale in the wavering light of the moon.

I know that my night will linger, that I won't know sleep any more than I know Randy or Connie or the rest. So I lie and

---

84 Brigham Young's requirements for each family of five pioneers heading from Winter Quarters to what would become Salt Lake City: "One good strong wagon, well covered. 3 good yokes of oxen between the ages of four and ten. Two or more cows. One or more good beeves, some sheep if they have them . . ."

wonder what Jaimy might be like now. Her ghost in Connie assumed Connie's youth, Connie's porcelain skin. But like the terror of a real haunting it took on nastiness, shouldered a new hate. How could she have changed? How could I? How can I even trust what it is I think I remember of her?

The television comes on. Or I think it comes on. Maybe it has always been on. Or maybe since the accident I receive a signal from Utah directly into my brain. There's Hot Rod Hundley[85] in my head giving me the play-by-play. And when the cameras hover over the arena, waiting for a commercial that won't come, there is Jaimy sitting, no, standing in the aisle near the floor. She's looking

---

[85] Hot Rod Hundley is one of only two men who have worked for the Jazz since their humble beginnings back in New Orleans. He was the first player taken in the first-round of the NBA draft (out of West Virginia University) in 1957. Hundley immediately signed for the relatively modest sum of $10,000, one day's pay for many current NBA stars, with Minneapolis, the team that drafted him. He famously claims that whenever he sees his mother he asks her: "Why didn't you wait?"

Hundley is one of the most respected color men in professional sports and has made a name for himself in Salt Lake through such distinctive euphemisms as his trademark: "Softly put that baby to bed." Hundley, well liked by nearly everyone within and outside of the organization, has also been known for some of his unJazz-like habits and practices. Former coach and team president, Frank Layden, once said: "We could fill the Salt Palace if we just invited the people Hot Rod owes drinks to." And his ex-wife, referring to his then newly published autobiography, claimed: "If all his old girlfriends buy it, it'll be a best-seller." As he said of himself:

"They talk about transition from offense to defense in basketball. I had to make one from Bourbon Street to here."

Hundley, like the Jazz, is a relatively unknown commodity within the sports broadcasting community. The only times he consistently gets to call games is during the NBA playoffs, and even there NBC, who has the NBA contract for weekend games, often gives the assignment to their own team of broadcasters.

When the Jazz take the court at the Delta Center for game three against Seattle, Hundley is on the air, and the Jazz rip the Sonics 96-76. They do this in spite of a particularly poor outing from All Star point guard John Stockton. He shot only 2 for 9 from the field, begging the question(s) about his health. Stockton has suffered a hyper extended elbow, a deep thigh bruise, and a pulled hamstring all in recent weeks, but coach Sloan seems unconcerned about Stockton's low scoring: "He could play 48 minutes, not score, and still help you win. That's the kind of player he is." But Karl Malone tells the media after the game that "95 percent of the players in the league wouldn't be playing with the kind of pain and health problems Stock is going through right now."

One thing helping the Jazz back into the series was the return of Bryon Russell. In spite of the fact Seattle coach George Karl repeatedly refers to him in the press as "By-ron," the small forward out of Long Beach State has another star-making performance after going 0-4 in seven minutes in game two. Russell comes into the game with 5:03 left in the first quarter, subbing for Chris Morris who had been getting burned badly by Seattle's Detlef Schrempf. "The last three days," says Jazz assistant coach Gordon Chiesa, "we've been talking Bryon up. Give us energy Bryon, give us energy." And Russell responds, going 8-14 and 3-6 outside the arc. He even adds three steals and hauls down an amazing ten rebounds from the small forward position. "He brings havoc," says Chiesa. "We needed that today."

directly into the camera, and as she begins to speak, the crowd of thousands hushes, as if to hear what it is she has to say. But just then the graphic advertising the Utah lead of 80-74 appears, fading into the image of a new Jeep perched on top of one of the arches in the southern corner of the state. What is she saying to me? She looks worried, as if trying to warn me about something. But what is it?

I see that look on her face as we're walking out of the clinic into the hot splash of air that greets us in Wendover. I try to take her arm, and she shrugs me off with a jab of her elbow. She's especially frail and sickly now, and I open the door of the Bronco for her and stand back as she stumbles inside. I see there's blood there, on her backside. "Jaimy," I say. "Should we go back in?"

"Get me home," she says.

We drive back past the Tree of Life and the broken fruit on the ground shines hard against the setting sun. I put on some music, the Replacements, I think, and let some air in the window. Jaimy's hand snaps to the dial and the music is gone. What am I thinking about, I wonder? Is it that I've got to tell my father? I don't fear God in this, though surely I fear the church. And why do I fear the church? Shouldn't I have had the faith in their prescience? Shouldn't I have come to them first?

I remember so much. So many things I can piece back together like my father stitches his quotes into a quilt to drape over any subject. Yet I can't piece together motivations. I can't recall faith. I can't recall what I'm feeling for Jaimy. Is it fear? Pity? Sorrow? Guilt? Hopelessness? Loss?

I hear the cock crow out in the yard. It is one of many details that come through with the yellow morning light. I've slept in my clothes. Or I've lain on the bed all night in my clothes. Either way I smell like charred remains. Inside and out, I think as I catch a whiff of my own rotten breath.

There is a toothbrush for me in the bathroom, as there has been all along. There is a towel, threadbare but clean and folded on the shelves above the hamper. I just wish they'd taken the mirror down.

Even my good eye doesn't look too good. The red veins pulse out like side roads on a map calling to me. My bad eye looks worse, swollen and red like the crown of my sister's head being born into the world. I haven't shaved in days. Or Connie hasn't shaved me. I let my clothes drop to the floor and turn on the water. It is hot and soon the bathroom is steamed against the chill of the morning. I can't work free of the bell and collar on my wrist so I leave it be and step into the hot water.

I like to let the hot water do its work. Soap always seems like salve to me against the cleansing power of really hot water. It hurts the trench in my arm, but I let it burn down all the way to my wrist because today I am going to drive myself home.

"Do you want me to wash those?" It is Connie.

"Sweet Jesus!" I say. "I'm in the shower, Connie!"

She jerks the curtain open and I try to cover myself with my hands. "There's nothing on you I haven't seen before," she says, and then, just before pulling the curtain shut. "Though it looks like you shrink up a little in the shower."

She takes the clothes and I hear her open the door again. "I'd turn down that heat, because in a few minutes that washer is going to kick in and you'll really get a burn."

When I get out of the shower I have just a towel to cover myself with. I take it into my room and lie back down on the bed. It seems the house is awake already. I hear voices in the yard and then a familiar clattering sound. "Hey-yah! Look out here, Chief!"

I go to the window wrapped in the towel. Randy is standing in front of a cherry-red Bronco. It is the same make as mine, and from the pleased look on his face I can tell it is mine. It is meant to be mine. "What do you think, Chief?"

"Is that my car?" I say.

"That's your ride home," he says. "We just got that rotor working. I think something was wrong with the first one. But listen to that baby purr. Like a fucking house cat."

"That's not even the same car," I say.

"What?" he says.

I start to answer him when I hear the door open behind me. At first I think it is Connie again, but it is Suzanne, and she seems embarrassed. "Breakfast," she says, averting her eyes from my nakedness. "But it isn't come as you are."

"What?" Randy says from the yard, and he kills the engine.

XXXVI. The Renunciation

Breakfast is more meat. Sausage patties and sausage links glisten on Bailey's white plates. Suzanne is in the kitchen with Connie and they both whirl angrily from stove to counter to table and backward again. I'm not sure if I'm underestimating my welcome at the table and I offer to help sling the hash.

"You just sit down," Suzanne says. "You've got a heck of a long haul ahead of you today."

"You pushing straight through?" Randy says.

"I don't know if I'm up to it, really," I say.

"That's what? Eighteen hours about? If you really hit it?" Randy looks as fresh as a daisy. His fake hand lies on the table and he grabs at Suzanne's skinny butt with his real hand, but she gives him a withering look before he makes contact. The real hand descends under the table.

"You can't make that," Connie says. Her hair is pulled back and she has a zit on her forehead. She doesn't look much like Jaimy this morning, and I feel thankful for that.

"I don't sleep," I say.

"Could've fooled me," Connie says, and she finally sits down to her own breakfast.

"Listen," I say. "You have all been really wonderful to me here. Fixing the car and everything," I say, hoisting a sausage link in the air for evidence. I'm still a little bothered by the idea that they might not let me get out of here. That the red truck doesn't belong to me.

"Hey," Bailey says. "Anytime you want to get run over, you just be our guest."

"Thanks," I say.

"We'll leave a light on for you."

"Your dirty clothes will be done in just a minute," Connie says. Maybe she didn't say those things, I think. And maybe, I think, even if she did, she's young enough to grow out of them and into some real ideas. Maybe ideas like that only hurt when they're applied theories, when there's cause to do harm. And then, maybe this is how I talk myself into stupor.

Out in the yard I actually feel scared to climb into the truck. Bailey and Randy have done a stellar job on her. The rust is gone and the interior's nearly all new. There's no floor mats, a cheap A.M./F.M. stereo where there once had been a Kenwood, but everything else seems to be really improved. The keys are even new, and they gleam in the morning sun as Randy dangles them from his plastic arm. It looks so real in this light, the dust on the forearm glistening like a growth of fine hair.

"I guess this is it, Chief," Randy says, and as if by magic the keys drop out of his hand and into my own. The others fade back into the yard, and Bailey disappears altogether.

"Should I call you, or something?" I say.

"You afraid to get lost?"

"Nothing like that," I say. "Just to let you know I made it okay."

"You already made it okay," Randy says, and he pats me on the shoulder. It seems for a moment that he might hug me, but something comes between us and I stand to receive his hand onto my shoulder with all the stiff regality of someone being knighted for a long journey.

"Are you going to get back to Utah, then?" I say.

"Sometime. Not now."

"Your kid?"

"Doesn't know me now. Won't know me tomorrow. You just leave the conscientious stuff to the pros, okay?"

I nod. "Thanks, then. I guess." I wriggle my wrist and the small bell jingles.

"You look like a fairy with that thing on your wrist," Randy says.

"He probably likes to look that way," Connie says, and I realize that she's still there.

"Connie!" Suzanne says.

"Hey," Randy says, stepping back behind Suzanne to give me room to pull away. "How 'bout those Jazz?" It's an evasive thing to bring up, but it's also a graceful way for me to leave. Randy's telling me everything is safe.

"They might do it yet," I say.

"You think of me out here when you watch those games, all right? You give us a thought once in a while."

Connie cocks her hip, folds her arms, and looks at the ground all in one motion.

She's still standing that way when I pull out of the driveway, only I see her raise her head in the rearview mirror just a little as I get near the road. Suzanne and Randy wave me off and Randy puts his arm around her waist and tries to pull her to him, but she pushes him away and walks into the house. I watch the little scene unfold as I pull onto the road. Randy follows her, unsure, it seems by his body language, of what has made her upset. Connie just stands her ground, angry, and slides off the side of my mirror as I come out of my turn. The car runs great.

I can't quit staring into the rearview mirror, and I'm almost off the road. Driving feels strange, like something I haven't done in years, or something I'm just learning to do.

They've even given me a full tank of gas to start the trip, though Bailey warned me to watch that the fuel gauge doesn't plunge when it gets to a quarter tank. He thinks it might be squirrelly. And he cautioned me to check my oil every stop. Or at least every other stop if I'm going to be driving straight through. He's mostly worried about driving around town.

But the car handles fine, and I crank the window down a while later when I find myself back on familiar I-80. The corn has grown since we came to Nebraska. Or maybe it's not corn. Maybe it's just something green, but it's all grown taller and fuller since I've been laid up. I lay my wrist on the window. The arm is stiff at the elbow, and the little bell whistles furiously as I pick up speed.

Within a few miles the green earth flattens out before me so that I think I can see its curvature against the blue sky. Only billboards and phone lines and the gradually lessening clumps of hundred years oaks intrude. One sign is black with white lettering: "JESUS SAYS 'WHERE'S THE BEEF?'"

Further down the road a sign with the same white letters tells me that God doesn't doubt my existence. The denomination claiming these signs is written too small for me to see before I whiz past. This is office humor or kitsch, not the word of God written large. These are items stolen from Dee Dee's desk and cast on the highway with all the terrible hollowness they had back home. I wonder if she read them every time she sat down to her work in the mornings, or if they just became like the pictures and the postcards, the same dull reminders of a greater world filled with greater promise outside of the office.

I remember that I want to see to it that Dee Dee gets baptized when I get to Kaysville[86]. I don't have a temple

---

[86] Mormons believe that I Corinthians of the New Testament invites baptism of the dead, and that this was a practice lost to Christianity for centuries before Joseph Smith reclaimed it through his translation of *The Book of Mormon*. While this practice is officially ignored by the Catholic church and found explicitly distasteful by many Jews (whose families died in the Holocaust), the church has a long history

recommend, and Dee Dee is not my people, but I know it can be done. If Zach were home, I'd ask him. As it is, maybe Luke. Maybe my father.

I feel giddy, as if remembering the office has made me realize that I'm not only escaping Nebraska, and Randy, but that I'm escaping many places all at once. And though I feel better knowing I'm on a busy interstate, and knowing that I left Randy behind with Bailey and Suzanne and Connie, I still feel his presence in the car. I see his shiny hook out of the corner of my eye. Maybe that's what he meant by thinking about him from time to time. Maybe it's that I'm so conspicuous now, with the bright-red paint job. Maybe it's because I feel like I've come back to a home I no longer live in. That I'm really in Randy's car, and no matter how far I drive I won't outrun that.

If I wasn't so drained by the experience, and I wasn't so fearful of stopping until I'm nearly running on empty, I'd trade the Bronco in for whatever I could find. One of Dad's most ubiquitous maxims was that better isn't always better, and though the Bronco has certainly been reborn into some red heaven, it is not the same car. The spots of rust told a story of its years in Michigan.

As I sail past the Lincoln exits I'm startled when I hear cars honk at me, terrified when they roll down their windows and call out to me. But I realize now, after following this white van

---

of baptizing the dead, and indeed keeps some of the most detailed genealogical records in the world. While the church officially restricted these baptisms to family members in 1995, the general view is that even if the ceremony is performed it is not a given that the deceased will enter into the kingdom of heaven. This ceremony would have to be performed in the Temple, and without a Temple recommend, Brian could not carry this out.

with the giant red 'N' on the spare tire cover for several miles, that the Bronco must make me look like the world's biggest Cornhusker fan[87].

I stop for gas near Grand Island and I'm surprised and pleased that my credit card still works. I feel as though I've been erased from the world and only these little miracles exist to tell me that I'm still alive. I stand and stare at the phones near the entrance to the gas station as I fill the tank, but just then a big rig comes rumbling into the diesel pumps behind me, and I decide to just grab a sandwich from their cooler and keep moving.

In the rest room there are the names of cities and towns written in the grout between the tiles over the urinal like a big, square map. Spokane, Little Rock, Bismarck. These lead to a rusty condom machine on the wall between the stall and the urinals. The machine advertises SAVAGE PLEASURES, a special condom with thousands of tiny fingers, and photos of women, and MYSTIC OILS guaranteed to keep me aroused for hours. People have written on the machine as well as the wall, and have scratched pictures of tiny phalluses in various stages of erection.

I hear someone making his business in one of the stalls and I wonder if any of them have Randy's inky codes. If there's anything to be learned from the numbers and names on the stalls. It's foolish, I tell myself, but I know that the codes are in there and that the codes in these the stalls make a web that could catch me up yet. When the man comes out of the stall he looks at me and walks quickly out of the rest room.

When I come to the sink I remember what my face looks like, and I think it's a good thing I won't see Rhoda for a little

---

[87] The mascot of the University of Nebraska is Herbie the cornhusker, and the school colors are red and white.

while longer. I look like a Frankenstein's monster with the red cable running down my arm, the scabs sprayed across my face like fish scales, my bad eye puffed out and bloodied. These wounds made me vulnerable a few hours ago, and now they just make me angry. I won't need a Jazz game to remind me of Randy and Connie and Bailey and Suzanne and the rest.

A few miles down the road I eat my dinner. My sandwich is stale and bitter and I'm tempted to toss it out of my window, but I see a state trooper hanging behind me. He finally pulls off at an exit near Ogallala. I'm close to the Wyoming border now, and chasing the sun over the horizon. The fields are making way for the desert. It's still a long drive all the way into Kaysville, but I feel that rubber band take a hold of my guts again. It's snapping me backwards to my parents and my family.

There's nothing shameful in what's happened to me, I tell myself. There's no need to crawl home with my tail tucked between my legs, as if I'd crashed my car drunk, or been beaten in a fight. And yet I can't help feeling that this is one more disappointment in my life. One more time I'll come home to a quiet house and the sagging face of my father as he rises from his easy chair.

There is stunned silence when any one of us does something my parents think we shouldn't. They don't carry on, like Rhoda's family might. Rhoda has so many stories of screaming fights between her and her mother I imagine they must be deaf to each other's conversational voice. Then there's the huddled up and consoling sadness of Jaimy's family. Jaimy's family ultimately huddled so tight that they squeezed me out altogether and then stared out at me, like a herd of yaks guarding their wounded at the core. My parents breathe out long sighs and then begin with their litanies of rhetorical questions aimed at illuminating our culpability and everything they'd done to keep us from failing.

XXVII. The Light Net

The sun is nearly down well before I reach Cheyenne, and I can feel the weight of my escape tiring me out. Maybe I should get a hotel, though it seems like a waste when I know I won't sleep. Edward Hopper said the American spirit was in the hotel room. Or maybe it was said about his art. I'm tired and the details are blurring and leaden. But I know I always misunderstood the quote and believed it meant that those places were haunted. And when you first misunderstand something that misconception is forever coupled with your understanding. When I drive past the great American motel and gas station with all its hundreds of pumps I feel the ghosts of all the dead souls there calling out to me, and the cacophony is too rich. Just too rich, so I let the car glide as far as it can. It seems to know the way.

When the sun fades, like Bailey's bar-b-que pit did, it leaves great, smoky clouds over all of the Wyoming sky. The desert air is warm and dry and the road is so straight I can let my hands completely off of the wheel. I could shut my eyes if I wanted. I could lay the seat all the way back and sleep my way home. When I get in, and answer all of the questions that I know are waiting for me, I decide I will tell my parents about Rhoda.

I miss her. And I try to imagine myself back with her, lying in her bed, her tumble of hair washing over my face. When I first met her it was at a bar and I remember seeing that hair from across the room. She stared at me briefly and I thought she had said something, from all the way across a crowded bar. I thought she had told me her name and then "Do you like the mountains?"

When I walked over to her she pretended to be talking to her friend Leslie, who she doesn't talk to anymore. I said: "Did you want to know if I like the mountains?"

She laughed, and Leslie, who I didn't like anyway, said: "Go away, creep." As I remember I stood there and tried to reach into her, to get her to tell something else.

"Well," she said. "Do you?"

"I'm from Utah," I said. "There's not a lot of choice there."

"In Utah?"

"In whether or not you like the mountains. It's hard to like or not like something when you're inside of it." I wanted to reach into her hair, to stroke it with my hand. I wanted to kiss her on the mouth right in front of her irritating friend Leslie who cut in with something like: "Well that's absolutely fascinating, Guy. But we were in the middle of a conversation of our own, so why don't you find your lonesome way home?"

"Do you like the mountains?" I said.

"I don't know," Rhoda said. "I like the stars though."

"You should see the stars in Utah," I said. "In the spring they fall out of the sky and if you climb into the mountains you can see them come down."

"Those would be meteors," Rhoda said. "You wouldn't want stars to fall."

I told Leslie I would go back to my table if Rhoda gave me her phone number, which she did. And I went back to my table and watched them talking. I tried to tell her things, to put my thoughts into her mind. Rhoda would sneak a look at me through her hair from time to time, and after a little while she walked away from Leslie and came over to my table. Leslie tried to pull on Rhoda's arm, I remember, and begged her like a little girl begs her mother not to go.

"That's not my real phone number," Rhoda said.

"Whose is it?"

"It's a hotline for alcoholics anonymous," she said.

"That's usually the best place to send the kind of guys I meet at bars."

"Do you meet a lot of guys at bars?" I asked.

"More than I'd like to by a mile." She took my hand in hers and I realized what big, strong hands she had. She wrote her phone number on my palm and told me I should probably memorize it for good measure.

Leslie came walking up behind her and added: "So you'll still have it after you're done whacking off tonight."

"Your friend's a real romantic," I said.

"She's jealous," Rhoda said, and they left together.

There are a lot of rules about how long you should wait to call someone you're interested in, but I called Rhoda the next afternoon from work. She was still in bed, and I thought I heard the first, faint murmurs of Mr. Mysterious speaking to her from another room.

I have to stop in Evanston for gas, and Bailey was right, the gauge is tricky and it drops in a hurry after a quarter tank. I come coasting in on fumes and I land at the Diamond Shamrock. What a terrible irony that would have been to run out of gas on the lonely Wyoming interstate late at night. Even the highway patrol goes home after 11:00 P.M. I'm almost there now. I've picked up an hour on the trip somewhere inside of Nebraska, but it will be late when I pull into the driveway.

I know Rhoda will have told Zach and I know Zach will have told my parents, my brother and sisters. And I wonder if they will be asleep tonight? If they've gone along with their lives just like everyone and everything else has since I was rebuilt by Randy and his gang? And if they sleep, will they have dreams of me?

As I pull away from the gas station and the lights of Evanston I think I see the shadows of an elk herd at the top of the hill that descends into Utah. They are in silhouette against the starry night, clearly too large to be deer, and frozen against the sky like the silhouette cutouts I'd seen in the yards of farms. I reach over to the glove compartment and pull it open. It used to be full of maps and cassette tapes and there used to be a light that came on when it was opened, but now it is dark and empty save for Randy's two gifts: the silver shell and the ear. I fumble around for the ear and feel the shell casing at my fingertips, though it gets away from me.

The ear is hardening now, the blood is gone or dried, and it is the shape of a garden trowel. The hairs are rough, like the whiskers of a new broom, and I hold the ear in my lap and run my fingers over it a few times while I watch the silhouettes of the elk disappear in the dusk of my departure. Good luck. The absolute best of luck.

I see the signs for Echo Canyon and Echo Lake, where a girl I knew broke her back once. We'd been jumping off the cliffs into the water, a bunch of us from Davis High the summer of our junior year, and her top kept coming loose when she broke the water. She was a good Mormon girl and had nearly burst into tears the first time her top came loose.

We convinced her to keep jumping though, some of us thinking it'd take her mind off her humiliation. Some of us, I remember, thinking it'd be fun to see her lose her top again. But she tensed up so stiff on the drop into the water, holding her arms tightly against her chest, that the paramedics said it was more like jumping off the roof of her house onto the front lawn than jumping into water. When the ambulance arrived she was still going on about her top, afraid that the paramedics might have to cut it loose for some reason, and the rest of us might see her breasts again because we all gathered around her. It was the most fearful I think I've ever seen anyone.

There have been mountains since half way through

Wyoming, but now, at night, they are closing in around me, like two giant shadow hands. It feels familiar and safe, even though the road is curvy and pitch black. There are repeated warnings for big rigs to slow their descent and increasing percentage points on the yellow signs. And then, it seems like suddenly I'm out of the canyon between Ogden and Layton. I can see Great Salt Lake in the palm of the great hand holding the reflection of what little moon is left. Only the mountains and the road taking me through them look the same. There are new signs, new homes, new exits coming off of the highway.

When I reach the top of the big incline that takes me to the edge of Layton I see the orange glow of a sortie of jets from Hill Air Force Base. The four exhausts converge into one faint bloom like a giant, spectral eye fading out over the valley.

I can see into the valley now. The Project 2000[88] is coming to a close, though the Olympics will likely make things much worse. There are lights strung through streets that didn't exist when I was in high school. They are more chaotic than the lights of Salt Lake City, but they make a pattern. They cast a net over the blue valley and over all of the places I used to go.

---

[88] Project 2000 was begun in the 1980s to help raise consciousness about the potential and projected boom in Utah's population, estimated to double in the twenty intervening years. In addition to the L.D.S. Church encouraging young mothers to stay at home and raise children, a healthy combination of relatively (by California standards) affordable property, incentive-based tax structure, and Utah's healthy computer science, mining, and military industries continue to draw thousands of Californians to the state. The effect of this migration has been disastrous on the marsh and wetlands around Great Salt Lake and the mountain desert climates. Great Salt Lake has vacillated between flood and drought, and there is real fear about providing enough water for all the residents in a desert state.

XXXVIII. An Empty House

The path home is so familiar the car finds it without my help. I feel as though I am nothing more than a passenger, and when I come to a stop in the driveway it is like sitting before the house of a stranger. I let the engine clatter to a stop and turn the lights down. There is no movement in the house, no lights inside the house, no one at the door.

I stroke the ear in my lap and then put it back into the glove compartment. When I open it up the light comes on. A minor miracle, if I can believe some of the things Rhoda believes. What Jaimy believed. Inside, huddled near the back of the empty box, is the empty shell giving off its faint shine.

The air outside is cold, and the sky is cloudless. The air always feels the same in Utah. Every year. Every decade. The seasons come on time like they are beholden to God Himself, and I can smell spring in all its chilly impertinence hustling out the winter. I breathe deep, taking the dry air into my lungs and into my blood, and then I walk to the front door.

It is unlocked. When I push it open it is like the husk of the place I used to live. The family portraits are gone from the wall. The green and red throw-rug Mom bought twelve years ago at ZCMI is gone. The furniture is gone. The lamp is gone from the table that is gone too. Even the familiar smell of home is fading out of the house. "Hello?"

And suddenly there is a dark figure in the hallway. It is my mother. "Brian?" she says. I walk toward her. She seems so much older. So much smaller than the woman I remember as my mother. I am only the pieces of her son.

"Brian," she says, and comes to me and she starts to take my hands in her hands. Her hands are cold and soft. They feel unfamiliar to me. She is crying now. This outpouring is not my mother, and this is not my house. She touches my face near my injured eye, and I think that this is not my body. This is only the recollection, the counterfeit stage of my memory playing me out in meager little details, hollow little scenes.

There is another figure suddenly behind her, and it is my father, who immediately begins spouting aphorisms and recitations. "Rejoice with me; for I have found my sheep which was lost." He puts his hands on my shoulders and the three of us embrace, but his touch feels even more perfidious than my mother's hands. Of course I am crying, but the crying is like the mechanisms of my machine breaking down. The gears in my guts throwing a rod, the cogwheels and sprockets blundering into each other. And the tears rip at my injured eye. The choking finds pain inside of my body in places I never knew were alive.

I cry until all of my pieces have fallen into their arms, and their tears begin to ebb as they realize their newfound trouble. There are questions, but they are not the questions I imagined or secretly hoped for. And they come at me from both directions at once. The tone of both is absolute disbelief. How could I have survived in the wilderness for fourteen days and nights? Who were these people who sheltered me? Did I ever once lose faith?

I'm about to venture something to the last question when another figure appears, and then another, and another and another and they are each smaller than the first, each more tentative.

"Brian, my goodness! For the love of Pete, we thought you were dead!"

"It's all right, Zach," I say. "How did you get out here?"

"On a plane, you dope. When that girl in Kalamazoo told me you were on your way back . . ."

"We were so worried, Brian," Michelle interrupts. And then the whole tone of the reunion changes to something more like an interrogation. My mother brings me ice for my eye wrapped in a paper towel, because there aren't any real towels left. They're all packed or up at the condo. I tell her it's well past the time to put ice over it, but she can't believe that, and she stares at my eye until I cover it with the moist pack, out of modesty.

And I find out, between descriptions of Randy and a story about how I must have fallen asleep at the wheel and drifted off the road, that Zach has actually been out here since a day before he heard from Rhoda, and that he has a U-haul packed up and ready to tow back if I think I'm well enough to drive now.

I can't bring Rhoda into this empty house. Not yet. Not until things have come to a point and adjourned somehow. I know everyone is holding back just yet and that this too is water behind the dam. I tell them I'm all right. I tell them there was a car wreck and that I was a little spaced out for a couple of days after I returned from my coma. The word nearly unhinges my mother. I tell them I'm sorry they worried. I'm sorry I woke them. I'm sorry I can't stay awake any longer, and I walk down the familiar hall to where my room is.

There is a twin bed left in the room and one of Zach's progeny follows me inside, jetting around as I bend to take off my shoes. He throws himself onto the bed. "Michael," I say. "What do you think you're doing?"

"This is where I'm sleeping. We were here first."

"Michael, do you see this eye?" I pull back the lid with my index finger and give him a good look into the blood of it. "I'm going to do this to your eyes if you're not out of my room by the count of three. One. Two."

"Mom!"

The pillow smells like a little kid, so I turn it over and I fall asleep, really deeply asleep, for the first time since I was with Rhoda.

XXXIX. The Affirmation

In the morning, after a silent breakfast of cold cereal in plastic bowls, Zach insists I call Carly back at the office and tell her I'm all right. It turns out that L.T. has not only been promoted once, but twice in this short time. Zach tells me later that two deaths in one office always make the company brass dole out condolence raises. Keeps the morale up.

I have obscene thoughts about getting Geoff promoted at Zach's expense. Geoff is the last of Amigos, I think. I picture him sifting through his car magazine at the cafeteria and I wonder if L.T. still comes down to see him. They stagger the lunch breaks at F.O.A. so that there's not a lot of co-mingling among office branches. Maintains the hierarchy and hegemony. I wonder about Kitty, but I don't ask after her, or anybody back there. I tell Carly I'm fine and that I'll be back to work in a few days. I'm a terrible liar. I don't know if I've just misled Carly or myself.

Then I have to call the cops and the F.B.I. and suddenly I'm struggling to remember my story from the night before. What was it that Randy said? My memory makes me dangerous? I worry about the cow's ear and bullet casing out in the truck, and after breakfast, when Zach and my father take another load up to the condo in Park City, I hide them above a ceiling tile in my old bedroom. And then I call Rhoda.

Rhoda is home and she again breaks into weeping when she hears my voice. She says I've been cruel, and I tell her that's something I'm only realizing just now. I ask her again to get a flight out here, but she thinks it isn't a good idea just now. Some vibe she's gotten from Zach, plus the fact that my parents are in the middle of a move and there's a lot of family around. She's absolutely right.

But there's something more. She tells me something's happened, and that she thought I'd abandoned her. At first I think it's something with Mr. Mysterious, but then I fear the sound in her voice is the same as it was in Jaimy's right after we found out. Rhoda won't say it out loud, and I can't bring myself to ask yet.

My parents are certain that I shouldn't do any work on the house, but I assure them that I can at least pack some boxes, carry some lighter loads out to the van when it gets back. It's only when I go out into the sun that I notice the U-haul Zach has rented and how long and full it seems. I don't know if my truck could even pull such a load out of Evanston.

The work continues all day. And the boxes get smaller and smaller and more and more fragile and important-seeming. My things have already been packed up, and though all of this has certainly put me into a nostalgic mood I know I should probably wait to examine my memorabilia and put Rhoda through a very serious look at my childhood when I get back to Michigan. But I have no idea when that might be.

There is a call from the Kaysville paper saying they want to run a story on my return. The reporter, a young woman with a lilting voice, asks me a few questions about how long I was unconscious and what did I think my family had gone through. Then she says the paper will probably run the story without a picture and that I can look for it tomorrow.

That evening Zach and my father arrive back at the house at the same time a cop comes by. I know I'm visibly nervous when she comes to the door, but she seems completely uninterested in the details of my disappearance, asking my father instead how much they were asking for the house, how many square feet? Case closed, and I can feel Randy's gloat come whistling across the plains.

We sit around the living room floor at dinner eating some

heated up pizzas from Papa Murphy's, a new concept in pizza over in Layton where they assemble your pizza but you take it home and cook it. Dad and Zach think it's a stroke of genius. Everyone avoids asking me questions, and at the end of our dinner Zach announces he and Michelle are moving to a hotel. The house is nearly empty, hollow sounding.

My father has insisted that the big screen television be one of the last items to move because he had mistakenly paid his cable bill through until the last of the month. He asks Zach to stay until the Jazz game is over, but Zach says the kids are tired, which is always his excuse when they start whining.

It gets darker and darker outside as I help carry some of the few remaining boxes out to the truck to take up to Park City. But the little boxes begin to add up and soon I have to find a better order for them. It is dark in the van and I have to feel my way along, working slowly, making sure I'm not piling anything heavy on top of anything fragile. It's relaxing somehow. All of my parents' things are in boxes now, save the television and a couple of suitcases. These are their mementos, the things they have collected to make their home, that made our home.

When I finish up I pull the sliding door of the van closed and lock it. It looks like rain tonight, I think. The air smells like the air in Michigan. It is completely dark now, and there are no stars shining through the clouds; only the smallest portion of moonlight is making it down to me in my parents' driveway.

When I look back into the house I see my parents. They are standing in the living room and my father is talking to my mother as if he is explaining something very difficult to her. They are standing close, facing one another, lit gas-fire blue by the giant television screen behind them. And then something extraordinary: my father takes my mother's hands into his own and tenderly brings them up to his face and kisses them. She throws her arms around his neck and they kiss again, tenderly, and with such complete attention to each other that I feel humiliated in watching. They are in love, I think. Maybe not every minute of every day of their existence, like the times my father snaps at my mother about not bringing the packaging tape back into the room he's working in, or when my mother gives one of us that exasperated look of hers. But here they are, clutched together in the pale light of the television, and in the husk of the house where they assembled a family, revealing their love.

XL. End Game

When I finally come creeping back into the house it is clear my parents have remembered the secrecy of their marriage, and the politeness of our family. My mother is picking scraps of paper out of the carpet, and my father is grousing about our not leaving any chairs for the game. I sit down next to him on the floor and he stares at me. I can feel a hundred questions in his stare, but the only one that surfaces is, "Why don't you go get us a couple of beers? There's a six pack of Wasatch in the fridge."

"This is really some game, Mother," my father says. "Can't you stop picking at that rug for a minute and sit down with us?"

"I just don't want to leave such a mess for the next people," she says. "This is such a lovely house."

"I don't think a few scraps of tape ruin the looks of the place. Brian, get your mother to sit down before she drives us all insane."

"C'mon, Mom," I say, returning with the two beers. "Sit down and watch the game. They look like they might have a chance."

My mother lets out a terrible sigh, as if she was giving up on life itself, and sits down on the floor next to me. "I only like the fourth quarter anyway," she confesses. "Or when we go to the games."

"Maybe we should go to the game?" I say to my father.

"If they win here, I could see about getting a couple of the tickets from work. But as Samuel Goldwyn said, I could probably sum up our chances in two words: *im* possible."

"Don't be such a sour-puss," my mother says. "I think it would be wonderful, given the way things have been around here, if we could all go to a game."

My father now gives a sigh and continues to stare at me: "He mixt in all our simple sports; They pleased him, fresh from brawling courts / And dusty purlieus of the law . . . You know," he says. "We can keep on with this, or you can just tell us whatever it is you're not telling us, son."

"I don't know what you mean," I say, though the words come out so softly I'm not sure I'm really speaking at all.

"Who is Rhoda?"

"Rhoda?" I say.

"Why would you call her before you called your own family? How do you think it makes us feel to hear that our own flesh and blood has . . ." My father pinches at his eyes and then looks up at the ceiling. Everything from here on out has the inflection of a question, an accusation. "And then we have to hear through someone we don't even know that you're coming home. That you're okay. We thought it was some kind of sick joke. That surely our own son, our own flesh and blood." My father pauses here, and I'm sure he's searching for just the right scripture to bring his point home. But it doesn't come to him. "Damn it all, Brian. How could you do that to us?"

"I won't tolerate that in my presence!" my mother says, obviously upset by his cursing in front of her.

"She's a really nice girl. You guys would really like her," I say. But again, I'm not sure I'm really speaking, that my words can be heard at all. My father shakes his head, drops his shoulders, and turns his attention back to the game and mutters something from Shakespeare under his breath. I can't hear it, exactly, but I've heard it all before. When Zach nearly got his license suspended for driving double over the limit, when Luke broke the Thompson kid's nose in a fight over a baseball card, when the dust settled with Jaimy. "Go, bind thou up yon dangling apricocks, / Which, like unruly children, make their sire / Stoop with oppression of their prodigal weight." The tonnage of my prodigal millstone is the least of his burdens and of my failings. I know he devoutly fears I am a son of perdition[89] and that my soul will perish. That what Jaimy and I did constituted murder, and I imagine he will see Rhoda as a sign I am rejecting the church, and by extension, my family, forever[90].

My father's quotes have always unfolded like maps of our family's existence, and usually they resound in my ear like a call back to a home even when I recognize them on someone else's lips, or when I stumble across them in some different text. But he wields this one at me, quietly and with deliberate inarticulateness, like I am the prodigal son who never really tries to return to the fold.

Since the accident I have attacks of stabbing back pain and I excuse myself. My mother tries to rise and follow me outside, but my father clears his throat and she returns to the floor. I go back outside with a beer in my hand. The rain isn't coming and the clouds have moved back over the mountain releasing the light of the stars to shine down on Kaysville. I drink the beer and I think of Rhoda, about how difficult things would be for her if she came out to meet my family. Even for my mother, I know, it would take years before she could think of Rhoda as something more than the

---

[89] Only a very few of what Joseph Smith obliquely called "the sons of perdition" are relegated to the Mormon hell.

[90] Mormon heaven is conceived in a three-tier system. The celestial kingdom is open to L.D.S. Members in good faith and service. The middle, or terrestrial kingdom, is for good people who have not accepted and received the gospel according to Jesus. The lowest, or telestial kingdom, is for nearly everyone else. The implication here, for Brian, is that his father will believe very strongly that without a much stronger and evident commitment to the gospel Brian will be lost to the family in the afterlife.

Gentile trollop who seduced her son. There's a soul at stake, and I'm not sure that Rhoda's family wouldn't feel the same way.

I don't even imagine we'll have the same talk we had about Jaimy and my father's concern for my eternal soul. I don't imagine we'll find a way through any of this. The facts and events of my life have been laid before me, and my father, being a firm believer in Jesus Christ and His concession that we must all decide our eternal fate for ourselves, will merely struggle on. I imagine I'll leave here with even less than I came with, and that leaves my heart like an empty bucket.

My parents just sit on the floor and stare at the television. If they're talking they talk like ventriloquists, through closed mouths. I stay outside, looking in at the last, Spartan bits of my childhood, until the fourth quarter begins. The game is back and forth, and it's soothing to my father in that way, it draws him into its world and he can, for the moment, let the other world, the world he and I live in, go. It's also a world where he can uncloak his emotions from whatever he keeps them cloaked in during the day. He nods at my mother when Malone hits a fade away and he pumps his fist into the air when Stockton steals the ball from Gary Payton. And in the waning seconds of the game, when Shawn Kemp, Seattle's boisterous, arrogant center blocks Malone's tie-breaking shot he slams his fist down hard onto the carpet. When Malone steals the ball back from Kemp at the other end, sending the game into overtime[91], he points at the television with the

---

[91] After Malone steals the ball back from Kemp the Sonics' bench and Sonics' fans erupt into a chorus of boos, feeling the referees have cheated them all series long. Seattle coach George Karl has been particularly critical of the Jazz, stating repeatedly that they always use illegal defensive formations (a complicated rule designed to increase scoring and speed up the game) when the other team has the

fervor of Charlton Heston's Moses commanding his people to look at God's miracle. After the game he embraces me in a perfunctory hug: "Wow," he says. He takes a breath: "Why don't we talk about this in the morning? You get some rest, I'll get some rest, and we'll come at this with a new set of eyes." I nod.

"My heart is beating like a drum," my mother says.

"In the morning then," I say.

"My goodness," my mother says, still caught in some of my father's impetuous delirium. "That certainly was exciting."

———————————

ball. And every time Malone steps to the line to shoot a free throw the Seattle fans continue their thunderous counting, attempting to unnerve and undermine Malone with every point he scores.

Malone says to the press after game five that the fact that he saw Seattle fans buying tickets to the NBA finals against the Chicago Bulls was extra motivation for the team who all feel as though they have been slighted by the press and the basketball-viewing country. The uphill battle for respect seems more and more important to the Jazz than simply winning the series away from the Sonics.

The overtime session against Seattle turns for the Jazz with 3:10 remaining in the period. Malone kicks the ball out to Jeff Hornacek who buries a three point shot, giving the Jazz a two-point lead. Payton makes a lay-up to tie the game again, but after a Bryon Russell miss Stockton sneaks inside Kemp and steals the rebound for a put-back and foul. On the next possession Payton bobbles an inbound pass and Stockton steals it away. He gets it to Hornacek who is fouled and the Jazz have the chance to go up by four points with less than eight seconds remaining. Hornacek, one of the all-time deadliest players at the line misses one of his free throws. The Sonics swing the ball to Payton who misses badly on a three point shot, and the game ends. Utah returns to the Delta Center, still down 3-2 in the best of seven series. A game seven would be played back at Seattle.

XLI. The Two Tickets

Again, I sleep soundly in the empty house. There is no noise from the other rooms, and no noise from outside of the house. And I don't dream at all again, not even the insipid dreams I sometimes have of the ceiling or of the wall-just infinite empty space. I can't even know I could come out of the terrifying void by myself. It's my mother's soft voice that finally brings me around. She whispers my name from the doorway. "Brian." That's all there is. "Brian."

"I'm up," I say.

"Your father went to get some breakfast," she says.

"So we're going up to Park City today then?"

"I think maybe," she is nervous. "Maybe you might want some time to think about things. Zach is going to be coming up and Michelle will be staying in town too, so I don't know."

"You don't want me to go, Mom?"

"What? Don't be hysterical," she says. "I mean. Look at your eye, and that nasty, nasty scar on your arm. And why won't you take off that ridiculous cat bell? It's making your father crazy."

"This?" I say, raising the collar on my wrist up and examining it as if I'd never seen it before. "I just can't get it off."

"Well, maybe we can unpack some pruning shears. You just rest. I mean, you could just rest somewhere here in town and we could get the van unloaded and you could just get your head together. Just rest your brain before you come up to the house," she says. But I don't need any more rest.

When my father comes home with the breakfast I hear him let out a whoop in the driveway. It's as if he's gone mad since our fight last night. And when I come into what used to be our living room he is clutching two purple tickets in his hand. "I got them! Can you believe they just let me have them?"

"They gave you the company tickets?" my mother says, looking up at the tickets as if they were the golden plates themselves.

"I just stopped by to tell them that Brian had come home and they all conferenced for a few minutes and BINGO! They told me everyone had been talking about this for days. Can you believe it? Days!" He's really animated now, waving the tickets as he struts around the living room, as if he were a Buddhist monk blessing the house with incense.

"Well, you two should go, then," my mother says.

"Us?" I say. I'm not sure I want to be anywhere alone with my father yet. "Why not you, Mom? You said you like the live games." My father's expression has softened out of its excitement.

A few minutes later and Zach and his tribe pull up, and before anyone has a chance to mull over whether my mother or I should go, Michelle mentions that Zach has been absolutely dying to go to a play-off game. We all look to my father, who looks nervously at the tickets and then at his watch. "Let's take this outside," he says.

He goes into the garage and the rest of us parade out the front door. "Let's get these cars off the court," my father says, orchestrating the maneuvers like a field general. "You there," he says to one of his grandchildren. "Make sure this ball is pumped up enough." And Michael is dispatched into the garage to retrieve the pump from one of the boxes.

He lays down the rules. A single elimination tournament, seven points wins the game, single point per shot, at least two non-combatant adults must call a foul, one free throw per foul and one point per free throw, for the second ticket. He'll play for my mother and Zach and I will play for each other. Zach and I, being younger, will play first. We all lock hands in a semi-circle in front of the hoop, even Zach's kids, and Dad says a prayer.

Since I blew my mission calling, I've always felt as though I was playing along, rather than believing. I suppose I expected some immediate, thunderous judgment, but when none came— from God, from the church, from my father whose leathery hand feels heavy and dry in mine—it felt as though I was either beyond redemption or beyond contempt.

Zach takes a shot from the foul line, the spacing between the cement slabs in the driveway, and misses. I make my shot and so I take the ball out to begin the first game.

My mother protests that I'm still recovering, but Zach convinces her that I'll be fine. It's not a contact sport. I could use the exercise, the fresh air in my wounds. And we can always stop. Zach's entourage ensures home court advantage, but I blow by him for a simple lay-up and score my first point.

"He elbowed me out of the way!" Zach protests. "Mom, c'mon. He can't elbow!"

"Elbow!" Michelle says, and the kids begin to chant: "Cheater! Cheater!"

"Your ball, Zach. Quit whining and play," Dad says. Michael boos until he gets a hold of one of Dad's looks.

Zach takes one dribble and clangs his shot off the front of the rim and I rebound the ball. I have to take it back behind the foul line and circle around Zach for another lay-up. "That wasn't behind the line," Zach complains, but again, only Michelle will call for a violation.

Zach is out of shape, though we're both winded by the altitude, and so he's reluctant to dribble much. He clangs another shot, only this time he shoves past me for the loose ball, knocking me down in the process. My knee tears across the concrete.

"Foul!" my mother says. "Foul! Foul!"

"That was pretty blatant. You have to agree, Zach," my father says.

"Blocking foul on Brian, you mean," Michelle says, hoping, I can sense, to buffalo my mother with her superior basketball knowledge.

"C'mon," Zach says. "He ran straight into me!"

I make the free throw. The sound of the ball slapping the net hangs in the air like an insult, and I wish it could be replayed on the jumbotron of our roof, revealed to the neighbors and reiterated to the skies of Kaysville. And I continue to score around Zach all but once. He sinks two outside shots in the row at the end and he and Michelle are convinced he just needed to warm up. And then it's me and my father.

He checks the ball to me and I toss it back. I'm winded from playing Zach, my knee is bleeding a little now, and my weak arm throbs all along the scar. There is some blood leaking out in places and I know my father is a fierce competitor. I give him some space on his first possession and he burns me for a point. Zach and Michelle's kids go wild.

When it's my turn I fumble the ball away, my father recovers and hits an outside shot to go up 2-0. I have to stand with my hands on my knees and catch my breath. I look down at the blood on my knee, and the skid looks as if it were quilted into my flesh. The blood on my arm has also broken the surface, but refuses to flow. "We'll allow one time out," my father says.

"You're used to this mountain air," I say, huffing my words.

"You can always forfeit," he says. And I probably would've, just to give my mother the ticket. But his challenge is clear. This isn't just for the ticket. I wish I could slam dunk the ball right on his head.

As it is, I settle for another lay-up. He scores again from the same side and I realize that if I corner him away from the left side of the drive he'll have trouble scoring. I try another lay-up and miss, but the ball bounces away from my father's fingers and I have the great satisfaction of knocking into Michelle and one of the cheering, jeering children to grab the ball before it hits the lawn, out of bounds. Michelle keeps tugging at her shirt and I realize that my blood has spilled onto her in the collision. I body into my father and he gives at first, giving me space to shoot up and over him. My outside shot is there and I hit it, thinking I really ought to get three points for the hustle and the length of the shot. But after all the effort it is still just one point.

I body Dad over to the right side of the drive and it works. His shot hits the side of the board with a thud. Though he pushes past me and rebounds the ball, his follow shot is just as bad and I snag this one and pretend to take it back out slowly, catching him flat-footed for another lay-up. Each point begins to feel like it takes on more significance, as if, somehow, it was worth more than a single point. I shake my arm near my father's face so that my bell chimes its little toll just to irritate him. I want to taunt my father, and this is the only forum I know I'll ever have to take advantage of him verbally. This is the only forum I've ever had. This is where I get to play hero and villain in the same act.

I throw the ball into his chest with some authority, and though I'm sure Mom and Zach and Michelle and the others don't understand, I know from his glance at the ball that he's feeling something like fear. He's not sure that this is the same game we began, and he's not so confident that his will is greater than mine. He's breathing harder now than he was before I gave over the ball.

Dad is no complainer, though. When the mudslides tore down the mountains in Layton in '83 I remember him hauling bag after bag of wet sand when men half his age sat in the tail gates of their pick up trucks, sipping at their steaming cocoa and rubbing their backs and their shoulders with the palms of their own hands. He worked until morning building a wall against mud, and so we did too. Zach and I cursed him then, for not slowing down, for doing what needed to be done and not taking time to rub his shoulders or ours. Now Zach cheers him, and we're all breathing harder. And I'm still just doing the things that need to be done and no one's complaining at all, really.

And I'm really winded now, like I might puke, but I can feel the sweat start to break. I don't really feel my arm any more, and there's a sharp ache in my bad eye. I push Dad into the corner again. He's not bad, I tell myself, and neither is he overly good. He makes choices and decisions just like I do. It's the only time I can remember feeling his body against mine, or mine against his. I lean into him until his return pressure is the only thing holding me from falling onto the ground, and we stay that way for several seconds, two convergent pressures, and there's nothing that will happen until one changes direction. I give him the weak angle he has to put up another bad shot, and then it's off to the races for another clean lay-up.

Dad misses again, and this time I can see that he is getting tired. Tired and irritated. He pounds the ball into the pavement after I juke him for another lay-up, and the sweat is rolling off of my forehead, disappearing into the cool morning. He fakes me inside and then finds his way back to his favorite spot and sinks a jumper. I've been found out, but I also know that I can work him at will from the top of the key. He's winded and it slows him down more than me. I dribble backwards and forwards, to the left and back to the right. I can dribble past him, I know, so I work his defense until I'm sure his feet are out of position. There's no stopping me from the top of the key, and if this were a film we'd be in slow motion. It feels as though the ball is rising and falling, falling and rising in slow motion, the ball is the sun and my hand changes night to day, day back to night. I slide past him for another lay up, putting me up 6-4, but when I go to check the ball and body him up I feel light-headed and my bad eye won't focus. I see my mother staring at me as my father lowers his shoulder into my stomach. Then I see nothing but pale sky. I hear my mother shriek and I hear the ball whipping through the net.

I know I've been knocked down, but I don't feel any of it yet. I bring myself up onto my elbows and I slowly raise my knees, my bloody knee now throbs and I can feel the blood on my arm has decided to run. My parents and Zach gather beside me, my father putting the ball emphatically down on the pavement near my arm and then using it as a stool to sit on. My mother rubs her fingers through my hair, and it is a gesture I know I should have made when Jaimy was on that table. "Are you all right, Brian?" she says. "Out stop!" She yells, "out stop! He needs to take his time out now," she says, and she shoos Zach's kids from the driveway like a coach.

"Don't over do it, Brian. If you want to go so bad, you can have my ticket. This is about all the basketball I can stand right now."

"They're making secret deals," Zach says to my father. My father just stares at the two of us, breathing hard. He is a much older man than I ever remember him being. In my mind he is always in his late thirties, when I was a child and there wasn't any distance between us yet. My body is so tempered by my experience that I know we're evenly matched, but there's a lot of distance everywhere else. The present is some long justification of our past we keep arriving at, only we can't ever really arrive there. So we're all of us, Mormons, Catholics, Hindus, part of a broken engine that won't ever stop. Always arriving somewhere and finding there's somewhere else to arrive . . .

"No," I tell my mother. "I forfeit. You win, Dad. I can't go on right now. I can't go any farther than this. The altitude." But as I look over the shadowy mountains and into the sky, and feel the immediate presence of my family, the sensation of my own blood coming down my arms and legs, I know that I am gripped with questions I couldn't dare ask of myself before. My child is in heaven, I know, but who will care for it there? Who tends to heaven's orphans? How do you love something that doesn't exist? That never has? And who will tend to Dee Dee, and the other baptized dead who have no one but the ignorant living to shoo them into heaven the clumsy way I shooed Jaimy into, and then back out of, my family? Will Dee Dee simply wait for me there? Will my child wait for me there? Or does it grow, like it has grown inside of me all of these years? And will it forgive me? Can a child forgive his father?

"We can wait it out a few minutes," my Dad says. "You had to play two games to my one." There's something condescending in his tone, but I don't care.

"No, the tide had turned. You got those two right there at the end. I'd puke my brains out if I had to do another lay-up right now."

"Why don't you go in and lie down?" my mother says, and I can hear the kids cheering my father.

After I cool down and we have the cold breakfast Dad brought home, it's clear the decision to leave me at the empty house has already been made. "There's some more of your things out in the garage that you ought to go through," my father says. "And that little color television is yours if you want it."

Zach overhears this and protests, "Why does he get it?"

"Oh, come on, Zach," my mother says, and she gestures out the front window toward the u-haul filled with Zach and Michelle's new loot.

I hang around outside the door to the truck going up to Park City, and when my father finishes giving instructions to Zach and Michelle he comes over to where I'm standing. "You going to be all right down here?"

"You'll be back," I say.

"Yes. Yes. But I mean will you be all right?"

"Are we going to talk about all that?"

"I think enough has been said," my father tells me, and I know that he is putting an end to the conversation right then and there. "But I want you to think about what you're doing with your life. I know you probably are doing that already, but I want you to think about how these things affect your brothers and sisters and your mother and me. Think about where it is you want to end up." He puts his hand on my shoulder and gives it a squeeze. "Pray on these things, and you'll find the right answers." He pats my shoulder, climbs into the truck, and they caravan out of the neighborhood.

The phone is still turned on and I call Rhoda. There is no answer there so I leave her a message. "I really miss you. I wish you'd think about flying down here. It might be a little rough, but we'd have the ride home to get things sorted out . . ." I want to keep going, but the machine cuts me off.

XLII. The End

I only see my parents for a little while the next day. My father is excited about the game and he insists he and my reluctant mother travel down to Salt Lake City several hours early just to enjoy the mood. "To get into the vibe," he says, and we all get a good laugh at that.

Zach and Michelle invite me to their hotel room to watch the game, but I know nobody wants that. "I'm just going to finish going through my stuff, get it all packed up, and then head on up to the condo," I tell them. And as Michelle and the children step into their car I pull Zach by the arm.

"Do you think you could baptize Dee Dee before we head back to Michigan?"

"Dee Dee?" Zach says.

"The woman from my work who died."

Zach smiles at me. And puts his hands on my shoulders. "These things take some research and some time, Brian. But I'd like to do that for you, sure." I thank Zach, though I feel like Zach should be thanking me. I smile, too, at the thought of Dee Dee as a still physical presence, the Snack-Machine, being lowered into the ceremonial baptismal font in the temple, supported by the thirteen alabaster bulls. It is a kind smile.

Luke stops by, but then quickly gets beeped from his work. Jessica calls; she tells me, after we talk for a few minutes, that she's worried my hitchhiker friend might have followed me out to Utah. For a moment I forget that I haven't told them everything, that she's just worried about some freeloading weirdo. Rachel calls. Everything seems eerily business-as-usual.

After everyone leaves I haul the little television into the living room and put it on top of one of my boxes that I already know I'm taking back to Michigan. I don't want to forget my talismans from Nebraska so I go and take them back from the ceiling of the house. The ear is more shriveled now, bristly like a piece of wood torn from the side of a tree. I set the ear on top of the television between the antennas. I prop the ear up on one of the antennas and I think maybe I'll get one-third better reception this way. Maybe I'll find new channels.

The shell I let roll back and forth in my hand, the bell on my wrist jingles softly, and as I do I find the pain in my arm once again. It aches up and down the stitching as if it were coming apart from the inside. When I stop the rolling motion and set the silver shell down on the floor next to me, the pain gently ebbs.

I take a warm bath and let the water glide over my head, lying in the bottom of the tub like I have drowned there. It feels like the scene of a crime since my mother packed up all of the extra towels and the pictures and the soap dishes. It's just a bathroom.

I walk back out to living room, carrying my clothes and with a towel wrapped around my waist. But as I reach down to pick up a dropped sock, my towel falls away. This accident first produces embarrassment and shame, but then I lay the clothes down on the floor and stand naked in my parents' old house. The house I grew up in. It is a dry cold, but it is deliverance, as if the move has confiscated every last thing I had to struggle against and left me refreshed and anointed; it has blessed and sanctified the house. How could anyone have a feeling like this and not believe that God was once a physical presence? Not imagine His flesh in our flesh.

I sit naked on the towel on the floor and began to piece apart the boxes from the garage. They are a minor history of my childhood, and though my mother has obviously worked very hard on keeping these things organized and separate my childhood seems to spill into my sisters' and brothers'. I find Jessica's junior high school diploma, and one of Luke's baby teeth like a small pill in the bottom of an orange prescription bottle. There are photos of Zach and Michelle at one of the Davis High School dances. They look like children. I wonder why I remember them as older and my parents as younger? If there is a median age of existence for the way I conceptualize my family? Why do I now imagine my own child fully formed and waiting for something more from me?

And then I find the pictures of Jaimy. She looks so very young, and the photos have all faded and gone silvery in the dry heat of the garage. The effect on Jaimy's image is overwhelmingly ghost-like. She seems to float on the page, her skin white and smooth and flat like the backs of the photos. Her diaphanous spirit seems utterly incapable of sex, and I wonder how it ever could have been any different.

The phone rings and it is Rhoda, back from another day with her brother. Mr. Mysterious could be pleasuring her with his flat, gray tongue while we talk on the phone and I couldn't care less. I miss her deeply, profoundly, and I tell her.

"Do you really want me to come out there?"

"You've never been to Utah," I say. "There's a planetarium in Salt Lake."

"Can it see over the Temple spires?"

"We're closer to the stars out here," I say.

"I've got the game on," she says, and I tell her she's wonderful.

"My parents are there," I tell her. "Maybe you'll see them?"

"How could I know?"

"Hold on," I tell her, and I plug the television into the wall and drag the rabbit ears out of the base. The signal is strong, though the tube is going and it takes several minutes for the picture to fill the frame. Maybe I will let Zach have it after all. The game

341

hasn't started yet, and the camera keeps lingering on a close-up of Karl Malone chewing his gum with great, deliberate strides, and staring straight out into space. "He doesn't look like his mind is on the game, does he?" I say.

The camera remains with John Stockton, the choirboy, during the National Anthem. It follows Larry Miller[92] out of his seat and down to the sidelines. I hear what sounds like Hot Rod Hundley's voice, away from the microphone, say very distinctly among the thousands of screaming voices: "It's a fucking cacophony in here!"

---

[92] When the Jazz were facing their darkest financial hour in Utah local car dealer Larry Miller was approached about limited partnerships in the Utah Jazz. Miller, a long-time baseball and football fan, was very aware that if the Jazz left town, Salt Lake wouldn't see another top tier professional sports franchise in his lifetime or in the lifetime of his children.

Miller bought the Jazz and immediately made his presence known. He took a locker in the locker-room, with a placard that read "Larry Miller-9" over the door. He insisted on good values, strong discipline, and consistency. All things Frank Layden promised to work toward when he arrived.

But Miller's hot temper threatened to undo his authority in matters of values, and indeed the Jazz franchise. In 1987, as the Jazz struggled through a four game losing streak on the road, Miller called team president Dave Checketts and woke him up, screaming epithets and curses into the phone. It took Checketts several minutes to figure out who was calling him, and when he did he was faced with Miller's demand that coach Frank Layden be fired immediately. Checketts, a fellow Mormon who normally tried to accommodate all of Miller's

"I'll tell you when I see them. They're Dad's old office's seats. They've held those seats since they played in the Salt Palace, and they're in the fifth row behind the Utah bench."

"Brian . . ."

"What Rhoda?"

"I don't know," she says. "I don't know what to say."

"What do you mean?" I say. My first impulse is that she's pausing to say something like good-bye. That Mysterious has somehow claimed her.

"Are you really sure you want me to come out there? I mean, won't it be hard? I know your parents are not going to like the fact that I'm Catholic, and I'm not about to pretend that I'm not."

---

demands, told Miller to go to bed. Had Layden been fired it would have spelled disaster for a team slowly rising out of mediocrity.

In 1994, as the Jazz faced the Denver Nuggets in a playoff game, Miller grew so angry that Malone was having a sub-par game he began yelling at coach Sloan to remove him from the game. Ignored by Sloan, and taunted by a Denver fan, Miller then charged into the stands and grabbed the offending fan by the throat. In another game, one where he thought his star players were being roughly treated, Miller tried to provoke a fight with L.A. Lakers' center Eldon Campbell.

Miller, a father, and by all estimations, in spite of his occasional outbursts, a good father, and Malone have a particularly interesting relationship. Malone, who operated for nearly his entire career without an agent, alternately fights with and embraces Miller. In the years since this playoff series there has been a parade of tearful, very public orations by Miller expressing his deep love for and friendship with Malone, and his commitment to keep the Jazz in Salt Lake City.

"My dad has a joke," I say. "There's this young Methodist couple and they die in a car wreck."

"Sounds like a laugh riot."

"No, listen. And they go to the Pearly Gates and one of the angels at the gate signs them in and tells them to follow him. And so they're walking along and there's this great, beautiful field with people running and playing and drinking wine and everyone is really happy, and the angel says: *These are the Catholics.* And they keep walking and there's this beautiful desert where all the plants are in bloom and the people are engaged in these really fascinating discussions and everybody is really happy, and the angel says: *These are the Jews.* And they keep walking and they come to this high, ornately decorated wall and the angel says, okay, I want you to be really, really quiet as we walk by this wall. And as they're creeping along beside the wall they hear great choirs of angels and they hear people having a wonderful time. And when they get past the wall the young woman says: *Why did we have to sneak past that wall?* And the angel says: *Oh, those are the Mormons. They think they're the only ones here.*"

"Ha ha ha," Rhoda says.

"I don't know which frightens me worse—the idea that the end is the end, or that arriving in heaven is the end that never stops. Both seem like tunnels with a light at one end you keep moving away from. Both are hopeless, really, and I think a tertiary heaven, where there's that knowledge of something better, could be the best thing to hope for."

"You're not exactly a romantic, are you Brian?"

"I'm not exactly anything, but at least thinking about these things keeps my soul in motion." I want to ask her now if she's pregnant. Or if she even thinks she is.

"That's supposed to make me come out there?"

"No. *I'm* supposed to make you come out here. But it's like my dad's joke. I think we can work with that."

"Do you really think you're the only ones in heaven?"

"No. But I think we think we've got the best seats. Isn't it that way with everybody?"

"Shallow people," Rhoda says. "I suppose it is for shallow religious people."

"And there's Kay's Cross," I remember suddenly. "Did I tell you about Kay's Cross?"

"No."

"It's not that far from where I'm at right now. It's a huge cross, maybe fifteen feet tall, made out of brick and mortar, and it's just sitting out in the woods."

"I thought you didn't like the cross as an icon?"

"Maybe it's an invitation," I say. Jaimy and I used to walk out there sometimes. She said it felt spooky, but she liked to be out there, in the woods, kicking at the remains of the fires left from the nights before. At night the heavy metal kids from Davis High would go out there and drink beer and, rumor had it, they would enact their own cultish rites. But all we ever found were charcoal stumps and burned up cans of Coors. "There they are! Right there behind Bryon Russell's head, up and to the right. Did you see them?"

"Is your father wearing a purple Jazz sweatshirt?"

"He must have gotten that at the game. Direct evidence of spontaneity." It feels strange, talking to Rhoda so many miles away, and seeing my parents at the same time. It makes things seem possible. It makes belief seem possible. If we can baptize the dead we can believe in an eternity of decisions and possibilities. If we can get past what needs to be done, if we can imagine an eternity, or if Rhoda and I can even imagine ourselves imagining an eternity at all, my difficulties appear small. Mr. Mysterious seems so powerless against this belief; all of my lies seem like miserly sins at worst. My failures are the failure of imagination.

My sins diminished, if not burned completely away.

There is a time-out on the floor, and the Jazz are absolutely killing the Sonics[93]. And then I see her, walking. Behind the fifth row of seats there is a walkway and I swear I see her walking back and forth behind my parents. Her face is hidden behind a thick swatch of black hair, but she hovers there, floats over the chairs. "Do you see her, Rhoda?"

---

[93] The Jazz torch the Sonics at every corner of the court. They hold the Sonics to 41 percent shooting, force 23 turnovers, and shoot 60 percent for the game. From the first whistle the Jazz jump out to a 12-0 lead they would never relinquish. Karl Malone scores 32 points (his jersey number), grabs ten rebounds, and hands out seven assists as the Jazz destroy the Sonics 118-83.

"We saw this in Portland. We saw this in San Antonio," says a chastened Sonics coach George Karl. "But I didn't think it could happen to us. Even if we had played well tonight I don't think we would have won."

Seattle's high-scoring, all-star point guard Gary Payton is completely out-hustled by his Jazz counterpart. John Stockton holds Payton to 3-7 shooting and just ten points. The Utah fans mercilessly chant his name "GAAAAAA-RY!" through-out the Delta Center every time he steps to the free throw line and each time he misses a shot. They lustily boo Kemp when he touches the ball, and their overall raucous din clearly affects the Sonics.

"We were alive defensively," says Jazz Coach Jerry Sloan afterwards. "We're not going to have much of a chance to beat this team unless we're alive like that." The Jazz help exorcise some of the doubt and recent failures with this victory, but they still have the daunting task of beating the Sonics in Seattle in game seven. "It's a one-game series now," says John Stockton. "Do or die, and

"Do I see who, Brian?" As she asks me this, my father looks directly into the camera and stands from his chair, mutters something to himself, and walks out of the frame. I hear his voice, inside of my head, quoting Dickens at me: "*My name is made illustrious there by the light of his. I see the blots I threw upon it, faded away . . .*"

Rhoda repeats my name, and I wish I could catch that sound like a thing and hold it in my arms. There's no closure in what I have at this moment, though, only the cold resonance resonating. I should say something simple and romantic instead. "Do you see someone behind the chairs?" The doorbell to my parent's empty house rings, and the sound echoes through the empty rooms.

----

it should be fun. But it's over now. The only thing you can do is be normal. Do what you always do, like the day before and the day before that. You go home, your wife and kids are there, and it's like 'Let's talk about something else.'"

After the game Malone didn't want to talk about his play, however. "There's some things more important than a game. I've got my little friend over there, and he's not doing so good right now," referring to the 13 year old boy suffering from leukemia who Malone and his wife Kay befriended on one of their trips to the children's hospital in Salt Lake City. Malone had arranged for the boy to have court-side seats for the game, and he greeted him immediately after the game was over, bear-hugging him out of his wheelchair and presenting him with his game jersey. "It's just a game, and we forget all of that at times like this," Malone says, gesturing behind him to the falling confetti, the indoor fireworks, the wild celebrations. Malone ignores the reporter's repeated attempts to discuss the game, to ponder how they might handle the Bulls if the Jazz can get by the Sonics in the next game. He lets the tears come and looks directly into the camera, "Hang in there Danny. You're my angel. My angel."

"There are literally thousands of people behind your parents, Brian."

"I know," I say. "Oh God, my father, do I know." I keep watching the impossibly small screen, the camera pulls back and the place waiting for my father to return to his seat grows smaller and farther away. Any moment now it might disappear altogether. I pull back the blinds and look out at the doorstep and see what looks like the other guy from that truck stop in Nebraska, the one I called The Cello. I wonder if that cycle's about to rev up again: running away, returning, repair. Or end. If I am about to be sent, sucker-punched, to the next world just when I'd had my first glimpse of how I might be able to stand it there. "There's someone at the door, Rhoda," I say. "There's someone at the door right now."

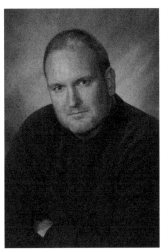

photo by Jeff Nooyen

Darren DeFrain is the author of numerous short stories, essays, and screenplays. He is a graduate of the University of Utah, Kansas State University, Texas State University's M.F.A. program, and Western Michigan University, where he received his Ph.D. in creative writing in 2000. He now lives in Wichita, Kansas with his wife, Melinda, and two daughters, and he is the Director of the Writing Program at Wichita State University. You can learn more at www.darrendefrain.com.

New Issues Poetry & Prose

Editor, Herbert Scott

Vito Aiuto, *Self-Portrait as Jerry Quarry*
James Armstrong, *Monument In A Summer Hat*
Claire Bateman, *Clumsy, Leap*
Michael Burkard, *Pennsylvania Collection Agency*
Christopher Bursk, *Ovid at Fifteen*
Anthony Butts, *Fifth Season, Little Low Heaven*
Kevin Cantwell, *Something Black in the Green Part of Your Eye*
Gladys Cardiff, *A Bare Unpainted Table*
Kevin Clark, *In the Evening of No Warning*
Jim Daniels, *Night with Drive-By Shooting Stars*
Darren DeFrain, *The Salt Palace* (fiction)
Joseph Featherstone, *Brace's Cove*
Lisa Fishman, *The Deep Heart's Core Is a Suitcase*
Robert Grunst, *The Smallest Bird in North America*
Paul Guest, *The Resurrection of the Body and the Ruin of the World*
Robert Haight, *Emergences and Spinner Falls*
Mark Halperin, *Time as Distance*
Myronn Hardy, *Approaching the Center*
Edward Haworth Hoeppner, *Rain Through High Windows*
Cynthia Hogue, *Flux*
Janet Kauffman, *Rot* (fiction)
Josie Kearns, *New Numbers*
Maurice Kilwein Guevara, *Autobiography of So-and-So: Poems in Prose*
Ruth Ellen Kocher, *When the Moon Knows You're Wandering,*
    One Girl Babylon
Steve Langan, *Freezing*
Lance Larsen, *Erasable Walls*
David Dodd Lee, *Downsides of Fish Culture, Abrupt Rural*
Deanne Lundin, *The Ginseng Hunter's Notebook*
Joy Manesiotis, *They Sing to Her Bones*
Sarah Mangold, *Household Mechanics*
David Marlatt, *A Hog Slaughtering Woman*
Gretchen Mattox, *Goodnight Architecture*

Paula McLain, *Less of Her; Stumble, Gorgeous*
Lydia Melvin, *South of Here*
Sarah Messer, *Bandit Letters*
Malena Mörling, *Ocean Avenue*
Julie Moulds, *The Woman with a Cubed Head*
Gerald Murnane, *The Plains* (fiction)
Marsha de la O, *Black Hope*
C. Mikal Oness, *Water Becomes Bone*
Elizabeth Powell, *The Republic of Self*
Margaret Rabb, *Granite Dives*
Rebecca Reynolds, *Daughter of the Hangnail, The Bovine Two-Step*
Martha Rhodes, *Perfect Disappearance*
Beth Roberts, *Brief Moral History in Blue*
John Rybicki, *Traveling at High Speeds*
Mary Ann Samyn, *Inside the Yellow Dress, Purr*
Mark Scott, *Tactile Values*
Martha Serpas, *Côte Blanche*
Diane Seuss-Brakeman, *It Blows You Hollow*
Elaine Sexton, *Sleuth*
Marc Sheehan, *Greatest Hits*
Sarah Jane Smith, *No Thanks—and Other Stories* (fiction)
Phillip Sterling, *Mutual Shores*
Angela Sorby, *Distance Learning*
Russell Thorburn, *Approximate Desire*
Rodney Torreson, *A Breathable Light*
Robert VanderMolen, *Breath*
Martin Walls, *Small Human Detail in Care of National Trust*
Patricia Jabbeh Wesley, *Before the Palm Could Bloom: Poems of Africa*